Golden City

Sirpa T Kaukinen

Golden City

Golden City

Dedicated to Reijo and Sointu

Chapter One

The letter fell from the mail-slot onto the porch floor. There it lay under the magazines until Sylvi, who came first, picked it up.

"An airmail letter really!" She said to herself and sat on the bed. "Must be from Canada," and so it was once she checked the sender's name and address on the back.

"Should I open it?" Slipped into Sylvi's mind, but once she realised that the letter was addressed to Aarne, she placed it on top of the radio. There sure would be something to yell about if she opened Aarne's letter and then there would be something to tease about for a long time when he would say: "Why have you women opened my letter? Just read your own letters."

As she was taking off her coat Sylvi thought: "I don't understand that Aarne. Why did he start to bother with this – it's not going to come to anything."

Sylvi herself being calm and somewhat stubborn, did not understand her quick-thinking and fast-moving man. So, she left the whole matter there, put her beret on the shelf, and started to peel the potatoes.

But the letter bothered her curiosity and her mind kept asking "I wonder what Aarne's brother writes in it? Is it going to be a disappointment to Aarne or a life-changing event for the whole family? I wish that Aarne would come and then we would learn what it says."

Kaarina came in the door unexpectedly pushing Sylvi's thoughts back to reality.

"What are we eating today?" Was an everyday question from the fourteen-year old Kaarina.

"Potatoes and pork-gravy," Sylvi replied evenly.

"Always the same. I don't like them."

Sylvi didn't bother replying because she knew that it wouldn't make any difference.

"I'm going out mother," Kaarina folded her skirt on the chair and pulled on her corduroy slacks. She added her gray short jacket which had been made from Sylvi's old coat.

"So, I'm going now!" Kaarina went around the central dining table and chairs and was already at the door before she saw the letter on the radio. "Is that letter from Canada?" She asked and stopped at the door.

"Yes. That's where it's from," Sylvi tried to sound indifferent knowing Kaarina's thoughts about the whole thing. Sylvi knew that Kaarina's circle of friends were the most important fact in her life and the thought of a move seemed to loom like the end of the world in her mind.

Knowing that the letter would not be opened before Aarne came, Kaarina slipped out. There she walked without seeing or hearing; while her thoughts circled in her head.

"I don't want to go. I don't want to go," pounded in her head. Nature replied with its nearness, the tree branches bent in the wind and the slushy first snow at her feet reminded her of the coming winter, but the reply didn't come. She walked until she came to the rock cliff from where you could see the river and the surrounding landscape. The familiar scene comforted and gave her peace.

"It'll all turn out okay. Father's brother won't give the money and without that the whole trip will be impossible." With these thoughts Kaarina turned and started to run; soon forgetting the whole letter.

Sylvi glanced at Marja who was playing on the floor and she felt good about the fact that her younger daughter's even nature seemed to give her strength to deal with problems at times of stress.

Marja's round child's face looked at the world

calmly and her big blue eyes lied about the churning thoughts racing inside her right now. After she had returned home from school, she had also heard some of Sylvi's and Kaarina's conversation and questions had also risen in her mind.

"What are they saying? Going to some Canada. Where is that?" Random thoughts rose from her subconscious – a long trip – a train full of travelling children – momma in Sweden – always new people – a new language – a new home – the return trip – a ship full of children – a girl who kept whispering in her ear – "sister, sister; I'm your sister. Don't you remember?"

And she couldn't remember her sister on the ship, nor her mother or father on the shore, and a year went by before she learned Finnish again and started to settle in. So, she learned to keep her thoughts to herself and only revealed a surface shell of her inner feelings to the outside world.

Marja pushed Molla-Maija carefully under her covers. "We are not going anywhere, not ever!" She promised to Molla; laying down beside her on the floor.

Dusk was already hovering on the streets outside when Aarne turned from the gate into the yard. Kaarina arrived there at the exact same time and the letter came again into her mind.

"Hi father! That letter came from Canada?" Came out more like a question than a statement.

Aarne didn't reply until at the door, "yes, did your mother already read it?" however, showed his interest.

"No. No, we didn't read it," Kaarina replied quickly.

Aarne smiled without showing interest but Kaarina could sense his inner tension.

"Keep that door open so I can get the bike inside."

Kaarina obeyed automatically and Aarne lifted his bike into the porch and headed straight inside. Kaarina pulled the door closed behind her and followed after him.

"Oh. So here comes Aarne already," Sylvi said half to herself, half to Marja, who was still pretending to sleep on the floor.

Aarne took off his working jacket and hung it by the door. His cap he threw on the shelf and without waiting he went straight for the letter.

"You haven't opened it yet?" He commented to Sylvi.

"I haven't opened it. Why don't you just read it."

Aarne opened the letter. Sylvi stirred the gravy. Marja pinched her eyelids together and Kaarina waited holding her breath.

"Hm, hmm, hmm," Aarne's eyes scanned the lines back and forth.

"Well, say it already!" Sylvi became nervous with the tense atmosphere.

"Well, the money is coming! Jussi is loaning the travel money. Now we just need to get the passports ready and then we boys are going!" Men from the district of Ostrobothnia in Finland often referred to themselves as boys even in their adulthood. Aarne's face revealed all the pent-up feelings he was holding inside.

"So that Jussi is loaning the money?" Sylvi repeated without understanding. She had not thought this to be possible. "What are we going to do there?"

"We are going to carve gold!" Aarne laughed with relief.

"You are so stupid. It's not going to come to anything!" Sylvi could not release herself from all the home things. She felt it to be impossible to leave home, home city, home country, relatives and friends; and go to God-knows where.

But in Aarne's mind the idea ignited and took hold. Finally, this gray every-day-ness would change into a new life. Hope for something better would push him to sacrifice all kinds of things. On the other side of the ocean lay possibility, possibility for money, education for children, perhaps for his own house, everything that a person could hope for. Aarne put the letter back on the radio and sat down to the set table purposefully at the same time saying: "It's clear now that we are going. Don't ask about it again. Just keep your mouths closed until it's all for sure!"

Sylvi set all the food on the table while her thoughts jumped here and there.

"Come on Marja up from that floor. Come and eat, and Kaarina, take your jacket off!" Small everyday matters calmed her mind.

Both girls obeyed and sat down reluctantly.

"Don't start crying and starving! Now swallow your food down promptly!" Aarne's command made the girls eat even though the pork-gravy and potatoes seemed to stick in their throats.

In the evening Aarne read the letter again.

"There is a job already waiting in the mine. Housing is cheap, I hear. Money is not so hard to get as here. Jussi has three houses!"

"What do you know about anything? You have never been there. It might all be lies!" Sylvi dared to oppose.

"Well, they have not returned from there," Aarne commented.

"Who is going to speak that English there because you are not going to learn it?" Sylvi questioned, surprising Aarne only for a moment.

"It might be so that I will be the boy who speaks English first. Come to bed now. We are not going to stay up all night!"

The command came with such conviction that Sylvi went to pee in the slop-pail and returned to her own side of the bed in a hurry.

But sleep did not want to come to either one of them that night.

In the morning the alarm clock pushed Aarne to get up at six o'clock. He got up, added wood to the stove and dressed. After coffee and breakfast he washed his face and brushed his teeth, combed his brown hair back, pulled his cap on and pushed Sylvi at the same time saying: "Well, Get up now! You can't sleep all day!"

Sylvi opened her one eye and asked: "What time is it?"

"Six-thirty. Well. I'll go."

Sylvi lay for a while after Aarne had closed the door but the thought of coffee pushed her to get up too. There were enough morning chores to last until it was time to go. She made the daybed, dressed, drank her coffee and organised Marja's clothing. At last she released the roll-blinds so that they whizzed up with enough noise to wake the girls too.

Kaarina muttered: "Be quiet. We don't want to wake up yet."

Sylvi ordered anyway: "Get up now. The time will soon be eight o'clock. I have to go now."

"Yes, yes. We'll wake up. We'll wake up."

Sylvi made sure that the girls were really on their feet before she closed the door behind her.

"Awful, I don't like that!" Kaarina looked at the oatmeal porridge which Sylvi had left standing in a small pot on the side of the stove.

"I don't like it either. Do we have to eat this?" Marja asked Kaarina.

Sometimes the girls emptied the porridge into the slop-pail and made sandwiches instead but you couldn't do it often because Sylvi or Aarne might find the porridge lumps in the slop-pail when they returned home. Kaarina did not want to risk anything now.

"Let's eat this. I don't dare to throw it out. And do we have hardtack bread so we could make sandwiches?"

"I don't know," Marja wrinkled her nose but started to eat. "Do you think we are going?" Yesterday's discussion came into her mind now.

"Don't talk about it. I don't want to talk about it. I don't think we are really going." The tightness in Kaarina's voice silenced Marja.

They poured coffee into the cups and continued to eat as they both stared out the window in their own thoughts.

They put on their pleated skirts and pulled on their wool sweaters. Marja buttoned her short coat and pulled her toque down on her head.

"Shall I take my mitts?" She asked Kaarina about everything if Sylvi was not there.

"Take your mitts. For sure it could be cold out there."

Once Marja had found her mitts, she took her schoolbag and left for school.

Kaarina looked in the mirror. She was satisfied with her blue-green eyes and her round face but not with her straight light-brown hair. Every morning she tried to tease her hair into a new style, but in the end she had to comb it down both sides from the part in the middle, as always before.

"Why don't I have curly hair?" Was left without an answer when she noticed the clock to be almost half past eight.

"Oh my God! Now I'm going to be late!" She grabbed her coat and satchel and rushed out the door. Her key fell twice from the nail hiding it under a rag behind the corner. From the gate she could see Leena, her best friend, standing at the streetcar stop waving her hand.

"Why are you so late? I've waited two streetcars already," Leena worried when Kaarina arrived panting at the stop.

"We'll make it, aaha, aaha, aaha. I was combing my hair."

Leena accepted the answer without quibbling.

In the streetcar the girls discussed school matters.

"Have you already cut your dress?" Leena asked.

"Yes, I cut mine yesterday at school."

"What is yours going to be?"

"I'm going to make the one which has a wide skirt and long sleeves and a tight bodice," Kaarina explained in detail.

"It's the same one that I'm making. Almost everyone in our class is making that one because it's the easier style. Isn't it fun that we are going to have the exact same dresses?" Leena enthused beforehand.

Kaarina wanted to talk about the banned subject with Leena, because they told each other everything, but where to begin and what to say was confusing.

"What are you thinking?" Leena interrupted Kaarina's thoughts.

"I'm not thinking of anything," Kaarina replied. She would have to say something sometime but now the matter was left dangling somewhere in the future. The present was more important and Leena, her best friend, with whom she had played since the first grade. Kaarina pushed the future further and together they started to plan the sewing of their dresses.

Aarne worked with trained hands, fast and with

sureness. One perfect gray clay bowl appeared after another from his hands at the electric potter's wheel. Skill and speed combined in him so that hardly anyone could match his work. Sometimes when he was drunk, he would boast to others: "The machine was first, but I was a fast second!" And no one would contest his boasting.

The manager said, "Hello Kalliokoski," as he passed Aarne.

"Hello."

After a while the manager continued on his rounds without saying anything more.

Aarne smiled faintly. He had fifteen years of experience. He loved his work and his workplace, everything except his pay. From the pay he received on Saturday, only a few pennies remained in his hands by the following Thursday. A fat bank balance was a dream that never came true. Aarne glanced outside the window and sighed – he was still young – only thirty-six years old – perhaps this would be his last chance. He picked up another slab of clay and slapped it on the potter's wheel. Let Sylvi and the girls say whatever they want! They were all going for sure! Let his brother send the tickets for the trip.

Sylvi looked at the large apartment with envy. If they could get something like this – came into her mind – but she knew it to remain a dream for a long time to come yet because of the dire housing shortage in Finland.

"Good morning Sylvi," Mrs. Koskinen greeted as Sylvi entered.

"Good morning Mrs. Koskinen."

"Well. Since you are already here, I'll go to work then."

"Go right ahead. We'll be fine here."

Mrs. Koskinen worked at a drug store in the same building.

"Make these blocks into a house, make them!" Pekka was so used to Sylvi that he didn't miss his mother much.

So together they built the house of blocks and after that Sylvi started her workday.

Marja and her best friend Aila jumped and ran in circles in the schoolyard so they could stay warm during the recess. Sometimes they would start to run, jumping over puddles, skipping over some but landing in the middle of others. Wet and shivering with cold, they ran inside when the bell rang.

It was a very ordinary November day for an ordinary Finnish family in the year 1952.

Chapter Two

"Are all these people going to Canada?" Marja demanded to know from Aarne as they stood in line for the x-rays.

"Keep your mouth shut. No, they are not all going there. Some could be ill," from Aarne silenced Marja for the time being. In her mind the line seemed to be moving at a snail's pace.

"It won't be long any more," Sylvi pacified her.

As soon as the line moved even a little Aarne hurried his womenfolk: "Go ahead again!" He had taken a half day off and was still irked about his boss' curiosity yesterday.

"Kalliokoski wants a half day off? I see, I see, of course, you're not often away?"

"There was a question in his eyes but he didn't dare open his mouth," Aarne explained to Sylvi.

"Why didn't you tell him that you're going to Canada?" Sylvi teased.

"When I have told you that we are not going to talk about it yet!" From Aarne ended the conversation there.

Everyone in their own thoughts they waited for their turn.

After the x-rays Aarne rushed to work, at the same time cursing all unnecessary waiting.

"It's going to be passport picture-taking time next week," he planned that evening for the next week.

"I have to stay away again. I can't," Kaarina resisted. "The teacher will soon ask me why I'm away again when I'm not sick."

"Say what you want but on Tuesday make sure you are at the photographers by three o'clock in the afternoon! There'll be more work-time wasted," from Aarne stopped any protests.

"You can pick her up," Aarne nodded to Sylvi, meaning Marja.

"I'll pick up Marja," Sylvi acquiesced as always.

The following Tuesday they were sitting in their best outfits at the photographer's who was organising them one-by-one for taking their passport pictures: "Mrs. please sit here. Yes, yes. So then. Very good. And now Mr. And then the older girl and after that the younger."

The pictures were taken. Especially to Kaarina everything seemed unreal. Time had taken on wheels and rolled along effortlessly.

Soon it would be Christmas and Aarne pushed everything along without letting go. "In the spring, in the spring, it will be the right time," Aarne said often and organised everything towards leaving then.

Just before Christmas a short letter arrived from Jussi in Canada.

Aarne read it aloud to the whole family: "Good brother. Have you applied for the passports? Everything is ready here. Get your tickets from this travel agency. The name and the address are on these receipts. They have been ordered and paid for from here. You can pay everything back here as you earn money. Write more in the spring as to when you are coming.

Your brother Jussi."

The letter was short and to the point as was usual for Jussi's letters.

"Well, he is not going to write some novel," Aarne snapped to Sylvi when she began to ask more closely about everything in Canada.

"It's good over there. They haven't come back from there!"

"But the girls schooling will be interrupted; you are not thinking of anyone but yourself only?"

"Damn. I'm thinking of you. I'm trying to make things better for all of you."

"The girls don't want to go," Sylvi repeated.

"They're only kids. What do they know about life? Let them talk when they have worked for a while," Aarne got up with determination and searched for a piece of paper and a pen to write Jussi a reply.

Christmas came and went; in passing for Aarne; in trying to organise a traditional Christmas feeling into the midst of rushing for Sylvi; in hoping for gifts for Marja and in thinking for Kaarina.

"Is this our last Christmas in Finland?" Kaarina asked Sylvi several times.

"Don't think in that way. We'll come back from there yet," Sylvi promised.

"When? Why are we going there at all?"

"Don't ask all the time. We have to go because of father."

And there was no better answer.

As was his annual custom, grandfather came to visit at the beginning of February. Sylvi's father was the only relative left from that generation and even he was seventy-two already. The girls called their grandfather, isopappa, and Sylvi and Aarne called him, pappa.

In the girls' minds isopappa was now a very old man, nice but unique. He read newspapers almost all day and listened to the news from the radio in the evenings and tried to even talk about the latest news with the girls.

Sylvi had not written anything to him about going to Canada and so it was a sad task for her to tell him about it now in person. As they were drinking their welcome coffee Sylvi started: "So, that Aarne has now got it in his mind that we are going to Canada."

Isopappa poured more coffee on the saucer; put a sugar cube between his front teeth and drank noisily before he asked: "Where are you going? Is that somewhere there in Ostrobothnia where he is from?"

"No, it's not there, but on the other side of the Atlantic, in America. On the other side of the world. Aarne is thinking that we should go there to earn money. We have almost all our papers ready, only the consulate has to be visited any more and that Aarne's brother Jussi is loaning us the money for the trip," Sylvi felt easier inside once she had told him about going.

"Well, if you are going there, then we won't see each other again," isopappa said as if to close the subject.

"Don't be like that now. We are only going for a couple of years. Don't be like that now!"

"Yes, it is so."

And nothing more was said about it at that time but isopappa's holiday had now somehow lost its good flavour. Everywhere she went with her father now made Sylvi think and ask – is this the last time that I am going together with pappa here? But she didn't put her thoughts into words.

Isopappa left for his country cottage when the request to visit the consulate arrived. "Well, Sylvi, write to me when you are leaving. I'll come and say farewell."

"Well, of course I'll write to you. Goodbye until then."

"So long." Isopappa closed the door behind him and left.

Sylvi wiped her eyes and turned to collect the dishes. Pappa would be left so alone and without protection. Of course, her sister Lempi would be here, but even then. Why did life grab one so deeply sometimes? Sylvi sighed. One had to divide into so many pieces. Aarne wanted one thing, the girls something else and now pappa. Everything soured her mind and especially the Canadian matter.

"So much trouble already, and we haven't even left yet," Sylvi said to herself. "I wonder if anything good will follow this?"

But silence hid the future and did not give a reply.

"Time will tell, time will tell," the clock seemed to be ticking.

The bus-trip to Helsinki seemed long for the girls.

"Should we eat more of our food?" Marja asked as soon as the landscape outside bored her.

"No, not again," Kaarina was ashamed of Marja's childish over-eating. "Just be quiet! My stomach is already full."

The trip continued at its own pace and they arrived in Helsinki in the evening. There they rushed directly from the bus-stop to Aarne's brother Matti's home.

"Welcome, welcome. Come on inside now," Matti greeted at the door. "Well, what are you writing to me, that you're going to Canada? I guess you are really serious about it?" He asked Aarne as soon as they sat down.

"Well, that's where we are going. Everything is ready. Only the consulate now," Aarne explained the situation.

"Can you just go there like that?" Doubted Aili, Matti's wife.

"Well, none of us others are in a rush to go there, except for Aarne," added Sylvi on behalf of herself.

"Damn wife, for God's sake, stay here! I can go by myself. Let go now! Can you hear!" Aarne was embarrassed by all public displays of emotions. In his mind, as in the minds of most men, feelings were a thing apart, to be discussed in private.

"Come for coffee then," Aili asked and the

evening was spent in talking, and in Aarne's case, in anticipation.

The next day as the Kalliokoskis were striding towards the consulate, the wind whipped at the people on the streets of Helsinki.

"It's a very cold wind! Good thing we can go inside. Well, here it is now," Aarne said at the door as Sylvi and the girls almost running caught up with him. His face was red with anticipation and from the cold wind.

Inside they were made welcome and were asked to wait. Aarne leafed through his papers and prepared himself to be ready. After a moment they were asked to come inside.

"Mr. and Mrs. Kalliokoski and two daughters," the man sitting behind a desk began, occasionally glancing at the papers.

"So it is," Aarne felt the tension of the moment but he answered evenly.

"You're going to Canada and your brother is expecting you?"

"My brother has been there for about twenty years and he'll help us out at the beginning," Aarne explained.

"How are your language skills? Does either one of you speak English?"

"I think we'll learn. My brother has learned;

gets along at least. I think we'll learn."

"I'm sure we'll learn," Sylvi dared to help.

"I see. Well, everything seems to be in good order. You have a job waiting for you at the mine. How is the situation with the girls' schooling as it's left unfinished here in Finland?"

"The girls will go to school there," Aarne assured.

The man turned his gaze to Sylvi and the girls.

"What do the girls think about this trip?"

Kaarina glanced at Aarne but closed her mouth when she saw his tight expression, whereas Marja kept her gaze riveted on the floor.

"I guess they are too shy to answer. Well, what about Mrs. Kalliokoski?"

"We are all going!" Sylvi declared on behalf of the girls and herself.

"What is the reason for your immigration, Mr. Kalliokoski?"

The question flustered Aarne only for a moment but now his prepared answer came out of his mouth almost automatically: "Well, they are these conditions. These wages and this continuing lack of housing here in Finland."

The man lifted his eyebrows: "But everything is going well for you. You have a well-respected job and these conditions will be improving as we go along."

"Well, improving, improving, but we now have this opportunity and everything is ready," Aarne was searching for reasons from his memory.

"So, so. We only try to point out that there also can be difficulties to overcome in the New Country, especially if you have great expectations of carving gold from the streets, as they say. But you have everything well prepared, as you said, and especially since your brother is willing to help you get started, difficulties can be minimal. I wish you a good trip and much success in the New Country," the man rose to shake everyone's hand in turn.

Outside the same wind whipped at their clothes but Aarne didn't notice it any more. The biggest hurdles had all been taken away from their immigration. The needles had been given, the x-rays taken, and the consulate visited; only the passports were needed and they would be received in March. He sighed with satisfaction and said: "Well now, everything is ready then. Why don't we go to Stockman's and buy some travel clothes."

"Can I get a new coat like you promised?" Marja asked.

"Well, we'll see."

"So, we are going then? So, we are going in the spring?" Sylvi repeated to herself.

"We are going and that's that!" Aarne declared

with certainty.

Sylvi shook her head still not accepting the decision.

Kaarina wiped her eyes – it felt like the earth had been taken away from beneath her feet and she was floating in some timelessness without an anchor. There would be no point in crying or questioning because everything had been decided on her behalf.

Marja didn't understand the seriousness of the situation and she accepted her parents' decision on her behalf.

At Stockman's Marja was purchased a spring coat and Kaarina a pair of rubber-soled shoes.

"Well, are you going then?" Matti asked as soon as they returned.

Aarne laughed with relief: "Well, why not? We are going right away, this spring."

"So, you are going?" Matti was left without words, but later in the evening when the women and the children were sleeping, he gave his support to Aarne in a quiet voice: "Go ahead. You'll do well there and return then when you've got enough money together. I would go too if I didn't have these four children. Good luck to you."

The passports were received in the middle of March and from that time on Aarne's travel fever continued to rise. The day of leaving had already been decided – May 4th.

"Well, we should pack everything we are taking with us and hold an auction for the rest," Aarne planned at the beginning of April.

"Sell all the rest?" Kaarina asked in horror. "I think that's terrible! Where will all our good furniture end up?"

"Sell everything?" Sylvi stuttered as well. "It took us fifteen years to collect all this and now they are being sold! I can't bear it!"

"Oh, for God's sake! We have to sell them!" Aarne went out to chop wood so he would be able to avoid the women's questions and crying.

"Mother. I'm not selling Molla-Maija," Marja declared stubbornly.

"No. No, we are not selling Molla-Maija," Sylvi wiped her eyes. Because of the girls she had to hold her tears and cry them at night when the others were sleeping.

The auction was held half-way through April. The beautiful dark dresser with the oval mirror was sold fast.

Sylvi felt bad when she saw Mrs. Niittynen buying the dresser. The dark square table and four chairs were also sold to her at a good price.

"Well, they won't last long at her house. Trashy people as they are," Sylvi said quietly.

"What are you mumbling about? We should get a good price for the sewing machine and our bed," Aarne hoped.

"Are we selling the sewing machine? You always told me that I would inherit it." Kaarina looked accusingly at Aarne.

"Don't grieve about that now. You'll be getting a much better inheritance there," Aarne promised but Kaarina turned and walked away from the auction area.

"We won't have anything left but the slop-pail and the water pail, or what?" Sylvi dared to ridicule Aarne after everything had been sold.

"Well, the rest of these couple of weeks will be spent like this." Aarne replied.

"We still have some of these books snd other small stuff. I thought we would bring them to Lempi's" Sylvi planned.

"Throw them out. Don't think that you're taking them with you!" Aarne ordered.

"But what will we read there then?" Sylvi wondered.

"English," Aarne laughed importantly to give emphasis to his words.

Sylvi shook her head and tried to collect her thoughts. Nothing in her life had prepared her for this and each new obstacle felt insurmountable. She had grown tightly attached to her everyday life and could not detach herself from it in the same way as Aarne.

"Well, put your books wherever you want but you're not taking them with you!"

"I will leave them at Lempi's place. I can always get them from there then." The thought soothed Sylvi somewhat. The books would remain safe there and in their own way would be calling them to come back.

Saturday all the books and small items were collected into an old large trunk woven out of straw, which they were preparing to take to Sylvi's sister Lempi's place.

"Oh, Holy Peter, I say! What will you do with this junk? What are you saving them for?" Aarne was becoming exasperated with it all.

Sylvi and the girls stood stubbornly on the other side of the straw trunk.

"We are not burning these good books. My school exercise books and all?" Kaarina pleaded.

"And my small rubber doll and its clothes and everything. I'm saving them for when I come back," insisted Marja too.

"Well, save them then," Aarne wanted to laugh at the girls seeming importance and he allowed them to have their moment as it was not that important to him.

"Well, go ahead then!" He grabbed the one end

and Kaarina the other.

"Carry this trunk across the whole city!" Aarne cursed all the way to the streetcar stop.

"No, don't do that now. These are all still good things." Sylvi defended.

"Shut your mouth and go!" Aarne pushed the trunk with Kaarina's help to the back of the streetcar and left it there for the women to look after.

When they left the streetcar, the old straw trunk creaked ominously and Aarne wiped his hands from the whole thing by saying: "If it breaks here you can collect all your stuff on your own!"

But everything worked out well and the trunk was successfully maneuvered to Sylvi's sister's place.

"Come on in," Lempi invited "and take the trunk straight to the attic!"

"Well, go on then!" Aarne ordered Kaarina.

Together they carried the trunk to the attic where Aarne pushed it to the farthest corner.

"Stay there for all I care." He wiped his hands and went down.

Kaarina looked behind and promised in her thoughts: "When I come back."

"Come down. It'll stay there," Aarne commanded.

"I'm making coffee," Lempi bustled about.

The sisters were different. Where Sylvi was of a

normal height, plump and peaceful, Lempi was short, thin and fast-moving. Only their similar faces, big blue eyes and wavy wheat-coloured hair gave away their kinship.

Even now Lempi busied herself in the kitchen and started to make coffee whereas Sylvi sat down to rest on the daybed in the living room.

"I brought you this doll," Marja offered her cousin Leila a rag-doll made by Sylvi.

"And this is for you," she gave almost a similar one to Liisa.

"Oh look! These are cute and all their clothes and all! Thank you, thank you!" Their cousins admired.

After a while Lempi called from the kitchen: "Come and get it. Coffee is on the table."

"Yes, well thank you. I'll come right away because we have to leave and start packing," Aarne's continuing rush to leave didn't give him a minute's peace.

"Where are you rushing now?" Sylvi was getting fed up and wanted to spend the Saturday evening with her sister's family.

"Well, there is the packing and all," Aarne drank noisily while the coffee was still hot.

"Well, sit down for a bit. You're not in such a rush," Toivo, Lempi's husband, urged and was able to get the visitors to sit down for a short while.

The children played and the adults discussed the trip details while drinking coffee, but everything was stamped with the upcoming trip.

On Sunday Aarne and Sylvi together packed dishes into a large wooden box, fitting towels and other clothing in between.

"Let's take this milk carry-can and the small cream can and four of each plate," Sylvi planned firmly. The kitchen was the only area where Aarne allowed her to have the final say about things and she enjoyed using this for her own benefit.

"Good thing you remembered the milk carry-can. At least we can buy and carry milk home," Aarne erred in praising Sylvi against his usual style.

The box filled fast and Aarne straightened to look at the room which seemed oddly empty and large even though over the years it had often oppressed him with its closeness.

Nothing else was left except the necessary food stuff and the dishes, the water and slop pails, the worn curtains in the windows and the old bed clothes on the floor.

During the week before the last week, so much still remained to be done that Sylvi doubted whether they would be ready on the day of leaving. On Tuesday morning she went with Marja to her school.

"Why are you coming to school with me, mother?" Marja asked while she hung onto her mother's arm.

"We need to get the report card earlier."

"Does everyone need to go to school in Canada?"

"Yes, all students need to go to school there. Of course, they all go to school. Students go to school almost everywhere," Sylvi agreed half to Marja, half to herself, though it seemed wrong to ascertain anything to a child when she didn't have any sure knowledge about things there.

If she dared ask anything from Aarne, the answer was always the same: "Well, we'll see it in good time."

"Oh, my goodness! So that's how far Marja is going! This sure is a surprise! Marja has been so good in school. Let's hope that this move is not detrimental for her schooling," the teacher started to say when Sylvi informed her about the big move.

"Children become accustomed to things so fast," Sylvi repeated Aarne's much- used words even though she didn't believe in them much herself.

"Certainly, she'll get her report card, of course! Perhaps you'll come back soon. I can't think of anything to say when I'm so surprised," the teacher continued.

"Thank you. Thank you very much and good bye," Sylvi felt relieved and walked towards home with Marja following her.

On Wednesday she walked with Kaarina towards her fashion and sewing school.

"Will I go to work or will I go to school in Canada?" Kaarina asked.

"I can't say anything as I don't really know about anything there," Sylvi dared to confess.

Kaarina was promised a graduation diploma and they were soon walking towards home with light steps. Both girls would be receiving their report cards before leaving. Sylvi gave much value to report cards as she gave to written words in general whereas Aarne counted and trusted work that you could see or money you could count. Sylvi thought that everything was now in order for the trip. She had already left her place of employment weeks ago.

Aarne had left everything to the last moment. All the internal tension about the trip was so great inside him that he didn't want to talk about it with any strangers unless he had to.

"This is a sad disappointment to us that Kalliokoski is leaving. Surely you have thought about this matter?" The manager asked when Aarne told him about the trip.

"Of course. I have thought about this thoroughly. These wages are not getting any better so I have to try my luck elsewhere," Aarne reasoned.

"We might have raised your wages somewhat if we had known about this but I guess it's too late now to promise anything?"

"It's too late now. Thank you anyway. Well, let's see what happens to this boy?" Aarne collected his 'things and tools' as he often called them and closed the window from which a slight spring breeze had wafted inside all day. He twirled his potter's wheel once, feeling as if he owned it after such a long use. It was hard to leave everything even though he wanted to go himself.

"Let's see what happens to this boy?" Aarne repeated as he waved his hand to his fellow employees.

Chapter Three

"Yes, so you are leaving, or what?" Store owner Rantanen asked Aarne. "Where have you found a place to live when they are so hard to come by now-a-days that you can't find them anywhere?"

"Yes, we are moving, going out of the country. Going to Canada! Time is getting short now. How much does it cost to use this phone?" Aarne searched for his wallet so he would have it ready for paying.

"It doesn't cost anything for a regular customer. Well, Canada!" Store owner Rantanen was left to wonder after Aarne had already said goodbye and left.

"Did you hear Kerttu? Going to Canada! He just ordered a cab!" Rantanen shouted to his wife who was measuring flour.

"Who is going to Canada? What are you saying?"

"Well, come and see then! You can still see him if you open this door a bit."

Kerttu came and peered out identifying Aarne from behind: "Oh you mean that man. I know him. His children often drop in to buy donuts. You wouldn't have thought he would have that kind of money. If you live long enough, you'll see everything."

The landlord said the same thing when Aarne returned the key for their room to him. Of course, he had already informed the landlord about the move but not that they were going outside the country.

"So, you are going to Canada! Well, good bye then and have a good trip, , , I can't say anything now, , ,if you live long enough, you'll see everything!" The landlord was left to ponder.

Aarne didn't stay to hear the landlord's words; instead he took the few steps to the gate with determination while the landlord was left standing in the porch with the key in his hand.

"Mother, mother, did you hear that they are going to Canada, those Kalliokoskis? Oh my God! Come and see them mother from behind this curtain. They are standing there by the gate! Oh my God they have fine clothes! Can you look mother!"

"Well, I'm looking. Mr. and Mrs. and the younger daughter have new spring coats and I guess the other girl has new shoes! That's what I always said to you that Kalliokoski has a good job and he has money, and now they are going out of the country!

That's what I thought earlier in the week when a truck came to get a large load of their stuff, that they are going someplace further away. Look! Now a taxi came to get them, oh my lord Jesus!" There behind the curtain the landlord and his wife were left to wonder while the Kalliokoskis stuffed themselves into the taxi.

"Move as far as you can; and don't take up the whole seat!" Aarne told Sylvi. "You are sitting there beside your mother," was an order for the girls and "to the harbour, to the harbour," was meant for the taxi driver at the same time as Aarne himself jumped into the front seat beside the driver.

The car turned and left. Sylvi, Kaarina and Marja looked out the windows in distress. Everything familiar seemed to be disappearing too fast at the same time as the car drove away. The yard, the home windows, the lilac fence, the Rantanen's store, each one in its turn, disappeared from their range of vision.

"Good bye then boys!" Aarne lifted his Sunday hat as the taxi drove past the ceramic factory. He looked at the women but didn't allow a few tears to sour his mind. A boat trip away a greener pasture awaited to be cut; about this he was sure. Sylvi and the girls would get used to everything.

No one said anything on the trip to the harbour.

"Here we are then," Aarne straightened his shoulders once he was out of the taxi, "and that there is the ship." He pointed out the ship going to Sweden to the women.

"Like that!" Sylvi evaluated the ship with her eyes, but as she couldn't see anything wrong with it, she kept quiet. Her attention was drawn more to the streetcar which rumbled to its stop and from which family members came pouring out.

"Look! Isopappa and aunt Lempi and uncle Toivo and Leila and Liisa. Hi, here we are," Marja ran energetically to meet her cousins.

"Well, there you are," Isopappa noted to Sylvi.

"Well, here we are," Sylvi already felt overwhelming sadness and searched for the right words for the poignant occasion.

"The weather seems to be fair," Isopappa examined the May evening as if something timely and important could be said about it.

Lempi also tried to talk about secondary issues. Everyone felt uneasy. More and more people arrived to say farewell.

"Oh, my goodness! Are they all coming to say farewell?" Kaarina dreaded. She had been sure about Leena coming but the whole class and the teacher were a surprise to her.

"Here is a small memento from us, from your fellow pupils and me," the teacher began ceremoniously: "Remember your birth country, and don't forget your mother tongue in the New Country," she said at the same time as she pinned a small Kalevala broach on her coat collar.

"And here is this from me," Leena held out a packet from which a sheer, blue kerchief popped out.

"Oh, thank you, thank you! Thank you so much," Kaarina tried to speak normally but her gaze carried the feeling of imminent departure into everyone's minds.

"Write to me then and don't stay long!" Leena reminded her.

"Of course, we are coming back," Sylvi tried to ease everyone's minds.

"Time will tell," isopappa only believed in tried and true things.

"Come on then. This ship is sailing now!" Aarne ordered the crying women.

Sylvi leaned momentarily on isopappa's home-spun coat collar and held tightly onto Lempi's hands. From there she started to follow Aarne up the ramp to the ship deck. The girls followed her. On the deck they all congregated as close to their relatives on the harbour as they could.

"Write soon then Sylvi!" Lempi shouted.

"I'll write as soon as we arrive there!" Sylvi shouted back.

Isopappa stood beside Lempi, looking sometimes intently at Sylvi on the deck, sometimes at the sky, and sometimes at the sea which surrounded the ship in a dark green billowing mass. "Time will tell if they come back," he said more to himself.

"Of course, they are coming back," Lempi was quick to answer and shouted to Aarne on the deck: "Aarne! When are you coming back?"

"As soon as the money is together. A couple of years at the most!" Aarne shouted back and laughed.

"There you heard it father."

"You can't come back just like that. We'll see it then," Isopappa remained doubtful.

The evening coolness and the cold from the nearness of the sea made everyone shiver. Kaarina buttoned her coat and asked Sylvi: "They are all going home from here, but where are we going?" She looked at Sylvi and continued: "Mother, we haven't got a home any more."

"Don't now. We'll have a home again. Don't think of this as so final."

Three muffled, heavy whistles told everyone that the ship was leaving; and very slowly but finally it left the harbour.

Mutual waving of hands and blowing into handkerchiefs increased for a short while but diminished as the ship travelled further. The people turned away, waved once or twice more, and then left for good. Everything on the shore diminished and soon the Kalliokoski family could only see the harbour and the bigger ships in the dusk, and behind them, the old castle rising in its grayness, steadfastness and finality.

- - - - - - - - - - -

The morning started with a fog. A cheerless, cold wind on the sea almost cut through the people.

"Go behind the others," Aarne urged Sylvi when the ship landed on the shore. The line of people travelled through the customs where passports were checked. People rushed here and there, with everyone caught in their own busyness, and it was impossible to make sense of the babble of many languages spoken. A scary feeling like a small knife pushed into Aarne's chest for the first time.

"Why don't you ask when the train is leaving since you know some Swedish!" Aarne now ordered Sylvi.

"I'm not going to ask something like that. I told you that we shouldn't travel to other countries when we don't speak other languages. It's just not going to work out!" Sylvi reminded importantly.

"Well. You don't have to carry on so. You're not a language genius either. Try to unravel these travel details. I'll speak then when we actually arrive there."

"Well, we'll see what you speak there," Sylvi

wondered aloud, but as always when Aarne's orders were in question, she collected all her nerve and knowledge of Swedish, and was able to find out that the train would be leaving in the afternoon.

Aarne's reply to this was: "Well, let's look at this city area near here."

Somewhat timidly they ventured onto the streets. People rushed about there, adults to their jobs and children to their schools; everyone speaking a strange language. Without saying anything to each other, each one of the Kalliokoski family members observed the passing crowd carefully, hoping to understand something, but quickly becoming disappointed.

Kaarina put her thoughts into words: "Well, you could yell anything here. Hi, ugly old woman! You could swear in Finnish. No one would bother listening."

The whole idea was too big to think about and they all tried to find something else to talk about. The items displayed in the store windows seemed safe enough and Marja soon asked: "Oh, look at those beautiful dolls! Let's buy a small doll as a keepsake of this place, father?"

"We don't have money for that."

"But you told us that we would have a lot of money when we go to Canada. Don't you remember?"

"Now you're hearing the truth from the lips of a

child," Sylvi couldn't help adding.

"Oh, for God's sake! No one can wish for anything more irritating than to have three women in the same family. That's my cross to bear for the rest of my life!"

"Don't, not now. I didn't mean anything."

"Keep your mouth shut then! All this is enough for me. Start marching back to the train station!" Aarne didn't want to hear anything more.

The chilly weather and a continuing drizzle followed them as they walked back.

"Look now! There is one man we saw earlier on the ship when we came. He would be Finnish," Sylvi pointed out to Aarne at the train station.

Aarne approached the man: "Whereabouts are you going in America?"

"I'm going to Canada. From here on the train to Goteborg and from there to Canada."

"Well, that's where I'm going, to Ontario, to a mine."

"I'm going west, to Vancouver."

"So, what about , , , do you speak English well?"

"Enough to make myself understood. Not all that well. Best to go on the train. Shouldn't stand here in the way of everybody."

"That's where we are going. So, see you again," Aarne sighed with satisfaction, feeling that he had found a soulmate.

"Well, let's go on the train. Pointless to stand here in the way of everybody," he said to Sylvi when he returned.

Everyone straightened their clothing and boarded the train after Aarne.

"Same people that were on the boat," Sylvi whispered into Aarne's ear after they accidentally had arrived in the right train car.

"Yes, yes. Well, I would have noticed it for myself," Aarne replied.

People smiled slightly to one another but stayed close to the safety of their own families or behind their newspapers which is characteristic for Finns. Sylvi and the girls inspected their new surroundings each in their own thoughts. Aarne looked around too until he noticed a Finnish-looking older man on the other side of the aisle, and then he ventured to ask: "Which way are you going? To America or to Canada?"

"I'm going to Michigan, to America," the man replied.

"So, we're on the right train," Aarne smiled, "when you can't speak English or Swedish you can't always tell."

"No, you can't. You must be a first-timer? Your family is with you. That's the way it should be. You'll get along somehow when you've got your family with you."

"So it is," Aarne agreed but unsure about it as he remembered all the obstacles his family had put in front of him so far.

"It wasn't like that before. You didn't take your family with you. The women stayed in the Old Country and the men left for America and that's where a lot of them stayed too," the man continued his explanation.

Sylvi started to listen now too.

The man explained further: "This is my sixteenth time across the Atlantic. Could be my last. I'm an old man. It was in twenty-seven when I came the first time and I've been back home eight times."

"And it's gone well for you?" Aarne asked right away.

"It's all been life. Sometimes it's been good and sometimes not so good," the old man's eyes seemed to look somewhere far and the conversation ended when he fell asleep.

"What western wanderer is that man?" Sylvi whispered into Aarne's ear.

"How do I know everybody? Keep your mouth shut and don't ask!" Aarne ordered.

The train moved and started its journey towards Goteborg. The cityscapes changed to fields and forests and the populated areas became farmers' fields. The early evening twilight soon turned to darkness and you had to press your face against the window glass if you wanted to see anything outside. The girls fell asleep, each in her own corner. And it wasn't long until the adults fell asleep too.

In the morning, Aarne ordered the women to hurry in his usual way even though the train hadn't yet reached its destination.

He himself was ready in a few minutes but Sylvi and the girls dressed themselves reluctantly. Aarne admired Sylvi's wheat blonde hair, but did not say anything about it. Instead he showed in his assertive actions, as always, to be in charge.

At the harbour, the now well-known group of Finns, congregated together and moved into the Atlantic-crossing ship. Aarne stopped to talk with the same young man he had met at Stockholm.

"Here we are at the harbour," he commented to the man.

"Well, here we are," the man chuckled.

"Once we cross this ocean our trip will come to an end for a while," Aarne continued.

The man's reply: "I'll still have the same distance to travel again before I get to the western shore," made Aarne think and wonder about the vastness of the New Country. He felt in his thoughts, that there must be a lot of possibilities for everyone in such a large country. He didn't need to dress his thoughts into words. He had already understood that the trip in itself was enough of an adventure for Sylvi and the girls.

As Aarne was thinking his own thoughts the women were busy with everyday matters and Sylvi wanted to go to their cabin. Organising everything took a couple of hours so that when they finally made it to the deck, the ship was already on the open sea and the harbour was left behind without anyone giving it a thought.

Now it was hard to tell any more who was a Finn and who was not. Sometimes a person nodded to them, perhaps remembering them from Stockholm, but most of the people seemed to be strangers.

"How can I tell to whom I can speak here?" Kaarina asked Sylvi.

"I really don't know. Best that you don't speak to anyone until you know if they are Finnish or not," Sylvi replied.

Kaarina thought about it. Her world seemed to be shrinking and changing more and more, the further they travelled from Finland.

"Excuse me but are you a Finn? Is that how I should ask before I can say anything to them?"

"I don't know. Don't rush about that now," Sylvi sighed. "There is so much else to think about."

"Keeping your mouth shut is always the easiest

way," was Aarne's idea.

Everything worked out well until the morning of the third day when Sylvi started to vomit.

"Seasick," Aarne announced to the girls.

"But why are we not seasick then?" Marja wondered, "since we are here on the same sea?"

"That's all we need," Aarne said aloud but already the next morning Marja was seasick too.

"And now to the deck and fast or we'll all be sick soon!" Aarne ordered Kaarina: "If nothing else helps don't give in. Keep your mouth shut and that's how you stop it."

Kaarina tried to follow this example. In the fresh air the uneasy feeling slowly left her and Aarne and Kaarina ventured to eat together but the dining room was only half full.

"It's no wonder the food is so fine here. You don't need to make too much of it because half of the people are sick," Aarne decided.

Sylvi and Marja improved with medication and by the time the ship arrived they were able to return to the deck.

- - - - - - - - - -

Sharp, jagged rocks emerged from the sea on the shore of Halifax.

"There is your golden land!" Sylvi commented to Aarne.

"How do you know that there is not gold in these rocks here?" Aarne replied with a laugh.

"These rocks look gray and ordinary," Sylvi still insisted in reply.

They followed behind the others in a row leading to the station.

"Well, this is where we are now," Aarne pointed a bench to Sylvi.

"And I am hungry now that we were able to leave that ship," in Sylvi's words reminded everyone that it was time to eat.

"I have a last Finnish apple in my purse," Marja dug the fruit out for everyone to see.

"Don't eat it. Save it," Kaarina asked, "Let's keep it as a memento."

"Eat it now or I will eat it." Aarne said and caused Marja to take a big bite from the apple. Soon only the core of the apple remained and Aarne told Marja to throw it away too.

After a while Aarne went to buy packaged sandwiches from a vendor. Then they sat and waited.

The day seemed endless and it was already evening before they were able to board the train.

"Well, what can I say? You get used to this travel, bit by bit," Aarne commented to Sylvi.

"You might get used to it but we won't so fast," Sylvi replied.

The train moved and started its nightly route from Halifax to Montreal.

"Look how dirty we are," Sylvi commented to Aarne the next morning when they arrived at the Montreal station.

"Don't worry. We'll wash when we arrive. Being so hungry is more urgent. Best if we go out to look for a store," Aarne proposed.

Somewhat timidly they ventured out onto the street and in a short time they found a small store and a storekeeper who smiled from behind his counter.

"You ask!" Sylvi poked Aarne from behind.

"Shut your mouth." Aarne searched the shelves with his eyes and followed the other customers at the same time.

Like them he picked up a bread from the shelf and butter was also easy to find. He just couldn't see any cans of fish.

"What is a fish?" He asked Sylvi.

"I don't know."

"There I have a real interpreter! When I told you already before leaving to learn the important words, but no, , ,"

"I don't know them all in English," Sylvi replied.

"Kaarina, draw a picture of a fish here on paper and that's it," Aarne ordered.

Kaarina blushed but since Aarne had given the

order, she drew some kind of a picture of a fish which Aarne pushed in front of the salesman.

"Hm. Yes, yes." The salesman rushed to the shelf and carried back a small jar of fish smiling triumphantly at the same time.

He counted the purchases and announced the total sum from which Aarne couldn't understand anything at all except that money was in question. From the few dollars he put in the grocer's hand some silver coins were given back. Then they returned to the street.

An argument ensued outside which lasted all the way back to the station.

"Making a child draw a picture of a fish," Sylvi commented outside.

Kaarina retorted with a red face: "And I'm not going to a store in this country."

"Can our father not draw a picture of a fish?" Marja added innocently.

"We're not going to talk about it any more," from Aarne's mouth stopped the conversation there.

At the station hunger united everyone again and the bread and the jar of fish disappeared soon.

After eating the waiting continued uninterrupted the whole day. They walked back and forth and talked and sat and waited for the train.

In the early evening a blonde, young man pushing a child's stroller stopped in front of them.

"Finns or what?" The man asked in Finnish and took them all by surprise so that they were not able to reply right away.

"Well, yes," Aarne said finally with some uncertainty in his voice.

"They keep on coming," the man smiled and stamped out his cigarette with his shoe.

"Well, have you been here a long time?" Aarne's curiosity was awakened.

"A year and a half pretty soon. It's so and so. It depends on work and there is not enough of steady work." The man replied evenly.

"What kind of work do you do then?" Aarne asked.

"Construction. It's well paid but there have been layoffs, at least for new men like me," the man replied.

The strange word -layoffs -mixed in with the Finnish, so it was hard to even notice it, just weighed on Aarne's mind. He didn't really ask its meaning and didn't ask anything about Canada again. That much he added that he himself was going to Northern Ontario mines.

"Well, I have to go. The wife is coming from work. Well, good luck to you in the future. It'll turn around for me too. I'll likely be able to return to work soon." The man turned and walked away.

"Well, there is all kinds," Aarne tried to forget the whole matter.

"He didn't look well off," Sylvi determined from her point of view but from Aarne's tight expression she presumed that the matter wouldn't be discussed again.

Finally, the train arrived and left soon after they had sat down.

"This is the last train. Then we will arrive," from Aarne didn't soothe the girls or Sylvi who were all tired from travelling.

That night and the next day were still spent on the train until all the other people had departed, each one at their destination.

Only the Kalliokoski family remained and Aarne started to count his money.

"I have forty dollars left when you count it all," he announced as he put his wallet away.

"Yes," Sylvi replied automatically without taking any part in the matter as she didn't understand any-thing about the strange money. She understood from Aarne's previous explanations that soon they would be arriving. That was enough for her to think about.

"It's the next stop then," Aarne wiped his brow with his handkerchief. He was sweating. Everyone else felt expectant about this final arrival without showing it to one another. It was late in the afternoon. The train slowed down and stopped.

"This kind of a small village!" Sylvi announced her opinion as she stepped out.

"Well, here it is," Aarne determined for himself.

"And I want to go back home," Marja asked.

"I'm not going to stay long," Kaarina whispered without seeing the station through her tears.

The conductor and the station workmen carried all their things out of the train.

The suitcases and packages which contained all their previous life seemed strangely worn and battered and bound together, like the immigrants they were themselves on their arrival to the New Country.

"Jussi! There you are!" Aarne stepped quickly to greet his older brother whom he recognised from photos he had seen.

"So, hello, hello. I mean Good Day and welcome to Canada," Jussi said to everyone and shook Aarne's hand.

Chapter Four

"This is the place here," Jussi introduced the small city from the taxi.

"Yes, yes, yes," Aarne agreed without deeply thinking about anything. A strange small disappointment and tiredness had settled into his mind now that they had finally arrived, and he couldn't inspect the place thoroughly yet. At first sight everything was so different from what he had thought or expected it to be and even his brother sitting beside him seemed like a total stranger. "My head is so mixed up because we have travelled almost two weeks, that it'll take a while for it to clear," he laughed to Jussi.

"Well, I can understand that. It'll take a while," Jussi replied.

Sylvi inspected everything around her thoroughly.

The small city was bigger than what it had first seemed to be from the station but the houses were

generally one or two-story houses. Some higher buildings could be seen further away. The street travelled
away from the station in a straight line until it followed
the circular lakeshore, and then travelled again in another straight line through the city.

"Here is the Main Street," Jussi explained as the
taxi turned to another street which divided the city
once again.

"Yes, I see," Sylvi noted the few three-story brick
or plaster houses and the older, wooden houses which
had been left in between, but she didn't say anything
aloud yet.

All the houses were close together, some attached to one another. The goods displayed in the
store windows told in their own way about what was
being sold inside but the signs printed in English remained a mystery to her. After the last turn the scene
changed to privately owned houses sitting in the middle of their yards, surrounded by a few trees, bushes
and flower gardens. The taxi parked in front of one of
the white wooden houses with a smaller similar house
peeking from behind it.

Jussi paid the taxi and they stepped outside,
Aarne with a determined step, Sylvi straightening out
her wrinkled, dusty dress, and Kaarina and Marja on
Sylvi's sides as if they were glued there. No one was
able to admit to themselves, or to one another, that

they had truly arrived.

Kaarina, especially, felt that everything was so ordinary and small. Where were the riches and the rosy future which Aarne had spoken about for the past half year? Perhaps the people's well-being lived inside these small houses or rustled as money in their pockets but for sure you couldn't find it on the streets of this small city. That was her opinion.

The door of the house opened and a short, somewhat stocky brown-haired woman ran to meet them with her arms outstretched, greeting everyone at the same time: "Welcome, welcome. There you are. Come inside now!"

Jussi rushed to introduce his wife: "This is Aune. You know her from pictures."

They followed Jussi and Aune into the living room where there were more new people to meet.

Aune started to introduce everyone: "This is our son, Martin and his wife Nancy."

Martin shook everyone's hand and said a few words in Finnish but Nancy only smiled.

"She is English-speaking," Aune explained.

Sylvi didn't understand and greeted Nancy again in Finnish: "Päivää."

"She doesn't understand," Aarne explained in Finnish and Sylvi blushed.

Aune brought forth a small girl, about Marja's

size, and introduced her: "Here is our Irene. Say päivää in Finnish."

"Päivää, päivää," the girl repeated automatically.

To that Sylvi replied: "Oh, she can speak Finnish."

Everyone joined in the relief of laughter except Aune who added a bit sarcastically: "The young mostly speak English, and Finnish only at home."

"Yes, I see," added Sylvi.

Jussi invited all: "Come and sit down in the kitchen," which reminded everyone that it was time to eat. Aune organised the newcomers and their own family to a ready set table in the kitchen and even Sylvi sighed with relief in that she could sit down at a table that didn't move with the movement of a ship. Aarne and Jussi concentrated, like men mostly do on the food, and Sylvi also started to eat but the girls stared with wonder at all the food that Aune carried to the front of them.

"Eat now. Take peas and salad," she invited like a good hostess.

"We haven't eaten peas in this way," Kaarina dared to object.

"Oh, my goodness. You'll learn to eat peas this way," Aune declared to the girls with enthusiasm.

Slowly and reluctantly the girls chewed their

food hoping that the meal would end there but Aune was already carrying a glass bowl filled with red gleaming jelly for dessert.

"What is that?" Kaarina whispered to Sylvi.

"I don't know. Be quiet and just eat," Sylvi whispered back.

The red jelly seemed to glow in the dessert dish in front of Kaarina. She swallowed a spoonful and it slipped down her throat before she had even tasted it. But under Aarne's tight gaze she was forced to eat it all.

"Well, here we are then. I guess we'll get used to this new life as we go along," Aarne said and stretched out his arms and sat on the sofa.

"Well, let's take a little drink before we do anything else," Jussi suggested and brought out a liquor bottle from the kitchen cupboard.

He prepared strong drinks and sat beside Aarne and asked: "What's new back home? When have you last visited there?"

"I don't know what's new there. I haven't been there, wait now, it must be eleven or twelve years ago. It could be in between the wars, the winter war and the continuation war, when we visited," Aarne replied.

Jussi stared a moment at the floor and swallowed his drink before he continued: "Is that when you've been there last? It's, , ,let's see, , , it's about twenty-six years ago since I left. You were a ten or eleven years old little ragamuffin then so you don't even remember."

"Don't say that! Is it so damn long ago? I can remember when you and uncle Aukusti left, , ,and now uncle Aukusti has already been in his grave for years, , ,that's how time goes by," Aarne tried feverishly to remember the time they were now discussing but which he had forgotten. For his brother they would be his last, surely still vivid memories of Finland, but to Aarne they were childhood happenings which had been buried under new events. The drinks seemed to build brotherly feelings between them, and their futures united them for the next while, even though they didn't have many memories together.

Aarne changed the topic to the present: "I suppose I'll be going to work on Monday?"

"Well yes. I have organised everything ready for you. Don't worry about that," Jussi replied.

"Well, no! I wish I could learn English and then I could manage," Aarne declared to Jussi.

"You'll learn enough to get by. I've been able to manage with Finnish. I do know enough English though that they haven't been able to sell me," Jussi laughed.

Aarne joined in the laughter but decided that he would go to language classes and learn English soon.

Sylvi glanced at the liquor bottle, from which
Jussi added to the glasses, with worried eyes. She had
talked to Aarne about drinking earlier and had hoped
that there would be no drinking in the New Country,
but obviously people's bad habits as well as good, travelled with them wherever they went. Back home Aarne
had disappeared into the city on Saturday evenings
and returned full of liquor. Sylvi had resigned herself
to these outings but had never been in agreement with
them. So, she made up her mind to say something
about the drinking to Aarne rather sooner than later.

In the midst of Sylvi's thinking Aune dried her
hands from the dishwater and handed Jussi two more
glasses, saying at the same time: "Make drinks for us
too. You'll take a drink Sylvi?"

"And I'm not taking a drink!" Sylvi was appalled
at the whole idea.

Aune shook her shoulders and sat with the
drink Jussi had made in her hand, and even though
Sylvi sat at the same table, from that moment on she
moved Aune in her mind to a group of women she did-
n't respect very much. Now she was forced to continue
the evening and even wait for visitors that had been
invited to come.

A knock at the door broke the cooled-off mood
in the room and Aune rushed to open the door.

"Come on in," she bustled. "Here is Vilho Lahti and Taimi and Anita."

"Hello," Anita, about Kaarina's size girl, greeted.

Kaarina didn't say anything.

Anita's mother stepped in to help. "But Anita, now you need to speak Finnish! Kaarina doesn't know how to speak English."

Kaarina felt that Anita stared at her with annoyance but they stayed together in the kitchen after the adults had moved to the living room.

After a quiet moment Anita began to speak in Finnish: "How old are you?"

"I'm fourteen," Kaarina replied.

"I'm fourteen too," Anita said.

"Are you from Finland too?" Kaarina asked in turn.

"No. I was born here. My mother and father were born in Finland."

"But you speak Finnish?"

"Not much. You'll soon speak English," Anita added.

"I don't know if I'll learn. I'm soon going back to Finland. I'm not going to bother learning English since I'm not staying here," Kaarina declared firmly even though she noticed that Anita was surprised by her answer.

"But why are you going back there when it's so

poor there?" Anita asked surprised and added: "My mother and father have told me."

"It's not poor there. It's good there. It's not poor there!" Kaarina spoke so loudly that even the adults sitting in the living room turned to look at the girls.

"The girl is homesick, at the beginning," Aarne hurried to explain. "Those kids. They'll get used to things soon!"

"The girls will get used to things soon when they go to school and learn English," Aune added.

"Of course. Children get used to things so fast," was heard all around.

Only Sylvi understood Kaarina's homesickness and tiredness and she reminded others by saying: "The children are tired because we have travelled a long time and the new places and all. It would be best if we went to sleep." She yawned and the men's drinking annoyed her on top of everything else so much that she also hoped to lay down and rest.

"Of course. Of course, you are tired. I didn't notice it myself, , ,I'll come and show you to the small house at the back so you can lay down," Aune suggested.

After saying good night Aune directed Sylvi and the girls along a path to the small house in the back-yard.

"Jussi and I were talking that you could stay

here in the small house and live in your own way at the beginning," Aune explained.

"Yes, yes, it's good," Sylvi agreed but wondered at the same time what the words, small house, meant that Aune had said in English; but she was so tired that she couldn't bother asking anything. She was happy to have this small place to themselves where they could start to unravel the daily problems of the New Country.

Sylvi prepared to sleep.

Kaarina and Marja didn't have enough energy to think about anything, no homesickness, nor tomorrow, nor the new life. Totally exhausted they crawled into the old, large creaky steel bed to sleep.

While Sylvi organised herself to lay down on a similar bed beside it, Aune returned to get Aarne; and even though Aarne was beginning to be drunk, he agreed to leave the company and the drinking.

Sylvi was almost asleep and in no mood to start a sermon about drinking, so she turned her back to Aarne's caresses after he had settled into the bed.

"Just go the sleep," she demanded angrily. "You don't know if the girls are asleep yet. Don't!"

"They are asleep. Don't worry about them," Aarne tried but the drinks and the tiredness mellowed his wanting so that soon the whole family was sleeping their first night in the New Country.

- - - - - - - - - -

The Sunday morning sun played on the cover of Kaarina's bed teasing her eyes to open. She looked around and tried to remember where she was. The big steel beds almost filled the whole room so that only a narrow space in between them remained for walking. The window from which the sun shone on the cover was located above Sylvi's and Aarne's bed. Kaarina got up and tiptoed to the kitchen without waking anyone.

The kitchen seemed large because there was only a table, four chairs, and a small stove and a fridge. Peeking outside she noted that the only window in the room looked to the backyard whereas a door on the opposite wall, which she opened a crack, led back to Aune's and Jussi's house. Another door led to a small living room.

Everything was very clean but faded and old.

Kaarina found her way back to bed. Her thoughts returned automatically to Finland. – Was it a beautiful day there? What was Leena doing? - The tears started to flow and the crying eased her homesickness even though it didn't take it away.

Marja got up and warned in her precocious way: "Don't cry again or father will get angry!"

"Be quiet! I'm not crying," Kaarina wiped her cheeks dry and started to dress.

Aarne and Sylvi wakened too and put on their clothes. While Sylvi was making the beds, Aarne went to get the suitcases and carried them to the kitchen to wait unpacking. Then he reminded the girls: "And you are not going to complain about the food any more! You eat what you get in front of you and that's that!"

"Why don't we make our own foods? We don't like these foods," Marja started to suggest.

"We are going to make our own foods as soon as we get some money," Aarne promised.

"Well, how long are we going to stay here in other people's homes?" Sylvi asked on her own behalf.

"I told you that as soon as we can, we are going to get our own home and foods. Everybody is wanting something from me. One wants this and another wants that! Keep your mouths closed or you can go and work yourselves!" Aarne was becoming angry.

Sylvi didn't touch the subject any more and asked the girls to be quiet as they made their way to Jussi's and Aune's to eat.

"Come on outside," cousin Irene invited in Finnish as the breakfast ended. She spoke in the singular even though she meant both of the girls. As they didn't have anything else to do the girls agreed to go and followed Irene down the Main Street.

"This is a store and this is a doctor and this is another store," Irene explained.

"What is a doctor?" Marja questioned each English word with a child's normal curiosity but after a while Irene became tired of explaining and the talking ended there.

They turned at the lakefront and walked back.

At Aune's and Jussi's Kaarina collected several newspapers without looking at them carefully and carried them to the small house to read the rest of the day. She opened one newspaper after another on the kitchen table and then commented with disappointment: "I can't read these! Look now! I can't read them!" She repeated while swallowing back tears as she noticed each newspaper to be written in English.

"What are we going to read here father?" She asked angrily: "No one can understand these!"

"We didn't come here to read, but to work. Don't cry but start instead to put your clothes away!" Aarne ordered annoyed.

"Yes, put your dresses to hang on these hangers and your shoes under the bed. There's something for you to do!" Sylvi suggested.

"I'm not taking them out of my suitcase because I'm going back to Finland next year. I'm going back home! Why would I take them out for nothing?" Kaarina announced stubbornly.

Sylvi and Aarne exchanged questioning looks, each trying to find the right answer in the other's eyes, but not finding it.

"Well, let it be then," Sylvi warned Aarne with her eyes and said quietly: "She'll come around when she is ready if you don't force her."

And so Kaarina's suitcase stayed closed and she carried it to the bedroom where she kicked it under the bed.

Marja organised her only doll Molla-Maija to the new place. From the time she was small, she had hummed some monotonous tune alone if things around her had become difficult. This is what she was doing now and concentrated all her energy to folding Molla-Maija's clothes and making her a bed in a shoe-box at the same time disappearing into her own world.

New things were pushed into their lives in such a hurry that it was hard to accept them all. Kaarina ran back and forth between Aune's and Jussi's place and the small house the rest of the day and at evening she returned and informed Sylvi and Aarne: "That aunt Aune said that you don't have to be formal here and you don't have to address adults formally. You can just be informal with everybody."

"Oh, no that's not going to work out. You have to be polite to your elders and address them Mr. or Mrs."

"Well, I just thought because she said so." Kaarina muttered.

The milk carry-can with its lid and the small cream-can were also something that would not be needed in the New Country even though Sylvi had so carefully packed them for the trip. Aune informed the same evening that in Canada a milkman with a van delivered the milk and the cream to people's homes in glass bottles.

"You think that everything here is like in Finland. It's not like that. Look, it's different here," Aarne explained to Sylvi and the girls.

"It's all different here," Sylvi agreed sarcastically.

- - - - - - - - - -

That new and something different started Monday morning for Aarne when he woke up at five-thirty and joined Jussi in going to work.

At the bus-stop a large crowd of men awaited and greeted them by nodding or smiling or by waving their hands.

"Are all these Finns?" Aarne asked Jussi.

"No, they are not. There are all kinds here. There are Italians, Polish, French. There are all kinds."

"Oh, there are?" Aarne thought a moment about his new situation where he had to trust his brother's ideas about everything, whether he wanted it or not. That was new and different. He often felt that he couldn't get close to the new ideas and words but instead they were stamped with Jussi's interpretation of them. He had already decided that he wouldn't ask about every little thing but would instead follow what he saw others doing even though it was against his nature.

A yellow bus arrived and was soon filled with the men going to the mine. At the mine site it stopped and emptied and turned back to the city.

"It's coming back in the evening to get us. Go now!" Jussi urged Aarne from behind.

In the dressing room everyone undressed completely and put on their work overalls. Taking his cue from the others, Aarne pulled on his brother's large overalls and walked with everyone to the area where they were waiting for the elevator, called the cage.

Finnish men gathered around them and one after another they greeted: "Hi, Jussi! Is this your brother? Hello there!"

"Hello there. Hi! What's new Jussi?"

"Hello! Hi and welcome!" Several men said and nodded to Aarne.

Aarne tried to remember everyone as Jussi introduced them but soon gave it up as a lost cause.

"You'll get to know them as time goes by. Go with Eikka now. He's your partner; I mean you'll be working with him. We'll see each other in the evening."

"We'll see each other then."

Jussi disappeared to his own area of work and Aarne was left standing somewhat forlornly beside a large, blonde, Finnish man.

"Hello! I'm Eikka Kuronen. You're coming with me," the man spoke in a Karelian dialect.

"Well yes. So, we are going together?" Aarne asked.

"We always go together here! You can never go alone. Well, here she comes!"

Everyone stepped into the elevator and Aarne followed Kuronen. The operator pressed the button and the trip down started. The top half of the cage was open and you could see the square timbers supporting the corners and the gray black wet wall of rock, which continued down, until Aarne felt sure that even Hell couldn't be any lower, but finally the cage stopped and everyone stepped out.

Kuronen turned on the light of his safety hat and Aarne did the same.

After he became accustomed to the semi-darkness, Aarne looked around. Jagged, dark, rock walls stared back at him with hardness, and the air seemed to be filled with very fine dust so that it was hard to breathe. But there was no time to think about that because Kuronen started to walk in front and he followed close behind him.

"This is what we make, supports to hold up the

ceiling and loose rocks, stairs and handrails," Kuronen pointed around him. Aarne noted the strong mine timbers that held up the ceiling and walls but the breathless feeling did not leave him.

"God damn if all this crashes and falls down, we'll be done," Aarne commented to Kuronen.

But he did not reply, just pointed to a large, long timber and lifted up one end of it. Aarne understood and grabbed the other end and together they started carrying it.

Kuronen's peaceful and happy manner soon calmed Aarne down too.

"And you get used to everything," Aarne thought at quiet moments, "it's only work. It's not what I thought it would be. Damn it! Where is that gold here? I wonder if I'll ever even see it," Aarne thought, but his first day was mostly spent in trying to get used to the nearness of the rock ceiling and walls which surrounded them at all times.

In the evening Sylvi met him at the door and asked: "Well, what about the working man? How was your day?"

Aarne replied with a small laugh: "Well, what of it!" But later when Sylvi asked more about the new workplace, Aarne looked to the ceiling and replied after a long silence, "Well, it's a kind of an abyss, a deep hole." And Aarne didn't say anything more, and Sylvi didn't ask about the new job for a long time.

- - - - - - - - - -

The girls started back to school after a week's holiday; Marja happily, hoping that school would bring friends and things to do into her small life; Kaarina without expecting anything. They were directed to a teacher's class who had Finnish ancestry.

"I am Mrs. Niemi and this is the fifth grade. I will speak to you only in English. Here are books for you. Look at these and I will speak to you when I get time."

The girls were pointed to the back of the class. Kaarina had trouble fitting into the desk with an attached seat no matter how she tried. She also felt herself to be different from all the other pupils who seemed to be about ten years old.

No matter what, the school day started. The class counted, read and wrote in the English language. Marja tried to follow the lesson but as she really couldn't take part in it, her initial enthusiasm waned slowly and she started to leaf through her book. Kaarina turned to look out the window beside her and allowed her thoughts to fly back to Finland. Soon she didn't see or hear the teacher, nor the other pupils.

"Kaarina!" Someone called her back from her reverie. "What is your name?"

Everyone turned to look at her.

"Name, name, name?" Echoed in the classroom as the teacher repeated the word many times.

"What did she say? What does she want? I can't understand what she wants?" Kaarina whispered to Marja in Finnish.

But the teacher continued speaking and using so many English words before she consented to explain: "What is your name? My name is Mrs. Niemi."

"My name is Kaarina," she tried at last.

The other children smiled and some laughed.

Kaarina sat down and stared outside again, and she stayed that way until it was time to go home for lunch.

"We're not going back there. They laughed at us and we were put into a class of small children," Kaarina cried to Sylvi.

"Don't cry. It's going to get better. They'll forget you! They won't laugh long," Sylvi tried to console the girls but they couldn't eat much because they knew they'd have to return to the school.

In the evening Aarne encouraged the girls, "they are only beginner's difficulties. You are going to do well soon."

And the school continued.

Sylvi's and Aarne's predictions came true and in a week the teacher and the pupils alike left them in peace.

Chapter Five

Life in the New Country started to come around slowly, sometimes getting caught in disappointments, sometimes moving happily, but always moving forward like life moves forward at its own speed; in the same way that the world turns.

The Kalliokoskis became acquainted with other Finnish families and especially with Vilho and Taimi Lahti. Vilho Lahti was an easygoing, mostly happy man, in contrast to Aarne's fast-moving ways and quick temper; and Sylvi found in Taimi Lahti a similar person as she was herself in her love of home.

The Lahtis encouraged the Kalliokoskis to become independent and to try new things on their own without Jussi's or Aune's continuing guidance. This time Taimi was printing names of spices in English on a piece of paper and telling Sylvi the exact shelf from where the spices could be found in the local grocery store.

Vilho was discussing with Aarne world politics and sports and now also the tightening work situation in the city, at the same time that they were playing cards in the living room.

"Has Jussi told you that there might be a strike?" Vilho asked.

"He did say something one evening but since he didn't mention anything more about it, I haven't said anything either. You would think he'd have said something! And Eikka hasn't said anything. And I can't understand much about what happens here. I just don't have enough English to understand anything about what's being said. There is no need for a strike, not in my situation!" Aarne was becoming angry.

"It's not going to happen to us. We don't even have a union! It's just coming to the Hollinger Mine. We'll see then if it starts in the other mines. They've been wanting it for a long time because wages are not going up. What can you do? Nobody needs a strike and I know you don't need it for sure! Let's hope it's only a short one. You never know about these things beforehand," Vilho explained.

Then they continued to play cards while talking at the same time.

"And take this and this! Devil! This card will hold for sure! Now you're going to lose Vilho!" Aarne threw cards on the living room coffee table accompanied by swearwords. He was becoming annoyed with the small city and all the difficulties that fate continually dealt him.

"And now a strike! And I thought I was coming to a better place!"

"Well, don't say anything more. Damn! It's not going to mean anything good for a small place like this!" Vilho added.

The women were drinking coffee in the kitchen but they also heard what the men were saying and Sylvi now asked with concern: "What is Vilho saying about a strike? Are they planning a strike here?"

"That's what they are saying. A strike is coming to the Hollinger Mine."

"Oh my God! I hope it's not for us. We've just arrived. We haven't got anything at all! Not even our own place to live!" Sylvi didn't know what to say. She stuffed a new piece of coffee bread into her mouth and started to chew it furiously at the same time as she drank her first cup of coffee.

The men's card playing and swearing continued in the living room. Sylvi and Taimi stared helplessly at each other and uttered blessings into their coffee cups while hoping that the girls in the bedroom wouldn't hear the men.

But the girls were deeply immersed in their own pastime so that they didn't hear anything. Anita had a large collection of movie star magazines which they were all leafing through with great interest.

"Look! Isn't she lovely?" Kaarina showed one picture after another to Anita and together they admired each one. Although Anita didn't fully meet Kaarina's expectations of a best friend, at least she was the same age and the only young person with whom Kaarina was able to have a conversation because of her lack of English. Anita pulled Kaarina into her life and circle of friends and the homesickness which was always on Kaarina's mind, she often forgot while she was in Anita's company. Marja also accompanied them because she didn't have any friends of her own.

Now, Anita reminded the girls of the upcoming festivities: "Come with me then. It's a big celebration. Mother, what is the name of it?"

"The queen of England will be coronated and there will also be a great celebration in Canada. Go with Anita girls."

Kaarina and Marja promised to go to the local baseball field the following Sunday with Anita.

The day of the celebration dawned with rain but improved as the day progressed and when Anita arrived in the early afternoon, the sun was peeking from behind the clouds. Anita had on a pleated skirt, a short jacket, low white shoes and on her head a colourful kerchief. Kaarina looked in the mirror and evaluated herself. She had taken out of her suitcase a skirt and her good shoes. Her short jacket was acceptable, if she kept it open, but she didn't have the right kind of a kerchief, so she hurried to Aune's place to borrow one. She asked in Finnish: "Aunt Aune do you have a kerchief to loan me, the same flowered kind that Anita and everyone has?"

"Let's see what I have on the closet shelf," Aune replied and after a short search she found a kerchief which she handed to Kaarina saying: "You can keep it! It doesn't suit me."

"Thank you, thank you." Kaarina put the kerchief on her head and tied it under her chin.

She looked once more in the mirror and sighed with satisfaction. Now she would look almost the same as others of her age, and even though she didn't know it herself, it started with that kerchief, her becoming a Canadian, not fast, nor easily but with time; as these things happen in this world.

The field was full of people from the elderly walking with canes, to babies being carried in their parents' arms. A strange flag flew in the flagpole.

"It's the flag of England," Anita explained. "Canada has no flag."

The band started to play music and people began to sing with Anita joining in the singing. Kaarina tried to copy the other people's mouth movements and to hum a tune she didn't know. Small boys were giving out brass coins and small flags. Marja inspected the queen's picture on the coin and started to wave the flag back and forth, like the others, but Kaarina turned her flag downwards and slipped the brass coin into her jacket pocket. Suddenly everything from her past came back and she wanted to go away from the celebration.

"I don't like being here! We have to go home. We don't want to be at a celebration like this," Kaarina explained to the surprised Anita and started to pull the stubborn Marja away from the field.

"I like it here; we just came here!" Marja resisted but Kaarina didn't let go of her arm until at the home gate. Even there she kept pushing Marja to keep going inside.

"Don't push me! I would have stayed there. Why did we have to leave?" Marja kept asking.

But Kaarina didn't reply; instead she walked to her bed and turned to the wall to think and cry. Changes continued to crowd into their every day lives. The language change she could understand but many of the other changes came as a surprise and became too heavy for her to bear. It felt that the bottom was falling from underneath the life that she had always known.

Nowadays Aarne kept asking Jussi about the

strike almost every day and Jussi's complete calmness about it irked Aarne to no end. Finally, while they were all sitting in Aune's and Jussi's living room one evening, Jussi announced that the strike was about to start the following week.

"It's starting on Monday. That's what I've heard," Jussi announced.

"So, it's starting?" Aarne wanted to know more. "You haven't said anything to me for many days even though I've asked you several times! And Eikka hasn't said anything either."

"It's not going to start for us. Our mine isn't even in the union. Don't start now! We'll be fine," Jussi tried to calm Aarne.

"Is that what you think?" Aarne laughed shortly even though he didn't feel like laughing at all. He always felt so alone and uneasy because he didn't have English, and couldn't really follow the news in the newspapers or the radio; and couldn't keep up with anything in the New Country and didn't know about its customs or happenings. The future seemed more and more difficult. The language classes wouldn't be starting until the fall.

In the evening Sylvi poured more salt into his wounds by saying: "And now they're going to have a strike! What did you tell me that it was different here? What if you get laid off and become unemployed and we haven't got any money? What do we do then? And neither one of us speaks English?"

"Don't for God's sake tell me more! Do you think that I don't understand that? It would be best if you went to work too!"

"And what work will I find? There is nothing for women here except cleaning or a dishwasher's place at the men's boarding house that Aune has talked about. And when do they need someone there? I don't know!"

"Best to be looking for work! Otherwise what will we do?"

School ended too and this freed Kaarina and Marja from their daily grind. They didn't feel that they had really learned anything.

"Well, after the next year you're going to be talking English perfectly," Jussi predicted to Kaarina.

"We're never going to learn!" Kaarina laughed in reply. It was much easier to take sun in the back-yard than to think about the fact that now they were the last and the least smart pupils in their classes. In Kaarina's mind it was pointless to take part in the life of Canada because she would be returning to Finland already the following spring. If some adult dared to suggest something different her reply was always the same: "I don't want to stay here! I'm not going to start learning English! I'm going back to Finland."

The summer started very hot – it was unbelievably hot – said everyone.

The paralysing heat continued without end; it
tired everyone and Sylvi didn't want to think about any
job but now she felt she was forced to look for one.

They also often visited Eikka and Vieno Kuronen. When Vieno talked about her job at the men's
boarding house, Sylvi quickly asked: "Do they ever
need anyone to work there?"

"Yes, they sometimes do," said Vieno.

"Well, if they need a dishwasher or a cleaning
woman, I could come right away if you'd let me know,"
Sylvi replied.

The matter was left to lie there but Sylvi felt easier because she felt she had started to search for work.

Everything was so uncertain as it always is in
life. The heat excited the striking men to demonstrations and to small acts of violence. Some reporters
had taken photographs of the agitators and the
demonstrators and these had been published.

Calmness and patience were now most important and even Aarne concentrated on his own life and
was just happy to be working steadily. Slowly he was
becoming used to the mine and to the many Finnish
men there: To Vilho Lahti, to Eikka Kuronen, to Kalle
Paalanen and to Jaska Ylinen. His everyday friends
now included some English-speaking men too, and he

had learned to reply to their greetings: "Hi! or Hello!"
But if anyone added something more to the greeting,
Aarne could only reply by smiling.

The work in the mine was the same for everybody whatever language they might be speaking and
there Aarne and Eikka made up a perfect team. Where
Eikka was somewhat slow, there Aarne was faster
than two men put together, and where Aarne's
strength was not enough, there Eikka didn't yield an
inch. Sometimes at quiet moments in the mine Aarne
stopped to think about his work in Finland, the electric potter's wheel, the ready bowls, the pliable gray
clay which he had moulded to whatever shape he had
wanted. He had been the master of that clay and now
he was a servant of this mine. That was a difference.
There were many. One day when he was deep down in
the mine where the heat, and the dusty air felt that
they were pressing his thoughts very low, he remembered the spring breeze which had blown from the windows of the factory in Finland.

"And God damn it, leave those thoughts now!"
He swore to himself. "Don't I have enough to do aside
from these thoughts?"

And there was a lot to do. Paydays were full of
work to make the money last long enough to pay all
the bills. Aarne paid Jussi fifty dollars a month for the
cost of the trip to come to Canada, and he had counted

that it would be two years before he would have the trip paid. And then he paid Jussi rent, even though it wasn't that much; then there was food which was also economical; but there also were the girls and the winter clothes they needed; and something would need to be done so that a bank account could at least be opened.

That something became timely when the Kuronen's younger son, Mikko, knocked on the Kalliokoski's door and puffed to Sylvi: "My mother told me to come and say that there is an opening at the boarding house!"

"Yes. Well, tell your mother that I'll be coming to see about it tomorrow morning," Sylvi promised.

"Who was that?" Aarne asked Sylvi from the living room.

"It was just Mikko Kuronen. I guess they're needing a dishwasher."

"Will you be going?" Aarne asked and came into the kitchen.

"I guess it would be best."

"Well. Do what you want," Aarne replied.

The next morning Sylvi walked towards the boarding house, which turned out to be one of the more rundown buildings on that street, a three-story wooden structure with a collection of old garbage cans leaning against it. Sylvi opened the door and stepped into the semi-darkness from the morning sunlight outside.

"There is our dishwasher coming. Hello!" Someone welcomed her and after a while she realised the person to be a small, dark-haired woman who was smiling at her with a cigarette hanging from the corner of her mouth. She also saw Vieno Kuronen's blonde, plump form standing beside the stove, and leaning by another door, a blonde woman with a tray in her hands.

Sylvi stayed by the door.

"The manager-lady is coming soon. Sit there and wait. You'll soon be standing when you start to work!" Vieno urged.

"Don't say another thing! I've been washing these dishes here for two years now and there's never been an end to them!" Added the same small woman who had welcomed Sylvi inside. "My name is Martta and Vieno already told me that your name is Sylvi. Come here now and I can show you how all this is done so you know it when I leave!"

Sylvi hurried to Martta's side and tried to remember everything she was showing and telling her.

Right after twelve noon plates started to collect on the shelf in front of them where the men left them after eating, and from there the two women rushed dishes and utensils through the dish and rinse waters and Sylvi dried the plates and organised them into a stack, from where the waitress retrieved them to put on the table again. Sylvi helped where she could but her attention was more drawn to the cigarette which hung precariously from the corner of Martta's mouth. Sylvi waited for the ashes to fall away any minute, but when they hung long at the end of the cigarette, Martta swung her hand to dry on her apron and knocked the ashes on the floor and pushed the cigarette back into her mouth. Martta had a hardened, man-like quality about her which proved that she had survived many of the New Country's trials and she knew her worth. In Canada's northern bush and mining camps everyone knew these people by their work.

In the midst of all this activity the manager of the boarding house walked into the kitchen. Sylvi turned to look at the small round woman who was tightly bound inside her cotton dress and white apron. Her gray hair caught in a bun at the nape of her neck added to her businesslike and tight demeanor.

"Martta has explained all the finer points of dishwashing to you, I presume. Did you say what the pay was too?" The manager asked with a strict look on her face but with a hint of a smile in the corners of her eyes.

"I haven't had time to talk about the pay."

"Well, everyone knows that the pay is twenty

dollars a week and all you can eat while you're here. So, if that's satisfactory to you, the job is open."

"It's fine," Sylvi rushed to say although she didn't understand anything about the pay.

Martta shoved a dishrag into Sylvi's hand and turned on both faucets to fill the two large tin sinks full of new, hot, steaming water and from that moment Sylvi's dishwashing career began.

The manager supervised everything, by walking from near the stove to the dishwashing area, and by checking through the serving opening to tell the waiter, Seija, to take some needed food to the dining room table.

At two o'clock everything became quiet and Martta spat out her eternal cigarette stub on the floor and stepped on it to put out the fire. Then she stuffed her apron into a brown paper bag and left. Where? No one was sure but everyone knew that she'd be going to work somewhere, to a boarding house or to a bush camp. These experienced Finnish workers had stellar reputations which travelled before them. They were always able to find work.

"Now we're going to eat," invited Vieno while she ladled soup into everyone's bowls and they all sat down to eat.

"When will the day here end?" Sylvi dared to ask once the manager had left to check on the cleaning woman upstairs.

"Those who just ate will be going to work on the afternoon shift. Look how I have put their ready lunch boxes on the shelf beside the serving opening. The day shift men will come to have coffee after three o'clock and we'll also have coffee then. After that you'll be tight for time all afternoon to wash out their coffee cups and lunch boxes before supper starts at five o'-clock."

"Yes, so we'll be going home about seven o'-clock?" Sylvi understood that she wouldn't have much time between lunch, coffee break and the washing of lunch boxes. As the day turned to afternoon, she noticed that the prolonged standing made her legs and back ache and sweat poured continuously down her face. As Vieno had told her, at three o'clock a new group of men pushed into the dining room and placed their empty lunch boxes into the serving opening to be washed, and then they sat down to have their coffee and a piece of Finnish coffee bread.

"And those too!" Sylvi said while she drank her coffee with Vieno, but she was able to finish washing the lunch boxes, the coffee cups, the dishes and pots and pans by the time it was seven o'clock. Completely worn out she followed Vieno out the door.

"Don't worry now. Tomorrow you'll be doing dishes like somebody experienced." Vieno comforted her.

Sylvi didn't reply; she was barely able to say good night to Vieno.

"Well, how big is your pay?" Aarne asked right after Sylvi sat down beside him on the side of the bed.

"Don't start asking anything because my legs and my back are aching so much. Just be quiet now!" Sylvi said more to herself.

"Well, you've worked before! You know it's not play. Say what your pay is so we can figure out if it's worth for you to be going there at all!"

"It's twenty dollars a week and you can eat all you want while you're there."

"Well, the pay is nothing to brag about!" Aarne said, "but at least you'll be able to eat there. Be that much cheaper here at home."

"As if I ate the most of all of us here!" Sylvi retorted to Aarne's hand that wandered around to squeeze her bottom at the same time.

But Aarne didn't really have anything else on his mind as he immediately went to the kitchen to tell the girls who were doing the dishes there: "Are the dishes done yet? From now on the two of you can do all this housework here because your mother is working now!"

Sylvi smiled to herself thinking about Aarne's order to the girls and the thought that he was satisfied about her going to work, even though it wasn't that much of a job. The last sentence that she understood before she drifted off to sleep was Aarne saying: "Well, it won't be long before we look for our own place to live."

The heat continued. Sweat poured down Sylvi's face while she washed the dishes and she may even have lost a few pounds. Together with Vieno they often wondered how the waiter Seija was able to keep the powder and make-up on her face in the continuing heat.

"How does she put it on and keep it on?" Sylvi started many times.

To that Vieno often replied: "And she still adds more stuff on her face when I have to throw my clothes off me pretty soon."

And Sylvi's days never felt so long and difficult any more as Vieno's lively talking and ready laughing spiced them up.

The rhythm of the day was ruled by the work. Sylvi left home a little before eleven o'clock in the morning and returned at seven in the evening. The morning's dishwashing chores ended after lunch. Then she and Vieno ate and spent a few moments discussing the city's and the whole world's problems. The waitress Seija ate very little because she was trying to lose weight. She preferred to sit by herself and read love stories or leaf through movie magazines or fix her face.

Almost every week Vieno also brought to work magazines and weekend issues of newspapers which they had ordered from Finland. Usually the Finnish papers arrived in Canada about four to six weeks after they had been published in Finland but the events and news from Finland continued to be very popular with all Finns in Canada. Jussi and Aune and the Lahti's all received magazines and newspapers which they had ordered from Finland. Especially to Sylvi these Finnish papers were now becoming an important connection to her home country. There was not yet enough money to order papers from Finland but she often heard the fresh news from Vieno or from the Lahti's and then read the pertinent points later from the borrowed newspapers.

But now the women read together in a state of agitation: "It's happened at Isojoki. Her name is Kyllikki Saari. They haven't found her. Oh God and she is a religious girl too! Where has she gone that she is so lost? Has she gone somewhere else? Where is this world going to?" Sylvi repeated as she read.

"Don't say anything more. A young girl too!" Vieno added.

"Bring the next issues of the papers as soon as you get them," Sylvi added and Vieno promised to bring them.

If Vieno's son or Sylvi's girls happened to visit the boarding house when the women were having their afternoon coffee, the youngsters were also given a cup of coffee and a piece of Finnish coffee bread. All this activity took place while the manager of the boarding house took her afternoon nap; she needed it after having risen at five o'clock in the morning.

- - - - - - - - - -

The most difficult problems of the spring and summer months had been the daily black flies and the vicious mosquitos of the evenings. The bites on the newcomers had swollen and itched all summer while the permanent residents hardly noticed their bites as they were used to them. The midsummer's heat had killed the black flies and now the mosquitos died at the end of the summer. The high heat ended with thunderstorms in late August. After that the sun shone during the day from a clear sky but the evenings brought with them a coolness and sudden darkness in contrast to the long evening twilights of Finland.

- - - - - - - - - -

Looking for an apartment or a flat to live in was now becoming the most important item in Aarne's and Sylvi's lives.

"We're not going to live here for years," Aarne repeated almost daily.

"And we have to pay rent here too. What are rents in this city anyway?" Sylvi tried to guess but also wanted to leave the small backyard house of Aune's and Jussi's.

"I'll ask Jussi about that," Aarne replied.

As soon as Aarne asked about the rents in the small city, Jussi replied: "Bill Paananen said last week that he has an upstairs flat for rent if you're thinking about moving. The small house at the back isn't meant for winter. It's not insulated."

"Well, what is the rent for the flat?"

"I guess it's thirty dollars a month," Jussi thought and said that the flat would be fairly close, only a couple of streets away.

"Put something on and let's go with Jussi to see if that place is liveable," Aarne ordered Sylvi when he returned to the small house.

Sylvi pulled her sweater on her shoulders and hurried along with the men.

The apartment turned out to be an upstairs flat with a kitchen, a living room, a bedroom and a bathroom, and half of a woodshed at the back.

"This is good," Jussi guessed.

"I guess it is," Aarne agreed with his brother and Sylvi nodded her head in consent.

"Well, there would be enough room here," she said more to herself but was still unsatisfied with the fairly large flat. Something permanent and steadfast was missing from the place, the same quality that was missing from the small city in general. Looking closer everything was constructed in a hurry during the high time of the gold rush. The houses had been fixed to be more liveable once the small city had become a permanent fixture on the Canadian map. Only the later constructed post office, two banks and the city hall, represented well built buildings; everything else was flimsily put together or poorly fixed.

The Kalliokoskis moved into this older, fixed and somewhat flimsy flat on their first autumn in Canada.

"Well, now you have a good winter place to live in!" Commented Jussi.

"But where are we going to get the furniture from? Tell me that?" Aarne demanded.

"Take the furniture from the small house. I think you can get started with them."

It was settled.

Sylvi missed the familiar, former good furniture in Finland but did not say anything to Aarne. Instead she used her energy to packing small stuff in suitcases and cardboard boxes, now for the second time in the same year.

Aarne and Jussi moved the small house furniture in a wheel barrel along the Main Street a couple

blocks to Crawford Street – which Aarne now renamed
– Kraafort Sreet – with his Finnish accent.

The girls' steel bed was collected into the bedroom. Three similar wooden packing boxes were put
side by side to form a dresser with a curtain to cover
their contents, and on top of that Aarne nailed a small
mirror. Sylvi placed a colourful rag rug on the floor.
There was already a woodstove, which was heated with
firewood and coal in the kitchen, and now they carried
a table and four chairs there. Aarne's and Sylvi's steel
bed was put into the living room. Beside it Aarne
added one more wooden packing box to form a side
table and on top of that he placed the alarm clock.

"Well, now we have our own place," he boasted
to Sylvi once Jussi had gone.

"Oh, it's better this way. It's always better in
your own place," Sylvi added satisfied.

She put the coffeepot on the stove and started
the fire at the same time that Aarne concentrated once
more on counting his money.

"The rent here is thirty dollars a month and
we'll spend about eighty dollars on the food; that
makes about a hundred and ten dollars in a month;
wait now; fifty dollars to make the trip loan payment;
let it be; that makes a hundred and sixty dollars. Our
wages together make two hundred and forty dollars a
month; so, we'll have about eighty dollars left over

every month."

"But we have to buy at least one dresser, and the girls need winter clothes, and then there is electricity and water, and we have to buy wood and coal for the stove,'" Sylvi reminded.

"Well, yes, well, we'll have to do all that and buy clothes once we can get going here. Let's start saving after a couple of years once we have this trip loan paid."

"Oh, my God! I thought we'd be back in Finland by then, after two years! What are you saying?"

"Well, what the Devil! You must understand that, a grown woman, that we can't haul that much together so soon!"

If nothing else, Aarne's look and the tenor of his voice shut Sylvi up.

Aarne went, muttering to himself, into the living room, and Sylvi stayed in the kitchen to drink her coffee. Neither one of them touched the subject again until later when they went to bed. That's when Aarne explained: "I'm not saying that it's like I hoped it would be here, but we can't return now either. Or do you think that Jussi will also pay the return fare for us?"

"Well, I didn't mean that but why didn't you listen in Finland when we were trying to tell you that we don't want to leave from there? That's what I meant."

"Well, I've heard enough about that. This is just

how things are in the world, and nothing more," Aarne started to sing half playfully in Finnish. "We'll put together a jackpot of money yet and return!"

"We'll see," Sylvi sobbed shortly in reply. She felt it to be impossible to think that they might have to stay in Canada longer than two years.

"You have to take life one step at a time," Sylvi still was repeating to herself the next morning when she walked to work. "What's the point of planning this or that because everything can change in one minute. The ordinary person is just in Fate's hands." She opened the boarding house door at the same time that Vieno ran towards her with a Finnish newspaper in her hands.

"Now I have bad news! Read that! They have found that girl's bicycle from the Isojoki swamp. I'm thinking they'll find her there too!" Vieno opened the newspaper in front of Sylvi on the big kitchen table of the boarding house.

"Don't for God's sake! From the Isojoki swamp! And they have written in those papers that Kyllikki Saari is here or she is there and she's gone to Sweden or somewhere! And she's likely not gone anywhere. Something very terrible has happened to her! I can't understand anything any more. Where is she really?" Sylvi and Vieno read together.

Sylvi added still: "Let's not tell the kids anything

because I don't know if they really read these papers. Well Kaarina reads them but I don't think Marja does! Does Mikko read?"

"No, he doesn't read anything. He plays outside all day."

Aarne read the newspaper in the evening and put it right back into Sylvi's workbag to be returned.

School started again.

Where the girls had gone to school happily in Finland, they didn't seem to want to go now at all.

"Do we have to go? Do we really have to go?" Made Sylvi nervous altogether.

"You have to go. Someone really has to learn English because I don't think that our father will ever learn it. I've not noticed him speaking English!" Sylvi dared to complain to the girls.

The girls were now put into the seventh grade but like in the spring they were pushed to the back of the room as if to be out of the way. The teacher's first week was spent in organising the class so that it was already the start of the second week before he had time to see the girls. Kaarina and Marja sat with their eyes downcast under the gaze of the new man teacher.

After a long talk, of which the girls understood nothing at all, the teacher gave them new green picture books and pencils. Marja opened her book with interest and started right away to fill the empty spaces in the sentences under the pictures. By the time it was recess she had already filled three pages.

"Why don't you write something?" She demanded from the uninterested Kaarina.

"I'm not going to learn this English because I'm soon going back to Finland."

"We are not going back for many years. I heard father say to mother."

Kaarina took this piece of news without feelings and didn't reply to it in any way but in the afternoon she took up her pen and slowly started to fill her book.

On their way home she asked Marja: "Do you understand anything about what you're writing?"

"Not that much."

"I don't either."

"Where are the dictionaries?" Kaarina asked Sylvi in the evening.

"They're there in a box under the bed."

Kaarina leafed through the one dictionary for a while and then announced with glee to Marja: "Listen Marja, if you say, I am and look at the picture, then you know that she is saying, I am. Do you understand?"

"I understood it from those pictures already."

"I'm taking this dictionary with me tomorrow and every time I don't understand a word, I'm going to look it up in this book or in the other one."

"Take them and I'll use them too. We can both use them when we are in school," Marja was enthusiastic.

The next day both girls filled five pages. The teacher checked their work during the recess. Once he noticed the dictionaries on Kaarina's desk he picked up the English one and after checking in it he said, "I – minä" pointing to himself.

The girls understood that the teacher was trying to say, I in Finnish, and now it was their turn to laugh at him. The new teacher seemed fun.

In the evening the girls asked Sylvi: "Hi mother, do you know what this means – I am Sylvi. I live on Crawford Street?"

"I guess it must be that my name is Sylvi and our house is on Kraafort Sreet."

"It's not exactly like that. But try, I am Sylvi. I live on Crawford Street."

Marja continued: "You say it father."

"I am Aarne. I live on Kraafort Riit."

"You can't either. You can't even say it as well as mother," the girls laughed together.

"Don't laugh! We are soon going to English classes and then we'll talk rings around the two of you," Aarne was getting somewhat annoyed.

"Well, we'll see it then. Let's not say much yet," Sylvi settled it.

Sometimes in the evenings when Kaarina and Marja were practising their English by speaking to one another, Sylvi looked at Aarne with a question in her eyes, and once asked out loud: "What's going to happen to us when the children are no longer going to speak the same language as we do?"

Aarne did not reply at all.

The language school started at the Finnish church and Aarne and Sylvi went there with high hopes; especially Aarne, had waited for the time when he could live in the New Country without an interpreter.

"Well, here it starts," he commented to Sylvi several times as he and Sylvi were walking towards the church.

Sylvi replied: "Don't rush now!" Didn't deter him at all.

In his usual way Aarne wanted to start right away and didn't want to hear about any doubts.

At the church pastor Linnala directed everyone to the back room where there were already sitting some shy and serious adult language school pupils. Vieno and Eikka were the only people Aarne and Sylvi knew there.

The pastor started by explaining:

"Welcome. I will try to teach you this new language and I believe that if you try your best, for sure you will be able to speak and read and perhaps even write English. Let's start by introducing ourselves in the English language. "I am pastor Linnala," he said and directed Vieno Kuronen to continue.

"I am Vieno Kuronen. I don't remember that Mrs, how to say it right, something missis, can you remember?" She broke into a laugh and poked Eikka who was sitting beside her.

"Yes, that's good," the pastor rushed to support her.

"Eikka Kuronen," only said his name.

A young man who was sitting beside Eikka introduced himself correctly in English: "I am Seppo Kaunisto. My name is Seppo Kaunisto."

Aarne and Sylvi introduced themselves quite well too so that the pastor was able to direct everyone to try some harder sentences.

"I am pastor Linnala. You are Mrs. Kuronen."

"So, I is me and you is you. I'll soon be talking in English," Vieno explained enthusiastically in Finnish.

"Say that again in English," the pastor tried to follow his prepared lesson.

Vieno repeated the sentence in English but pronouncing was not easy for her. They all had the same problems. Some spoke English with a Karelian dialect, some with the Ostrobothnian, or the Savo dialect, and

Sylvi with the Turku dialect, so that it was almost impossible for them to understand each other.

However, they were able to finish their first lesson and leave the church.

"And now we can start doing our homework. I can figure out that it's not going to be easy. This is my second year. I'm an old man and too old to learn to speak new languages, but you Aarne, you're a young man. You'll soon be speaking English," Eikka Kuronen said to Aarne on their way home.

"We'll see," Aarne replied shortly.

At home Sylvi showed her book to the girls.

"Oh, I have the same one all filled out already. We have the same books," Marja boasted and Kaarina added: "We know all that already!"

Sylvi couldn't reply in any other way except by saying: "Well, soon you'll be teaching us how to talk!" And she went to bed.

School, the New Country, and especially the new language, stepped in between the adults and the children. In so many ways it was necessary to give in without knowing if that was the right thing to do or not. Would that have happened in Finland? Sylvi wondered. Certainly, the children would have left home as they matured, but this New World was not familiar, and she and Aarne had not lived here. The girls were still so young and innocent that they were not readily able to discern the wheat from the chaff, but instead brought everything home: The language, the customs, all new ideas, without being able to separate the good from the bad. And not only that, Sylvi thought, but also that when the girls became acquainted and acclimatised to the New World very fast, they often instructed Aarne and Sylvi. Aarne didn't approve of that at all and let everyone know about it each time, but Sylvi tried to smooth everything that the girls brought home, so that some peace there could be maintained.

Sylvi fell asleep thinking her thoughts.

Aarne tossed restlessly in his sleep. This time it felt like he was wading in a deep snowbank somewhere in the wartime Karelia; he was being careful, alert and ready; while inspecting the surroundings; he was also waiting for the unexpected. Suddenly he was on his skis, sliding down a steep hill, then thrown into a snowbank, then feeling that he was drowning in snow which was squeezing him into a cold embrace, until the top bedsheet tightened and tightened its grip around him. Then he fought and pulled himself awake and free. "What God damn! Where am I?" He swore on the floor!

"There you are on the floor! Are you having a nightmare again?" Sylvi asked into the darkness.

"Yes, that's it! Hell! It'll pass. You go back to

sleep!" Aarne climbed back into bed again. They were both used to Aarne's wartime nightmares.

Sylvi smiled faintly.

Her own dreams were a wonderful time when she could return to Finland just by closing her eyes. Home images and familiar people often visited in Sylvi's dreams. In the morning when she woke up and looked out the windows, for a few moments it seemed that the whole of Finland should be there too – but instead the morning brought with it an ordinary day and reality, and a strange land – and the first winter in Canada.

Chapter six

Winter forced its way into the north already on October the 13th and from that day onwards the continuing snow falls and freezing cold temperatures and dry inland weather touched all life and activities in many ways. The icy cold and the growing snow banks cut out all outside comings and goings or made them as short as possible. Going to work and to school were necessary; going to the mail box and to the grocery stores had to be done but all other trips were cut out. By the end of November, the cold lurked in all the corners and any openings of houses; the northern lights tore the dark night sky with blue, green and yellow zig zag lines. The dry snow creaked and crunched underfoot when walking, and the snow banks grew.

Sylvi's longing for home and Finland grew in the same way as the snow banks. She missed her own culture, books, newspapers, movies, and her whole previous life. There was a constant need for Finnish books and newspapers. She had rifled through Aune's and Jussi's small collection of books and read everything already twice. Presently she had to be satisfied with sewing, knitting, writing letters and with the language school.

The girls now competed with each other about which one could learn English faster. Marja did her homework carefully and with time, Kaarina quickly and carelessly. They still didn't have any other close friends except Anita. The biggest obstacle there was the fact that all the other young people spoke English while Kaarina and Marja spoke mostly Finnish.

"Why do they laugh at us?" Marja often asked. "When they are not able to speak Finnish at all even though they have Finnish parents!"

"Well, and do they really know English very well? How do we know that when they speak it so fast that no one can really understand them?" Kaarina added.

"And all Finns here speak all wrong. They don't even know Finnish! They say 'mie' and 'sie' like Karelians; or they talk like father 'kolome' and 'nelejä' in the Ostrobothnian dialect. So, try to understand all that! Mother why do they laugh at us?" Marja wondered aloud.

And Sylvi laughed at the girls although she knew herself what they were talking about. Men at the boarding house reminded her almost every day that she left all words half ways. Even though she didn't take notice of the men; just did her dishes and worked dutifully and spoke mostly to Vieno, when they sat down to think and talk about the local happenings and the news from the larger world.

Sylvi's longing for Finland was an almost every-day issue and beginning to these talks and Vieno had to console her daily: "Are you homesick again? Can you remember what I told you yesterday? That you're not the only one who is longing for somewhere. Do you not think that I long for Karelia? But I doubt that I'll ever get back there again. Don't you grieve."

"Yes, I do understand that you are right in this matter but I'm not only grieving for myself but I'm also thinking about our girls. I don't know if they are going to learn English and they are still longing for Finland too!"

"Don't fret about them. They'll get used to everything quickly. I was worried about our boys too when we first came! And now they don't want to speak Finnish at all!"

"You will learn something because you're going to language school. But if I don't learn, then I'll speak Finnish! Soon you'll also have to be careful that you don't forget Finnish before you learn English!" And Sylvi couldn't keep from joining in Vieno's infectious laughter. Their days seemed to rush by with talking and working in harmony.

In the evenings when Aarne started to do his language homework Sylvi often sat down to help him; because if Sylvi was unsure about her English, Aarne was coming to the conclusion that he might not ever really learn English. At the church language school he sweated and blamed the English language or the pastor for his own inability to learn English.

The pastor on his part, constantly corrected mistakes that all the pupils made continuously.

The atmosphere in the language school was very serious.

"What am I supposed to put there? And what word is missing from that?" Aarne cursed to himself at the same time that he quickly rifled through his dictionary.

"All the words are in the lesson already. You don't need to look them up in the dictionary," the pastor reminded him but this only drove Aarne to become angrier than before.

"It's easy for him to open his mouth because he already speaks English," Aarne whispered into Sylvi's ear.

"Don't for God's sake say anything but just write the words down and be quiet!" Sylvi warned him and started to collect her books.

The pastor got up to say the evening prayer which usually signalled the end of each week's lesson: "Go with God's blessings and we'll see each other again next week."

"We'll see each other next week! What does that help if we speak English here for one hour when all Finns only speak Finnish to each other all of the other times?"

"Now you're speaking right," agreed Eikka. "There is no sense to this because I speak Finn at home and at work."

Finnish was spoken between all Finns, at all the Finnish owned stores, at work, at church and in the city, as well as at home and when visiting other Finns.

"That's the worst side of this that we don't use enough English," Aarne added to Eikka when they separated.

Sylvi never took part in these discussions; just continued reading and studying in her own steadfast way; whereas Aarne left his home work to the last evening before the next English class.

"Tell me now what word is needed there?"

"When I told you already that you have to do the home work right after the lesson so the words are still in your mind," Sylvi answered from the kitchen in a loud voice.

"Don't yell! You're not a language genius either," Aarne slammed his book shut.

The pastor had already started to become tired of the pupils' slow progress in their lessons and at the next class, as soon as the previous work had been taken up, he began to talk about addresses and numbers in a fast way.

"Where do you live Vieno?"

"I live hundred two Main Sreet," Vieno tried.

"Good. Correct," the pastor smiled.

"I live sixty-tree Kraafort Sreet," Sylvi replied.

"Aarne, you are next," the pastor continued.

"I live same place," Aarne said.

"Well, what is the address?" The pastor demanded. "What is the address in English?"

"Kraafort Sreet," Aarne left the number unsaid because he knew that he couldn't say it correctly.

The pastor started to help him by stressing each word while smiling kindly at the same time: "Say sixty-three Crawford Street."

But Aarne didn't say it and he closed his books and charged out the door as soon as the class was over.

"And that's the end of the language class! You're not going to laugh at me a second time! Now I'm going and not coming back!" He boasted to Eikka who was trying to keep up to him.

"He smiled even though there was no reason for

it. It's his needless joke. I don't care about him either!"

But Aarne had had enough.

"That's going to be the end of that. You go but
I'm not coming!" He repeated to Sylvi at home.

Sylvi shrugged her shoulders and started to do
her new lesson on the kitchen table.

The next week Aarne ordered the Finnish Canadian Vapaa Sana newspaper and read that and other
borrowed magazines from thereon forward and did not
return to the language school.

The girls were now left in the strange situation
of having to become their parents' interpreters. Especially Kaarina was appointed, when the need arose, to
accompany Aarne and Sylvi, and she had to talk on
behalf of her parents the best she could. If clothes
were needed to be bought, or the electricity bill or the
water bill needed to be paid, the whole family went together. Aarne and Kaarina stood together in the front,
with Sylvi and Marja behind, and Kaarina spoke with
Aarne giving orders from behind on what to say. Often
Kaarina also consulted Marja to determine if a word or
a sentence was correct by whispering with her. At first
Kaarina felt unsure about interpreting because her
own grasp of the language was not yet perfect, but with
time she learned and became a good interpreter, and
even haggled with merchants to get cheaper prices on

products at Aarne's demands; Marja also learned similarly. On these trips they saw other children, some much younger than themselves, who spoke on their parents' behalf. And this was not only true for the Finns but for all the immigrants in the city. It couldn't be helped because adult immigrants did not easily learn English.

Aarne still felt that he knew all the news thoroughly, because he now received the Vapaa Sana Finnish Canadian newspaper twice a week and could read in it all the world, Canadian and Finnish news when they were fresh, and study the Finland and world news at depth when he received the Finnish newspapers later.

Late in the fall he and Sylvi together read in the Finnish newspapers the final outcome of the missing Kyllikki Saari when her beaten and murdered body was found in the Isojoki swamp. The raw murder and sad burial upset all Finns everywhere but otherwise the crime was not solved.

As months passed all happenings in Finland and in the larger world seemed to shrink and moved to the back of everything in general. Everyone's own life and the New Country's news demanded almost all possible attention.

Once when he was returning home from the mine Aarne stopped in front of a magazine and newspaper store window and tried to make sense of the large-print headlines on the newspapers displayed inside. He could understand some names such as USA, Canada, Europe, and the Korean War in the headlines, but couldn't make anything out of the small print. He went inside however and bought the paper with the headline – Cost of the Korean War - and folded it under his arm and rushed home.

Marja and Kaarina were studying at the kitchen table when Aarne pushed the newspaper in front of them and asked: "What does it say here?"

"It says that, what was the cost of the Korean war, like how much did it cost," Kaarina started to explain.

"Well, isn't it all wrong when the words Korean War are at the end of the sentence and the word cost is at the beginning of it?"

"Yes, the words can be in the wrong order in Finnish but in English they are in the right order and have to be written in that order," Kaarina explained.

"So even the order of the words is wrong or you really don't know either," Aarne shook his head in confusion and left with his newspaper to sit in the living room and try to make sense out of the headlines and look more closely at the pictures in it.

As the winter unfolded Aarne also started to visit the local hotels and speakeasys with Vilho Lahti.

The small city and everything in it had started to irritate him: such as the smiling pastor, the language school, the mine work and the whole nothing place.

"Come to the hotel Vilho. Let's have a decent drink and I'm buying this time!"

"Let's do it," Vilho agreed, "but let's not stay late or Taimi is going to start a racket and then she'll preach at me all Sunday. But I can take two or three drinks or beers."

"All the women preach. Sylvi preaches too but now we boys are goinna drink and we're not asking anybody's permission!"

From there they headed straight to the hotel on the Main Street which was full of miners celebrating their payday. Everyone was feeling high at all tables and by the time it was midnight Aarne was so drunk that his talking had changed to singing out loud in a big booming voice for everyone to hear.

"Let's sing the *Vagabond Waltz*. Where does it start now – it goes like this – *The counts celebrate their weddings in castles, the bride wears a wreath on her head*, , , but who is coming in now Vilho? It's Kalle Paalanen! The Devil! Come here Kalle! All the other reckless guys are here! Listen to this now Kalle: *The blood of Vaasa doesn't tremble, and the iron from Kauhava doesn't rust.*"

"Don't Aarne in the name of Satan! Shut your

mouth! The whole city is goinna wake up to this. I'm looking at that Selma there – if I could join her. Now there is a woman, boys! No one man is goinna be enough for her. That's what I've heard!" Kalle moved to join Aarne and Vilho at their table.

"What do you mean by God! Is she goinna need three? And I'm not going! I'm not that drunk! I know how gossip travels here like a wildfire! If I go with you Kalle by tomorrow some looselip is goinna sing to Sylvi that there is Aarne busy in Selma's bed. And that's goinna cause an uproar. I'm not completely crazy! But bring more beer! Where is the waiter? Beer here and now! Take some Kalle. That Selma is goinna wait."

The men continued to drink until they were shoved out the door with the last men leaving the hotel after midnight. Selma had long gone home and none of the men remembered her. Kalle left on his way and Vilho and Aarne left together on their way.

"*If I could join a pretty girl once on my way and hug her*, , , where are those words now, give me, , , *He had seen many countries in the world, seen the east, seen the south*, , , and now I'm goinna fall because this road is so slippery, , , oh for Satan's sake, , , where are you Vilho?"

"Here I am. Hold onto that fence there so you can stand up."

"I'm holding and you hold on too. It's no wonder that my feet don't wanna hold me up because it's so slippery. Well, I'm turning here now. Go straight home Vilho."

After he had turned at the street corner Aarne was left to walk alone the rest of the way. He fell in the snowbank and crawled up from there to the side of the fence, and by holding onto it, he staggered home. He grunted and pulled the downstairs door open and made his way onto the stairs. From there Sylvi helped him upstairs.

"Where have you really been when I have already waited for you for two hours? It's so awfully cold out there that if you lay down to rest in a snowbank, you're going to freeze there! And look at your clothes because your pants have split at the bottom and where is your hat? Where have you left your good hat?"

"I don't know. Close your mouth now while the weather is still good! I'm goinna go to sleep. You go where you like," Aarne grabbed the rag rug and pulled it under his head and curled to sleep on the kitchen floor. Much later Sylvi woke up to Aarne crawling into bed with all his clothes on.

"Go right now on your side! O for God's sake how you smell! You have vomited! Don't come so close!" But Aarne pushed much closer than what Sylvi would have wanted at that time.

On Sunday morning Sylvi washed the kitchen floor and the rest of the day she preached to Aarne who was trying to sober up on the couch from his drunken stupor.

"We'll never be able to return home from here; and surely never become rich if you're going to start drinking. Then all the money will go to drinking, , , and then you split your good pants! And we haven't even opened the bank account yet!"

"Well, if that's going to shut your mouth, then take it from the next week's pay. Take ten dollars from the grocery money and let's open the bank account with that. Let's eat that much less. We have potatoes and carrots in the cold pantry. Well, I'll come straight home after work on Friday and let's open the bank account together then. But now close your mouth!"

And Sylvi closed her mouth and was happy about the fact that something good had come out of something bad.

But this act of releasing his pent-up anger became a habit with Aarne and from there on, perhaps once a month, he spent an evening at the hotel and discussed his problems with men. There he could relax in a way which was impossible at home and spend a few moments by himself or with men he knew; drinking beer, talking about work, swearing and singing, or just carousing, as he had a habit of saying.

And even though Sylvi never approved of these evenings, she became used to them and released her own angry feelings the next day, preaching and accusing Aarne of whatever was annoying her at the time.

Sylvi started to prepare for Christmas and the girls helped her. Already halfway through December they retrieved all the Christmas decorations brought from Finland and started to plan on buying new ones.

"Have you seen the silver and gold balls that they have in the stores here? I want at least one of those for each of us, or do they only sell them in half dozen boxes?" Kaarina suggested.

"Yes, we really like them. I saw some in the window of a house I passed when I walked home from school. Let's buy them! And then they have electric lights in their trees. I have also seen lights!" Marja became excited.

"I don't know if we'll buy any electric lights. I was planning to make gingerbread cookies and two cakes. Why would we start to buy so many decorations? We are not going to stay here for years," Sylvi concluded.

"Well, we'll help you in that baking. Isn't that so? And then we can taste the cookie dough like in Finland," Kaarina asked.

"Well, you could taste a little of it," Sylvi smiled.

"And will father soon get a Christmas tree?"

Marja questioned still.

"Yes, father will get a Christmas tree. They have so many trees here in the forest!"

"And he could get a tree right away because many people here have them already decorated," Kaarina declared.

"It'll be left to the day before Christmas eve or to Christmas eve. What would it be doing in here with its needles coming off everywhere?" Aarne ordered.

"Let's bring it in at least a couple of days before Christmas eve and then we can decorate it very nicely," the girls suggested importantly.

They seemed to be happy that the celebration of Christmas would be similar to the ones before, but they were also interested in the Canadian decorations that they had seen in the stores or other people's homes, and Christmas customs that Anita had talked about.

Aarne and Sylvi, on their part, tried to hang onto the traditional Finnish Christmas and they visited grocery stores to check out turkeys and hams. The turkeys were much cheaper and for that reason they settled on buying a turkey.

"I think I can make this bird because I saw them being done at the boarding house," Sylvi planned. "They made several for Thanksgiving which was in October."

"We liked it when we ate it at aunt Aune's and uncle Jussi's," Marja announced.

The celebration preparations worked out without problems almost to Christmas until Jussi and Aune invited the Kalliokoskis to visit on Christmas Eve.

"I don't think we'd come on the eve. That's when we celebrate Christmas. Don't you on the eve?" Aarne wondered to his brother.

"Yes, some Finns celebrate on the eve but here the celebration is actually on the Christmas Day. We celebrated on Christmas Eve at the beginning but the kids wanted to change it to Christmas Day. You'll see it soon enough yourself that the kids change everything to the way it is here."

"We'll see," Aarne didn't argue against this as he had at the beginning.

Stubbornly they enjoyed Christmas on Christmas Eve but the New Country's customs pushed into this occasion and changed it to something different from what it had been in Finland. Surprisingly Aune, Jussi and cousin Irene walked in the door after dinner and put small gifts under the tree and sat down to enjoy the evening. And it wasn't long before the Lahtis knocked on the door and also stayed to have coffee.

Kaarina and Marja didn't want to open their gifts while the visitors were there.

Aarne teased the girls until late into the evening after the visitors had all gone away. "Look at your gifts tomorrow morning. Doesn't this country's Santa Claus come then? That's what I've heard. I mean that Sand Kalle." Aarne replied.

"What Sand Kalle are you talking about?" Sylvi wondered out loud.

"It's Sand Kalle, the Santa Claus in this country," Aarne replied.

"It's not Sand Kalle, but Santa Claus," Kaarina corrected. "You're talking that Finglish again – the mix of Finnish and English - and then you think that it's real English."

"Well, tell me some of those Finglish, those mixed up English and Finnish words? I don't know what you're talking about," Aarne said doubtfully.

"Well, say an English version of the Finglish word paanari is actually partner, and when you say ressi or tressi, it's actually a dress in English and vili-paru is wheel barrel! I don't know all those Finglish words that Finns here are making up, but they are not real English," Kaarina explained.

"Yes, we know a lot of those words too but they are not real English," Marja repeated after Kaarina.

"Now you're hearing the truth from the mouths of babes!" Sylvi laughed, "you should have kept on going to language school."

"You can think what you want to think but I don't need those words at work," Aarne ended the discussion there.

The strike ended after Christmas and the buses filled again with men going to work. The whole city seemed to stand more upright, and each man returning to work and his family started once again to live the normal life of a working man, where there were no big monies, or even hopes of big monies. A long time went by before all last marks of the strike were gone from the city, and many families carried with them a load of debt in their lifestyle for another two years. The coming of spring however seemed to make everything brighter. All the mines also gave small increases to everyone and this seemed to promise an easier lifestyle in the future.

Aarne's feelings about everything also seemed to brighten for a few paydays but since no large wage increases seemed to be forth-coming he was soon complaining again: "Well, these new wages are not going to carry me far. That's what I'm telling you. Should I go to bonus work instead so I could earn more?" Bonus work was usually accompanied by more risk from which men earned an hourly wage and a bonus on top.

"Don't think about that! That's so much more dangerous or then you have to work so fast that you might hurt yourself. That's what I've heard. I mean that you have to work fast so you can get that bonus," Sylvi explained importantly.

"There is more danger there, but there is also a difference in the pay. Death comes to all of us any-ways, I mean to everyone, , , to you and to me!" Aarne added with fervour.

"Well, I know that; but do you have to start looking for it?"

"I don't look for it. I came to look for gold and money. But it seems that gold and money and death always walk hand in hand."

Aarne's words came true for Kalle Paalanen al-ready the next week when it was heard that Kalle was killed by a large boulder falling on top of him while he was scaling for loose rock in the mine. The word was carried in the mine from level to level, and Aarne heard many versions of it, but finally he learned the actual true story of the events from Vilho who had been Kalle's partner at the time of the accident.

"Well, that damned Kalle rushed there, , , we had just blasted before that, , , and he is goinna start hitting and scaling the loose rock from the ceiling with the bar right away! Even though I had always told him to start from the sides and slowly; doesn't he poke the bar into the middle, , , and doesn't a huge loose boul-der like hell come down directly on top of him! It was good luck that I didn't also end up under it too! I just turned for a minute. I tried to move the boulder on my own but it didn't budge! Then I hurried to get nearby men. We needed eight men before that huge rock moved at all. A couple of English-speaking guys grabbed his legs and pulled Kalle away from under it, while we others moved the rock with the bars and timbers, , , but he had died, , , oh for God's sake that awful day!"

That early spring Aarne didn't talk any more about bonus work; just let time go by and saved what he could from his small pay.

Aarne and Sylvi and even the girls, each in their own way, began to understand during this first winter about the small city's limited and narrow life which all depended on the mines. Insecurity lurked directly behind unemployment; and where would you go if this ended, if you didn't speak English, and you didn't have marketable skills, where would you go then?

There were no good answers to these questions. No one needed a potter here, Aarne had already learned. Somewhere far, more south or west, there were large cities where there were other employment opportunities; everything wasn't dependent on one industry like it was in the small city; that's what he had heard. But now Aarne didn't dare to take one step. How could he go anywhere and look for work when he didn't have the language or any other marketable skills? That was always on his mind and bothered him, but there were no good answers to that. He just had to be satisfied with this and now and wait for life to give him a chance and open up and live up to its promises.

Chapter Seven

The first year had gone by. For Aarne and the girls the actual day almost flew by without their taking any notice of it, but Sylvi's thoughts returned to Finland and the time of leaving. Somehow that time seemed as near as yesterday and at the same time as distant as war-time.

"We haven't gone far," she sighed to herself while working.

In the evening when she really concentrated on counting out loud their achievements during the past year, it didn't warm up Aarne's thoughts either.

"There is only fifty dollars in the bank. So, if we save as much this coming year, then we'll have a hundred dollars in the bank!" Sylvi said half to herself, half to Aarne.

And Aarne couldn't add anything to that. He knew as well as Sylvi that the everyday life of Canada ate almost all their income the same way that it had eaten it in Finland. The only thing they didn't save on was the food.

"We have growing kids, by God! At least they can eat enough. I know myself what it's like to be with an empty stomach. And my kids are not going to know that even if it takes my last dollars!" Aarne announced if someone dared to suggest saving on food.

And Kaarina and Marja didn't look starved but instead they had grown and stretched in everyone's eyes. Especially Kaarina was starting to change into a young woman. In some people's eyes she looked to be ready for work but Aarne and Sylvi hoped that she would continue her education. The past winter had gone well in school and Kaarina had taken unbelievably long strides in English. The teachers had foretold of a good future for her, finishing high school and going from there on to as far as university. Since she was a year older than the other pupils, the principal had promised to help during the coming summer by supervising her studying at home, so that she could write the final exams for public school in August, and go to high school in September.

For the summer she was going to work as a waitress at the boarding house because the waitress Seija had married and moved away from the city. If Kaarina liked the work, as a healthy young woman she could always find a job waiting on tables in a boarding house, or at the bush camp, and if she didn't like that she could 'get married', as aunt Aune often suggested, 'I was eighteen myself.'

But Kaarina couldn't think of herself together with any man yet; the thought of marrying seemed to be waiting in the far future.

On the first day at the boarding house the manager helped Kaarina by showing her how to set the two long dining tables and ordered: "A soup bowl at both ends of each table. And always remember to check if the soup is hot! They serve themselves but you keep watching that everything is on the tables."

"Yes, okay," Kaarina agreed, trying to remember the manager's orders at the same time that she straightened her apron, and checked her lipstick and hair, on a small pocket mirror.

At twelve noon when the men started to fill up the dining-room, she placed herself at the door between the kitchen and the dining room, and listened half-ways to the manager giving her additional orders in a quiet voice from the kitchen.

"Look at that bald man there near the door. Always sits there. It's Jack and he's been here for ten years already. Well, go now to see if there is soup! Well, go fast! Okay Jack, she coming, she coming!" The manager pushed Kaarina towards the table.

All the men's judging eyes seemed to be going

through her but somehow she collected the big bowl given to her by Jack, and she quickly made her way back to the kitchen while followed by the men's calls and whistles.

"Look at that girl! Hi, where's the new waitress from?"

"Don't go running so fast! We're not goinna eat you alive!"

The English-speaking men satisfied themselves by whistling.

Kaarina blushed right down to her neck and she tried to make her face seem expressionless as she carried the hot full soup bowl back to the table. And on the first day she didn't dare to look at any individual, but instead concentrated on changing the cups and plates on the tables, and cutting bread and filling the bowls.

When she collected the dishes after the men had left the dining room, she found a coin under Jack's plate.

Kaarina's question: "What am I going to do with this?" seemed to make the manager laugh.

"It's for you. Jack likes you. Otherwise he wouldn't have left the money. And he's not going to leave money every day. Certainly, the men will try to give you bigger sums of money but then they'll expect bigger services. So, think carefully girl before you take those monies!"

Just the talk of something more made Kaarina blush again and the manager patted her shoulder at the same time saying: "Oh, you poor girl, you're so naïve! Well, I guess the world will teach you too!"

Sylvi looked at everything from the sidelines but didn't say anything; just hoped in her mind that Kaarina would stay that way for a long time to come. Only now, with her daughter at the boarding house, the men's dirty talk came to her mind like a nightmare.

"Well, they're not going to talk like that!" She placated herself. And the men didn't talk dirty while Kaarina was there, but understood themselves that the new waitress was very childish and conducted themselves accordingly most of the time.

Kaarina collected the dishes and Sylvi started to wash them, the manager disappeared upstairs and Vieno started to make coffee.

"You're goinna come and have coffee Kaarina?" Vieno asked.

"Yes, I'll come."

"That's the way! I won't give up coffee for anything. That's what keeps me going with this cooking. How did I get stuck with this kind of work? Me who doesn't wanna stand on my feet all day!"

Kaarina wanted to laugh at Vieno's quick and humorous way of talking in the Karelian dialect but she held her face serious and listened to the women's conversation while she drank her coffee.

"Well, how do you like this waitress work?" Vieno questioned. "I know that this work is not fancy but if you don't speak English, you'll be going to the bush camp or trying to find a cleaning job. And I'm not going to the bush camp! Where am I goinna shove Eikka and the boys then? They can't get along without me! I'll be cooking here for the rest of my life!"

"Kaarina will get used to it," Sylvi consoled.

And Kaarina did get used to it all; to the cockroaches that ran around the cracks of the old boarding house; to the steaming summer heat and to the swarm of flies that buzzed around the garbage cans; to the mosquitos that woke in the early evening to lie in wait for their prey; Kaarina became used to it all. After a month she didn't blush any more when the men whistled. On the contrary, she dared to smile to a couple of young men that seemed to want her attention. She didn't allow herself to think of doing anything more than that. Aarne's constant reminders, 'remember to act in an honest and upright way!' caused her to be afraid of all communication beforehand.

But Kaarina and Anita thought about all kinds of things that summer.

"When you get married," Kaarina often started the conversation, "do you want a long or a short dress?"

"Let's speak English and then I can speak better," suggested Anita and they carried their conversation on in English because Kaarina spoke it quite well now.

"There is a good-looking young man at the boarding house. His name is Erkki. I like him a little bit," Kaarina started.

"Does he speak English?" Anita asked.

"I don't know. I have never spoken to him."

"He probably doesn't speak it. And he works at the mine. Don't bother thinking about him. Get somebody better."

"Oh." And Kaarina didn't mention Erkki after that. And Erkki didn't seem so handsome any more but appeared to be stiff and older than before. As the summer went on and as she learned more English, Kaarina didn't smile shyly to him any more, but in a condescending way, to let him know that she had high expectations.

And the summer went on and the manager at the boarding house liked her better and better.

"Stay here Kaarina. You'll get a raise at Christmas and the men will buy you gifts. Keep looking at Erkki for a year or so and you'll get a good husband from him. There is no point in thinking about something else."

Kaarina smiled in reply but didn't say anything.

And Sylvi didn't say anything either; but waited for Kaarina in the evenings, to make sure that no one accompanied her home.

Aarne on his part had started to recognise that Kaarina was able to manage her life fairly well and he let her know this in his own rough way by saying: "Put your money in the bank and that's how it'll start to add up. Well, it's good that you've been able to keep your job."

But slowly the life of the immigrants who didn't speak English was beginning to dawn on Kaarina. The mines and boarding houses would always stay the same and would never offer anything more than menial hard work; whereas school and education would open a way to good language skills and with that to good jobs and a better position in life. By the end of July Kaarina was sure about her decision and Aarne didn't object much either when she let him know about it: "I'll have to quit the boarding house now because I'm going to write my exams in three weeks and I have to study more for them."

"Then you're going to lose all of August wages!"

"I know that, but I have to continue with school!"

Perhaps something in the girl's stubborn determination reminded Aarne of his own continuing struggle towards a better life and he said: "Well, go then but remember that in this house you don't go to the same grade twice!"

Sylvi smiled at Kaarina and encouraged her to confront the boarding house manager the next day: "You'll be able to get these kind of boarding house places any day whereas you'll only be able to go to school this once. Keep your head and quit."

And so Kaarina quit to the annoyance of the manager and the men, but they were soon placated by the hiring of a new waitress Liisa, who moved freely amongst the men and laughed easily to their hints if the manager wasn't there.

Kaarina spent the next three weeks reading her books and studying for the exams.

At times she felt hopeless, and at other times everything seemed to be going well. With a dictionary she felt confident but how would she do without it?

The day of exams dawned cloudy and rainy. Kaarina felt very tense. And the principal began by giving her the math exam first; math had always been a hard subject for her. This was followed by geography, history, science and English. It was two o'clock in the afternoon when all the exams had been written. Feeling tired out, she waited for the principal to finish marking all the papers.

"Pretty well Kaarina," the principal remarked.

"You received 55% in math, 74% in geography, in history 71%, in English 72%, and in science 70%. You have passed them all. Tomorrow we'll visit the principal at the high school."

In the morning they walked together to visit the high school principal with the marked exams on hand. After a long conversation, in which Kaarina didn't take part, the high school principal asked Kaarina if she thought that she would be able to keep up with the studies there.

"I don't know but I would try my best!" Kaarina replied and it was sealed.

The high school principal laughed and said: "Come then when the school starts. You can try. There are many here who don't even want to try!"

The principal and Kaarina walked home together.

Kaarina ran the steps up to their flat and yelled to Marja: "I got in, I got in!"

"So, you're going to high school?"

"Yes, I'll go there as soon as it starts," Kaarina fell on her bed in relief.

"So, we won't go together any more?"

"No, we won't go any more. But we didn't go together in Finland either."

"Well. I'll go together with Donna then," Marja was satisfied.

She had found a new best friend. Donna was a second generation Finnish Canadian and they were nearly the same age. From the outside Marja was still the same small girl who had left Finland, but there were a lot of new ideas inside. Sometimes when she was alone and she thought about things, she remembered something from Finland, but it was usually just a momentary memory. Some events like the time of leaving had been edged in her memory and she could view them like photographs; but the everyday events seemed to disappear into the shady shadows of early childhood, and she was satisfied with the new life and didn't really miss the past.

During that summer the Kalliokoski family purchased two new technical pieces of furniture: A washing machine for clothes and a refrigerator, both second hand. The washing machine was old, made of enamelled steel with three legs, but the refrigerator was almost new.

Usually when families moved away, they sold or gave away their large items of furniture, and the newcomers readily bought them. It was the style in the west – the distances were long – the final destination might not be known or it might not yet have been firmly decided – that's why it was better to travel lightly.

During the first year Sylvi had washed their

clothes in Jussi's and Aune's basement. Now she had her own machine which she wheeled from the top of the stairs to the kitchen early on Monday mornings. When the clothes had been washed, she dragged them pail by pail to hang up on the clothes line, which ran along a small roller from the window on the upstairs landing, to a high pole on the other side of the yard.

The refrigerator was perhaps even a better purchase. Up to this point milk and all food products that might spoil had been stored in cold water in large bowls placed in the bathtub. Now they didn't have to watch that the water was kept cold and change it when it became warm.

But when the girls asked for a phone, Aarne's patience was worn out.

"We don't need a phone," he replied with certainty.

Sylvi was of the same mind: "We don't need that. Who would phone us?"

"Yes, but we need it!" The girls tried.

"What would you need a phone for? Barely grown children! We're not going to buy it or rent it and that's that!" Aarne was becoming angry.

Jussi and Aune had a phone and so had the Lahtis, but Kuronens didn't have one, and neither did many others that they knew. The city was small. People saw each other almost every day at school, at the mine, in the stores and when getting the mail. Aarne decided that the small sum of money that might have been spent on a phone was better to be saved, and the matter was left there for now.

The high summer heat was now most intense in the middle of the day and the evenings brought with them a coolness. The midsummer in the north might be sweltering hot but it was not long; instead it burnt itself out by the end of August or the beginning of September.

The rain that started in September took away Kaarina's good humour from the first school day morning forward. In the high school everything was new and strange again. The new teacher called several times: "Karen, Karen, Karen," before she realised that she was being called to answer. The students took their cue from the teacher and also called her Karen even though she wrote her name Kaarina. Sylvi and Aarne didn't like this but they became used to it with time. By the end of October, the girls tried to even change Kalliokoski but Aarne wouldn't hear of it.

"It's not Kallio, and it's not Koski, but Kalliokoski, and that's that! And it's not going to be changed; don't even think that!" Aarne decided even though the girls muttered against it.

- - - - - - - - - -

On Saturday mornings of that fall and winter,

Kaarina and Marja attended the Finnish confirmation classes. Kaarina felt herself to be somewhat too old, and Marja too young, but so were all the confirmation pupils, all of them different ages. The youngest were fourteen years old and the oldest had already turned eighteen, because siblings came together, especially if the trip from outside the small city was long. The boys looked after the heating of the small woodstove and carried in wood and coal from the woodshed, and the girls brought with them prepared sandwiches for lunch, and made tea, everyone in their own turn.

The other youngsters like Anita learned everything at the confirmation classes in English, but Kaarina and Marja in Finnish, because Aarne and Sylvi had decided on behalf of the girls that the classes would give a good opportunity for the girls to keep up their Finnish language. But especially Marja felt herself to be more and more uncertain. Her English was not that good yet, and especially difficult were the words in the Bible; but she didn't have perfect Finnish any more either. At home she often asked Kaarina or Sylvi whether the words 'siellä' or 'tuolla' were written with one 'l' or two, or how many k's or s's were in some other words.

"Two 'l's! What do you mean that you can't remember?" Sylvi wondered.

"I just can't remember for sure," Marja said uncertainly.

Marja had also noticed that it was very hard to make up sentences without the knowledge of Finnish grammar and that English was becoming her stronger and more certain language.

On Sunday mornings the girls hurried to the church again; the confirmation class had been told that it was their duty to attend Sunday morning church. The church was a stronghold in the immigrant community and the support of it was important with taking of collection, and organising coffee, luncheon and dinner events, and this all demanded the attendance of every church member. Sylvi and Aarne also attended church even though Aarne was not very enthusiastic about it after his disappointing language classes.

The fall and winter also brought with them new causes to argue about between Kaarina and her parents. Anita had obtained permission to attend dances at the Finnish Hall and Sylvi and Aarne had reluctantly agreed to let Kaarina attend also, even though they had both been against it.

The girls began to prepare feverishly. Kaarina couldn't dance at all, and Anita had only practised with her father, but now they danced every day after school to the music coming from the Lahti's radio.

The need for clothes became another issue to

argue about, which only surfaced when the girls were ready to go to the dance. Anita's and Kaarina's see-through nylon blouses were not suitable in the eyes of Sylvi, and especially in the eyes of Aarne.

"In God's name, it's like you have no clothes on at all! Why don't you go naked? Now you've lost your money on those clothes!"

"I saved this money myself! Can't you see there is a camisole underneath it?"

"It's not much to talk about," Aarne continued.

"And that kind of skirt! That taffeta is going to wrinkle so much and such a tight waistband that you can hardly breathe at all," Sylvi complained.

Kaarina's curled hair was the last straw which changed her face to look strangely adult-like.

"It's not going to last long when it comes down and your head is going to ache from those curlers if you keep them on your head a long time," Sylvi placated herself.

"My mother curls my hair with a hair-curler that you heat up on the stove," Anita explained on her own behalf.

"Oh, those old ones that they had when I was young in Finland?" Sylvi marvelled.

"And be at home by eleven at the latest! Can you hear? After that the doors are goinna be closed here; just so you know!" Aarne reminded her for the third time.

"I'll be coming, I'll be coming, but now I have to go. Bye then!"

The girls closed the door and changed the conversation to English as soon as they were outside.

"They didn't want to let me go to the dance," Kaarina said.

"Not my parents either. They said that I have to be home by ten even though the dance starts at eight o'clock," Anita added.

But the parents were forgotten as soon as they arrived at the hall and joined the other girls there. Almost all the girls were strangers to Kaarina even though she had seen them at school, whereas they were Anita's friends from childhood whom she had often seen when visiting, at parties or at the Finnish Church. Now Anita introduced them to Kaarina.

"Shirley, this is Kaarina, well Karen."

"Linda, this is Karen."

"Marlene, Liisa, Helena, this is Karen," Anita introduced everyone in their turn.

Kaarina smiled and mumbled something suitable to everyone but couldn't particularly remember their names after five minutes.

The music of the first waltz livened up the group of men who seemed to rush towards the girls in one mass. Anita disappeared from beside Kaarina and

Kaarina's own hand was soon held in the hand of some man who was pulling her towards the centre of the dance floor.

"I can't dance," she tried to say.

"You'll learn," the man replied assertively and pulled her towards him.

Very stiffly and counting her steps Kaarina followed the man.

"What's your name?"

"Kaarina."

"I'm Matti."

The man pulled her slightly more towards him.

Kaarina became confused and mixed her steps up so that she stepped on the man's shoes.

"I guess this is your first dance?"

"Yes," Kaarina wished she could go away from the floor, away from the man's tight hold and nearness, back to the ladies' corner. At last the dance was over. She grabbed onto Anita's arm and repeated: "Listen. Let's go away from here. I can't dance really well and that man is holding me too tight."

"No. I don't want to go. You'll learn how to dance. Follow the man and then it's easier," Anita rushed to a new dance in a new man's embrace.

At the same time someone took Kaarina's hand and led her to dance a tango with sureness and grace; he held her at arms length and moved so smoothly that it was easy to follow him.

"I can't dance very well," Kaarina said.

"What! You dance like an angel and look like an angel too! I can remember you from the boarding house. My name is Yrjö. You remember me? Do you wanna go walking outside?" The man suggested smoothly.

"No! I can't go outside. I'm here with Anita," Kaarina told the man.

The man laughed in reply and continued: "Another time then. After you grow up a bit or what?"

Kaarina blushed but smiled back without replying and returned to Anita.

"Was that Yrjö who asked you to dance? A lot of girls like him. He's a ladies' man," Anita whispered in English into Kaarina's ear.

"Who said?" "A lot of girls have said."

"He asked me to go walking outside."

"Don't go! He might kiss you or God knows what!"

"I'm not going!" Kaarina snapped back. Some kind of small self confidence had returned inside her.

At the intermission the girls drank soft drinks and exchanged their opinions about the men.

Anita's friend Shirley walked back and forth showing everyone who wanted to see it, her engagement ring.

"And Shirley is only eighteen and now she is already engaged!" Kaarina marvelled. "I don't want to become engaged so young!"

"But at twenty-one you'll already be an old maid," Anita informed her importantly.

The music called everyone back to the dance floor. Matti and Yrjö both asked Kaarina to dance again and Yrjö repeated his request to walk her home, this time, but Kaarina answered him negatively. It didn't seem to deter him at all.

"You'll come one evening," Yrjö prophesied and laughed.

This caused Kaarina to blush and her cheeks burned still when she and Anita started to ready themselves for going home.

On the way home Anita was full of talk about men, clothes and everything that had happened at the dance. Kaarina listened with half-an-ear at the same time thinking her own thoughts.

At home Sylvi and Aarne waited for her with mixed feelings.

"If we were in Finland, would Kaarina have gone to a dance so young?" Sylvi started, "when she has only just turned to be sixteen!"

"How would you know that she wouldn't already be engaged if we had stayed there?" Aarne replied.

"You are completely crazy! She wouldn't be!

No. She is coming now. Be quiet, and don't make noise!"

"Keep your own mouth shut and I'll keep mine."

The next day no one mentioned the dance at all but Sylvi and Aarne felt that Kaarina had started to grow up and even Kaarina herself felt that she had taken an important step into something new and unknown.

No one spoke any more about going back to Finland, as if it was about to happen in the near future. Finland and the home there were often in the minds of everyone but as they all knew that they wouldn't be able to return now, they each pushed these thoughts under everyday life and thought about them privately, when there was time to think. The new life was full of something to do and work.

Chapter Eight

Kaarina well remembered the day in Finland when uncle Matti had sold his radio to his brother Aarne because they were moving to Helsinki and would be buying a new one there. At first only Aarne had been allowed to open the radio but very soon they had all understood that through the radio a new, vast world had opened up for them all. They had listened to sports, news, popular music, Uncle Markus' Children's Program and sometimes even a late evening mystery play.

When the Kalliokoskis moved to Canada, the radio had at first been like the newspapers to them, they had not understood any of it at all.

"What do we understand about it?" Aarne had asked when Jussi and Aune had told them to listen to the radio. "It's good if we can understand when people are talking to us right here; never mind the people that we can't even see."

But with time, the Canadian radio pushed itself into their lives. The radio spoke and played music in homes and restaurants; and people listened to it in cars. The manager at the boarding house turned it on after supper and the men sat in the front room to listen to its message, to smoke cigarettes and to watch the life on the streets.

With Anita's encouragement, Kaarina began to listen to the music coming from the radio. At the Lahti home radio music was played constantly so that it seemed like background music to life itself. Kaarina could also listen to the radio at Aune's and Jussi's when she visited and even turn its buttons with Aune's permission.

The more she learned English, the more she understood the radio programs and then learned more English again. Sometimes Aune asked her to interpret news on the radio, because Aune's and Jussi's English, like the English of most immigrants was quite poor. But Kaarina herself wanted to listen to the music that was played almost day and night. Music was the same to everyone and its message was universal. In between the music, the radio presented advertising of products, such as cars, stoves, refrigerators, clothes and all that people could possibly need or desire.

Music gave rhythm to life; it told stories and

made people remember. America's Wild West country music and ballads told tales of early times with native Indians, horses, riding cowboys, sunrises and sunsets, broken hearts, far away places, and longing for somewhere else. All that music was played and accompanied with banjos, violins and now-a-days mostly with guitars.

Blues was also played on the radio, as well as spirituals and jazz: Southern America's own music where cornets, trombones, trumpets and bass violins played captivating and melancholy Southern American blacks' own stories and to which drums added the typical rhythm of jazz, Ella Fitzgerald sang beautifully, or Louis Armstrong accompanied his trumpet solos with a husky voice. Anita had told Kaarina that jazz had been born in New Orleans when the Creole descendants of the mixed races of Spanish, French and Africans had mixed blues with European classical music and popular music, and made this music into loud and rhythmic ragtime music. This music was played at dances and the blacks marched to its beat at their funerals. The work songs and the field calls of the blacks also belonged to this music.

Soon jazz had travelled to Chicago and Kansas City. Anita had told that this music which was often played by Count Basie, Benny Goodman, Glenn Miller and many others had been transformed in the 1920's and 1930's into New York City's big band swing dance music and had travelled from there through radio and jukeboxes to all over America and Canada. At the same time Duke Ellington had developed jazz suitable for orchestras and singing. The Second World War had taken this unique American music and dance style to England and to Europe. Played quickly jazz became fast-moving and passionate jive music. After the war jazz changed again when Dizzy Gillespie and Charlie Parker started to play fast and lyrical bebop music. In the hands of Miles Davis jazz had become soft and peaceful and had made its way to the west coast where it began to be called Cool Jazz. Jazz was free, every musician's own interpretation of a musical mix, which invited everyone to listen: Jazz spoke of democracy, the right of anyone to live their own life and to be free.

Bing Crosby and Frank Sinatra made singing to music popular. America's popular golden voices of Bing Crosby, Frank Sinatra, Perry Como, Doris Day, and Rosemary Clooney sang on the radio almost constantly. Every week some new discovery performed new music. It was popular for a short while and soon escaped into history. But for some time already, a new, energetic, loud and rhythmic music accompanied by drums and singing, had played from the radio into people's ears. Known by their name as *Bill Haley and*

His Comets, they counted the new time with rhythm: *One, Two, Three O'clock, Four o'clock, Rock.* It seemed that the young people of the world demanded more versatile and different music, where the drums and tempo were played to a fever pitch, and that the American music and culture rushed towards the 1950's and the whole world with a very powerful force.

The girls talked about the radio constantly to Sylvi and Aarne and about all the new things that it would bring to theirs and to everyone's lives.

"It can wake you up if you want it to," Marja informed Aarne.

"As if I have ever been late anywhere," Aarne laughed.

"And you can hear all the news on it," Kaarina added.

"Well, it would be good to hear them. But we won't be able to understand it. You're going to have to interpret if we buy it," Aarne said assertively.

"We'll interpret all that you want," the girls promised without thinking about it.

So, a small plastic radio was purchased for the whole family as a gift that Christmas. It was placed beside the alarm clock on the wooden stand beside Aarne's and Sylvi's bed.

Most days the girls turned on the music coming from the radio as soon as they woke up, because Aarne had already left for work, whereas the adults were able to listen to the radio after supper. The girls interpreted as much as they understood.

Anita received a much-wanted small record player for a gift that Christmas and now she bought a new record almost every second week.

The small city was surrounded by beautiful nature, or in Aarne's words Canada's backwoods, but otherwise there was not much to do or any entertainment. There was a library and three small restaurants, of which only two were open in the evenings; in the summer there was baseball played by the young and in the winter, there was hockey. In addition to these there were movies, dances, beer parlours and churches.

On Friday evenings in the winter, Kaarina and Anita went skating. On Saturday evenings they went to the movies, or if there was a dance at the Finn Hall, they went there. On their way home they met at the young people's local gathering place and played music on the jukebox there. In many movies, music played an important role as the singers themselves acted in the leading roles, and the music of those movies was played endlessly on the radio and in the jukeboxes. Through their performances in the movies, the actors and singers felt very close to their audiences; they were almost like friends. The movie stars on the wide screen were Kaarina's and Anita's role models and icons now. They ruled the styles and tastes by which the girls purchased lipstick and rouge or how they combed their hair. Anita's hair was tied into a ponytail which moved if she moved her head; and Kaarina curled her hair like a famous movie star did.

Some well-off people like doctors or mine managers with their families, took their holidays in Southern Canada or in America, and brought back with them news and fashionable clothing, but the best information and latest styles Kaarina and Anita acquired from the radio, movies and magazines. And even though they lived so far from everything, through the radio, movies, magazines and the music, they were in very close touch with their icons and the styles and life needs which were ruled by them.

And it was music that carried Kaarina and Marja to embrace the new life. When she was skating with Anita on Friday evenings to the tune of the Tennessee Waltz, something of the New Country's history seemed to be coming through the music into Kaarina's thoughts. The words told about ladies and men, of long silk or taffeta gowns, which swished along to slow waltzes, somewhere in a large hall, in Southern America a long time ago.

"Where is Tennessee, Anita?"

"It's somewhere in the south of America. I don't

know for sure. It's just a nice song. It's fun to listen to it. Anita was always satisfied with the small city. It was the only place she knew and where she had ever lived, whereas Kaarina understood the true size of the world after she had crossed the Atlantic Ocean.

"When school is over, I mean the whole high school, it would be nice to go on a holiday somewhere else," Kaarina suggested.

"I don't know. I have never thought about anything like that. Everything is so far," Anita replied.

Saturday evenings when they went to the Finn Hall, the familiar Finnish music was played there: *The Vagabond Waltz, the Säkkijärvi Polkka*, or a schottische. Sometimes the band also played something new but usually the hall dances were nostalgic times for the Finns to relive their own culture again, and to speak in Finnish, to eat the Finnish style open-face sandwiches, to enjoy their own music and culture, and to tell their jokes in their own language or dialect.

Marja had also started to listen to the radio, as the radio was always on at Donna's home as well; and in the same way that Kaarina and Anita had done before them, they sang the songs they heard, and tried to move along to the music.

In the American South, in the city of Memphis, in the state of Tennessee, a recording studio owner, Sam Phillips, had long searched for a white singer who could sing the black music in a clean and embracing way to the whole world. He had himself seen and experienced the powerful force in the Southern American churches of the black people, when the blues and gospel music was played and sung and the people moved to its rhythm. But because of segregation, this kind of music and singing was still played and sung mostly by the blacks, and shunned by the whites. Sometimes when Sam Phillips left his recording store, he reminded his secretary to record and keep a copy of a white singer who could sing in the black style, he was so sure that the black music would then spread across America and the music would start to give opportunities to black and white people to communicate and to live and work together more equally and harmoniously.

A short time after the Kalliokoskis moved to Canada, a young American truck driver walked into the Phillips recording studio with his guitar, and sang and recorded two songs which he made for his mother.

The secretary saved the two recordings to the studio recording machine and wrote down the man's phone number. In the summer of 1954, the singer Elvis Presley and the band were requested to come again to the Sam Phillips Studio and during a break, the young performer relaxed and performed-*That's All Right Mama*-in the style that Sam Phillips had been looking for. Combined in his singing style were American folk ballads, the blacks' blues and gospel music, the boogie style, and the new rhythmic beat, and Elvis' own wild swinging of his hips and moving across the stage. Later that July disc jockey Dewey Phillips played *That's All Right Mama* and *Blue Moon of Kentucky* records on the radio. American youth demanded by phone that they be played several times that day. Sam Phillips had found Elvis Presley and his Rock an' Roll, Rockabilly music, was soon played on all the American and Canadian radio stations and in the year 1955 its music and rhythm started to change music and life around the world.

Kaarina's and Marja's white confirmation dresses, that Sylvi sewed for the girls in the spring of 1955, were exactly the same. When the small northern Finnish church filled up to celebrate the confirmation of the young people, they were like a new flock of birds, the boys in their navy suits and the girls in their flared white dresses, almost ready to take flight into the play of life.

All the parents had given their child or children a small gold-plated watch which increased the momentary feeling of satisfaction, one generation towards the other.

Aarne and Sylvi sat proudly amongst all the other parents. It was just now that they both really

recognized how much the girls had grown and matured in the past two years. When they had come, the
girls had really been children and now they were beginning to change into adults, almost too quickly.

That spring there was also another matter to
celebrate and cause satisfaction; the trip to Canada
had been paid in full at the end of May. Jussi and
Aarne together printed by hand and read the important receipt: Aarne Kalliokoski has paid in full his trip-
loan to his brother Jussi - $1,000.00 – one thousand
dollars. Cousin Irene printed to the end of that in English – All Paid in Cash – and both Jussi and Aarne
signed their names underneath. Aarne put the receipt
into his right-hand pants' pocket and pulled it out in
front of Sylvi's eyes in the middle of the kitchen once
he got home.

"Today is a day to celebrate! The loan for the
trip has been paid! Now we boys are on our own!"

"What are you really rushing and shouting
about? Are we now going to start to save for the return
trip?" Sylvi asked right away.

The girls who had been doing their homework
at the kitchen table voiced their opinions against this
in unison: "We can't go! We can't go in the middle of
our school! We don't really have to go again?"

"Well, we have to think," Aarne was looking for
words and Sylvi joined him in replying: "We have to

think now."

"Yes, but we can't really go now!" The girls made sure they were heard by repeating their opinion many times.

The matter was left there without anyone touching it until later in the evening, when they were all in bed, Sylvi said to Aarne: "Well, didn't I tell you that once we were ready to return, the girls won't want to go back any more! So, what are we going to do now?"

"Well, I don't know. I guess they have to finish these schools first. We have to save the return fares too and we have to have more money saved to start there again. It's going to take a few years for that too. For God's sake, we'll both be forty years old pretty soon, in a bit more than a year!" Aarne replied.

"That's what I told you when we were leaving that those girls can't start to travel around the world like some adults! Marja can't properly write Finnish any more and Kaarina is already too old to start again in another school and she has no experience in any kind of work except as a waitress! We just have to wait now!" Sylvi continued.

"Well, just two more years and during that time we have to save money for returning. Can you hear me?" Aarne ordered.

Sylvi didn't say anything. Privately she thought

about the time of leaving Finland, when the girls and she had been against going to Canada. Then Aarne had wiped all their arguments to the wind, and now it seemed that Aarne was looking for her support in returning, which Aarne seemed to want as much as she did. But at the same time Sylvi also felt that there might be more obstacles in the way of returning, than what there had originally been in the way of coming to Canada; and she couldn't really think of any rational plan for such a large undertaking. It was much easier to breathe in the fresh air coming in from the windows and go to sleep.

The next morning when Sylvi was writing her monthly letter to Lempi and pappa, she didn't really know how she would touch upon the matter of returning to Finland. Lempi's and pappa's constant questions – Are you coming back soon? – demanded a reply.

It was impossible to think that the reply might really be: "I don't know, I don't know when we are coming back, or are we ever coming back!" It was difficult to write at all because everything was so different from what they had thought when they were in Finland, and it was hard to compare the new life to what life had been like in Finland. Some things, like a larger apartment, was a good thing in the New Country; some other things, like the change of language, and the loss of one's own culture and the loss of relatives and friends, were very negative things. At home in Finland they had lived in a fairly large city, and here they lived in a small city, almost in the country.

In the New Country everything had to be started from the beginning and one had to be independent and resourceful and take chances and risks, even in everyday life. Sylvi thought to herself that if there was a saying in Finnish that applied to this style of living, it was, *"The weak fall on the road of life, the brave, take it in stride!"*. She felt herself to be without striding or daring. But something had to be written and Sylvi jumped over these thoughts, and she wrote more about the fact that the girls were doing well in school; they had been confirmed and it was a lovely spring. She glued the envelope closed and mailed the letter on her way to work.

When the regular miners took their holidays, they usually spent the time at home, or they might not even take any time off; but instead took their holiday pay and worked through the holiday-time instead. Work was respected by everyone; that's the reason everyone had come, and the money.

Jussi and Aune had told them about their one holiday, taken to go to the American side, and about the Finnish Grand Festivals they had gone to, when they had been given a ride from someone they knew, and had spent the nights at someone's house they knew from before. The Lahtis had also visited relatives in a large Southern Canadian city and they sometimes spoke about that to Sylvi and Aarne.

"It would be nice to go," Aarne suggested to Sylvi, but still somewhat doubtful, "but can you just go like that without knowing the language?"

"Well, we can't really speak anything! That's the thing! And these others have always had some friend or relative taking them there and back, and speaking on behalf of them, but we don't have anyone because Jussi and Aune are not going to go anywhere far any more!" Sylvi added.

The whole world described by the radio, and shown by the movies, was always somewhere south or west, always behind a fence, or on the other side of the sunset, Aarne felt; and the small city and its Finnish society, had become for them and the other Finns, a place of deceptive safety and security. Jussi had asked for Aarne's help in fixing his roof, and instead of any hoped-for holiday, Aarne and Sylvi had to now be satisfied with this choice. The first week was spent in fixing the roof; and the second week they spent with Marja and visited the few nearby beaches. Aarne was going over the roof-fixing in his mind while lying on a blanket on the beach. It had been worthwhile in two ways. First of all, Jussi had paid him. Now he had a bit of extra money, and some new experience, like having gone to buy the roof supplies with Jussi. There Aarne had noted that they had been able to purchase everything without hardly saying a word, but just by pointing to the items they wanted to buy.

Of course, they had always bought the groceries together with Sylvi, but there were young Finnish workers to help at the grocery store, if they had to ask for anything. Sylvi had also visited fabric and clothing stores with the girls, and even on her own. They had time for that, Aarne thought, and Sylvi had some English; she was still going to language classes; whereas Aarne's time had gone to work and some small repairs to their flat, and fixing of furniture; so that the visit to the roof store had been his first language test aside from work, and he felt that he had passed this test successfully.

The fixing of the roof had gone well although Jussi's work had been minimal. The first day, as soon as they started, Jussi had climbed up, sat on the side of the roof and shown Aarne how the roof tiles were nailed on; but then right after lunch Jussi had stayed on the bottom of the ladder and said: "You go on the roof. I'm so dizzy and it's so hot too. I'll open the bundles here on the ground and give the roof tiles to you as you go up and down the ladder."

At that point Aarne had understood that he'd

be fixing the roof on his own, and on top of that, he would run up and down the ladder as well. That's why he had taken the money Jussi had given him, because he had understood that Jussi would not have been able to fix the roof on his own. Aarne had noticed Jussi's shortness of breath and his worsening cough at the early spring potato planting field, where Jussi had moved slowly, his face beet red, a crooked cigarette hanging at the side of his mouth, continuously getting up to cough, so that Aune had finally ordered him to go and make mojakka – Finnish beef stew - in the kitchen and they had all planted the potatoes. But it wasn't until the roof fixing that his cough had really become overwhelming, and Jussi's breath had not been enough; and the height of the roof had made him dizzy on top of everything else.

When Aarne had asked about it, Jussi had replied: "It's that silicosis cough. All the miners get it. Don't ask about it. You're goinna get it soon too."

And Aarne hadn't asked about it. He had just thought about the fact that Vilho often had a cough too, and Korpi Niki and Kangas Paavo; all men that Aarne worked with and went to the hotels with on Saturday evenings.

Jussi didn't go to the hotels to drink hard drinks or beer on Saturday evenings, and they really didn't have that much in common anyway, aside from potato plantings and pickings, and few visits back and forth. But it had been good in the roof repair work to hear Jussi say to him: "You nail just like our father did in his day. You move and do that work in just the same way that he did!"

Then Aarne had thought and tried to recollect their father in his carpentry work and had said to Jussi: "Is that so? I can't remember the way he did his work. You'd remember that better from the days you worked with him before you left for Canada. Father had already died by the time I started to do any work."

"It's in your blood," Jussi had kept repeating and Aarne had thought that perhaps it was so, as he had always liked doing all carpentry work.

After the roof was done, Jussi and Aune had asked Aarne and Sylvi to dinner, and given Aarne money and thanked him. After they had left, Aarne and Sylvi together had gone to look at the roof from across the street, and determined the work to be very well done. The fact that the new part of the roof was of a brighter colour than the original one, didn't make it any worse. All roofs in the north were fixed much in the same way; they were only done if it was really necessary. At that point and now, as he was thinking about it on the beach, Aarne decided that he would ask the landlord of the flat if he could get some paint and paint the flat, so that Sylvi and the girls would have something positive to think about. It would be good to think about the flat having been a nice place once they had returned to Finland.

Sylvi sat on the beach with her sunhat shading her eyes and watched Marja's swimming. How time had gone by! Now Marja was the same age as Kaarina had been when they came, and they were still here. She saw how Marja spoke to other children of the same age, and seemed to be enjoying the hot summer and leisure time the same as they all did. It was now the first time for the whole family to stop and breathe in and think about the fact that they had truly arrived, and Sylvi didn't really want to think about where they would get the return money. She felt that she and Aarne now lived at some kind of a stand-still place; whereas the girls seemed to be living every moment of every day in the New Country. Would they still want to return? This was something she didn't dare to ask the girls any more at all.

Kaarina had found employment for the summer in a small ladies clothing shop. It was a step up and gave her the opportunity to use English every day. Because of her new job she had been given permission to wear nylons with seams at the back and shoes with small high heels. Most of her pay went to purchase underwear and slips, skirts and blouses to wear at work.

The whole world was changing. There was talk in the city about some new metal, uranium, and the place where it had been found - Elliot Lake. First Aarne had heard about it in the beer parlour. He had walked from table to table without saying anything and listened to the men talking. Then he had rushed home. He had searched for the place on the old map they had brought with them from Finland, but he hadn't been able to find it there. After that he had woken Kaarina up and demanded her to check on her new school map, but they hadn't found the place there either. Sunday morning, he had walked quickly over to Vilho's place and found out there that Elliot Lake, which the men were now talking about, was in the province of Ontario, in between the cities of Sudbury and Sault Ste Marie, very near Blind River. Vilho also knew that uranium, which America was buying for its nuclear stockpile, had been found there.

"Well, are you going there?" Aarne asked even though he knew well that Vilho had never mentioned it.

"I'm not going. Taimi doesn't want to go and our girl is not interested in going at all. And I'm too old to be going. Are you planning to go?"

"Well, I've been thinking of going, but haven't mentioned it to Sylvi yet; so, don't you mention it to

her either. I'm goinna first ask who might be going
and if I can get a ride. I'm just wanting to take a look.
That would only cost a little bit of gas money for the
one who has a car and could give me a ride, and
enough for a couple of nights in a hotel." Aarne was
planning as he was talking about it, and the thought
of going grew bigger and surer as he spoke. Maybe his
opportunity would be there and this time he would go
alone! No one would stop him any more, not Sylvi, not
the girls, and not Jussi. Now it would just be Aarne
alone, only him and the future; the future which now
seemed to be running into today; so fast were coming
all kinds of changes, like washing machines and
phones, and all kinds of radio singers, in front of an
ordinary person.

In the same way as Elvis was fashioning new
music for a new age; Aarne now started to think about
planning his own life in a new way. In his mind his
life had evened out to be what it had always been. He
went to work, and Sylvi went to work, and the girls
went to school; the only difference was a larger flat and
that they were now living in Canada and people here
spoke English. They would be returning to Finland in
two years, but in this time before leaving, Aarne
wanted to make money. He felt that now it was his
time to live and experience life; whether he knew English or not. He thought about the vastness of the New

Country and its opportunities. This first move across the Atlantic, would not remain to be his only move or opportunity; he didn't want to be like Jussi, getting older and sitting around in this small city, talking about times gone by, coughing and eyes watering.

"I won't be doing that, that's for sure!" He decided it then and there and told Vilho. "It's goinna be so that this boy is going, even if I have to go alone! As soon as I can get a ride to that Elliot Lake."

Chapter Nine

Canada's mineral riches are most apparent in the Canadian Shield, which is also called the Laurentian Plateau. This shield-shaped region of rock and stone covers most of middle and north-east Canada and is one of the richest and most productive mining areas in the world. This rocky area which was formed in the prehistoric times millions of years ago has gone through many changes, and these tumultuous alterations through times, have shaped this area into a very mineral rich place. The wear and tear that has happened during millions of years, and the changes wrought by ice-age, have slowly brought these mineral riches near to the earth's surface, and even made them visible to the people on the ground.

From these areas have been found and mined silver, gold, copper, nickel, iron and now uranium. Already in the year 1930 pitchblende or uranium oxide ore was found on the shores of Great Bear Lake in the

Canadian north-west. A second similar large find was made in the year 1952 in northern-Saskatchewan. Uranium was also found in Ontario, on the northern shores of Lake Superior; but it was only at the beginning of the 1950's that uranium was found near a populated area, in the forest, near Lake Lauzon, east of the city of Sault Ste Marie.

All this Aarne heard from the men he worked with and his friends when they discussed these matters during lunch hours in the mine.

The first ore samples had not shown to be all that promising but samples obtained from deeper levels had proven to likely be very uranium-rich, and geological maps had shown that in total, this find would likely measure a hundred square miles in area.

Canada's mining claims have to be landmarked and written formally as claims within thirty days of discovery in order that a claim holds up legally. It's likely that this discovery, mapping and writing up of a claim, begins the usual fever that strikes all those who have had anything to do with mining claims. So, it was now as well. The original mine finders, who were experienced in their field, must have been like ill with fever to claim as much as they possibly could before anyone else came to the area to make a claim. One of these men, a well-known New York mining financier, also owned a mine in Northern Ontario, and this mine's hourly paid men were on a strike at the time. He organised the personnel that worked on monthly pay to come and measure, mark and map, their new finds and so this huge 56,000 -acre area was marked, mapped and claimed within the required time. After the world heard about this claim, a thousand more claims were mapped during that summer, in addition to this original claim.

Pronto Uranium Mine was built in the southern area of the claim and mining had already begun there. The northern area belonged to Preston East Dome Mine and to a new concern named Algom Uranium. Work there would begin soon at two mines called Quirke and Nordic. The Canadian government's representative organisation, Eldorado Mining and Refinery, was ready to buy all the uranium produced in these mines and sell it to American and British stockpiling concerns. The province of Ontario's planned community, called Elliot Lake, was feverishly being built in 1955.

Newspapers told about the finds, radio talked and explained about them every day; both informed all continuously about the huge size and opportunities of these finds. It was as if a wildfire had started to burn the province of Ontario, and especially the northern mining area, so fast the news spread. The uranium finds gained more shimmer and their reputation more fame every day. With gossip and rumour they became the largest and richest of all remembered gold discoveries. No one really knew anything for sure but everyone knew something and talked about it all the time, and the gossip and rumour grew as they spread. The northern miners started to travel there, taking a couple of holiday days with some made-up excuse such as a sore back or an upset stomach. Everyone wanted to see what the place might look like; and to ask what wages would be paid there, and when could they come to begin work.

Aarne was also like sitting on hot rocks – if he could get going – he thought every moment – or how he would talk about going to Sylvi – if he could get going. If he heard the words Elliot Lake being spoken between two men, he joined them right away as a third one, and asked: "When are you going? Do you have room in your car?"

"Well, yes. Come along. I have room. Come on with me," Kassu Mäkinen replied to Aarne's questions. "There are already three but you can fit in too."

Aarne asked and talked to others but at the end he settled with Kassu because he knew Kassu well, and with Kassu there would also be other men going he already knew, like Kuronen's older son, Pekka, and Jaska Ylinen. That felt good. It also felt good to be going with his own money. He wouldn't need to take on any debt. Sylvi would be staying at home with the girls, but not be happy about it.

Sylvi had stared at him with an alarmed expression on her face when Aarne had started to talk about the matter: "Well, that's what I thought when I heard others talking at work and that you had also been seen talking with Kassu and he is going! And Vieno said that her Pekka had said that you are going in the same car as he. That's what I already thought that this is where it would end up! Why didn't you tell me right away that this is what you're planning?"

"Well, I can't tell you anything because you're always crying right away that you can't go there or that the girls can't go there or some other Hell's reason. I have to go now! Be it what it may be! I have to see what's there and if it's worth going there and it's best that I go alone. Those girls can't stay away from school and it's best for you to stay and work. I'm not doing anything else now, just looking. If it's not worth going, then we are not going there, but I have to see it! And we are going on Sunday and we're staying with Kassu's friend for the night. It's all in some backwoods! And then we're going to go and look for work on Monday and sleeping the night and driving back on Tuesday and then going back to work here on Wednesday! There is already two days pay gone and I have to pay for the night to sleep, and for the food, so just keep your mouth shut while it's still good weather."

And Sylvi shut her mouth when she saw that Aarne wasn't going to change his mind.

She dried the dishes, sniffled at the wall, and walked into the living room to continue her knitting, and to think about more reasons why she couldn't move again to somewhere else. She wanted to return to Finland and as quickly as possible.

The girls stood at the bedroom doorway.

"Where is our father going now?" Kaarina asked Sylvi.

"Why are you yelling and fighting?" Marja complained.

"He is going to that Elliot Lake to see if he could get more money there."

"Do we need more money? I don't want to go!" Marja was against it.

"And I don't either. We're not going again mother! You don't want it either!" Kaarina stressed.

"Well, I sure don't want it. I didn't want to even come here. I want to go back to Finland," Sylvi repeated like a child and as stubbornly as the teenage girls.

And even though Sylvi and the girls continued to be against going, for the whole of the following week, Aarne prepared for leaving coldheartedly. He made sandwiches and packed them and poured fruit juice into a couple of bottles. He packed a work shirt and pants, underwear and socks. He put on his dark outside jacket and pressed a working cap on his head. That much he had already learned about rural Canada, that there was no point in packing any Sunday clothes.

Now that they were sitting in the car, going to Elliot Lake, Aarne stared at the continuing fall forest scene unfolding outside the car window and said to the others: "There is a lot of forest here, I say!"

"Don't say anything more. I saw that when I came as a young boy on the train. I said to my father, are you coming to do bush work or what? It's all the same if you're in the bush, or the mine," Pekka Kuronen remarked. "I want a lot of money! Money is what I want!"

"It's money, we're all after!" Jaska Ylinen joined in.

"I agree with that. Why are we driving in this Satan's bush otherwise? I have a wife and kids at home, and I have a good home, so that I'm not coming here for two dollars any more. Are you crazy? We have to get good pay and bonus work! Get the money together and back home as fast as possible. What do you say Aarne?" Kassu asked.

"Same for me. What do you think the wages are there? Are they twice what we're earning now?" It came into Aarne's mind that he hadn't really asked that from anybody, but it didn't seem that anyone else knew that either.

"I don't know but everybody has boasted that the pay is good!" Jaska added with conviction. Aarne wondered if Jaska was talking about those men who had been there and returned, and knew facts, or who was he really talking about; but he didn't have the nerve to ask about that particularly.

"Well, what is it like to live there?" Seemed like a better question to ask.

"I don't know. It's not that fancy yet. They've only just started to build houses there, and some are just ready. It's all still in the backwoods. It's a good thing that it's not early summer or we'd be eaten alive by those Hell's blackflies. It's waiting for us there, that El Dorado, that golden man or was it the golden place, boys? That El Dorado is there in the middle of the backwoods," Jaska said and the others laughed.

"There it is," Aarne agreed.

It came into his mind to ask what uranium really looked like: "What does that stuff look like? Is it the colour of gold?" Aarne asked now.

"I haven't seen it," Kassu replied.

"I don't know what it looks like but that much I know that they make atom bombs out of it, from that uranium," added Pekka. "I know that. It's dangerous.

I've read it in one book."

That didn't sound very good.

"Well, how are you goinna take it then if it's so dangerous, or if it explodes?" Aarne continued asking.

"Well, I don't know that. I'm not touching it. I'm goinna shove it in the wheel barrel and bring it to the captain and say, give me the pay in hand. Here is the wheel barrel full of uranium," Pekka joked.

"Well, is it safe if they make bombs out of it? Are you sure? Well, I'm not touching it at all! I'm just shoving it in the wheel barrel and taking it away like Pekka," repeated Jaska laughing.

The trip continued and the men spoke less often. Sometimes either Kassu or Jaska broke the silence and said something more about the subject, now more peacefully.

"It's a starting job here in Elliot Lake. It's not like it's up north where everything is ready for you, I mean houses and stores and school for the kiddies. This is in the middle of the bush. They're building it the whole time but I don't know exactly what there is now," Jaska explained.

Kassu continued: "I don't know either. The only thing I've heard is that they're building houses and schools and making streets. What they have now is just camps and trailers and tents."

In the afternoon they stopped for coffee and

donuts and continued on their trip.

For a moment Aarne thought – is this what it would be like without a family, like being a damned orphan on the road drinking old, bitter coffee and munching on a dry donut?

"Pretty soon it's Sudbury, the city of Sudbury," Pekka announced.

"Well, I guess that must be a bigger place." Aarne suggested aloud.

"It's bigger. You haven't seen anything like it yet. Stone and rocks everywhere and the trees are stunted like they're in Lapland. It's like you were on the moon. It's that chemical stuff and sulphuric acid that's eaten all the trees and bushes away. The lakes are so beautiful blue and green, but if you drink the water, you'll get sores in your mouth," Pekka explained.

By the time they arrived in Sudbury, it was almost pitch black outside, so that Aarne didn't really see anything at all. – Well, what does it matter – he decided in his mind – I'm not going there anyway. Later he fell asleep for some time but woke up as soon as Kassu announced that now they were already near Elliot Lake.

"Hang on boys! This road is really bad. That's what I've heard!"

Everyone took a hold of something. Kassu

steered his car carefully on the wet and slippery clay-topped road. Everything was dark and desolate and seemingly black forest grew on both sides of the road.

"Is this some kind of a cow path?" Jaska asked.

"No, it's not a cow path! It's just a normal Canadian backwoods road," Kassu replied.

They could see a glimmer of light, as if coming from an opening in a tent, and from elsewhere someone directed a flashlight towards the road. On the tall wooden poles lining the sides of the road, hung electric lamps with lights shining onto the shanties and trailers on the sides of the road.

The car swerved half-ways around on a long curve and almost slipped sideways into the ditch.

"Oh, for God's sake, in the name of Satan, don't go into a ditch!" Kassu swore.

Aarne thought – if the car was his – would he be driving it and punishing it in such a way in the middle of the night on this backwoods road? - But he din't say anything to Kassu.

The car jerked and swerved some more; Kassu swore and turned the steering wheel and pressed on the brakes. Everyone held onto something within the car and peered outside into the darkness.

What they could see in the darkness, was not looking good. The sides of the road were lined with shanties, tents and trailers. On the sides of the biggest road there were large trailers with wheels, and on them signs announcing their purpose to everyone: store, restaurant, bakery and barber. Only the bank was located in a real building.

"Well, it's not much, I say!" Jaska announced.

"Well, not these places, that's for sure," Aarne agreed.

Kassu stepped on the brakes slowly and long, and stopped the car in front of a low shanty covered with tarpaper, and they went inside.

"Well, hello Kassu! You found the place?" Someone invited them inside.

"Well, just by accident. Listen, we are so tired that don't start doing anything for us except show everyone where to sleep, and these boys will all go and lay down," Kassu answered.

"Well, let's at least have a drink," Kassu's friend, Sulo, offered anyway.

"Well, we could always take a drink. Then we'll sleep that much better. It's really a terrible road, I wanted to say!" Kassu shook his head.

"Don't say anything more. Every day someone goes into a ditch or someone else into the bush," Sulo continued.

"Well, it's no wonder!"

The drink given to each man warmed up their insides and soon they all crawled into roughly fashioned beds made from sawn boards and fell asleep.

The morning was in direct contrast to the previous night's gloominess. A bright fall sun lit up the slippery and wet clay road, and when they drove to the mine office, the whole city opened up in front of them like a large building area. In every direction you could see just finished basements; other houses that had been covered with the skeleton of a roof, and some completely ready houses.

"This is goinna be a fairly big place," Aarne estimated.

"This is goinna be very big. This is only the beginning. As you can see new houses are being built everywhere. This is goinna be a really big place. This is only the beginning," Sulo repeated.

They drove to the mine office and everyone tidied themselves to be presentable enough to ask about work.

Kassu's friend Sulo spoke a few words to the secretary in the front office and they were then asked to come to the big office to talk to the manager there.

Sulo spoke and Kassu spoke, and at the end the manager shook everyone's hand and spoke to them in English: "Well, as I told you, why don't you all come in the spring. That's when men are needed. Everyone will get a job. Give your names to the secretary there, and Kassu, you stay here right now! I need captains and shift bosses. You can start right now."

Kassu smiled and spoke a moment longer, and they all shook the manager's hand and even Aarne was able to say, - Thank you – in English.

Pekka took his hat off and said: "I will come in the spring. Bye for now. See you in the spring!"

They all gave their names to the secretary and then went to the nearby large trailer which served as a restaurant.

"Well, what did he say about the hourly pay?" Aarne asked.

"They start at a dollar and a quarter and bonus on top, and they go to three dollars an hour, and there is as much work as you can possibly do," Kassu explained with the help of his hands.

"Well, are you coming right away as I heard him say to you – rite away?" Aarne asked Kassu.

"Well, I'm coming. I'm coming and bringing my family later, and I'm goinna buy a new house here! You guys come in the spring," Kassu encouraged the others. "That's when they need all the men they can get to come and work. That's what he said. You all heard him."

"Well, I'm coming. I'm young and free. This is where I'm coming!" Pekka was enthusiastic.

"Well, I don't know. This is a big place but does my wife wanna come and the kids. That's what it's hanging on for me," Jaska guessed.

"Well, I'm coming, right away in the spring," Aarne promised on his own behalf. What he would say to Sylvi, he hadn't thought about yet, but he would have the whole winter to think about that.

- - - - - - - - - -

When he arrived home, the radio blared with loud music and some man with a big, low voice sang: "You load sixteen tons and what do you get? Another day older and deeper in debt!"

The girls danced to the rhythmic music.

"And turn that radio lower!" Aarne yelled into the middle of the music, and right after that he announced to Sylvi and both of the girls, that they would all go to Elliot Lake in the spring.

"And we're not going anywhere any more!" Kaarina yelled back to Aarne: "I'm going to stay here with uncle Jussi and aunt Aune. I'm not going again!"

"Shut your mouths!" Aarne was angry.

"I'm not listening to you any more. You just wander and wander and you can't find a good place to settle!" Kaarina started to cry.

"Listen to us for once now. We are not going any more!" Sylvi continued.

"I don't want to go either," Marja said quietly.

"Shut your mouths!" Aarne shouted and prepared to go to sleep.

The next day's newspapers and radio told about a young, popular, film star, James Dean's death in a car accident, somewhere on an American highway. Both of the girls cried and talked about it for many days, and glued more of his pictures from magazines onto their walls. And it wasn't long when the world heard and read about American president Eisenhower's heart attack.

Aarne heard from his friends that Kassu had put his house up for sale and had gone to Elliot Lake. He also heard that his family would follow him in the spring.

Chapter Ten

The new rhythmic music echoed loudly from the high school gymnasium walls. The teenage students danced wildly in a motion of turning and twisting to the boisterous music with a beat. The teachers walked amongst the pupils directing pointed glances at those students that seemed to be acting too enthusiastically. The new music was unexpected and unnerving in the minds of the teachers. The teachers remembered couples, who had danced too closely in previous years, and now they were forced to recall them as good and tame. In the late winter, early spring of 1956, it seemed that the young people of the world had been released from all restraints. Each dancing couple moved together and apart, at arm's length or twirling in a circle; sometimes grabbing each other, and then energetically continuing with their own dance. In between the new jive music, which was now called rock'n'roll music, slow music was also played and Kaarina felt that she might be able to try dancing to that, but no one came to ask her. Anita, who was standing beside her was asked to almost every dance but Kaarina was not asked. It was sad and embarrassing to stand in the group of girls and try to look busy, or not wanting to dance, or wanting to dance, at the same time. Finally, when Kaarina thought that the evening would pass with her standing, leaning against the wall, one of Anita's friends asked her for a dance, and then another; and by the time the evening ended, she had danced a half a dozen dances, the last one with a boy who had said that his name was: "Bill, or you can also call me Billy."

"Who is he?" Kaarina asked Anita.

"Billy Newman. He is fun but pretty wild. Dances and moves around and always asks all the girls. He is pretty wild. Don't think about him at all," Anita said firmly.

"There is something magnetic about him," Kaarina replied.

"Are you crazy? Just when we came, we were talking about looking at boys that are upright and serious, and will take us home early, and whom you can ask home later; and then you start looking at a guy like Billy! He always has girls around him and all the girls are after him. Are you going to be able to take it if you like him, and he is always looking at others and going somewhere?"

Kaarina had had enough of Anita's continuing advice and explanations. She thought about the fact that Anita was always directing her to some safe harbour; when Kaarina herself felt that she wanted to live and experience life. Somehow, she was tired of always studying, and always trying to be good; always having to put forth the stamina and work of two people; just so she could be a normal teenager in her new home country. Kaarina was starting to think that Anita didn't really understand or know her; she was sometimes so thoughtless.

When Kaarina thought about the matter further, she felt that Anita lived in her own perfect world and didn't know, or didn't even want to know anything about the variety of life, whereas Kaarina wanted to live life to its fullest; whatever that meant; she was not yet really sure about that.

"Well, bye then," Anita said when they parted later that night. "I'll come and get you tomorrow. Let's go and have a coke at Smithy's restaurant. When I was dancing with Warren, he said that he and Albert are going there at about two o'clock tomorrow afternoon."

"Well, bye. Okay. Come and get me then," Kaarina agreed.

Kaarina went inside, threw all her clothes here

and there and went to bed to think her tumultuous thoughts. She didn't really want to see Warren and Albert, who were both goody, goody boys. Instead she thought about what Billy had said: "I'll be seeing you," and what he had meant by that. "See you soon again," was left as a question. Kaarina remembered his dark hair which had fallen in a careless wave on his forehead, and how Billy had stopped in front of her and grabbed her hand, and started to twirl her towards the floor at the same time saying: "Come on, dance!"

"Why are you kicking and turning and like you're mad about something? Was it not fun at the dance?" Marja whispered, almost aloud.

"Be quiet! It was pretty much fun. I'm just tired," Kaarina snapped in a loud whisper; hoping that Marja wouldn't notice that she really didn't want to talk about anything at that moment. Kaarina felt that she was living through some state of crisis, of which she didn't know the ending yet.

Sylvi and Aarne were sleeping in the living room.

Sylvi's dreams were usually peaceful, tied to the home and everyday life; whereas Aarne's nightmares were often full of terror and memories of the war.

He often lived again those first days of the war, when as a part of a group of young men, they pushed forward in a snowy forest and from nearby they could hear the directions: "Forward, don't stop, forward, go ahead!" Everywhere it crackled and somewhere further it exploded. "There, there, load, aim, aim and shoot!" The directions continued.

Aarne loaded his rifle, aimed and shot. Then they all ran up the small hill where the men they had just shot now lay; and the nightmare always ended with them ascertaining that the men were dead. But in Aarne's mind remained their vacant, open eyes staring into eternity, without seeing anything.

The war memories repeated in his dreams sometimes with the feeling of such reality, that Aarne's heart beat with a strong force, even after he awoke. And as soon as he closed his eyes again, elusive images slipped with stealthy steps out of his subconscious, and they reclaimed their life as ghosts who waded in the snow, turned to look back, and waved for him to join them: "Hey, Aarne, come, come and help!" But when they turned to look at him straight in the face, he could see their vacant eyes and staring gaze, and he remembered that they had died: Veke, Reino, Väiski, Antti, Yrjö, had all died. Sometimes when he was awake and drunk, he repeated all the memories and situations, and tried to find answers, or arguments in favour of why something had been done or not done.

Sylvi was tired of taking part or giving replies,

and she really didn't have any answers; just allowed Aarne to unload his problems. Only if Aarne started to talk to the girls, then Sylvi tried: "Well, not now; it's all over a long time ago. There is no war here any more!"

In the morning Aarne woke up and purposefully walked into the kitchen. He knew from experience that it was better to stay with the rhythm of the day and the time and go forward with those and not allow himself to concentrate on the war memories, no matter how they returned at night with such reality that he thought himself to be on the battleground again. He went to the kitchen window and looked out at the late winter, early spring scene and that already made him feel more peaceful and think about today and about going to Elliot Lake. That much he had already decided, that he wouldn't be staying here in the backyard of life; no matter how many obstacles were put in front of him. When he returned from work in the evening, he carefully checked the newspaper he had just bought again. In the English-language newspapers there were often news from Elliot Lake, and Aarne tried his best to understand them, or then he ordered the girls to explain the newspapers to him.

Sylvi looked and listened to these explanations from the sidelines and often said: "It's pointless for you to read these things. We're not going there."

But usually Aarne didn't reply to Sylvi's comments in any way. There would be no big decisions made until the spring. Until Kassu sent some new information, they would have to wait quietly.

The next afternoon Kaarina and Anita walked to the Smithy's Restaurant in the middle of the city and as Anita had already told her, Warren and Albert were already sitting and waiting for them there.

"Hi, come on here!" The boys invited the girls to their table and the girls gave their orders to the waitress.

All the youngsters came from the same kind of homes and they all knew that none of them would have the money to buy anything more than a coke, and a grilled cheese sandwich; and often that had to be divided between them all. The boys were both in grade twelve, and Anita in grade eleven, and Kaarina in grade ten; but they all spoke about the same school matters. Young people came and went from the restaurant doors; some greeted them; some others looked for their friends. Spending Sunday afternoons at the Smithy's restaurant had become a habit for them all. There was really nothing much else to do; but in the late winter, early spring months of 1956, Warren spoke about something new that had arrived in Southern Ontario.

"On the American side and in many places in

Southern Ontario, people have televisions," Warren started and continued: "There is a lot of talk about television on the radio. In America they pretty well have a television in every home and they have good programs, like singing and musical programs; sometimes they show movies; there is comedies, and all kinds of informational programs and animated programs, well all kinds of programs."

Albert asked: "Where would you have seen a television? They don't have them here. How do you know all that?"

"When our family was on a holiday in New York there was a television in the hotel room and you could watch it all day. We hardly went anywhere because mother and father wanted to watch television all the time. Well, it likely would be my family that might be the first to buy a television here. They would have enough money. They cost about a thousand dollars, at least the biggest ones, so it wouldn't be something that everyone could buy."

Warren's father worked in a high managerial position in the biggest mine in the city, and Warren knew that if there was someone that could buy something expensive, it would be his family.

Both of the girls listened and stared with round eyes at Warren.

"Are they coming here, so far north, do you

think that?" Anita asked.

"They'll come here for sure. For sure televisions are coming here in the fall and then life here will change. Believe me. People are going to be watching them all the time," Warren promised.

They loitered home before supper. They jumped and slid in the wet snow, like they had done as children; with the boys pushing and pulling each other, trying to show off to the girls. There was a promise of spring in the air, but in the evening and especially at night, you could still feel the iron grip of the freezing cold descend on the small city.

"Bye. See you at school tomorrow!" Warren grabbed Anita's hand into his own and they left running towards Anita's home.

Albert and Kaarina continued to walk towards Kaarina's home.

"Do you not like television? Listen, it might be a lot of fun to watch it," Albert watched Kaarina's reaction.

"I really don't know what it is. Everything changes all the time. I have to read and read and study all the time because I have to keep up with the others, and then there is always something new. I think it's just going to bring a lot of difficulties into my life. I really don't know. Let's see if I like it or even if I ever see it. I don't think we have the money for a television," Kaarina replied.

"I think I'm going to like it. Well, bye! We'll see each other at school tomorrow," Albert turned back to the centre of the city and towards his own home.

Safe, good and ordinary Albert! - Kaarina thought. - Wonder where Billy is tonight? Well it doesn't really concern me! - Kaarina said to herself and went inside.

As always Marja was sitting at the kitchen table with her books and exercise books in front of her doing her homework.

"You better start doing your homework," she said to Kaarina quietly in Finnish. "Pretty soon we have to clear the table so we can set it ready for supper."

Kaarina found her books and exercise books and started doing her homework without enthusiasm in the bedroom. She only had a little bit of time before setting the table.

Marja collected her books and also went to the bedroom. She was now in the last year of public school and doing very well. She very rarely thought about Finland any more. Only if Sylvi received a letter or a card from relatives, then she would listen to the news her mother read, smile and might say: "Well, when you write back, send my greetings to Liisa and Leila, and of course to isopappa!"

In previous Christmases she had sent and received a card from Aila and her teacher in Finland, but now a lot of time would pass before she even thought about the old life. There was so much new in the everyday life in Canada.

Now she thought about buying a new, beautiful dress for the public-school graduation in the spring. It seemed that there might not be anything available in the few stores of the small city, and for that reason she had borrowed Aune's department store catalogues. Often in the evenings Marja took out the catalogues and leafed through their pages of fancy dresses. The dresses were very beautiful, and the models all looked like movie stars, and the colourful clothes fitted them perfectly. Marja looked for her small purse which she had hid below her underclothes and counted her money again. There was $19.00 in her purse and there was still time. If she ordered a dress from the catalogue office on the Main Street, it might take a week for it to arrive from the big Southern Ontario city of Toronto. After that she could go and try it on, and pay for it, or send it back and order a new one.

In the previous summer Kaarina had ordered a blue summer dress, and they had together gone to try it on, but it had been a big disappointment. The material had been very cheap and the dress had been so wrinkled that they had not been able to get it straightened out even with the help of the salesgirl. Kaarina had returned the dress. Marja made up her mind to ask Kaarina to come with her if she ordered a dress from the catalogue. Perhaps they could together ask about its quality before ordering it.

"Have you already picked out your dress?" Kaarina asked Marja. "It's so hard to know what size to order from those catalogues. I wonder if it might be better to buy one from these stores here. What do you think?"

"I don't know, but you better start doing your homework. I'm going to go and set the table," Marja reminded once more.

"Well, I'm doing and thinking about them all the time!" Kaarina snapped back.

The late winter, early spring days seemed to drag on. She always waited for the weekend when she could go either to the Friday evening dance at school and perhaps see Billy, or to the Saturday dance at the hall, where she still danced a lot with Yrjö.

At the following Friday evening dance Anita danced almost the whole evening with Warren, and they seemed to be more and more taken with each other. Kaarina looked for Billy but didn't see him anywhere. She sighed and noted to a blonde girl standing beside her. "It's not that much of a dance."

"No, it's not. I have only danced two dances so

far. My name is Margaret," the girl introduced herself and continued: "Someone said that you're Finnish. My mother is also Finnish. My father was a Swedish-Finn but he left for the west a long time ago. I can hardly remember him. Now I have a stepfather and he is a Finn but I can only speak a few words of Finnish," Margaret explained further.

That evening Kaarina walked home with Margaret and after that they started to go together to the school and Finn Hall dances.

Marja and Donna still walked together to school and back. On Saturday afternoons they also sometimes met at Smithy's; drank a glass of coke or ginger ale and visited the counters where magazines, candies and cigarettes were sold. From there they bought Donald Duck and Mickey Mouse magazines, and spent the afternoon laying beside each other, either in Donna's or Marja's bed, reading the magazines together.

One morning when Sylvi walked along the Main Street on her way to work, a familiar-looking Finnish woman tugged on her sleeve and announced with alarm to Sylvi: "There was an accident at Elliot Lake and that Eelis Ranta died. A rock fell from high up in the shaft and he got hit and that was it! That Alma is going with her girl to bury him."

"Oh my God! Eelis Ranta! He wasn't more than

a couple of years over fifty and they have that girl, that Mirjami. Same age as our Marja. Oh my God!"

The woman already continued on her way but reminded again over her shoulder: "Tell that Vieno Kuronen because I heard that their boy is going there too!"

Sylvi found a serious-looking Vieno in the boarding house kitchen and before she was able to say anything, Vieno started anxiously to explain: "That Eelis Ranta died. Did you hear? What shall I do now? Our Pekka is going there at the end of this month. He already gave his notice here at the mine! That's where he is going! I can't hold him!" Vieno spoke nervously at the same time as she moved the pots on the stove here and there without any purpose.

"Well, I heard just when I came. I don't know what that woman's name is, but she told me about that accident. That's where you always see her, some-where in the city, going to the grocery store or some-thing."

"You mean Saima Kallio?"

"That's the one. He is going to be buried there; I mean Eelis. That Alma and their girl, that Mirjami are going there. That's what she said," Sylvi remained standing without being able to say anything more. It was difficult to alleviate Vieno's anxiety in any way.

"Pekka is not listening to us. He's decided. He's

not listening to us old ones. There is always the same worry over them even when they grow up!"

"So, it is! Our Kaarina doesn't want to study any more. Where does she think she is getting a job from then? I just don't know. Marja studies and studies, but Kaarina is like she is tired of it all. It's not easy, this life of ours," Sylvi continued.

"No, it's not! You said it," Vieno wiped her eyes.

They both started their workday without any enthusiasm.

After a couple of weeks, when Alma and Mirjami had returned from Elliot Lake, the Finns in the small city learned more about the accident, but that didn't help anything. Their lives were going to get more difficult. Alma was going to become a cleaning woman at a hotel and Mirjami would help her there on Saturdays. Perhaps Alma would get some small government assistance later but no one seemed to know about that yet. The ordinary people would have to be satisfied with what they could earn from their daily work. It would be pointless to plan for an unknown future or old age beforehand.

The following week's Saturday Kaarina and Margaret met at the Smithy's and they both bought a movie star magazine. Both magazines had photographs of Grace Kelly and Prince Rainier. Their love story was like something taken from storybook pages.

After meeting the summer before, they were getting married in April of 1956. All newspapers, radio and magazines told about the Hollywood movie star's and prince's love story. The girls had seen Grace Kelly acting in the movies *High Noon* and *Mogambo* and the year before she had been seen in a movie called *Bridges at Toko-Ri* with Bill Holden, and in a suspence movie called *The Rear Window*.

Margaret pointed to Kaarina: "Can you see this? Here it says that perhaps thirty million people in the world are going to be able to see their wedding on television and we have no television at all! Where are we going to see their wedding then?"

"There is nothing here that a person needs!" Kaarina added angrily. "I'm in the same position that my father often says he is, which is that, I'm in the wrong place at the wrong time!"

"This is such a backwoods place! There is nothing here! As soon as school is over, let's go together somewhere else. Somewhere else in the world or somewhere south, they at least have televisions. What do you think about that?" Margaret challenged.

"Go away from home? It's a bit scary. I have thought about that sometimes but not recently," Kaarina was a bit unsure about Margaret's idea.

"Think about it now! We can't stay here forever. What work can we find here? Or get married to a miner or a bush worker. That's our future if we stay here," Margaret added.

"So it is, but now we need a television so that we could see the wedding," Kaarina said.

"Perhaps we'll still see her in the movies. We haven't got anything else," Margaret added.

Aarne heard that Kassu Mäkinen's house was sold and he walked over to ask Martta Mäkinen about when Kassu might be coming home to help pack and move with his family.

"When is Kassu coming?" Aarne began the conversation.

"He wrote that he'll be coming at the end of May when this house sale is final. There is already a new house there, at Elliot Lake," Martta explained.

"Oh, there is! Well, I'll come and visit at the end of the month again when Kassu is here," Aarne promised.

Aarne went home and took out his bankbook. There was a few hundred dollars more there, but would that be enough, and where would he live there, and how would he send money to Sylvi who wouldn't be coming there right away? He had heard about men at the bush camps, giving money-letters to friends to bring to their wives, and the money being spent on drinking before it was delivered. He started to think about these things as he sat down on the living room sofa.

"What are you looking at that bank book for? Do you think you're going there? There is no point in a family as poor as ours to be living at two different places! And it's also not going to work out for the girls to go again, and look what happened to Eelis Ranta! Is that what you're looking for yourself and us?" Sylvi started talking.

"Keep your mouth shut!" Aarne replied; got up and went walking again to get some peace and to think more about things.

That much he knew, that after Eelis Ranta's death, Sylvi had been very upset if he mentioned any-thing about Elliot Lake.

"What am I going to do then if you die there? I don't earn enough money to support myself and sup-port the girls too, and how will you pay the rent here and there for yourself? Just tell me that. It's not going to work out! That's where all the extra money will go then if we live at two places!" Sylvi yelled as soon as Aarne came back from his walk.

Aarne washed and went to bed without saying anything more. It took him two weeks to enable him-self to turn his thinking around to the fact, that there was no way he could go to Elliot Lake, exactly for the reasons that Sylvi had said aloud.

Kassu came to get his family at the end of May.

"Well, are you coming there?" He asked Aarne as soon as they saw each other at the hotel beer parlour. "Men are needed now for all kinds of jobs."

"Listen, I have to tell you that I can't come now because those girls have to finish their schools and Sylvi doesn't want to go just now. That's what I came to tell you." Aarne explained to Kassu.

"Well, it's not going to work out if you come there alone. It's too expensive for you to support your family here and be yourself there. That's where all your pay will go then, for rent and living. Come later when your whole family can come. It's not going to end there. Elliot Lake will always be there."

"Yes, it will be. I'll still be coming. You'll see!" Aarne left for home in a dark and dismal mood and didn't say anything to Sylvi about the fact that he had seen Kassu. - Let Sylvi live with her own uncertainty, at least for a little while longer – Aarne thought.

And he didn't mention anything about the matter any more; and Sylvi didn't say anything about it either; even though Aarne knew that Sylvi would soon hear about Kassu and his family's leaving.

Kaarina often saw Billy at school, and almost always as they passed by each other, Billy said something to Kaarina: "See you soon or are you coming to Smithy's on Saturday? Will we see each other there?"

Kaarina didn't know how to take these half-hearted invitations to see him. Should she agree to go? If she went to sit at the restaurant, would it seem that she was too eager to know him, and if she didn't go, would he stay interested?

But on Saturday Kaarina went to Smithy's and Billy motioned her to come over to his table.

He was sitting with his friends, Jimmy and Tommy, and Linda and Diane. Billy ordered Kaarina a coke and the evening was spent in talking about all kinds of things. Every now and then Billy would ask her to interpret a word: "How do you say that word in Finnish, or that one?" And Kaarina tried to interpret as best she could. The longer the evening went on, the more Kaarina felt like she was accepted into the group and belonged with them. Everyone was relaxed and they all seemed to enjoy themselves late into the evening. Finally, they strolled home and Billy held her hand long and tightly. Kaarina was already opening the door leading upstairs when he took her into a strong embrace, and pressed her against the wall and ran his other hand over her breast, down to her waist, and at the same time kissed her lips and even her neck.

"We'll see each other tomorrow," he said.

"We'll see each other," Kaarina agreed and ran up the stairs with her cheeks burning.

Kaarina went to bed in a cloud of happiness.

Billy had seemed to be interested in her all evening; she was sure about that, and it seemed that he would be interested in her in the future as well. After all he had said: "See you tomorrow."

But Kaarina didn't see Billy until the following Friday and then he just passed by her and waved his hand at the same time saying: "How is it going?"

"Well," Kaarina replied with uncertainty and stopped, ready to talk, but Billy had already gone on his way. Blushing, Kaarina left to walk to her next class. She sat down with a feeling of dejection and opened her book.

In the evening she went to the school dance with Margaret and didn't see Billy there either. On their way home she asked Margaret: "Did you see Billy at the dance?"

"No, I didn't see. I'm sure that he wasn't there."

And Kaarina didn't say anything more about it.

During the week when she was coming home from school, Billy ran behind her and after he caught up with her, he asked: "Do you wanna go to the Friday evening dance at the school?"

"Perhaps, perhaps not," Kaarina replied uncertain about his intentions again but agreed to go with him anyway. Perhaps he was busy – Kaarina thought – and was just happy that he had asked her to be with him again.

At the dance Billy pulled her very close to him and they danced all the dances together. At Kaarina's home door, he took a hold of her waist and held her as if she was glued to him, and kissed her many times.

"Don't hold so close. Go a bit further," Kaarina tried to hold him away.

"Hey, you're not a baby any more. Don't tell me that!" Billy looked at her long.

"I have never done anything like this," Kaarina tried again.

"Well, it's time for you to learn," the man laughed and grabbed both of her breasts in his hands at the same time saying: "Doesn't this feel good? Take your blouse off and let me feel you a little bit and then you're goinna feel even better."

"No, no, I don't want anything like this," Kaarina repeated.

"You'll want this yet. Just wait. Well, bye. We'll see each other soon," he let her go and walked away from her.

"Bye," Kaarina replied and ran up the stairs.

Aarne waited for her in the kitchen. "What are you whispering and talking about so that the downstairs people are going to wake up yet?" He looked at Kaarina with a stern expression on his face.

"Oh, it's nothing. It's just Billy Newman. One English-speaking boy," Kaarina tried to reply with a blushing face.

"Well, ask him in the next time," Aarne ordered.

"Yes, yes. I will ask," Kaarina promised.

Sylvi and Marja went to buy a fancy dress from one of the better stores in the city and new shoes for Marja's graduation.

"See. We are just living our own small life. We're not always thinking about something else," Sylvi explained importantly when Aarne looked critically at their purchases.

"Well, it's good for you to talk. You don't need to feed and support anybody." Aarne added.

He was becoming sure that Sylvi had already heard about Kassu's coming and going back to Elliot Lake but didn't want to say anything to Aarne about it.

The following Monday Kaarina started to study for her spring exams. She first studied all the subjects that she felt somewhat sure about, and after that she studied subjects she was unsure about; but she had to go to the exams still uncertain, and the results were not very good.

"Well, this is not all that good a report," Sylvi looked at her long.

Aarne looked disappointed as well and said: "Well, you better start studying in a serious way if you're planning to go to schools. I told you that when you started there."

"Yes, yes. I know," Kaarina replied without feeling anything.

Kaarina returned to the boarding house for the summer. There was no other job available at the time. Now she was more adult and more able to stand up for herself and didn't blush so easily when the men joked or hinted at inappropriate things.

Billy left for Elliot Lake. He had been able to get a job in a mine and a room from people his parents knew who had moved there.

Even Marja was earning money by babysitting children on Saturday evenings when their parents went out.

At the end of July Aarne was sitting and listening to the radio after supper. After a while he asked Sylvi: "Can you hear that they're saying *Stockholm* and some *Antriatoria* many times. What are they talking about? Can you make out what they're saying?"

"I can hear it too but I can't make out what it's all about. Kaarina and Marja come on here. What are they talking about when they are saying *Stockholm* and *Antriatoria* and then they're talking about New York too? What has happened there?" Sylvi asked the girls to come in the living room to interpret.

Kaarina and Marja came in the living room to listen and explained slowly: "There are two ships that have run into each other on the Atlantic Ocean. One has been coming to New York and the other one has left New York, and they have run into one another sometime last evening or night, and the name of one ship is *Andrea Doria* and I guess that one has gone down and some people have drowned but that *Stockholm* has not gone down."

"Oh, my God!" Sylvi voiced all their concerns.

"We were in that *Stockholm*," Marja added quietly.

The news from the radio brought them all together for a short time. Marja walked over to be close to Sylvi; even Kaarina stayed in the living room and Aarne started to walk back and forth between the kitchen and the living room. The sinking of *Andrea Doria* made them all feel awful.

"How many people drowned?" Aarne asked Kaarina.

"I don't know. They're talking about forty but could be more after they have counted them all," Kaarina replied seriously.

"You wouldn't have believed it! How big that ship *Stockholm* was! I guess it has to be fixed and what was that other ship like? Even those big ships sink!" Sylvi repeated.

"Well, other big ones have sunk like the *Titanic* and the *Ilmarinen* during the war and many others.

Well, it's good we made it to the shore. We can hear more about this tomorrow!" Aarne turned the radio off.

Everyone glanced at each other. They had made it to the New Country and were still all together. It seemed that in the sea of life they were still holding onto the anchor of their own family, but for how long; no one could foretell that any more.

Aarne continued his evening walks. They gave him opportunities to think about things and to plan the future. He was slowly coming to a peaceful place about the fact that Sylvi had prevented him from going to Elliot Lake but now he thought again and again about what he could do to collect that big pot of money that he had come to make. Elliot Lake would always be there, as Kassu had said, but what would he do now; he thought about that and turned it over in his head during all his moments of leisure.

Almost every evening he finished his walking at Vilho Lahti's place and helped Vilho for a moment in the rebuilding of his house; work which he had started in June as soon as frost had gone from the ground. Vilho's long time ago made plans were now coming to fruition. In front of his small house, which stood at the back of the lot, was already a cement-block foundation, and the frame for the walls, was now coming up for the new part.

"I'm not making a full basement. That would take me the whole summer. As you can see, I'm just making a cement block foundation and on top of that, the frame for the walls," Vilho explained.

By the end of August Aarne and Vilho and two others together brought the addition up to the roof. Aarne nailed the roof tiles on as he had done for Jussi and the others installed the windows. Vilho paid them as much as he could.

"I have to thank you all for helping me get this far," Vilho spoke on the Sunday when they all drank coffee together at the Lahti's home. "Once I get the final floor on, I can always finish the rest inside by the time it's Christmas."

"It's going to be so nice that we'll be getting a real living room," Anita spoke to Kaarina who had also come to view the addition. "It's going to be big."

"Yes, it's going to be big and then we can hang our coats here by the door and the new steps are already going down to the front yard," Kaarina admired, "and then you're going to have your own bedroom beside this new living room."

"Wait till it's Christmas and then we can get a really big Christmas tree," Anita continued. "Now that we have so much more room."

Sylvi and Taimi admired the new addition and the two new windows which gave a lot of extra light.

"It's such a nice house now and so much more room," Sylvi talked to Aarne on their way home. "Taimi said that she's going to put her sewing machine in front of the old living room window and then you can see so much better than before in that small old bedroom."

"Yes. It's altogether a different house now. But he had to spend all his savings! Can you remember how he spoke about doing this addition already when we first came here?" Aarne continued and added: "And not only the money he had to spend on this but you also have to think that Vilho already had a lot and a house on it before. So, if you count all that, it's a long penny."

Chapter Eleven

Summer was over and the September rains arrived in the north. The rain which started in the afternoon washed the asphalt-covered streets in the centre of the small city shining clean, and streamed down the gravel-covered side streets to ditches, and then ran along to small creeks and into the lake. In the evening the rain drummed on the lake's surface in the same way that it drummed on the furniture store window; outside of which a group of people had gathered to wait for six o'clock and the reading of the news. Inside the furniture store stood the first television of the city, which was the only reason that these people had come out on such an evening. Kaarina and Margaret stood under their umbrellas amongst the others and peered towards the furniture store window. At five to six o'clock the owner of the store turned the television on inside the window and the test-pattern appeared on the television screen. Almost right away it changed into a man who started to read the day's news in a matter-of-fact way.

"Can you see anything?" Kaarina asked Margaret.

"Every now and then I see the man who is reading the news and then somebody moves in front of him. It has a fairly good picture," Margaret said. "But I can't hear anything. That man is moving his mouth but I can't hear anything."

"I can't hear anything either and I can only see a little bit. All the people are crowding in the front," Kaarina complained.

"It would be nice if we could hear something," several people said to one another but the store's owner had already left the window. If the spectators wanted to hear something, they would have to buy their own televisions. That's what he had planned.

The newsman on the television screen read and the people watched. After the news followed a short comedy show. People broke into laughs several times and poked each other to draw their attention to something funny in the program. "Did you see that? Funny! Hey, that was well done!" After the comedy many people left. A little bit later Kaarina and Margaret also turned to run towards home and then only a few teenagers remained to stand in front of the window. The store would soon close. The rain continued as before.

"It's a wonder, that television," Kaarina told Aarne and Sylvi and Marja. "You turn it on like the radio, and it's like some kind of a movie, but only small, but like a movie; but it was a bit hard to see because other people stood right in front of the window and you couldn't see all the time. And then it rained so much. You couldn't stay any longer."

"Well, I'll go and see tomorrow evening if the weather is better. Then I can see what kind of a device it really is. Everyone is talking about it at work too," Aarne said assertively.

And the Kalliokoski family was not the only family that talked about television that evening. The word travelled from one person to another and the following evening, a yet larger crowd of onlookers stood outside the window, waiting for the opening of the television. Kaarina and Aarne stood with the others. It was a better night; the weather was a little bit cool but clear and without rain.

Kaarina greeted Warren and Anita who held hands and also stared at the window. They walked to stand beside Kaarina.

"My father has already bought a television. It's arriving on Friday. Come and see it on Sunday evening with Anita," Warren invited Kaarina.

"I might come," Kaarina promised. "What time

would be a good time to come?"

"Come right after six o'clock. We are going to eat early because of the television. A lot of people are coming. I guess you didn't know that Elvis is performing on Sunday evening. Father and mother said that my friends can come and watch, because we have a television, and only a few have it yet," Warren boasted.

"Thank you for the invitation. I'll come with Anita. I don't know much about television. Elvis performing! I can't believe that we'll see him! Isn't that wonderful?" Kaarina became enthusiastic. "Is this the very television that's in this window?" Kaarina continued.

"No, it's not this one. Father has ordered a bigger one. It's a cabinet-model and pretty big, I hear. That's what he said. He ordered it already earlier, as soon as he heard that they are going to have television hereabouts," Warren replied.

At home Aarne explained to Sylvi and Marja: "It really is a wonder, that television! There are all kinds of performances there. It's as if you can understand everything better because you can see the picture. It might be that I will go and find out what it costs."

"Well, isn't it a little bit too expensive for us?" Sylvi was doubtful. "Wouldn't it be better if we kept that money in the bank?"

"Well, let's see now. We won't be the first ones

to buy it," Aarne replied.

Sunday evening Kaarina and Anita knocked on Warren's home door. Some of their school friends already sat in the living room and Warren's parents welcomed them inside too. Warren's father and mother sat regally in two big comfortable stuffed chairs and the youngsters all sat on two living room couches.

A man on the television read the world's and American news, and after that the Canadian and local news. All the boys had something to say about the Canadian hockey team. Even though they had heard the hockey news every day from the radio, it was only now that these seemed very real, as a previously taken photograph of the players on their home ice in Toronto was shown, and the game results were displayed in numbers on the television screen. But the girls were waiting for Elvis Presley's performance.

The show began. The announcer walked onto the stage, introduced himself shortly, and explained with a few words about the coming performance. All the girls glanced at each other, they were almost not able to breath while they were thinking about their idol, Elvis Presley.

"Well, good. Soon we'll see what kind of a young man this Elvis Presley really is," Warren's father said.

"We are not really that interested in him," Warren's mother continued, looking official. "I would much rather listen to Frank Sinatra or Doris Day or Bing Crosby. They are all good singers. We really don't know what this new performer is all about."

Elvis Presley walked onto the television screen dressed in a well-fitting dark suit. He accompanied himself with a guitar and performed *Don't Be Cruel,* and then thanked the announcer and the television audience politely that he and his band had been asked to come and perform. Next, he sang a peaceful ballad.

"This is not bad," Warren's father began, "we have heard so much about him that it was hard to know what to think."

But then Elvis changed his style and sang two fast songs. He swung his guitar back and forth in front of him, and moved across the stage as if he was dancing to ever-increasingly fast music. He turned and twirled rhythmically and swayed his hips as he moved on the stage. Everyone in the living room sat with their eyes glued to the television screen without saying anything.

"This is too much! Is this kind of music good for young people? I really don't know!" Warren's mother was unsure as she blushed, "and this kind of dancing on the stage! I have not ever seen anything like it! This is not suitable for adults and totally un-suitable for young people. Now we are going to close this television, father! I'm going to get some cookies and juice from the kitchen."

"Please, let's watch the program to the end," Warren's friend Roy's girlfriend, Jane, asked nicely. "I think that was his whole performance. He is already leaving the stage."

"Well, lets see the show to the end, if some other performer comes on, but this is odd that this kind of a program is being shown on Sunday evening when children and young people are still awake. It just comes to my mind to ask, how he performs in front of a live audience," Warren's father was not happy with the show either.

The young people didn't say anything. Especially the girls looked at each other with a supressed look of ecstasy on their faces; and the boys glared at the girls, questioning their apparent adoring of Elvis.

On their way home Kaarina and Anita talked to each other.

"I'm sure we'll see him again. I've read though that the older people don't like him at all," Kaarina wondered aloud.

"You could see in everything that Warren's mother and father didn't like the performance at all. The adults don't like Elvis' performances. It's not so much the singing but the moving around. That's what they are writing about in all the magazines. But all the young people like him and especially the girls. He is so wonderfully free. He is doing all the things that we ordinary people don't dare to do," Anita explained blushing at her own outspokenness.

"He is more daring than Marlon Brando is! Can you remember Marlon in that movie *The Wild One* when he only had on his jeans and a white under-shirt!" Kaarina continued smiling.

That night Kaarina went to sleep quietly but she was still thinking of Elvis. She picked up a movie mag-azine with Elvis' smiling photograph on the front cover and took it to bed. The man's wild singing and moving on the stage had woken up new feelings in her too. Perhaps it was those new movements on the stage, and the singing with sexual hints, that were the reason why the adults worried about his performances, and the young people wanted to see and hear more about them. Perhaps a part of his popularity was his ability to act out the young people's sexual feelings; he inter-preted the feelings that the young people didn't dare to think or talk about.

Early on Saturday morning Aarne marched into the furniture store with Kaarina. Six new televisions had just been delivered there recently and two men were already looking at them. Aarne and Kaarina to-gether checked each television front and back. Neither one of them understood anything about televisions, other than they were medium-size boxes with a few buttons on the side of the glass screen; they had four legs and on top stood a separate antenna, with two slim steel rods sticking up in the air.

The furniture store owner came towards them, and Aarne himself asked right away: "How much?"

"Four hundred and fifty dollars," the man replied.

"Did he say four hundred fifty dollars?" Aarne asked Kaarina in Finnish and once Kaarina said that he did, Aarne closed the sale by saying: "I take it," and then he slapped the correct amount of bills into the store owner's hand.

The man counted the money, which Aarne had taken out of his bank account on Friday, gave him a receipt and explained that the television would be delivered that very afternoon, because the store's small delivery truck would be going their way.

"You asked the price yourself!" Kaarina wondered aloud outside the store.

Aarne laughed: "Well, I've learned that much. I walked by here yesterday after work and I noticed that one of the televisions had a big tag on it where the price was printed, so I figured that the price would likely be more than four hundred dollars."

Aarne was proud of his purchase and boasted to Sylvi as soon as he arrived home: "Well, I bought that television for us and I spoke everything myself!"

Sylvi stared in wonder: "You spoke yourself?"

Kaarina added to that with a laugh: "Yes, father spoke almost everything by himself. I just checked that the receipt was correct and listened as to when it would be delivered, and they promised it for today."

Sylvi became worried: "Well, did you spend all our money from the bank? What do you mean that you bought such a thing?"

"Well, you can understand everything much better when you see things on it, rather than when you just hear them. That's why I bought it," Aarne answered tightly.

"Oh, those girls would have explained everything for us," Sylvi tried again.

But Aarne became more stubborn and replied: "They're not going to be here forever; they're going to school or get married or go to God knows where? You're not going to be able to interpret everything for me."

Sylvi didn't say anything more; but thought about what Aarne had just said more carefully; the girls would go to school, get married, or go to God knows where! All these choices felt bad to Sylvi. When she looked over to the maturing Kaarina, Aarne's suggestions seemed possible, but in the case of Marja, they were not possible yet.

Sylvi and the girls together mopped up the floor

and did the dusting in a hurry. Then they organized a good spot for the television into the corner of the living room, across from the sofa, which had been bought previously to replace Aarne's and Sylvi's old steel-bed. The girls spent the whole afternoon running back and forth to the living room window to check if the delivery truck had arrived yet. At last Marja reported that the truck had arrived and that two men were now carrying their television up the stairs.

The men set the television into the chosen corner, turned it on and situated the antenna so that the test-pattern was clear and in the middle of the glass screen. Aarne signed the delivery slip and the whole family sat down in the living room to stare at the stationary test-pattern.

"Well, that's nothing, I say! What is that supposed to be? That kind of an empty picture stands there now and it cost so much? Four hundred and fifty dollars! God bless us!" Sylvi rushed to say.

"Is something else coming on it?" Marja asked quietly from Kaarina once the television had been turned off to wait for the evening and the reading of news.

"There is going to be more in the evening when the news come on. Just wait. You're going to like it yet," Kaarina predicted.

At a quarter to six Aarne turned on the television with ceremony and they all sat down in anticipation of the test-pattern changing to the reading of the news.

Very soon a man appeared on the screen and started to read the news. This was followed by a short musical program where a famous woman singer performed a few songs. The girls admired her beautiful dress and the whole family praised her lovely singing voice. Just as it was on the radio, advertisements were presented in between all the performances, and fridges, stoves as well as cars were the main stars in these ads. At the end of the evening began a wild west movie which the whole family enjoyed.

"Well, this is fun. I'm going to make coffee," Sylvi said enthusiastically even though it was already ten o'clock in the evening.

"Don't make any for me. It's just going to keep me up, but make for yourself if you want!" Aarne was in a good mood once he saw that the whole family liked his purchase.

After the movie was over, the programming ended, and Marja said to everyone with satisfaction: "I liked that singing and musical program the best. That lady had on such a lovely dress and she sang so nicely!"

Later in the night, Aarne thought more about the television; there was a lot to think about. The former news in the papers and on the radio had been every person's own choices; buy this or buy that; listen to this or that; but this television, this one and only channel and new dimension, this acting and speaking person on the screen had become a part of the audiences life. The actors on television came to act into everyone's home and took part in everyone's life in a way that the radio, the newspapers and the movies, had never been able to do.

The Kalliokoski family's television sat in its own place in the living room, and even though it didn't seem to have any more life than any other piece of furniture did, as soon as it was opened in the evening, it demanded every family member's time and attention.

The following week the family gathered each evening to watch news and that evening's programs. The girls did their homework as soon as they came home from school and helped Sylvi with the dishes so that they would all have time to watch television. Soon they all had their favourite programs. Sylvi liked the comedy programs the best, Kaarina liked the musical programs, Marja also liked the musical programs and the guest-shows where several actors answered questions posed by a host, and Aarne liked the news, sports and the wild west movies.

The furniture store continued to be busy as televisions were looked at, purchased, paid for, and delivered into almost all the homes in the small city during that fall. At school Anita and Margaret both told Kaarina that their families had purchased televisions and that their families also watched them all evening. Marja visited Donna's home to watch their television. At grocery stores, in schools and at work, everyone had something to say about television programs.

One evening when Aarne and Sylvi walked homeward from the Lahti's, they noted the prevailing quietness of the streets, and Aarne asked Sylvi: "It's such a quiet evening. There is no one here. Is it some celebration evening?"

"No, it's not a celebration. They are all watching television. That's what everyone is doing every evening. There is no one out in the evenings. I don't think so."

And neither one of them thought about this very deeply; usually Aarne and Sylvi didn't go out much in the evenings. Kaarina might be the one to notice it the most; if she went out after dinner. There was really no one on the streets any more; only on Saturday evenings and Sundays during the days, would you see people on the streets, as you might have seen before the arrival of television in the small city.

- - - - - - - - - -

At work Aarne had become acquainted with Tony, an Italian man, who had joined the working group of himself and Eikka in the summer, the same as an Englishman named John had. John was quiet; he read newspapers or some book after lunch; but Tony talked all the time, and didn't listen to anybody who tried to suggest that others didn't understand him. Tony asked, explained and replied to his own questions; and it was about this time that Aarne started to take part in his continuing conversations.

"How you Aarne? How you Eikka and you too John? Today is payday. I get my million today and I go home to Iittali and take Sofia and kids and we go on a big holiday. Come on! We all get million today! Be happy! I bring pizza tomorrow. Sofia make it." Tony spoke mostly to Aarne but included everyone in his conversations.

"I get my million tollari shek today too. Sure. I go for holiday too. Maype I go to Finland," Aarne replied with laughter.

"What are you talking there? You're talking English! I can hear you. You're a real spokesman. Tell that Tony that let's work now and then rest once this is done. You're getting a million dollars; you're going to Finland and he is going to Iitali. I heard that. That's where you're going! Come on John. Is time to sit down. You sit down too Aarne," Eikka took part in the conversation laughing at the same time.

Sometimes Eikka let Aarne be the interpreter;

sometimes he spoke with John and Tony on his own. John hardly ever spoke; he mostly only smiled. Very rarely did he have something to say and he said it with such good English that Aarne, Eikka and Tony had trouble understanding him, because they were so used to their own simple and mostly incorrect way of speaking English.

At home Sylvi was surprised about Aarne's improving English and asked him: "Well, how does this Tony or Johnny understand you because you don't really speak the right kind of English? I don't believe it."

"Oh, it's easy for us! That Tony was in the war too. It was the same for them as it was for us, only in different places. Well, I don't know their places but the fighting was the same as it was for us and all over the world. That guy just talks all the time and he doesn't care if anyone understands him or not. That's how you just have to start talking. If the others laugh, let them laugh!" Aarne explained.

"Well, I speak Finnish okay but I can't really talk that good English. Except a little bit in the stores and I understand that television and Marja taught me that song that somebody sang on that television and she promised to teach me that *Mockingbird Hill* song. So, I do know how to say those things here at home," Sylvi said proudly on her own behalf.

"I guess you'll soon become one of those television singers, like that Elvis," Aarne teased Sylvi and she smiled. She especially felt that their life at home was more cohesive and more fun after the coming of the television; the girls were home much more and Aarne was mostly in a good mood.

After a few weeks of steady television watching, Kaarina went out on Saturday afternoon; she had had enough of sitting. She saw Anita coming out of the drug store and she called to her: "You have come out. I have too. Let's go to Smithy's; there must be some-body there."

Kaarina saw Billy right away and Billy motioned for her and Anita to come to their table.

"Hei. Where have you been? I can guess. You've been watching television like everybody else in this miserable little city. I had enough already a cou-ple of weeks ago. Hei Kaarina, I thought I would call Margaret's home and ask about exactly where you re-ally are, but then I came here instead. I have seen quite a few friends here today. Everybody's going to be coming back. You can't continue this; sit and sit and watch that box all the time. You'll go crazy that way! Let's all go to Wally's home tonight when his par-ents are gone. They went visiting somewhere farther and are coming back later tonight. Will you come?" Billy asked enthusiastically.

Anita said no right away: "Warren is coming to

watch television to our place tonight. I just came here for a few minutes with Kaarina."

"By the way, did you see Elvis on television?" Billy asked now.

"We saw him. Anita and I went to Warren's home to watch him," Kaarina replied.

"Ahaa! Now you have met one of the better families of this place! Warren and his friends think they are so important because their fathers are big bosses in the mines here. I hear Warren is going to Teachers' College next year like his friend Albert. Pretenders!" Billy said accusingly.

Kaarina didn't know what to say. She had never noticed that Warren pretended and Albert even less. Albert was from a very ordinary home too. Billy must be wrong. Kaarina thought for a while about what Billy meant by Warren's and Albert's pretending, but didn't say anything about that either.

"Warren doesn't pretend anything. He is just more steadfast and serious than what you are," Anita defended. "Don't you have any plans for your future? You've always said that this place is too small and miserable for you. Are you planning to go somewhere else when school is finished?"

"I don't know. I might go to the Air Force, perhaps I'll become a travelling salesman. I don't know yet. I haven't made any final plans. How about you

Anita? What are you planning to do when school is over, and what about you Kaarina?" Billy asked in his turn.

Anita explained right away: "I'm going to Teachers' College. It's the easiest way to a good career. My parents want me to have a diploma, or a degree, and a good career, even though we might get married right away after we are finished with schools and Warren has a job."

Kaarina replied: "I don't know how long I can continue. School is always more and more difficult the further I go. Now I have to learn French and Latin on top of English. Perhaps I'll go to Business College. That's where Margaret is going."

Kaarina knew that up to this point Sylvi and Aarne had made all the decisions in regards to everyone's future, but now they always seemed to have more and more to do and they also had their own plans; and no one asked about her future or what plans she may have. For a moment she thought about Aarne and his continuing struggle on behalf of his family, and what Aarne's opinion might be of Billy. But that thought went away from her head as soon as it had come.

"Perhaps you're more like Marlon Brando, some kind of a rebel, or like James Dean was?" She said and glanced at Billy.

"Sure. That's what I've been telling you all the time that don't expect anything from me. I'm just living this moment. At home we have several younger kids and I don't want to get married as soon as I leave school. I want to live my own life and I want to travel and see some of the world. Well, do you want to go to Wally's place?" Billy asked again.

"I have to go and eat and I really promised Margaret to go and watch television with her," Kaarina hesitated and didn't want to seem too eager.

"Bring her too," Billy encouraged and waved his hand.

"Are you coming to get me?" Kaarina asked.

"Do I have to come?" Billy tried.

"I won't come there otherwise. I don't know where Wally lives. Well, we have to go now. Come and get me after seven if you want me to come there," Kaarina said and turned towards home with Anita.

Billy came dressed in his outside jacket and jeans when he came to get Kaarina in the evening.

"Hello," he greeted Aarne and Sylvi and stayed near the door.

"Hello," the parents replied.

"Come home on time then," Sylvi added.

"Yes, I'll come at eleven," Kaarina promised.

"The doors are going to be closed here as soon as the news are over at eleven-thirty," Aarne reminded at the same time that he looked at Billy more carefully.

Kaarina and Billy went by to pick up Margaret too.

All of Wally's friends had gathered at his place. The record player was on at full-blast and everyone danced for a little while, but then they all started to sit on the two sofas and Wally turned the television on. Billy sat beside Kaarina and Wally beside Margaret. After a little while Wally turned the lights low.

Billy hugged and kissed Kaarina during every commercial and tried to slip his hand under Kaarina's sweater but Kaarina took his hand away.

A little bit before eleven when Kaarina announced that she would have to go home, everyone joined in to Billy's comments: "Now already! There is still something on television for a little while!"

Stubbornly Billy stayed at Wally's but Kaarina knew that she would have to leave; the same as Margaret knew that her family was waiting for her; and they started to walk home together.

On their way home Margaret said to Kaarina: "They want to hug and kiss all the time, and I don't really like them that much. I don't want to get into trouble. I saw when my mother was married to the man she loved greatly, what a difficult time she had when my father left her. I was nine years old then, and he never came back. Mother was bitter at all men. My stepfather has been trustworthy to this point, even though he is not the big love of her life, but at least he has stayed with us."

"I can't say anything to that. I have to start running home now."

They had arrived at Margaret's home.

Margaret continued: "I have to go inside. Well, how are you going to support your children if they arrive with the man who is not so trustworthy? You have to go to work. That's what my mother had to do. And it's not so much fun if the children are small and you don't have any skills. Think a little bit more about that. Did I tell you that next year I'm planning to go to business college? The course is only for a year and then I could look for a job. We don't have that kind of money to send me to some expensive school. I guess your family doesn't either; or what?" Margaret asked.

"I don't know if we have that much money that I could go to school somewhere farther," Kaarina thought aloud. "I haven't thought about the whole thing. Up to this point mother and father have decided about everything."

"You should think for yourself about what you plan to do, and where you plan to go, and pretty soon too. There is nothing else here but the business college. If you plan to teach, or to become a nurse, then you have to go down to Southern Ontario and it's going to cost money, perhaps a couple of thousand dollars a year. Well, let's discuss this more later. It's getting cold here," Margaret went inside.

- - - - - - - - - -

The following Thursday, at the end of October, when Aarne was at work, John opened up the local newspaper at the front page in front of Aarne, Eikka and Tony and asked: "Have you seen the news?"

"What's he saying?" Eikka asked Aarne and they all collected around John to look at the newspaper.

John read slowly and explained in English: "It seems that there is a revolution happening in Hungary and the Soviet Union has gone there. There are riots and they have started fires, and the Budapest radio has announced that these demonstrations have spread to the countryside."[1]

"Hungary?" Tony asked right away. "I have heard from my brother about riots. He said that they have also had riots in Poland and there the Soviet Union has promised to give people more freedoms. I don't know anything more."

"What is he saying?" Eikka repeated again.

"There are demonstrations in Hungary. Kaarina interpreted already earlier for me that the university students have joined together to make demands on the government. They want freedom in the voting and trade with western countries. There is food rationing there and the ordinary people's wages have been reduced," Aarne explained. "But I didn't think it would come to this."

Johnny looked at them all and said in English: "Let's see how long this kind of rioting is going to last. I wonder if this is going to be long?"

Tony was excited and tried to speak his best English: "Always something! There was few years of peace and quiet. Let's hope that these riots stop soon."

"Don't say anything more," Eikka joined the conversation in Finnish and said to Aarne: "These kinds of bad news. We are already old men."

"So we are," Aarne agreed.

Eikka continued: "Let's go back to work. We are going to hear more about this when we see new papers next week. And they're going to talk about this on radio and television too."

Aarne turned towards Eikka and said to John in English: "Come on John. Back to work."

The rest of the day Aarne's thoughts stayed with the Hungarian situation and he thought about what the radio and television would say about how the situation would continue there.

That evening's news told more about the riots and burning of places and property. Aarne didn't say anything to Sylvi but he did notice that she watched the news as closely as he did.

Kaarina and Marja waited for the last Sunday in October and Elvis' new performance on television.

"Why would we watch anything like that! What was the name of that moving and singing man again?" Aarne teased the girls several times.

And Sylvi said: "Why don't we listen to the radio on Sunday evening instead?"

Finally, Sunday evening came and Aarne turned the television on as always. Elvis walked onto the stage with assurance gained from his many recent performances. There were rumours that the cameramen had been told to cut the picture immediately if Elvis started to move inappropriately. And Elvis performed in a fine manner, until he started to move his hips in rhythm to a fast song, and the announcer walked onto the stage before the song was even finished. Then the cameras were turned away from Elvis. For his last song Elvis became serious, and sang a peaceful ballad, and the announcer thanked him and asked the audience's support for his performance.

"Well, I don't know what he is all about but I guess he can sing," Sylvi looked at Aarne for his support.

"Oh, he is so wonderful!" Kaarina praised

"I like him too," Marja agreed.

"Well, there is nothing wrong with his singing

but what are they saying about the moving of his hips and legs?" Aarne demanded but now with a small smile.

"O, we haven't really noticed that. We really haven't seen too much of that!" The girls said in unison.

"Well, that kind of swaying and swinging is going to last a little while, and then it's over. It's just something new," Sylvi commented.

In the following days Aarne started to think about something new again, when it was announced on November the first in 1956, that there was an explosion at the Springhill Coal Mine in Eastern Canada and many men had been killed.

After this Aarne crawled into the pantry on the side of the kitchen, where Sylvi stored newspapers to start a fire, and he collected the last few days papers, folded them into his armpit, and headed over to his brother Jussi's place.

"Did you see the news? There are demonstrations in Hungary. Do you know anything about them? Do you know anything about any news at all?" Aarne demanded from his brother.

"I saw those and I've watched television. They are all far away from here. They are not goinna come here except the refugees from Hungary. They are goinna be coming here. They are collecting money for them all the time and they're goinna be giving them jobs in places in Canada where they have their kind of work. And that mine accident was in a coal mine. There is a much greater chance for explosions in those coal mines than what there is here."

Aarne was put off with Jussi's apparent indifference and explanations. Sometimes he asked himself if Jussi was really his brother, and was he really aware of all the Canadian, and the whole world's happenings; he seemed so disinterested in everything. Or was the small city really so far from everything, that Jussi knew from experience that no happenings in the larger world, would ever really reach them. Aarne left then and there and hardly said Goodbye. Jussi had made him so agitated and angry again.

There was more news every day, but Aarne had a difficult time trying to ascertain the whole situation, when he really didn't know the names of anyone or on what side these names might belong.

Chapter Twelve

At the beginning of November, the Hungarian new government announced to the world that the riots were over, and that the government would protect the workers' rights and human rights. The whole short revolution and riots had only lasted about two weeks and it had taken hundreds of lives and caused thousands of injuries. The Hungarian refugees started to travel to America and Canada.

Aarne and Sylvi read and listened mostly quietly and together, to these announcements; the girls were not interested in them. The Hungarian fate felt close; the war itself still felt close; it was always underneath all the other issues; and now Aarne and Sylvi started to talk about it to each other. At the time it had felt that there was no time to talk and now it seemed that some unknown gate had opened at the same time inside both of them.

"Do you remember when it was announced that

Germany marched into Poland, and when France and England told the world that they were going to take up arms against Germany?" Sylvi remembered.

"Well, I had to go to the eastern border already early that fall. I can remember it all like yesterday," Aarne added.

"And then they started to bomb Helsinki and Turku and the street lights had to be put out and everyone had to have dark blinds to keep anyone from seeing our lights. And I had to go to mamma's and pappa's and Lempi came too. And the trains were full of people, women and children and the elderly. At least you could get some food in the countryside, whatever they had there," Sylvi continued.

"And do you remember the Continuation War? At times it was so quiet at the front that there seemed to be time to whittle wood and make some bowls and small utensils. I even made that small wooden suitcase for the girls when they went to Sweden to be away from the war for a short time." Aarne remembered.

"And everything was rationed and we made meat stew with mamma and pappa because that seemed to be the most economical food to make for everybody. Sometimes you could even buy some meat there."

"I was at Äänislinna that Juhannus – Midsummer Day of 1944 when the great retreat started. It was a very cold springtime then! It was terrible those last weeks, God help us! Well, you've seen those pictures. There they are in that box in the dresser. Then we came home that fall. We were able to keep our independence but had to start paying back the war reparations," Aarne continued.

"It was in the spring of '44 when Kaarina and Marja left for Sweden because we had a hard time finding any more food and there was no coffee or sugar at all. I don't know what we lived on! And then you came home in the fall and we could turn our lights back on in October. And the girls finally came home in the spring of '45. So, it finally felt that the war was over then. Although there really was not much food until the fifties. You couldn't even find potatoes at all in the spring of '45. But we were really lucky that we all survived without getting injured or without any of us dying," Sylvi added.

The whole evening was spent with them reminiscing about different details and happenings from the wartime.

When the book *The Unknown Soldier* was written by Väinö Linna and published in Finland, Aarne's brother Matti sent the book as a gift to both Aarne and Jussi. Aarne read it twice and after that Sylvi read it. Then Aarne loaned the book to Eikka and Vieno, who also read it. The book was made into a movie, which was brought to America and Canada at the beginning of 1957; and through the winter and spring of that year, the movie travelled from one Finnish location to another where it was shown to people and it had now arrived in the Golden City.

In Finland Aarne had been able to talk about the war with men he knew and had fought with, but in Canada the older Finnish people, like his brother Jussi, were not interested in talking about it. Aarne didn't even know if Jussi had read the book. But it did feel that a lot of Finnish immigrants had read it, and when it was shown at the Finn Hall, the hall was full of people. Aarne and Sylvi sat amongst the others in their Sunday best, Eikka and Vieno sat beside them, and Jussi and Aune behind them.

When Aarne looked around, he saw a lot of new immigrants, like themselves, but there were also a lot of older people.

"So, you came to see the moving pictures," Aarne turned to comment to his brother and Aune.

"Well, yes. We had to come here. You've been talking and talking about this for a long time and I read the book too," Jussi told Aarne.

"So, we do know something about it!" Aune added.

Aarne glanced at Sylvi but neither one of them said anything.

The lights were turned down and the film started. In the same way that the book was immediately liked by all who read it, the movie pulled everyone's attention to the screen. Many scenes in the movie felt painfully real to Aarne, and at intermission he started to reminisce to Eikka. "It was just like that, taken right from real life!"

"You are so right! How many close calls I had too, but I never thought I'd want to write about them," Eikka added.

"You wouldn't have been able to write like that!" Vieno informed everyone but was soon talking about her own memories too. "How many times I cried and missed you! It was such a heavy and miserable time, the evacuation from our home in Karelia and all; I don't want any of that back any more. I know you didn't have to evacuate Sylvi, but how do you like the picture?"

"Don't say anything more! I was on my own, well with my sister Lempi, first pulling along the one child and then two and trying to escape to the bomb shelters in the middle of the night! And worry about the old folks in the countryside; wondering how they are surviving and what's happening there, and are they still alive!" Sylvi and Vieno were soon competing with their war memories, with one another.

Aune and Jussi were quiet and seemed to be

listening. They and the other older Finns could only remember the civil war in Finland, which in its own way divided the Finnish immigrants into two groups. Aune and Jussi belonged to the group that had arrived in the 1920's and 1930's. To them Finland was a far-off memory: a poor home, a large family, no inheritance, and large-scale unemployment had driven them across the Atlantic Ocean to the New World. Only a few of them could remember anything positive from their childhood or youth in Finland. And the New World had not offered easy days either, but hard depression years; yet a kind of respect had taken hold inside them towards their new homeland that had given them work.

At the beginning of the war, Finland and their relatives there, had become heroes in the eyes of the world and the immigrants along with them. They had helped energetically when a *Help Finland Association* had been formed in many localities in Canada. They had assisted at the local *Song and Sports Festival* which was founded after the Winter War to help the war-torn Finland. They had also travelled to a few of the localities where this annual festival had been held. But when Canada joined the war, at first against Germany and then against Finland, the whole picture changed and the Finnish Canadians became enemies in their new homeland.

In order to find work and to assure their own neutrality the Finns in Canada had to change in a hurry. They tried to speak English the best they could; children were given Canadian names, and saunas were no longer heated in the small city. Finnish was only spoken in the immigrants' homes and the saunas were built at the cottages and no one mentioned the war. Everyone became quiet and careful.

Kaarina watched the movie with Yrjö from the back of the hall. Several instances on the movie screen brought tears to her eyes too but she couldn't show them while she was with him. Now she actually regretted that she had come to the movie with Yrjö. The man's hand squeezed her hand in the dark, at times tenderly, at other times more insistently, and finally resting his hand on her thigh.

Kaarina pushed his hand away from her at the same time whispering: "Take your hand away!"

"Well, can I touch it outside then?" Yrjö demanded.

"Don't ask anything like that!" Kaarina was starting to have difficulty trying to keep him in line; the man was eight years older than she: "Just watch the movie!"

"I'm watching the whole time. Give me your hand," Yrjö demanded again.

She didn't want to draw attention to them, so

she allowed him to hold her hand, at the same time looking on either side, knowing that all gossip grew as it travelled. Because of Aarne and Sylvi she wanted to behave properly. Kaarina knew that Sylvi didn't like Yrjö and she didn't like Billy either.

Sylvi talked about it every time there was a chance: "Think before you have to get married too young! And here I thought that you were on your way of getting something better for yourself when you went to school to learn something, and now you're already running around with men!"

If she listened to Aarne, he often said that Yrjö was as slippery as a bar of soap: "What does an old man run around with a child for? How old is this Yrjö really? I think he is close to my age. You went to school for nothing!"

And Kaarina herself was not sure about any-thing any more. She had learned English at school and after school she had learned how to use her charms to attract Billy and Yrjö. At the age of eighteen she felt ready to step into the swing of life.

The war on the screen ended and people exited slowly to the late winter, early spring evening, Kaarina and Yrjö among the first because they had sat at the back of the hall. Kaarina didn't want to meet Sylvi's asking eyes or Aarne's questioning look, so they ran into Yrjö's car as soon as they were outside. Soon the car enclosed them behind frosted windows, away from the people's inquisitive eyes.

"I'm so cold!" Kaarina shook from the cold in her seat while Yrjö tried to get the car going.

"Come on here. I'm going to keep you warm!" And she was in his strong embrace. Yrjö kissed her on her ears, her cheeks, and her mouth, stopping all Kaarina's conversation with his tongue. An enjoyable lazy feeling took over her body for a while and she really didn't push his one hand away from fondling her breast, and his other hand from stroking her in between her legs. All of sudden he turned to the steering wheel and put the car into gear.

His urgent comment: "Let's drive a bit to the side," woke Kaarina up, and when Yrjö stopped the car again, she had already cooled off, and was able to defend herself better.

"You're going to let me do it yet," Yrjö smiled with confidence when he let Kaarina out of the car at her home.

And Kaarina was no longer sure about being able to defend herself against him.

Everything was unsure. The end of high school seemed to be most uncertain. She would then be almost twenty-one! The quick thought – would she become an old maid? – entered her thoughts momentarily, but neither Yrjö nor Billy offered anything permanent.

Even the smallest hint of anything permanent set both men to laughing.

Especially Billy repeated his well rehearsed sentence: "Don't trust or count on me. I don't know what I want in my future yet."

Kaarina was uncertain herself. She felt more and more certain about leaving high school and going to business college. She had already spoken about business college at home and both Aarne and Sylvi had slowly come around to her thinking that it might be her best choice.

"Well, why don't you go there in the fall. You can go there for one year and then go to work. There is no point in continuing this high school if you're just going to leave it there," Sylvi had said.

"Well, do what you want but that decision is final then," Aarne had commented.

Kaarina had hoped that some adult would be able to help her in making the decision but that kind of assistance was just not there. Neither Aarne, nor Sylvi could yet understand the Canadian school system and they both felt that ordinary work might be the best choice for Kaarina because she so often complained about her heavy workload at high school.

"Then you can go to work at some office or store or any practical place that they might have here. Or you might even have to travel to a bigger place. That's what they seem to do if they can't get work here," Sylvi tried to help even though she understood at the same time that Kaarina was very young and naive to travel anywhere else, and she often took back her suggestion, as soon as she had made it. "I'm sure you'll be able to get something here; there are mining offices and grocery store offices, so you don't have to leave."

"I'm sure you can find something here at the beginning. There's no point in thinking about going away," Aarne stressed too.

He especially felt that it would be wrong to encourage Kaarina to go to some southern city which they didn't know anything about. How would things work out there in the long run?

The more Sylvi and Aarne together thought about the matter, the more they felt that the girls were the most important thing that they had, and it was very hard to think that the girls might want to leave for somewhere else, and then they would be left on their own in the north. All distances in Canada were very long, and because they didn't have a car, impossible for them to travel. Often Aarne ended the conversation by looking towards Kaarina and saying: "It's no point in you rushing somewhere because you don't know anything about the conditions there. We haven't been anywhere else and we really don't know anything more about the whole of Canada except for this one place."

- - - - - - - - - -

Pekka Kuronen didn't suffer from the lack of having a car, nor was he afraid of the future. He had travelled to Elliot Lake in the spring of 1956 and had worked hard; saved his money and bought a car for himself at the end of February of the following year. Pekka started to drive from Elliot Lake to the north around Easter of 1957. He had taken a week's holiday so he could go and show the car to his parents and his brother Mikko. He had had his driver's license for about a month; and he had gained driving experience on the small city streets of Elliot Lake. This is why he was driving his first car carefully. He looked steadily to the front and often to the back; he made sure the speed was correct for highway driving which was new to him. Thank God that the road was dry even though there was still some snow on the fields and in the forest.

"Yes serii, it's great! An American car, by God!" He said to himself. He felt that some of the songs he had heard described his car exactly. "*It's Wonderful! It's Marvellous!*" He sang out like someone he had heard sing on television.

The car was a 1956 Ford, blue on the bottom and with a white roof; already made in the fall of 1955.

He had bought it slightly used for two thousand and five hundred dollars. Now he still had two weeks pay in his pocket for his holiday and he truly felt that he was going from "*rags to riches*" like someone else had sung on television.

It was a new time now; it was peaceful; there was work and money, and you could buy anything with money! On the American side president Eisenhower had been voted to be a president again for another four years, and everyone hoped that his careful managing of all issues would continue for the future.

Work had given Pekka a feeling of self-confidence and self-worth, and because he had mostly spent his time in the company of English-speaking people while in Elliot Lake, his English had improved noticeably. He felt himself to be different from before and he could feel his manliness to be exuding from his whole being.

As he was driving, he started to sing some songs he knew out by heart: "*As a child I didn't know any sorrows,*" he sang out loud in Finnish and continued in English with a song about some yellow rose in Texas.

At the same time, he planned for his future. At home he would take his whole family on a drive, just to see the countryside. They had never had a chance for anything like that. And now that he knew how to drive, perhaps they could travel to Sudbury, or Port Arthur, or Sault Ste Marie, all cities with large Finnish populations. He would try to find a girlfriend, blonde and beautiful, who would sit beside him looking attractive.

He really had a lot of plans. In the next two years he would save so much money that he could buy a house, and then that girl. He would look for some good Finnish girl or at least one that had grown up in a Finnish home. Who that girl might be, he didn't know yet? He would go to a dance as soon as he got home and start seriously looking for the girl. Of course, she would have to travel to Elliot Lake; that was for sure. He would never go back to the northern Gold Camp. There would always be work at Elliot Lake. The mines were in full production mode all the time and spewed out great quantities of uranium for America, and for the use of the whole world. There was as much overtime work as you would ever want and the pay was much better than up north. Pekka had been lucky in getting room and board at a reasonable rate. He had mostly stayed at home to watch television and only gone out to see a few movies. He had seen several wild west movies and such pictures as *The King and I* and also Marilyn Monroe's picture *Niagara*. Pekka's whole body warmed in thinking about her curves and breasts and her behind, which had swayed back and forth as she walked across a bridge to the American side in the picture *Niagara*. That's what he would do! He would take his wife for a honeymoon at Niagara Falls. That would be a sight to see and something to experience.

Everything was possible with a car and with money. He took the next curve on the road with sureness and speed, like he had seen some great hero do in an American movie, freely, without a worry for tomorrow; he would drive to the future which would be full of roses.

The further he drove, the better he drove, and every curve taken, gave him more self-confidence. He was young, full of energy, and hungry for new life experiences and new things. There were so many new ideas and inventions which anyone could buy. Pekka owned a ballpoint pen, and at home his parents had a record player, which could be taken from room to room to play records for one's own and everyone's enjoyment. All homes had televisions now. There were all kinds of home machines. He had seen at Elliot Lake his landlady mix a cake with a handheld mixer. And then the best of all inventions – a car! All these new inventions and machines were taken up and used by young people. For them everything new was immediately suitable and after a few times, necessary; and not as new things were to older people, something to shun.

The young people were becoming the largest consumer mass in the world. This decade would be the decade for the young; that's what everyone said.

- - - - - - - - - -

Both Sylvi and Aarne were satisfied after they had seen *The Unknown*. After many conversations together, their opinion was that the movie was a statement to all who saw it. This was the truth about war: This shooting, rifles, the people's aggression and fear, the exploding of bombs, the injuries and the loss of blood, and death. Especially Aarne felt that he didn't have to be angry any more; he didn't have to explain to Jussi and Aune that this was the truth about war; this hell on the screen.

Now Aarne felt that he didn't have to measure Jussi like men were measured in Finland and Europe. Jussi would have another measure and he didn't know yet how Jussi would be measured. Now Aarne made up his mind not to be angry at Jussi any more as he had been many times before. Jussi would not change; he would just stay as stubborn as before, with his important Aune, and he would be an altogether different person than what Aarne had thought he might be while he was still living in Finland. The same as the New World was a different place from what he had thought it to be before he arrived here.

Whenever Aarne thought about his birth home

in Ostrobothnia and his mother's home, a large farm where there had been enough bread for many children and even their children: a grandmother who had taken her daughter's children on her lap when life had hit them too hard; and now this insecure feeling which was with him at all times, then it all tore his heart out, and his eyes watered for a moment, and he had to turn his thoughts to something else. He would never get any help from Jussi. For Jussi and Aune, Golden City would always truly be worth its name in gold. And nothing on this earth would ever move them away from here. This was their measurement, their coming here. This was their big adventure, and the bush camp where they had met, and Golden City; they were the measurements of their life, but Aarne knew that he had a different measurement. He was a soldier from the Finnish Winter War and the Continuation War. He was the Unknown, a soldier who had been tried in fire and hell, at least one of them. Now he didn't have to explain it any more. Väinö Linna had said it clearly in his book and the movie.

Or when he really thought about all this further back; the small plot of land that Jussi had inherited as a second son, hadn't given him a chance to farm; and the one cow that Aune had received hadn't helped them very far. You couldn't get work anywhere. Tomorrow didn't seem to promise anything better and after 1929 there was no hope for anything better in the future.

It had been the custom in Ostrobothnia to travel to America for generations and now they travelled to Canada. Some relatives had disappeared as soon as they left and no one ever heard from them again. Those that had returned to visit had praised their new life to be wonderful. They had visited in their fine clothes and brought gifts, and the next generation in Finland had followed them. So, perhaps it had been more like that, and not Jussi's laziness. Jussi had worked hard too and had earned a house for himself and Aune and that in itself had been a fine accomplishment. Perhaps Aarne had hoped for some kind of support from Jussi that only a more secure community could give, but Aarne had found it hard to agree with that.

Aarne had started to understand with a firm sureness that he would have to dare to do something on his own and independently, and risk everything once more. After all his walks and thinking, he had come to the conclusion that his only way of making money would be to buy a lot and build a house on it, and sell it, and then with that money he and Sylvi could go back to Finland. Would the girls go with them? That he couldn't foretell yet but perhaps if the going back happened fast enough.

When he really started to think about everything his whole life was pretty good now. He had the new device, the television, which helped him with his English and his understanding of the whole world and he still had a few hundred dollars of money in the bank. They lived in a clean and good-size apartment. They both had reasonable jobs, even though they didn't pay that well. Now if he really started to save, after two years he might be able to buy a building lot. A lot of other people bought lots and built houses. Nowadays people talked about bank loans that ordinary people could get. And he wouldn't tell Sylvi much yet; he would just save all he could, and he might even buy the lot without telling her, and then there would be no back talk. That might be the easiest way. But before all that there would be the education of the girls, which would also take money.

It was spring and he and Sylvi and the girls were all healthy and young. His wages would never be the same as millionaires' wages. The northern gold mining pay was generally low; the work was dirty and dangerous at times. The only way to get ahead was to try something different and independent, or live Jussi's life; stay at the northern mines and live like a small log-fire burning in between two strong pieces of wood; a fire which would eventually go out in the wind. There was no other choice.

Chapter Thirteen

Aarne was now firmly planning his family's future and in doing that he concentrated on the news he
heard and saw, and on all that was happening around
him. Kaarina was going to business college and she
was satisfied to be learning practical subjects like typ-
ing and book-keeping and happy about the fact that
these courses were going to lead her to a good job in a
year. Marja was already now reading about Canada's
and America's history because she was going to high
school. Almost every evening she told her family something about what she had read that day. This history
was something new to them all, and it was learned in
Golden City, like all other important things about the
New Country were learned on the spot. Kaarina had
also studied this history earlier but it was only now
that they all felt they had the time to concentrate on
it. They had seen from maps and heard from people
around them that Canada was a big country and even

though America was also very large, Canada was larger in land mass. But then America had ten times the population that Canada had. Aarne had also determined that the northern problems were different from the southern problems, and east and west didn't know much about one another. All the people that had travelled to the New World over time had hoped that there would be room for them and that they would all have equal opportunities.

History stated that Canada's and America's aboriginal people, the native Indians had come to the New World after the last Ice Age, making their way from Asia across the Bering Strait to Alaska, and from there south and east. This is what Marja told them. In between reading and interpreting either Aarne or Sylvi asked again about some detail, and Kaarina and Marja tried their best to answer these questions.

"You mean the Indians that we see around here?" Aarne wanted to make sure.

"Yes, that's who they mean. They told us that they could be related to Mongols because they have straight black hair and yellower skin than we have. All Indian Nations spoke their own languages. They all lived in small villages and their leaders were chiefs, but the different Indian tribes didn't have that much to do with each other because their languages were different, and because distances here are so great.

"Is that so?" Aarne commented.

"And then our teacher told us that there were a lot of Indian tribes in America too. All Indians lived by hunting and fishing, and they mostly hunted the caribou, because it gave them food and clothing, and they could also make tents, which were called teepees, out of them. It's an animal related to the reindeer."

"Don't forget that Eskimos lived here too. But there were only a few of them and they lived near the Arctic Sea and in northern Alaska areas. That's what I remember our teacher told us," Kaarina assisted.

"And then the French were the first to come to Canada from Europe, and they brought with them the Catholic religion and hoped that the Indians would also begin believing this religion. And the French in Canada started the fur trade with the Indians, and in this way got to know them, and learned how and where they hunted. The French exported the furs to Europe and started to make a lot of money from that. The Indians also taught the newcomers how to use snowshoes and canoes, and taught them the important water routes on the Great Lakes. The Indians' lives also changed as they learned how to use guns and shoot, and started to use iron and copper and steel in their pots and knives and tools, and wool in their clothing and blankets," Marja continued, "and then the natives also learned to drink alcohol, and they contracted communicable diseases from the Europeans, and hundreds of natives were killed that way."

Kaarina told them more: "Christopher Columbus came to America under a Spanish flag and he arrived at one of the Bahama's Islands in 1492. He and his crew founded a small colony called Hispaniola there. When Columbus came the second time the following year, he took the West Indies Islands for Spain, and in 1498 he went to Trinidad, and on his fourth trip to Central America.

Then came the Puritans from England. They believed in religious purity and the main purpose for their immigration was that they wanted to practise their religion in peace. They first went to the American northern states. And they say here that the history we are talking about starts from this time.

And more people came from many countries in Europe. Italian Giovanni Caboto came to Canada's eastern coast in 1497 because he hoped to find a new route to Asia. Jacques Cartier from France, was searching for China, when he arrived at the St. Lawrence River in 1534. He made a second trip and came to the site of Quebec City and also travelled to the area of Montreal. Our teacher told us last year that some story told that Leif Eriksson and Bjarne Herjulfsson came from Greenland to Canada's east coast sometime in the year 1000, but I don't know anything about that. Then about the year 1608, Samuel de Champlain came from France, and he founded a small place on the site of Quebec City because he wanted to build a fort there. The place is on a large river and there are profitable hunting areas near there. He became the New France's governor in the year 1627." Marja yawned and closed her book.

"And we'll continue tomorrow evening," Aarne ordered everyone.

"There is so much to think about here, that I really know nothing about, so read and translate more again tomorrow evening," Sylvi added.

And they all went to bed.

The next evening Marja started again: "Then in 1609 an Englishman, Henry Hudson, came to America under the Dutch East-Indian Company's flag. First, he came to the Delaware Bay area, and later went to the New York area, and the Hudson River was named after him. New York became very Holland-like, and the area became to be called Albany. Then in 1611 England furnished Hudson with funds and this time he travelled north, and this area became to be called Hudson's Bay.

Some time in the 1700's France and England began fighting against each other in Europe, and their colonies in the New World also began to fight against one another. This fighting went on for a long time and both sides received aid from their mother countries. Finally, in 1774 The English Parliament adopted the Quebec Act into law, and the French in Canada became English subjects but the Catholic Church was able to keep its rights. But soon the warring started again, and George Washington tried to take Canada but couldn't do it. At the Paris Peace Treaty of 1783 Canada was given the province of Ontario, and the American and Canadian border was drawn through the Great Lakes along the 49th parallel. America started to expand westward from there.

The people that had stayed loyal to England in the war became to be called, the Loyalists, and they started to move to the Canadian side once the war was over. Many moved to Quebec and Nova Scotia because they were given free land there.

People always had differences of opinion but it was hoped that Lower and Upper Canada could join together. In 1840 Lower Canada or Quebec, where people spoke French, and Upper Canada, or Ontario, where people spoke English, joined together to become one province and the name of that province became Canada. In May 1867 the English Parliament adopted the British North America Act into law, and it was published July 1st, 1867, and they say here that it's Canada's founding law."

"It's that July 1ˢᵗ that's always celebrated here every year," Sylvi said.

"You are right," Marja agreed.

Now Kaarina took the book and continued to explain: "There were more and more immigrants coming and the more that came, the more they all wanted land so that they could build homes and open up farming areas, and the Indian fishing and hunting lands became smaller and smaller. The Indians and the newcomers began to fight over the lands that everyone wanted now, and finally the Indians stopped their nomadic life and their fishing and hunting culture started to change. The government gave the Indians their own lands, and these lands with settled borders, became to be called reservations.

Then in the American and Canadian west, and in the prairies, where the Indians had hunted large bison, also called buffaloes, and from which they got their food and clothing; the Indians and the immigrants had slowly hunted these animals almost to extinction. When Canada started to expand west and northward, Canada purchased Hudson's Bay's huge land ownings from the company that owned them. On these lands lived the descendants of the French and the Indians, called the Metis, and they wanted to live there in peace. They tried to become self-governing but the Canadian and English soldiers were able to conquer this territory in 1870, and this place which had originally been named Red River, now became the province of Manitoba; and then the province of British Columbia also joined Canada in 1871," Kaarina finished and gave the book back to Marja.

"There is so much history here that it's hard to remember it all. I'm making coffee," Sylvi commented.

Aarne started to think about all that he had heard. A lot of Indians continued to live on their reservations, which were located in all areas of Canada and also in the Gold Camp; and now a lot of them went to schools and worked in the communities around them.

The longer Aarne lived in Canada, the more he also noticed that new immigrants usually stayed close to other immigrants from their own country, where they could speak their own language; and even though they went to schools and worked with all other nationalities, they usually spent their free time with those from their own country. Aarne smiled at his own thoughts and said to himself: "Everyone seems to have their own reservation, their own place of safety, I say." He had also noticed that it was usually in the next generation, that immigrants became used to everything, and started to take part in the politics and everyday life of the New Country with their full energy.

The girls' interest in history was short-lived. Everything new and what was happening in their life now, was much more interesting to them. New issues and new songs and singers like the 1957 summer's pop idol, Paul Anka, who sang his famous song *Diana* on the radio several times a day, were most important to them.

Aarne continued his evening walks and usually strolled along the Main Street and looked closely at the store windows where all kinds of items were displayed. He was most interested in new cameras and had for some time thought about buying one for himself. Once they were back in Finland it would be fun to show everybody pictures from their Canadian trip. Without asking anything from Sylvi, he bought the camera towards the end of August.

"Are you going to learn how to use that?"

"Why not. Other people have learned it. Stop there now so I can get a good picture! And smile a big smile!"

"Well, did you take it?"

"Yes. Now the two of you stop there!" Aarne ordered the girls, who had watched the picture-taking from the sidelines, but stopped in front of Aarne with a small smile on their faces.

Aarne determined the distance, loaded the camera and ordered: "Good. So. And now!"

Aarne took pictures of the house, from the apartment and from the street. He walked to the Main

Street and took a picture from there. One evening he rushed to meet Sylvi in front of the boarding house and he took a picture of that. On their way home he took pictures of two new-looking parked cars. The following week he had the film developed and they all looked at the pictures. Some pictures were clear, some hazy when someone had moved, but Aarne himself was very satisfied with the results and said to Sylvi: "Well, I'll improve as I take more pictures. That's how you learn at the same time."

Sylvi commented in reply: "It's just something new again."

Kaarina and Margaret signed up for the business college. They were given a list of the needed books and supplies and were told to come back at the beginning of September.

"I guess we'll have to go and tell them at the high school that we are not coming back there?" Kaarina asked Margaret.

"Of course. Let's go together next week."

The August afternoon was warm and bright with sunshine and Kaarina had a good and free feeling about the fact that she had decided to go to business college. It was good to think that she would be learning something useful and could go to work in a year, and she wouldn't have to wait any more for some far-off future.

Some car drove slowly close beside them and the driver called to Kaarina: "Don't you know me any more?"

Kaarina looked in surprise towards the car. Billy stopped beside her, looked out from the car window and invited: "Hi both of you, come on for a ride. Look what I bought with my summer earnings!"

"Heavens! It's Billy," Margaret said.

They ran to sit in the backseat and Billy turned the car onto the Main Street.

"You bought this?" Kaarina was surprised about Billy's return and the purchase of the car.

"What kind of a car is this?" Margaret inspected the car closer.

"This is a used Chevy 1953," Billy bragged proudly. "Mother and father were not happy because I was supposed bring my money home but I already bought this in Elliot Lake. I was not going to come back with my money in my pockets. They always have a need for something."

"This is really nice even though it's not new," Kaarina estimated.

"It's nice to see you but I have to go home. Can you give me a ride there?" Margaret asked.

"Sure, of course. Well, you're going to come for a drive with me?"

"I guess I will," Kaarina agreed and moved to the

front seat to be beside Billy once Margaret left the car.

Billy drove to the lakefront and parked the car, and grabbed Kaarina into a strong embrace.

"Hey, I missed you," Billy kissed her deeply and stroked Kaarina's breasts and waist. "Let me touch you. There was nothing else but work, and more work there. I missed you so much."

Kaarina was surprised about his ardour. She tried to remember where everything had been left between them, when Billy had gone to Elliot Lake, but couldn't remember anything except that he had wanted freedom and money; and he hadn't written any letters or cards during the time that he had been gone.

"Let's go to that lonely beach and let me see you naked?"

"I can't. What if somebody comes there? It's a bad idea," Kaarina refused.

"There is no one coming there," Billy started to drive along the quiet sandy road that circled the lake.

At the same time that he drove, Billy began to ask about the past summer and fondled and kissed her so that Kaarina had to yell: "Hey, look! A car is coming there. Stay on your own side!"

Billy smiled and straightened the car out to the right side and parked near the beach. They ran to sit side by side on the sand and soon their feelings overtook all caution. He opened Kaarina's blouse and took her brassiere off with experienced hands: "Let me, let me touch."

At first almost without wanting Kaarina went along with his wishes but soon she wanted him as much as he wanted her. Finally, she had to push him away from her and ordered him: "Don't come so close. Do you want us to get into trouble?"

"We're not goinna be in any trouble. Let's get something so we can really do it right the next time," Billy replied.

Kaarina didn't say anything.

"Let's go then. I'll take you home. We'll see each other in school. It's starting soon."

"No, we won't see each other there. I'm going to business college."

"You didn't say anything."

"You didn't ask anything about school."

Billy started the car and drove back to the city. Kaarina was quiet and listened to a new singer singing a popular song on the radio. The song's words told about a wonderful day on the beach, and love-letters a couple in love, had written on the sand.

Kaarina glanced at Billy who didn't seem to hear the words, and she became angry at herself. She felt that at the end of it all, Billy wasn't really interested in her, but only in her body, lips, breasts and hips, and the promise of making love.

When Billy stopped the car, Kaarina pulled the door open, slammed it shut, and ran up the stairs, feeling angry at herself. She had an empty feeling inside her when she went into the bedroom.

The next week Sylvi and the girls went together to buy new clothes for starting school. After they returned home, the girls tried the outfits on again in their bedroom.

"What's happening in here?" Aarne opened the door a little when he returned home from work.

"We are just talking that Kaarina still needs new slacks and a sweater and Marja can then wear her old clothes. Now we bought blouses and skirts for each one for the start of the school," Sylvi told him.

"Do you think I'm a millionaire? For God's sake! What does that business college already cost?" Aarne was horrified.

"Well, it's costing a hundred dollars now and then it's fifty dollars a month and the books on top of that. But I'm paying for all of Kaarina's school and then you can pay for all of Marja's when she goes somewhere," Sylvi tried to plan.

"Is that so," Aarne replied more calmly.

Marja immersed herself in her high school life, and started to enjoy her skills and knowledge in a different way, than what Kaarina had in her time. Marja took everything calmly and with sureness: English, history, science and mathematics were easy for her; she had had more time to study them. She also took part in playing basketball and in writing the school paper and on the week ends she went to the high school dances with Donna.

- - - - - - - - - -

As Aarne watched more television he noted that the American blacks living in the southern states of America were now demanding equality with white people. They were talking about civil rights and many times those two words were printed on the television screen, and Aarne repeated them to Sylvi. He had even looked up those two words but neither one of them really understood much about the whole issue. Everything in the New Country was so large and vast and the distances so very long.

"Is there anything in your book about these black people because they are showing them on television almost every day and we really don't know what they are talking about?" Aarne asked Marja one evening.

"I'll get my book. I'm sure there is something about that history but I haven't read it yet. We haven't talked about it yet."

Marja and Kaarina together leafed through the book for some time and then Kaarina started to explain. "There is something here. Well, you can remember that Christopher Columbus came first to America because we talked about that earlier, and then over time came all the other immigrants. The French and the English came first to Canada, and then came people from all of Europe, that could cut forests and clear land and begin farming; they were all people who were ready to do physical work. Most people just wanted to come for a few years and then return and live richly for the rest of their lives. There was as much work as anyone could want, because a railway was being built from east to west in Canada, and mines were being opened, and forests were being cut."

"Well, that was here but what about on the American side?" Aarne asked.

"Well, they say here that it was the same there as it was here. They too needed people to cut forests and open up land for small and large farming. First there came people from Spain, France and England, Ireland, Scotland and Holland, and later from all over Europe. The immigrants there also begin to live near their own countrymen, so they could speak their own languages, and live near others who came from their own culture. So, it was much the same there as it was here. Or did you want to know more about the blacks there?" Kaarina asked.

"Well, mostly about them because they are

showing them on television all the time. Is there nothing about them in your book?"

"There isn't anything about them in this book but I can get a book from the library and we can look at that."

The next evening Kaarina read and explained from the library book: "It was after 1500 when some Spanish and Portuguese explorers started to take African coastal blacks as prisoners and from these times began the transport and sale of black slaves. When these Spanish and Portuguese travelled to the New Country, they also begin to take aboriginal people there as slaves, but they couldn't work in the continuous heat. Then the African blacks began to be transported to the Caribbean Islands and to Southern America. There they farmed sugar, rice, coffee, tobacco and later in Southern America, also cotton, and the blacks were used as slaves and given only a place to live and food for their work. They did not have any human rights."

"There doesn't seem to be very many blacks here in Canada?"

"No, I don't think so," Kaarina replied and continued: "After the French Revolution the world started to demand the release of slaves. It was talked about in America too, but when they started to write their constitution, the blacks and their rights were not mentioned there."

"What is that constitution really?" Marja asked in between. "I was going to ask about it when we talked about the Canadian constitution one evening."

"Well, it's like a basement in a house. In the constitution are written all the laws and rights of the people who live in a particular country," Aarne explained.

Kaarina continued: "America expanded west and south and towards Mississippi and blacks were used as slaves on these farming plantations. Later some white plantation owners gave freedom to their slaves in their testaments, and the blacks then travelled to the American north and there they could live free and find low paying jobs."

"Well, this is not very good history," Sylvi said.

"Then England ended slavery in the West-Indies around 1833 and after that the sale of slaves was ended in all of England's colonies. Spain's South American colonies stopped the sale of slaves when they became independent. Slavery ended in the American north, as it had never really been accepted there, and the religious people there had always been against slavery. Northern states started to demand the end of slavery, and a civil war started there during the presidency of Abraham Lincoln, and the northern states won this war. President Lincoln was shot in 1865 when that war ended, but he declared the freedom of slaves, which became the thirteenth amendment to the American constitution. After his death, during President Andrew Johnson's presidency, this amendment was realised and the end of slavery, and civil rights, and voting rights, were promised to the blacks, but it didn't work out in reality.

The American south was almost destroyed in the civil war and the rebuilding of it, called the reconstruction, was begun. But the whites there did not want to give the blacks voting rights, and finally by the time it was 1876, everyone had had enough of the reconstruction.

After that the southern states started to make Jim Crow laws, and these laws divided the southern blacks from the whites. The blacks were organised into their own schools, and they had to travel in different train cars and buses from the whites. Their names were taken off the voter lists. Finally, by 1900 the blacks founded the National Association for the Advancement of Colored People, and it was supposed to stop segregation by law. Over the years, the blacks started to travel north, but even there, poor living conditions, poorly paid jobs and poorly built and overcrowded apartments, awaited them. The northern blacks were able to vote from 1928 on, but the thirties did not really bring anything new into their lives.

Things started slowly to improve after the war, when the blacks began to join the National Association for the Advancement of Colored People, and their leaders urged them to try to obtain their rights by peaceful means. President Roosevelt established that blacks were hired for government jobs, and were accepted into unions around 1945. By 1953 twelve states and thirty cities had accepted the fact that blacks had the same rights as whites, in being able to work under the same laws as whites, and their wages started to improve."

"Oh, you mean almost now. We haven't known anything about this at all. Well, there are very few black people here in the north," Sylvi commented on her own behalf.

Kaarina closed the book and added: "And these are the things that they are always talking about now on television."

"Well, it's good to know in case there is something on that television; we would then be able to understand it," Aarne agreed: "This much I wanted to tell you, that the more we learn, the more there is to know."

Before television had come into their lives, none of them had ever really thought about other peoples' lives so closely, but now they felt that they were on the frontlines of a very important viewing audience. The television news and information programs brought the world's happenings to everyone's homes, and forced everyone to think about other people's lives more closely. This is the conclusion that the Kalliokoski family came to that fall. During the day they all still listened to the radio as before, and the news given there received a visual confirmation in the television evening news; or if Aarne bought the newspaper, they felt they could check the written text on the evening news.

That fall Kaarina and Margaret saw the popular movie called, *The Defiant Ones,* where two prison escapees, white Tony Curtis, and black Sidney Portier, escaped from a jail in a southern state. They were able to live through many difficulties during their escape, and people watching the movie started to understand that, in the future of the American south there had to be room for all of its people.

One evening at the end of September when Sylvi came home Marja announced importantly: "Now they are playing *Finlandia* on the radio, mother."

"I wonder if Sibelius has died? He was old. I wonder how old he really was?" Sylvi wondered mostly to herself.

"They haven't said anything about that. Wait till it ends now and then they might say something," Marja said and they both stopped to listen to the music.

Once the music ended, the announcer advised that the composer had died at the age of ninety-one.

"Where did he live mother?" Marja asked.

"He lived in Ainola, in Järvenpää. Don't you remember that we talked about that when we went to Helsinki, that Sibelius lived at Järvenpää."

"I can't remember that. Is that Järvenpää near Helsinki?"

"That's where it is. Sibelius is Finland's most important composer. He is well known at least in Europe, and I guess here too, since they have announced it on the radio."

When Aarne returned home he predicted that the television news would also include something about the composer, and the news were also announced there, and there was a picture and a write-up in the next day's newspapers.

At the beginning of October the radio and television news advised people that the Soviet Union had shot into space, a small metallic ball, which was called a satellite and it had been given the name of *Sputnik 1*. There was talk of a new era. Kaarina interpreted from the newspapers that this ball had been made from shiny aluminum, and that it had four antennas, and it travelled around the globe at the height of many kilometres, and it would continue to circle in this way, until it would finally break up and disappear into space.

The paper also said that this kind of a satellite would predict weather and it would also be able to send radio and television signals down to earth. All this sounded strange and wonderful to the ears of ordinary people; but at the same time, they were afraid of some danger coming from space. It was felt that America had been left behind in the space race, especially when the Soviet Union sent *Sputnik 2* satellite into space in November, and it was announced that inside it travelled a living dog. The whole world seemed to stop and think that perhaps in some far-off future, people might also be able to travel to space.

"These boys are already late right from the start," Aarne predicted to Sylvi that fall, and especially after the first American satellite, called the *Vanguard* fell back to earth from a height of three feet, exploded, and burned out.

Aarne continued his evening walks and looked for building lots to the end of October, but with the coming of late fall, he had to stop going out. It was slippery again and cold, and in his mind started to play the dark and heavy music of depression, and the question: "Would it always be like this?" The next spring would come and summer; both would rush by at a quick tempo; and then would come the fall days and nights, which would weigh on his mind as heavily as the music of Sibelius' *Tuonelan Joutsen* – the *Swan of Tuonela*. With fall and winter, he would again have to carry fire wood and coal upstairs; and no matter how much of it he carried, the upstairs would never really become warm. On very cold nights, when he added more coal into the stove, a thought came to his mind about a spark that would ignite the insulation in the attic, near the chimney, and the question, would they all be able to escape down the stairs? Or if the fire started downstairs, how would Sylvi and the girls go down if the stairs had already burned away from under them? But then he had to forget all these thoughts. There was nothing else. If he would be able to get a very good apartment, it would have expensive rent, and then the purchase of the lot and the building of the house, and the going back to Finland, would all be that much further.

Late in the fall when Elvis Presley's new songs were playing on the radio, the announcer talked about him as the King of new music, but now Marja listened more to Buddy Holly's music, which he performed in a newer style yet.

"What illness from Hell comes over these young people when they hear this music? I can't understand any of it. I can't even understand any of the words," Aarne complained.

In November Kaarina saw Anita on the street and they stopped to converse for a few moments.

"Warren and Albert are coming home for Christmas. I think Warren will give me an engagement ring for Christmas. I'm pretty sure about that," Anita's face shone with happiness.

"Can that be true," Kaarina was happy also. "How are their studies going at the teachers' college?"

"Very well. Usually all teachers are able to get a job as soon as they graduate. There are so many children born nowadays, and new schools are being built all the time, and they need more teachers too."

"That's true. Are you going to go to teachers' college or will you get married in the summer already?" Kaarina still asked.

"I think we'll get married in the summer and I will go to teachers' college if Warren can get work near a college, and if not, then I'll become a housewife. Let's see what happens and what father and mother say too. They still want me to go to teachers' college and get a teaching diploma in case I might need it one day," Anita replied.

"I'm graduating from business college in the spring and I hope I get work right away, either as a secretary or a book-keeper," Kaarina said on her own behalf.

"That's good. Are you seriously keeping company with Billy now?" Anita asked.

"I don't know. We go out a lot and we are to-gether often but he hasn't spoken of the future at all," Kaarina looked at the snowbank.

"He needs to find a career too. What is he plan-ning?"

"He hasn't spoken about that. Sometimes he says that he is going to become a teacher, sometimes he talks about the Air Force. But his family hasn't got any money to educate him. They have many children."

"Well, then he needs to go to work in the mines. I'm in a rush to go to the mail. Let's talk sometime in the winter when we see each other. I'll say Hi from you to Warren, shall I?" Anita started to walk fast towards the post office.

"Say Hi to Warren and Albert too if you see him as well. See you in the winter," Kaarina started to walk towards home.

Chapter Fourteen

Marja began to decorate the flat at the beginning of December as she listened to Christmas music coming from the radio. *White Christmas*, sung by Bing Crosby, was played every day and so were most of the other popular Christmas songs.

"Why are you already starting to put decorations around the window?" Sylvi asked on the first Saturday morning of December when Marja and Kaarina together, fitted a small row of Christmas lights around the living room window, and also glued a few cut large white snowflakes on the window glass: "Don't put so many all over the place. This is enough for now."

"But if we don't put them up now, then when shall we put them up? These are only kept up for a month. A lot of other people already have their Christmas trees decorated. Just look when you go out!" Marja replied stubbornly.

"But not at our place. This is enough for now. Let's decorate more closer to Christmas," Aarne supported Sylvi.

Kaarina was left in between. She had got used to the decorated store windows which appeared at the beginning of December, and to the lights that burned long into the evening, but she still thought a lot about Christmas in Finland and especially Christmas Eve.

But Marja had become more Canadian. Nowadays she opened some of her gifts on Christmas Eve and the rest on Christmas morning. In the past couple of years, she had visited Donna's home on Christmas morning, after she had opened all her own presents. Then they had together inspected all of Marja's gifts, and after that Donna had rushed back home to eat their traditional turkey dinner. Marja and Kaarina together had pressed Sylvi to bake a ham on Christmas Eve, and a turkey on Christmas Day, and even Aarne had got used to this; that much they had given in to new customs.

The words of *White Christmas* spoke about the dream of enjoying a white and peaceful Christmas but Marja was daydreaming about her first boyfriend, Fred, who would be coming to pick her up for a visit to his home. Sylvi and Aarne were not yet used to Marja's maturing but they had to go along with it like they had gone along with all the other changes; after all, Marja was almost seventeen years old now.

That afternoon Fred came to pick up Marja and he spent a few moments trying to have a conversation in the company of Aarne and Sylvi in the living room.

"He is a polite boy but what do we understand about his talking?" Aarne asked Sylvi.

"He seems quite nice and I felt I understood a lot of what he was saying but not everything. It still takes me a long time to understand everything," Sylvi agreed with Aarne.

Later that evening Aarne said to Sylvi: "Well, I can't really say anything about this except that his father is one of the important big bosses at the mine. That's what Vilho told me when I told him that this Fred was Marja's friend."

"Oh, I see," from Sylvi allowed Aarne to know that she couldn't say anything else either.

Aarne looked at the afternoon winter scene. Huge snowflakes drifted slowly to the ground – "like Old Country furhats," – Aarne said to himself. "Look outside," he turned towards Sylvi, "I have never seen such huge snowflakes. Have you? They are like Old Country furhats." Then he thought for a moment of what he had just said and stopped in his thinking: - Was he becoming Canadian? – came to his mind – that was the first time that he noticed himself to have said, Old Country, like those Finns who had lived in Canada for a long time.

Billy came to pick Kaarina up for a drive, ran up the stairs, knocked on the door and called to everyone: "Hello! Are you coming Kaarina? I'll be waiting in the car. It's running out there. I can't leave it," and already at that moment he disappeared back outside.

"Why can he not come properly inside?" Aarne looked towards Kaarina.

"Well, he'll come in the spring when it's warmer," Kaarina replied and with one sweeping gesture she threw her coat on her shoulders, pulled her hat on her head and pulled the scarf around her neck.

"Take your mitts. It's cold out there," Sylvi urged: "and tell him to come inside next time."

Kaarina ran out to the warm car. Billy kissed and embraced her. They were going to join Billy's friends.

Just as Anita had hoped, Warren asked her to marry him on Christmas Eve when he visited the Lahti's, and gave her his grandmother's diamond ring as shining proof of his love.

On Christmas Day morning Anita ran to the Kalliokoskis to show her ring. She seemed to be bursting with happiness.

"Well, a lot of happiness to you; I don't know what else to say," Sylvi smiled.

"Congratulations," Aarne walked from the living

room to shake Anita's hand.

"Happiness always. Happiness always," Kaa-rina repeated and hugged Anita who then continued her trip to her next friends.

Christmas came and went and the yearly gnaw-ing winter settled on the small city once more.

One night, Aarne thought, he was back at the warfront again. They had marched all day and arrived at a group of the enemy's bodies. Some of the soldiers had run to pull out gold-filled teeth from the gaping enemy mouths; some others had stolen what still could be taken from the corpses, at the same time yelling to each other: "I have killed many of this same kind and will kill again!" Or asked each other: "Are there gold fillings there, or gold rings? That's what I'm looking for." However, most like Aarne had turned and continued marching, swearing at the same time: "Come away from there! You Satan's thieves!"

The nightmare ended as soon as it had begun and Aarne woke to think about life's hardness – Was it always so? Did you always have to steal everything that you could, everything loose, teeth, rings, boots, clothes, life itself, so that you could get ahead? Was this the eternal battlefield? No kindness, no pity, fight till you have breath left; and when there is a weak mo-ment; when you fall or tire out; someone hits you for the final time. Then others take you teeth, rings, boots, clothes, and finally your life. In war it usually happens fast, like a movie at a fast pace, in ordinary life it happens slower, but the final outcome is always the same.

Is that what is going to happen to me? - Aarne thought more, before I ever get to the big haul, I'll be an old and worn-out man? - His gums bled if he sucked them even a little bit. "God damn war-memories!" He swore and got up, ran his hand through his hair and looked at the clock and pushed the blankets and the day cover on top of Sylvi's plump and peaceful being; but the whole day, dark and depressing thoughts occupied his mind.

That same evening when Sylvi drank her coffee and took a bite of the Finnish coffee bread, Aarne reminded her harshly: "And you, try to stop eating so much! God damn it, you'll soon be looking like an elephant!"

Sylvi's blue eyes flew open as she tried to find words: "What is your problem now? Let me drink my coffee in peace!"

"Leave all that eating. Can you hear! Look at yourself sometimes!"

"And you look. You're not so young and slim any more either!" Sylvi dared to defend herself. She dunked her coffee bread in the coffee again, but when Aarne disappeared into the living room, she hurried to look at herself in front of the girls' room big mirror and straightened her now-tight dress, front and back; but it didn't help matters any, she had really gained weight.

Whenever Kaarina saw Anita that winter, she was full of her diamond and constantly spoke of her upcoming wedding in June, and what she would have to do before that.

At the end January when it was announced on television that America had successfully sent a satellite called *Explorer 1* into space, Aarne called the whole family to the living room and announced importantly: "They are a little bit late but finally they've been able to go, I say!"

"Well, I guess that's good," Sylvi estimated and stayed to watch the rest of the news with a feeling of uncertainty.

The girls were not interested in the news and turned to go back to their bedroom.

"We don't care about that, some satellite! Have you heard that Elvis has been called into the army?"

"And we don't care about Elvis at all!" Aarne said in his own defence.

Nowadays Aarne bought the English-language newspaper each Saturday and read it page, by page, during the following week. He compared news he found there with the Finnish Canadian newspaper,

Vapaa Sana, which he received twice a week. The most important Canadian news in 1958 was the election which took place at the end of March that year. The conservatives won by a large margin and John Diefenbaker was announced to have become the prime minister, already for the second time; he had been elected the first time in June 1957, although the conservative win had been modest at that time. What Aarne understood of the Canadian politics was very little, but he had read that the previous liberal government had brought Canada closer to the American way of thinking, and John Diefenbaker had promised a change in this matter.

Aarne also read that Nikita Khrushchev had been selected as the Soviet Union's new leader. He didn't know anything about this man or his leadership style yet, but he was sure about the fact that the world was changing in the west and in the east.

A shower or in Finglish, shaueri, was organised for every bride before the wedding. The word meant a downpour, more meaningfully a downpour of gifts, because every invited woman brought her own gift to the party; and it was hoped that these gifts together would make up a downpour of gifts. The Kalliokoskis were best friends with the Lahtis and Kaarina was Anita's best friend; and for that reason, Anita had asked Kaarina to be her maid of honour. Now Sylvi and Kaarina together had the honour of organising Anita's shower, and ask every invited woman to bring a gift and a plate of something suitable to eat for the coffee table.

Kaarina walked from one Finnish house to another and asked women to the shower, and at the same time asked for a small amount of money to purchase wedding gifts for the young couple. According to custom, money was collected from all Finnish friends of the bride, a dollar from here and a dollar from there, and with these funds much-needed and even expensive gifts for the bridal couple were purchased; sandwiches and cakes were prepared, which were usually brought to the Finn Hall where everyone was invited. But if the groom was English, then the wedding was held in a Canadian style, invitations were sent out and a more elaborate wedding was organised to be held in the finest hotel of the small city. This was their plan, Anita had told Kaarina. But most often the Finns collected money anyway, and gave a gift together to the young couple, especially if the young bride's parents were long-standing members of the community.

Kaarina hated the collecting of money because these occasions gave an opportunity for the givers of money, to ask all kinds of questions, while they were searching for money in their purses.

"Well, come on in! Kaarina Kalliokoski! I know your father and your uncle! They work in the same mine as our Eetu. Anita Lahti is getting married? Where is that money purse? There it is. I wonder if Anita is already in a hurry to make it to the altar?"

Usually at this point Kaarina blushed all the way to her ears and tried to say something negative which was usually swept aside. "Don't say anything! Good thing it is, if there is no hurry. I guess he is a good man even though he is English-speaking. There is my two dollars."

Kaarina tried to push the money given into the envelope, and at the same time give the card to be signed by the giver of money, but usually the torrent of words continued. "Anita can then collect for you. Can you make out our last name there? When is the wedding? An invitation is coming! That's the English way, but I'll come to the shower and I already gave you the two dollars for the wedding gift. We are very good friends with the Lahtis. Are you still going around with that Yrjö? He thinks he is some kind of a God's gift to women, but is he good for anything else? Or do you have somebody else? That's what I've heard. If you're thinking of that Billy, they have a bunch of kids; I think five altogether in that family. That's a catholic family and they have a lot of kids. Their religion already tells them that. So, think clearly for yourself before you go with him. So, think clearly girl!"

Kaarina thanked without saying anything more

and rushed outside to cool off her burning cheeks. People seemed to know about Yrjö and Billy too.

There was a kind of nostalgia in the air at this time of winter going away and spring coming. With a blue sky and days full of sunshine, it captivated Kaarina to remember times gone by. From somewhere in her mind came the thought of the fourteen-year-old girl who had cried her heart out about having to leave for Canada. How long ago that seemed! A momentary longing for somewhere filled her mind. For Finland? For childhood? She wasn't sure about that any more. She remembered the time of leaving, and the happenings before that, and the promises she had made to herself. Going back to Finland within two years had already long gone by and not come true; and like all the other immigrants she was more and more closely tied to her new life.

Spring and the wedding were coming. In Kaarina's mind, Anita seemed to be preparing for everything strangely calmly; being seemingly more interested in gifts rather than love; whereas Kaarina felt herself to be struggling more and more often with Billy and her own wild feelings about him, and she couldn't seem to understand Anita's calmness about it all.

Shower guests arrived on a sunny and beautiful early spring morning and filled the Kalliokoskis small flat soon. Kaarina and Marja had organised the chairs closely beside one another in the living room; some of the chairs were their own and some were borrowed from Aune. Sylvi and Aarne together had turned the kitchen table to be in front of the window and Sylvi had covered the table with her best table cloth.

The first guests started to organise the table and put several coffee pots filled with water to boil on the stove, whereas the guests who followed were seated in the living room. Anita and Taimi came last, looking seemingly surprised, although they had guessed the reason for the event.

Kaarina sat Anita on the best living room chair which was decorated with ribbons and flowers and the party started. Kaarina offered the gifts, one at a time for Anita to open; Kaarina read the card which was sent around with the gift, and then she stapled the bow which had been on the gift onto a paper plate. Once all the gifts had been opened, the paper plate with the bows would be tied on Anita's head, and pictures would be taken which she would save, and save the hat in her hope chest. She had received the hope chest from her parents and as was the usual custom, she would collect and store all the towels, sheets, table cloths and other gifts that she received now in it. At the end of the shower, the guests were offered coffee or tea, sandwiches and coffee bread and cakes to eat.

Schools were also finished in the spring and Kaarina and Margaret soon sat happily at their graduation from business college. After the ceremony and speeches all the pupils received their diplomas.

"Well, that went well and if we get jobs, I would be truly happy," Margaret looked at Kaarina as they begin to get ready to go home.

"Don't say anything else. Father said that now it's not such a good time as it has been before; there is a depression-time in employment and perhaps we won't be able to get jobs so easily." Kaarina replied.

"My stepfather said that last week he saw some young men who had come from Port Arthur to look for jobs here at the mines. If they are coming here to look for work, it means that there is no work there," Margaret continued.

"But we have to get jobs. Mother paid for my college and now my whole family is waiting for me to get a good job," Kaarina added, "as soon as I get Anita's wedding out of the way."

The young couple's wedding day started with sunshine. Kaarina and Anita got ready by waking up early in the morning. Anita's hair was combed to the back, and her veil was secured tightly to her hair with bobby pins, and the front of the veil was pulled to cover her face. Her long white gown changed her to look like an angel and made Kaarina ask: "Are you not afraid a little bit? That and everything.?"

"Oh, that?" Anita waved her hand: "I haven't thought about it at all. And you don't have to do it right away if you don't want to. Warren is a gentleman, and not some ruffian! Why do you think about that when there is so much more to marriage? You have to get along and the man has to have a good job if you have children." At this point Anita looked down and Kaarina noticed her uncertainty and she didn't ask anything more.

What was life all about? - Came to her mind. - Billy didn't own anything more than his car, and didn't want to, by his own admission own anything more, but Kaarina felt herself to be ready to start a life together by his side; whereas Anita wanted to make sure the man could support them without any fiery feelings. Which would be more lasting: the fiery love or the planned future? If she thought about her own parents, she wondered if Sylvi had made the best decision when she had always gone by Aarne's orders or wishes. Now they were immigrants and had that been the best decision, in Sylvi's case, remained a puzzle.

At one o'clock Anita's cousin Lenni came to drive them to the church. Kaarina hoped that Billy would also come to the wedding, and would in this way show that he was interested in getting married, generally speaking; but when she walked out of the church to the music of *Mendelson's March* and checked all the pews, she couldn't find him anywhere.

"Was he at the church?" Anita asked outside while people were wishing the bridal couple much happiness.

"I don't know," Kaarina replied shortly.

"He wasn't. It's just like him. Believe me. Don't' trust him anymore!" Anita looked deeply into Kaarina's eyes.

"I didn't look if he was there or not. It could be that he was there," Kaarina tried.

"He was not. I didn't see him anywhere," Anita ended the conversation there.

But Billy came to the evening ceremony, his hair combed neatly and he was handsomely dressed in a dark suit, and danced with Anita among the first of those who danced with the bride, winked his eye at Kaarina, and asked her to the next dance.

"Are you the bride?" He started: "You look so beautiful in yellow."

"Why didn't you come to the church?" Kaarina demanded.

"I told you I'm not coming to church. I'm not coming near any church. Don't even think that. Let's just dance and have fun. We can enjoy a wedding night without any church!"

"Don't try. I'm not having any wedding night

until we are married!"

"Well, then you're going to be without it. Don't try that," Billy looked at her lovingly, playfully, but at the same hurting Kaarina's feelings deeply.

And the wedding didn't have the shimmer and shine that it had started with, but instead Kaarina danced and smiled mechanically and didn't bother Billy with any more questions. It was late at night when they parked in front of her house and Billy took her into a tight embrace and whispered in her ear: "I love you in my own way," that she felt there was still something to hope for in their togetherness.

"Listen, let's go to the drive-in-theatre next weekend. There is a good movie there," Billy suggested before he left to go home.

"I don't know. I've never been," Kaarina replied.

"Well, that's a good reason to go there then."

So, they drove to the drive-in theatre the following Saturday. When Kaarina looked at the car parked beside them, at first it looked empty, until much later when she saw a couple sit up in the back seat, pull down their dishevelled clothing and then stare at the screen for the rest of the movie while holding each other tightly.

Billy slipped his hand under Kaarina's blouse, opened her brassiere and fondled her breasts at the same time saying: "Let's go to the back seat. We can get into a better position there."

Kaarina sighed without feeling much anything. When they opened the front doors of the car to go to the backseat, the cars beside them, honked their horns as if approving their move. Kissing in the backseat soon led to caressing and more heated feelings. It seemed that the culture of the day encouraged the young people to make love without saying it directly. The music from the radio, television programs and movies, and advertising, encouraged the young people to enjoy life and to buy everything which would bring with it a quick maturing, love and a happy future.

If Kaarina's life seemed to become smaller inside a car, then Aarne's, Sylvi's and Marja's seemed to become larger on the movie screen when they went to watch the popular movie called, *Gigi*. The *Gigi* movie took place in Paris. The actors were beautifully dressed and it was fun to listen to the delightful songs even though the story itself was strange to them. The young and naïve Gigi had been sent to Paris to learn how to charm men and learn fine etiquette in the hopes that she would become a rich man's mistress; but instead Gigi and the rich man Gaston, truly fell in love and at the end of the movie Gaston asked Gigi to become his wife. In the fall they had seen a movie called *Sayonara* which had also offered something different to think about. Where the *Gigi* story was light, the *Sayonara* movie had shown a story of prejudice and intolerance.

Many times movies showed different people and distant places, but whatever the place was, people always had problems; Sylvi thought to herself.

As they walked home, Marja admired aloud the songs and the dresses of the movie; whereas Aarne and Sylvi walked beside her quietly, both thinking about the new world into which the girls would soon step, without any of them knowing much about that world.

"Wouldn't it be fun to go to Paris, mother?" Marja asked.

"We can't go that far. You can't go there. You're only a student and you know some English but then you would again have to learn a new language. You better just finish your school here and find a job here," Sylvi replied.

"But I loved those songs and the fine dresses and everything," Marja continued.

"It's not real life," Aarne replied.

"We can make those fine dresses here too. And it's best for you to stay here with us," Sylvi reminded her again.

"Well, those clothes were a little bit old fashioned," Marja agreed. "But they were fun to watch anyway. And I'm not homesick for anyplace. I like it fine here."

Aarne noted quickly that this was the opportunity for him to tell Sylvi and Marja about his long-kept secret plans and he started right away: "It might be the time for all of us to think that the best plan for us all, is to stay here. I don't think these girls are really going to be able to return. So, if I start looking for a plot of land and build that House, and we stay here?" Aarne looked towards Sylvi.

"Really. You've been thinking all these thoughts on your own without asking me anything and here I thought that we were going back to Finland," Sylvi was opposed to Aarne's plan.

"Well, where are these girls going then? Are they coming with us or are they staying here?" Aarne tried again.

"I don't want to go back. I can't remember hardly anything about Finland. I'm staying here and I think Kaarina wants to stay here too," Marja announced.

Sylvi stopped to blow her nose and to wipe her eyes.

"Well, what do you think about the lot and the building of the house?" Aarne repeated.

"I can't think about those things now. I have enough in thinking about the fact that you are all planning to stay here."

"But if I build that house," Aarne tried once more.

"I don't know. Leave me alone," Sylvi didn't want to talk about the matter.

"I would like a house and then even more if I get my own room," Marja was interested.

"Well, let's go and see some lots," Aarne tried once more.

"And with what money are we able to buy a lot? We don't have any money," Sylvi was not keen about the idea. "And then you think about those things on your own. I don't know. I don't know," Sylvi repeated and the conversation ended there.

- - - - - - - - - -

Kaarina and Margaret visited the employment office to look for work. After that they went to all the Main Street stores and offices. They talked about looking for work to people they knew; like Aune, who had encouraged her when Kaarina had visited there. Aune had even promised to take all the phone calls that Kaarina was hoping to receive from prospective employers.

After looking for work for three weeks Kaarina was asked for an interview at the *Consumers Co-operative* which was owned by the Finns in the area, and she was hired, and given a desk and a chair, and an adding machine in an upstairs office. Other people who worked in the office were a secretary, two book-keepers and the manager. One of the book-keepers carried a large box to stand beside Kaarina's desk and instructed her to add up every store shopper's last year's purchases, so that they could be given a one percent discount on their next winter's coal purchases. Kaarina started her work with big hopes.

Margaret was hired for a bush-camp office book-keeper. She answered the phone, paid the bills, the men's wages and kept the books. The manager of the office picked up the cheques, delivered them to the men in the bush, and brought new bills for Margaret to pay.

The girls celebrated their first week's pay by buying new jeans and new checkered cotton blouses to go with the jeans.

- - - - - - - - - -

Pekka Kuronen came again for his holidays and visited the boarding house kitchen as soon as he arrived. Kaarina and Margaret happened to be dropping by at the same time.

"Hi girls. I'm Pekka. Kuronen's older son. You remember me Kaarina." Pekka spoke in Finnish.

"Hi," Kaarina replied and Margaret more quietly: "Hi."

"Come for a drive! I'll show you around this area," Pekka invited as he took his coffee cup and piece of coffee bread from Vieno's hands.

"What's he saying?" Margaret asked in English.

"He is asking us for a drive. Pekka is Vieno's son. Do you want to go?" Kaarina explained to Margaret in English.

"We can go, yes," Margaret agreed.

"We can come," Kaarina replied to Pekka.

"Nice car," Kaarina admired as they went to sit in the back seat.

"Sit down. I'll show you places around here," Pekka started to drive.

They drove through the city streets and then down the local highway to the lake area where many people had their cottages.

"Now we'll go and see cottages and saunas that the Finns own around here. Have you been here?" Pekka said. "But I'm not sure we can see them from the road here."

"No, we can't see them from here. But I have been here earlier visiting a couple of cottages with my mom and dad. I've visited the Mäkinen's and the Virtanen's. But it's a long time ago, a couple of years back," Kaarina replied.

"How about you quiet girl? Have you been here?" Pekka asked Margaret in English at the same time that he looked in the rear-view mirror to see her.

"No. I have not been here. I don't know anyone from here." Margaret replied in English and smiled to

Pekka in the mirror.

"We'll see each other again," Pekka replied as he drove back to the city and turned to drive home.

"He was nice-looking and seemed friendly. He seemed to mostly speak Finnish but I guess he must know more English too?" Margaret asked Kaarina.

"For sure he knows more English. He has lived at Elliot Lake for two years and has worked there the whole time," Kaarina explained.

"Where would I meet him then if he lives there? I don't know," Margaret doubted.

"I don't know either,"

The matter was left there.

After a few days Margaret ran to meet Kaarina after work and announced to her: "Do you remember Pekka? He waited for me outside my work last night and told me that he had asked his mother where I worked, and came to get me and gave me a ride home, and asked for my mailing address so that he can write to me when he goes back to Elliot Lake."

"Well, you didn't have to think about where you could meet him because he thought of it himself," Kaarina laughed.

At home she thought about her relationship with Billy and whether it would ever lead to anything more serious. If she asked him about the future , Billy always started to talk about going away to some big city, to the Air Force, to some school or to wherever, as long as it took him away from the small city; when he would have enough money; now he apparently only worked in the mine for the time being. Other times he spoke about the future as if they would be together; yet other times he asked: "What are you planning?" As if Kaarina was starting some important career. If she thought about the past, first Billy had been a fun friend, then he had become Kaarina's first boyfriend through whom she had met many other friends. With Billy she had started to live the teenage life that had been left unfinished in Finland, without a care or any plan; then she had fallen in love with Billy, but was Billy in love with her? When she thought about their togetherness and its future, she felt like she was falling into some deceptive swamp, without knowing its depth or its bottom. Her work was routine and didn't seem to be an opening to an important career; she might be able to become a secretary or a book-keeper. Usually women worked until they married or became pregnant with their first baby. All those thoughts turned in a circle in her head without any answers.

That evening when they kissed and Billy started to caress her breasts, it felt like he lighted a fire within the both of them. "This is nice, let me open the buttons." And one button at a time Billy opened her blouse and took it off. "And what is this? Let's take it off too." He opened her brassiere and undid the elastic bands holding up her stockings and took her panties off. He opened his belt, slid down his zipper and Kaarina lifted up her skirt out of the way. He pushed himself into her without asking, and finally Kaarina allowed it to happen, breathing deep when a sudden pain slashed her virginity into the past. With Kaarina sitting on the seat and Billy kneeling on the car floor, they made love for the first time, without her parents' approval, without a ring or a bridal veil, without the minister's blessing or a marriage certificate. As soon as it had happened Kaarina regretted it, but he smiled and looked at her for a moment as if she was some angel and said: "I love you. Don't worry. I was careful."

Kaarina struggled her brassiere on, straightened her slip and buttoned her blouse back on, and pulled her skirt down. She didn't know what Billy meant and asked several times. "Are you sure? Are you sure?" Now she felt she belonged to Billy.

"Well, let's go home," he suggested but Kaarina was afraid of going home. What if everyone at home would notice what had happened? They drove back to Kaarina's home in total silence.

They kissed as they parted and Kaarina watched at the gate as Billy's car disappeared behind the corner. She ran up the stairs and sobbed quietly as she went to sleep.

That fall's newspapers told that the dog that had been sent into space in the *Sputnik 2* satellite, had died from the excitement or agitation soon after the take-off.

"It's not right to be sending animals there. There should be some kind of a boundary, or something, I say!" Aarne commented to Sylvi and they both sat down to think about the world that seemed to be becoming more and more strange.

Soon the girls told them about the fact that the America's army had sent Elvis Presley to Germany.

"That was the end of that man's music, and a fine finish to a cat's meow!" Aarne laughed at the girls' news.

"It's not going to end there. He is coming back yet," Kaarina stated and Marja repeated: "He is still coming back. You just don't like him."

The next week's news told about a new mining accident at the Springhill mine and Aarne reminded Sylvi that there had already been an accident there two years' ago, and that the mine had been started again in 1957.

"What has really happened there?" Aarne asked while he was watching television: "Tell me that Kaarina!"

"Well, they say that there has been an underground explosion; like a sort of a big blast. They have taken more and more coal out from there, and that has created a large empty space and the timbers that were left to support it all, have given away, and everything on the top has fallen down. It has been very strong, that explosion, and many men have died there."

"Oh, for God's sake!" Aarne swore.

The bad news continued several evenings and the Kalliokoskis collected around the television to hear the depressing news. By the following afternoon it was announced that seventy-five men had been saved, and those that had been left under the debris, had mostly died right away. At some difficult areas the men sent to assist in the recovery, had kept the coal-seam open with timbers and their own bodies, so that the injured could be pulled to safety before the seam closed completely.

The relatives hoped and prayed on top of the mine, and five days later twelve more men were discovered in an empty pocket behind a collection of fallen rocks, and the last men were pulled above ground on the first day of November.

The small city was silenced into thinking about minework. The coal mines sounded dangerous, Aarne thought, when he heard about the difficult conditions that the men there worked under, but then the gold mines were not totally safe either; or was there any truly safe place in the whole world?

During that same fall the Trans Canada Pipe Line was completed and the news told everyone that the last link was joined in October 1958 near the Gold Camp at a place called, Kapuskasing. Now it was possible to deliver natural gas from the west coast of Canada to the east coast, and the pipes continued to America where the gas would also be bought; as America had been a very important financial investor into this huge project.

Chapter Fifteen

"Why, why are you leaving now?" Kaarina asked Billy when he told her that he had been asked to come to be tested for the Air Force.

"Perhaps this is my chance for education and a better life. Can you imagine! I would have to work for two years to save enough money to go to teachers' college for one year! And now this! Air Force was always my first choice!"

"But then, what about our relationship and our future?" Kaarina was worried when she thought about her own life if Billy was in the Air Force or in some far away school and lived somewhere else.

"I always told you that I'm not going to stay here. Let's think about our future later," Billy acted as if he wasn't attached to Kaarina in any way. "Hey, come on here. I'm going on Monday, next week. Let me, , ," He started to put his arm around Kaarina's shoulders and pulled her toward himself.

All of Kaarina's pent-up feelings and thoughts started to unravel into words: "What are you thinking of? You have promised this or that and that our future would be together and then you think that you can use me like some rag doll to satisfy your own wants!"

Billy stared at her with a surprised look on his face. "I thought you wanted it as much as I did!"

"No, I didn't want it! I'm in love with you and I trusted our future to be together. You have always said: 'I love you – I love you'," Kaarina retorted.

"Well, I do love you, but I can't think about any serious future when I have no profession, no money, nothing. I hope you're not thinking that I'm staying in the mine? I always told you that I'm not staying there, under any circumstances."

"But what if you have to. If you can't get anything else, or if I get pregnant, what then?" Kaarina demanded spoken answers to her long-thought questions.

"Well, sometime in the future but not now. I'm always careful. I'm always careful," Billy repeated twice.

"I'm always careful! I'm always careful! But what then if you're not careful enough and there is an accident? What then? And I have a bad feeling about it all. My parents would be horrified if they knew, and your parents! We are playing with fire and one day it's going to burn us!" Kaarina shouted.

"Don't start yelling and shouting! You are all worked up about this one thing and nothing has happened. Let's go home. I don't want to talk about this any more."

Billy started his car and drove Kaarina home. At her front gate, Kaarina charged out of the car and slammed the car door shut behind her without saying anything.

As she sobbed into her pillow she thought about the evening over and over and tried to remember where her relationship with Billy had started to go wrong. Kaarina knew herself to have been a rebellious and stubborn teenager, but when she thought about her time in Canada, she understood more clearly now, that she had been left without parental support when they had become immigrants. All the difficult times in the beginning and the huge daily struggles had robbed Kaarina of her parents' support when she had most needed it. Aarne and Sylvi had tried their best but the future in the New Country had come to them without any preparation on their part. It had been a daily struggle that they now had a reasonable place to live, a collection of some kind of furniture, clothes on their back, and food on the table, and that they had jobs and the girls were in school.

Kaarina knew that she looked like an adult on

the outside but felt herself to be immature inside; whereas Marja had been able to develop more slowly with time and she was already certain about herself and her future. She was planning to go to teachers' college and their parents now had time to help her with her future plans; whereas Kaarina felt herself to be drifting to her own future without much planning or support. Now and then she hoped that she could talk about everything with Sylvi, but it seemed to be very difficult to start unravelling her problems, that seemed to have no beginning, nor any end.

The next week she spoke to Margaret about everything and Margaret warned her about Billy and about all that had happened between them. "Listen Kaarina, don't do that any more. Stop it right now! What if you get pregnant? My God! Where are you then? And what if he leaves you, or if he is in a school somewhere else, will he come back here then and leave his school because of you?"

Margaret continued: "He is not really a nice guy. There is so much more to you than what there is in him. He is full of talk and promises and plans which will never come true. Remember how many told you about that when you started to go with him?"

"I do remember but I didn't want to hear anyone. Do you think that?"

"Yes, I think that. Pekka writes to me every

week and tells me about Elliot Lake and how he is saving money. He is coming to visit at Christmas and he has told me that he is hoping that our future would be together. Don't trust Billy. He will never change; he'll just use your time. If you are waiting for him to come and get you, after he has spent some time in the world; I don't believe in that. He is never going to grow up to be an adult! You will grow and mature but I believe that he'll look for another childish girl like you and start the same game all over again. Then he doesn't have to ever change. He is going to blame his parents all his life that he had to help his younger siblings and for the fact that they were poor."

"I've never thought about it that way. I'm so crazy about him," Kaarina still had a hard time trying to see Billy's weak points.

"Think of things as they are, and don't look at life through rose-coloured glasses," Margaret ended her advise.

Kaarina didn't see Billy for some time and heard from elsewhere that he had gone to try out for the Air Force.

Then Billy returned, depressed, disappointed and angry; and waited for Kaarina outside her work place.

"What are you doing here? I thought you went to try out for the Air Force," Kaarina didn't know what to think and say when she saw him.

"Hey. I want to talk to you," Billy replied. He stretched his arm to push the other front door open and continued in a bossy tone: "Jump in the car!"

"I have to go and eat. Mother has the food ready."

"Okay, we'll go," Billy drove Kaarina home and came to wait in the kitchen without asking. He even went to greet Aarne and Sylvi in the living room.

"We're going out," Kaarina said to her parents as they left.

"Don't stay late. Can you hear? You now have a good job and they are not easy to get on every street corner," Aarne reminded.

"Well, I know that," Kaarina replied.

Billy drove to Smithy's restaurant and they sat there for the rest of the evening while Billy told her about the Air Force exams: "I got through the written tests okay and then we learned about technical stuff, and then we all went in the airplane; but it all seemed different and strange in the cockpit. The next two days were more and more questions about what we would do if something happened; if there was an accident and how you would help others; and how you would act in the air and on land if you had to take the plane down in a forced landing. So, I replied honestly that I would first think about myself. Isn't that the most im-

portant thing? If somebody tells me that he thinks
first of other people and the airplane, that is a lie! Everyone is first thinking of their own life. But that made
me fail. They said that I was not suitable for a situation or work where I had to be responsible for others
and for the airplane. I have listened all my life to the
fact that I am the oldest and responsible for several
smaller children and I have had enough of that. I don't
want to carry responsibility for all the others. Let them
take care of themselves! I'll look after myself. The Hell
with the Air Force! I'm sure not going there! That's
for sure," he sat looking depressed at the darkening
evening.

"Well, that was too bad. What are you going to
do now?" Kaarina didn't know what else to say.

"It's back to the mine. I have to go back to the
mine! There is nothing else. Save more and apply to
teachers' college; if I'm accepted there. Let's go home,"
Billy drove her back home. They didn't talk about the
future any more.

That Christmas the Kalliokoskis had a lot of
presents and it felt that life was much better than it
had ever been after they had arrived in Canada.

Marja and Donna were now bold teenagers as
they repeatedly sang Ritchie Valens' new song, *Donna*,
just because it seemed that Donna now had her own
song, or then they sang *LaBamba* which was on the

other side of the same record.

"O, my God! They have to sing those same songs on the hour every day. *Donna* or *LaBamba!* Just be quiet for a while!" Sylvi was tired of the same music, first coming from the radio and then being sung by the girls.

"Have you heard the new Buddy Holly song?"

"You don't have to sing it again because it also comes from the radio on the hour." Sylvi said.

"Yes, but now Buddy Holly and the Crickets are so popular and Ritchie Valens too. After Christmas they are going on a tour in America and already now all the places where they perform are full of people. They are going to tour on a bus because they don't all like to fly. That Ritchie Valens is afraid of flying because he saw some airplane falling down," Marja explained.

Kaarina replied: "I haven't heard anything about that. I don't know much about them. I've heard their music but I still like Elvis. I wonder if he is coming back?"

"I just don't know. He might come back from the army but will he be as famous as before; we don't know anything about that yet. The songs have changed a lot in between!"

Kaarina didn't feel that she belonged any more with the teenagers who lived by the music of the day, like she had, when she had lived with Elvis' music. Anita was married now and lived elsewhere and Margaret was thinking about her own future with Pekka. Kaarina felt more and more like she didn't really belong to any group.

The Finnish Newspaper advertised that there would be a New Year's dance at the Finn Hall and she decided to go there alone.

"Can you go to that dance on your own or is that dance more for couples?" Sylvi asked when Kaarina was getting dressed.

"You can go there on your own," Kaarina replied and left bravely, but lost some of her bravery on the way to the hall. Once she arrived there, she joined a group of girls where she saw some familiar faces.

Several men came to ask her to dance and she danced with Antti, Mikko and Matti and even Yrjö, who now seemed to have a new girlfriend standing beside him.

At eleven o'clock, when a girl she knew, Paula Virtanen, was getting ready to go home, she joined her. It felt good to be free and without worry. In its own way the dance at the Finn Hall had been fun even though the music was old-fashioned, with polkas, tangos and waltzes being played, instead of the modern music. On their way home they talked about the future. Would it be with a Finnish mine or a bush worker, or with someone they had gone to school with; and would their life continue in the small city, or somewhere else? Several of their high school friends had already left to work elsewhere. Of course, there would be the possibility of staying single, working in the small city and living at home as long as you could. Kaarina shook her head when she thought about the unknown future.

Equally unknown was the world's future. At the end of 1958 the news often spoke about the island of Cuba and a man named Fidel Castro. Aarne knew that Cuba was the largest of the West-Indies Islands and that Christopher Columbus had arrived there on his first exploratory trip. Naturally beautiful scenery and crystal-clear waters had awaited him and his crew there. Cuba had developed into Spain's sugar and tobacco plantation colony, where America had invested money and also owned land. Later the Spanish immigrants who had come with Columbus and their descendants, who owned the plantations, had begun to demand independence from Spain. In the year 1902 Cuba had gained its freedom but America had been able to keep its navy bases, such as Guantanamo Bay, and Cuba was left to be dependant on the trade between America and Cuba. Employment was based on a need for workers at time of harvesting, and unemployment at other times. In the summer of 1952 Fulgencio Batista, a sergeant in the army, was able to seize power for himself and America accepted Batista's government. Fidel Castro, one of his students, turned against him, but he was jailed and sent to Mexico. There he became friends with Ernesto Che Guevara, who believed that the best future for Cuba would be behind a revolution. They attacked together in the summer of 1956, but Batista's army awaited them and they had to flee to the Sierra Maestra Mountains. In the year 1957 Castro undersigned the Sierra Maestra declaration where he promised to hold a free election in one and a half years if he gained power, and to return the 1940 constitutional rights, which had been stopped when Batista had gained power. In the mountains Castro and Che Guevara trained guerilla patrols and attacked the Batista army again and they were able to rob an army storage train which was full of weapons and food. At the end of 1958 Che Guevara and Camilo Cienfuegos marched as conquerors into Havana at the same time as Fidel Castro marched into Santiago de Cuba. On the television news on New Year's Day 1959, it was announced that Fulgencio Batista had rushed to escape from under Fidel Castro's army and he had gone to the Dominican Republic Islands. Jose Miro Cardona, a law professor, created a new government in January, 1959, and he became a prime minister, and Manuel Leo, the president. Jan

6, 1959, Fidel Castro arrived in Havana, and on the 7th, the American government recognized the new Cuban government.

Not only Aarne, but many other news watchers asked each other: "What is happening in Cuba?" But so many news that seemed important for a moment were soon forgotten and replaced by new news.

The end of January and the beginning of February were very cold and there was a lot of snow. It snowed profusely and a strong wind blew across the American Midwest where it was also freezing cold. The idolized young singers, Buddy Holly and the Crickets, had travelled with a bus and performed at a place named Clear Lake, Iowa, on the evening of 2nd of February. Holly was exhausted from the continuing cold and the slow bus, and he rented a small airplane along with a pilot, so that he could get sooner to their next performance in Minnesota. There were only enough seats for three, and after a draw, Holly, Ritchie Valens and J.P. Richardson, fondly called the Big Bopper, climbed into the plane along with the inexperienced pilot. The trip was very short; the plane crash-landed right after take-off and the young performers with the pilot were all killed a little after one at night, on the morning of February 3rd.

After that Marja and Donna walked around quietly and listened to the music of Buddy Holly and

Ritchie Valens and cried about their fate. A blanket of sorrow descended on the winter. They went to school dances but it took time for their former happiness to return.

About the middle of February Fidel Castro became Cuba's prime minister.

One late winter afternoon Kaarina was walking home from work and she saw Billy's car coming towards her on the Main Street and Billy and an unknown woman sitting on the front street. Billy was talking and looking with interest at the woman beside him. Kaarina kept staring at the woman as the car passed but couldn't identify her. When she thought about what she had seen, mixed feelings started to churn inside her. Who was the woman in the car? - Is this how our relationship will end? – Flashed in her mind.

Aarne began to wait for spring and for the time that he could continue his walks and look for lots. He knew now for sure that Marja would be going to teachers' college in the fall and the whole family would have to prepare to pay about one thousand and five hundred dollars for one year of education and room and board.

"It's a huge sum," he estimated to Sylvi. "When you think about the fact that our wages together are just under three thousand dollars a year!"

They already had the money saved up for Marja's education and the next year they would save more. After her school, Marja would be able to get a good job, and Aarne could then think about the lot and the future more precisely. But as soon as the snow melted, he started to walk across the small city streets again, and always noted on a piece of paper the addresses and phone numbers of the lots he found. After that he rushed over to Vilho's place and asked Vilho to call the numbers and ask for the lot prices. Vilho called and Aarne learned that one lot would cost two thousand, and the other lot two thousand and one hundred dollars.

Aarne shook his head. It would take two years again to save the price of the lot without even thinking of building the house.

"I don't know about the building of the whole house; how much it would be. This new part here was already over two thousand dollars, so think about it in that way. It might be a bit more than two thousand dollars to get it up to covering the roof, and about a thousand and a half so you can get it ready inside. Think along that line. Take a loan from somebody you know."

"Take a loan from somebody I know! What rich friends do I have here?" Aarne started to laugh at Vilho.

"Well, ask you brother. Ask Jussi."

"Does Jussi have a sum like that? I don't think so and he is getting old too. I can ask, just for fun, but I won't ask now because I have to educate Marja; and to save another two thousand for the lot, will take a year or two."

"That's true," Vilho agreed and Aarne left the matter there.

Then Vilho commented: "Our Anita got married and they went away from here and now Taimi is crying that she misses Anita and the house is too big!"

"Well, perhaps they'll come back yet, once they have a good start there," Aarne replied.

"I don't think so. They won't be coming back to this small city except to visit," Vilho was unsure about it.

"I guess time will tell," Aarne put his hat back on and started to walk back home.

That spring Vieno told Sylvi that Pekka had written to her that he and Margaret were going to get engaged.

"But can that girl speak Finnish? Or I guess Pekka speaks English fairly well?" Sylvi asked Vieno.

"Pekka speaks English well. He speaks a lot of English and he has written to her through the winter. It's nicer to go through life as a couple! That much I know that this immigrant life is not easy. Margaret is a nice and quiet girl."

"She is very nice," Sylvi added. "She has visited our place a lot too with Kaarina."

"They are going to live at Elliot Lake. They'll buy a new house there and get a good beginning. And there is some work for women too if Margaret wants to work for a while."

Margaret told Kaarina that she had seen Billy and he had asked to see her.

"If you see him again, tell him to come and visit me. I'm always at home in the evening," Kaarina replied to Margaret.

One evening Billy came and knocked on the Kalliokoski's door and asked Kaarina out.

They drove towards the lake. Billy stopped the car and said: "Well, how are you? What have you been doing lately?"

"Nothing much. What about you?"

"I've been thinking about you and I hope we can continue together without any engagement just right now?" Billy glanced at Kaarina.

"We can continue but how can we remain just friends? Do you have an answer for that Billy?" Kaarina said to Billy.

"You're a hard woman Kaarina. You want me to be almost holy and that's difficult for me. Let me try to be a friend," Billy moved next to Kaarina and kissed her on the cheek.

"Well, we can try. Who was that woman in your car a couple of weeks ago?" Kaarina turned to look Billy in the eyes. "I saw you driving together on the Main Street."

"Oh, her. That's Diane Blake. She lives a little bit out of the city. I gave her a ride home when I saw her at Smithy's"

Kaarina wanted to believe Billy and left the matter there.

The rest of the evening they sat looking at the lake and talking about things in the past; sometimes embracing and kissing, but later in the evening Kaarina still thought about Smithy's Restaurant and how many girls Billy had met there and where they had gone.

That same spring Margaret ran to visit Kalliokoskis and announced at the door: "Look at my ring! Look! We are engaged. Pekka visited on the long weekend," she held out her left hand for Kaarina to look at. "Mother will put an announcement in the newspaper and the wedding will be held at the Finn Hall. Will you be my maid of honour?"

"Of course, I will be. When is the wedding?"

"The last Saturday in August. I am so excited. Mikko will be Pekka's best man."

"How old is Mikko now? I guess he is already

eighteen. Can Billy come to the wedding?"

"Everyone is invited to the Finn Hall. Of course, he can come."

It had been announced several times on the news that the St. Lawrence Seaway Canal would open for travel that spring and the opening ceremony would be held on Canada Day, July 1st.

Aarne and Sylvi both sat down to watch the important ceremony on television.

"Oh, see there is Queen Elizabeth and Prince Philip and President Eisenhower, and from Canada prime minister Diefenbaker with his wife. It's so fine. But what are they going to do with that canal?"

"Well, those big ships can travel all the way from Lake Superior to the Atlantic Ocean."

"Oh. Will we travel to the shore along this canal when we return to Finland?" Sylvi asked.

"I don't think so. You have to go to Halifax. Leave those thoughts about returning for a while now, because there is money needed to educate Marja, and otherwise," Aarne shut the television.

"There is always something. Well, after that then. Isn't that so?" Sylvi tried to get a straight answer from Aarne.

"Well, we'll see. If we could get a lot and the house, and sell the whole lot, so we could get a bigger sum of money," Aarne planned aloud.

"How long is that going to take? We'll both be fifty by then. I want to go home now. Pappa is so old and getting older all the time."

"Well, it's the same for all of us." Aarne left the issue there.

The rest of the summer went by fast with Kaarina preparing for Margaret's wedding. All the prior events leading to the evening went smoothly; she already had the experience of Anita's wedding behind her.

On the last Saturday of August Kaarina put on her fine yellow taffeta dress which she had made herself.

"That is so pretty on you," Sylvi looked at Kaarina and thought how well that exact lemon yellow suited her, and how perfectly the tight bodice with the flared skirt, fitted her. "And then that small yellow rose bouquet; it's so pretty."

"You are lovely," Marja stopped to admire Kaarina.

"How expensive is this party really going to be for you? Do you have enough money for this?" Aarne smiled from the bedroom door.

"I have enough money but not much left over because I had to give gift money for those women who were collecting it for the hall, and I had to buy a present for the shower, that Margaret's aunt held for her."

"Well, I guess you'll get a lot of presents when you get married," Sylvi said. "I know you don't know yet where we'll be, and when you'll get married, but that's what I think." Sylvi estimated.

"I guess I'll get some gifts then." Kaarina agreed. "But now I have to go. Don't expect me back before one o'clock tonight. I'm sure it'll take that long."

"And act like a decent person," Aarne looked seriously into Kaarina's eyes.

Kaarina thought for a moment about Aarne's words and his look, as she hurried down the stairs.

Billy waited in the car.

"I have never seen you so beautiful," Billy gave his approval.

"Thanks. Now we're in a rush. Let's drive."

The church was full of people and Kaarina rushed to Margaret's side to ask: "Is everything okay? Do you need help dressing?"

"No Kaarina. Mother wanted to help with the dressing."

"Isn't she lovely?" Margaret's mother shone with approval, and Kaarina nodded her head in agreement.

"I wish you and Pekka happiness," Kaarina said to Margaret.

"I am so happy Kaarina! I'm about to bust and so is Pekka. Pekka is going to take me to Niagara Falls and from there to Elliot Lake, and then we'll buy a house there. We're going to live there. I already gave my notice at the office," Margaret said.

"You are going away too! Now the music is starting."

Pekka and Mikko were standing at the altar, both looking well-groomed, and Kaarina started her slow walk towards them.

The people smiled and admired Margaret's dress and her bouquet of deep red roses.

The Finnish minister read the ceremony in Finnish and English and after church the bridal group went to be photographed. Margaret's mother and step-father then invited the group to their home until the festivities would continue at the Finn Hall.

The people ate and drank and danced at the wedding. Everyone seemed to have a good time. The serving tables were laden with special foods: Smoked ham and fish, potato salad, lettuce salad, two kinds of bread, butter, cut cucumbers and tomatoes; their time was almost over, but just now they were at their peak best, dark red and sweet to the taste. At the other end of the table there was coffee, cake, coffee bread and to top it all off, a beautifully decorated white cake with icing.

Kaarina danced one dance each with Pekka and Mikko, and the rest of the evening she danced with

Billy, who held her tightly in his embrace.

"Kaarina, I want you so," Billy pulled her even closer.

"Don't, don't hold so close! Everyone is looking."

"Maybe in the car?"

"No."

"Take one drink."

"It won't help. You shouldn't have any more drinks either."

"Am I drunk? I'm not. We are just having so much fun."

"You are a little bit. It's noticeable that you've had too much to drink. Hey, they are leaving now. What time is it?"

"It's just before twelve."

"Now she is throwing her bouquet of roses! I have to catch it so I can be a bride someday soon too."

"Is that your rush? I have no rush except to enjoy the wedding night."

Kaarina ran to catch the bouquet of red roses which Margaret lifted up for everyone to see and then she threw them. People laughed and clapped their hands at the same time that they started to prepare to go out.

Margaret and Pekka thanked everyone for their gifts and hurried out towards their car, and disappeared into the night. Kaarina and Billy rushed out after them.

Billy drove to the lakeshore and parked the car. He grabbed Kaarina and hugged her tightly. They kissed long and passionately and Billy slipped his hand on Kaarina's breast and started to fondle her.

"We have to leave it here."

"I'm careful."

"Something might happen."

"Well, it's best to go then." Looking angry, Billy started to drive slowly along the gravel back road around the lake.

"Don't go this way! It's so lonely and dark here."

Billy stepped on the gas, and the trees lining the side of the road started to flash by the car windows.

"How long are you going to be this holy woman? I don't know how long I'm going to last through this!" Billy turned to look at Kaarina.

"Don't drive so fast! You promised to be a friend and now you want something else again. Look ahead on the road Billy! There is a parked car by the side of road!"

"I can see that. Some black car. I have a driver's license but do you have one?"

Billy stepped on the gas so that the car started to bounce on the gravel road.

All of a sudden, the parked car's head-lights

were turned on, and it charged beside their car.

"What! Where in the hell is it going now? Trying to push us off the road! Hold on Kaarina! Now we're passing it!" Billy stepped on the gas once more even though they were coming to a curve on the road.

The other car sped up too and with its full force it hit their car on the side.

Billy's hand grabbed the steering wheel in desperation, but their car swerved off the road and hit the opposite ditch-bank with full force; the car turned half-ways over once, and Kaarina felt herself to be thrown in between the back of the front seat and the back seat. The car turned again a second time, and with a huge thud it slipped on its roof to the side of the forest road.

Kaarina tried to grip the seat under with her hands. Then she grabbed onto Billy's suit coat bottom, but she couldn't get a firm hold on anything. The car windows rattled to pieces as they fell off. The whole incident was over in a couple of minutes.

"Billy help me!" Kaarina heard her own voice yell. She was stuck between the seats and her one leg was pinned under the back of the front seat. Her head was spinning and her nose was bleeding profusely, while she became nauseated.

No one replied.

The radio was still playing Bobby Darin's new

song *Dream Lover.*

Kaarina yelled again: "Billy help me!"

But no one replied.

"Billy help me!" She couldn't move and started to panic. Mixed-up questions started to churn in her head. Did the other car not see them? Why didn't Billy reply?

Kaarina tried to lift her head but the back of the front seat was in front of her and the smallest movement caused huge pains. The music and the entertainment continued on the radio. She began to shake and shiver in the cold. She tried to sit up but through the night her leg swelled and the pain in it intensified; and not only the leg but her head ached too, and the cold made her feel more and more helpless. Sometimes she woke to call into the darkness: "Billy say something?"

The stillness continued.

A rainy early Sunday morning came to wakefulness and she thought she heard the sound of car tires on the gravel. The car seemed to stop and she started to hear voices saying: "Look! An accident! We have to phone the police! There is someone in the car. I can see his or her head moving. Look at the other side of the car and the front! Looks bad!"

"But where is the driver or is that the driver there at the back? Do you see any others?"

"Help me, help me!" Kaarina called and tried to let them know that she was alive.

"Now she is calling for help. Wait a moment. I'll drive to the first house and ask them to call the police and the ambulance. Can you think we're going fishing and now this! I'll come right back. You stay here. We can't get anybody out of that car until someone helps us."

Kaarina lost consciousness. She came to her senses again when the men pulled the car doors open and she was able to say: "Billy, Find Billy. He's on the front seat. He is the driver."

Kaarina heard someone ask: "But where is the driver then?"

"Go look over the sides of the road or is he under the car?"

Kaarina was loaded onto a stretcher and into the ambulance. At the hospital her head was bound up and her leg x-rayed and put into a cast.

Kaarina was able to give her name and address. Mixed up thoughts continued to run around in her head. She soon fell into a deep sleep.

Much later she woke up to the fact that Aarne's, Sylvi's and Marja's frightened and white faces stared at her from the side of the bed.

"Just be quiet. Oh my God! Your one leg is broken and a concussion and cuts and bruises all over.

Oh, my God! Just try to be still," Sylvi spoke quietly.

Aarne wiped his eyes and Marja's tears ran on her cheeks in rivulets.

"Did Billy get hurt badly? That other car came so fast from the side. They put their lights on; then they crashed into our side and forced us off the road."

"We don't know anything. Marja spoke to the doctor but he didn't say anything. Marja will ask again tomorrow."

"I wonder who was in the other car when it came so suddenly from the side and just crashed right into us?"

"Just sleep," Aarne ordered with authority.

The next day a doctor and a nurse came together to tell Kaarina that the door on Billy's side had opened, or he had opened it and had been thrown under the car and had died right away.

"He died right away. His neck shattered and his back broke." The doctor said.

Kaarina was not able to say anything. She started to sob.

Later she asked the nurse if Billy's family knew and the nurse nodded and added that the burial would be in two days.

Jussi and Aune came to see Kaarina, as well as Nancy and Martin and cousin Irene.

The Lahtis brought a late summer flower bouquet and Kaarina thanked them.

As she stared at the flowers, Kaarina thought of Margaret's bridal bouquet and she tried to remember what had happened to it, and what had happened to her clothes. Where were they?

But Sylvi informed her the next day: "The dress is all torn and only one shoe was found. The other shoe might have been thrown out or is still inside the car."

Kaarina asked the nurses and friends who came to see her: "Did Billy look okay?"

But she couldn't find out anything for sure until much later when friends told her that Billy had looked like himself in the coffin. On the one side of his face there had been scratches and pieces of glass, but the coffin had been kept open as was the usual custom.

Billy's parents and his younger brothers and sisters had stood beside the cheap coffin and cried uncontrollably.

Aarne and Sylvi and Marja visited throughout the six weeks until Kaarina's cast was removed, and she could move on crutches. On the Saturday that she was able to leave for home, Aarne and Martin helped her upstairs and into bed. Jussi could no longer help anybody; he was barely able to climb the stairs himself.

Kaarina cried and read newspapers that Sylvi

had saved that told about the accident.

For a couple of weeks, the police had hoped to find the dark mysterious car which had charged into the side of their car; but it was never found.

If it was ever mentioned Aarne began to talk right away: "What crazy person goes on that back road at night? You're going to find out that you'll lose your life. Don't ever go there again! God damn it! We'll be lucky if you're ever able to walk right again."

Almost every day Kaarina read books and sat on the couch watching television. Albert sent her a fall postcard from Elliot Lake. He had heard from his parents about the accident and had also read about it from the newspapers.

Margaret wrote letters from Elliot Lake. In the early fall she told that they were very happy and that they had bought a new house and had moved into it. She had got a job in a mine office. And she never knew exactly what day it was, even though it would be remembered as a black day when history was written, that America stopped stockpiling uranium for the Cold War, and did not renew their purchase agreement that November in 1959. And so Pekka and Margaret had to travel back to Golden City. They stuffed all their belongings into Pekka's old small bedroom in the Kuronen's upstairs, and often at night they spoke of their new house far away at another place.

Elliot Lake became depressed; only a couple of mines gave work to fewer men now. Lovely, new houses stood empty on still streets; no one wanted them any more. Pekka was able to return to the gold mine, which job he was able to get with the help of his father; but the major part of his pay cheque had to be sent to the bank which had given Pekka and Margaret the mortgage on their house. Perhaps Elliot Lake would one day open up again. Margaret was expecting a baby.

Chapter Sixteen

Albert visited the Kalliokoskis at Easter. Kaarina walked fairly well now and her frame of mind was brighter than it had been in the winter.

"Are you starting to get over the accident?" Albert enquired.

"Slowly. I feel fairly well now. My leg gets tired if I walk a lot but the doctor says that it's getting stronger all the time. Otherwise I feel okay. I got Margaret's previous job. The pay there is better than where I worked before. I've been there for a while already."

"That sounds good. Billy didn't make it through the accident?" Albert asked.

"So it was. Billy died right away. The police said that he was thrown out of the car when the car started to turn on its side and he was thrown under the car. I was thrown between the front and the back seats, and my one leg was pinned under the back of the front seat, and I couldn't move. I called Billy's name several times and asked him for help but he never replied. I didn't hear anything else except the radio music and program. I was afraid I'd be left in the car for several days and might die in there slowly because I couldn't get out. It was very quiet on the back road. Early in the morning the car that saw our overturned car, came and saw us there."

"It's not good to go on the back road at night," Albert said.

"Father said the same. Billy didn't listen to me when I said that let's not go there."

"I heard that the other car crashed into the side of Billy's car. I guess that other car will never be found."

"I guess not. I remember it was a dark car, either black or navy blue or dark gray. Well, I couldn't even identify it, if I saw it again. It was so dark too."

"It's like that. Sometimes things happen that have no answers at all."

"Albert, can you take me there with your car? I would like to see the accident place."

"I can bring you there but it's best if we ask permission from your parents first. I don't want to bring you there if they don't know about it. I also don't believe that there is anything there. The fall rains and the winter snows have washed everything and cleaned up the place."

Very reluctantly Sylvi and Aarne gave permission for them to go when Kaarina and Albert promised that they would return before dark.

Kaarina was nervous until they were near the accident scene; then she started to feel unsure. Albert parked the car and started to walk.

"Perhaps here, or a little bit more ahead, or perhaps this place. Can you see anything? Are there no marks on the road? I think this was the place." Kaarina stopped suddenly when she understood that the car had charged off the road because Billy had pressed on the gas when they were coming to a curve.

"He tried to get past the dark car, I think. It came straight for our side and rammed us off the road but then it continued on its way. It could have been just right here. Why didn't they stop and come and help us?"

"I don't know. Perhaps they didn't want anyone to know that they were here. I think there is a small piece of bent chrome from a car's side here." Albert noted and lifted up the piece for Kaarina to see.

"It is this place; I just didn't see at night that we were coming to a curve. I remember that Billy was driving really fast. Albert, will anything be left of us?" Dark and deep questions started to turn again in Kaarina's mind.

"I don't know for sure. It's one of those big questions for all of us."

"Billy had a way of explaining everything with his hands and when he did that, he didn't look at the road. And he drove so fast. The whole accident happened so fast. I don't even remember what he said at the end. I told it all to the police. They came to see me one last time at home and they said that the whole thing was an accident and that they have not found the other car."

"Yes. Shall we go now?" They drove to Smithy's and Kaarina glanced at the restaurant side after she had paid for her magazine. There was a new group of youngsters there – almost children – Kaarina thought.

"I'm taking you home now, but can I call you sometime?" Albert asked.

"We have no phone. Father is saving money to buy a lot and build a house. We have to save on everything. Marja is going to teachers' college."

"I understand. We also had it tight when I went to teachers' college. Well, I better ask now then. Will you go to the movies with me on Saturday evening?"

"Yes, I can come."

"I'll come and pick you up right after six."

Kaarina didn't want to talk about the accident any more and now asked Albert: "I wanted to ask you what exactly happened at Elliot Lake, Albert? Why did it end so fast and so many people lost their jobs and had to leave their houses and their whole lives there? You were teaching for the second year there and I guess you also have to leave when spring comes? Where will you go?"

"My job will end and the school will close in the spring and I'll come home. I've already applied here and I think I'll be accepted at one of the public schools. If I later go somewhere else; time will tell about that. The Elliot Lake story is the usual story about *boom and bust*; about the phenomenal boom of the uranium rush and the eventual fast bust. The whole place was born because uranium was discovered there and America wanted to purchase a lot of it in order to prepare for the Cold War. When they stopped the purchase of uranium last November, then the mines started to close, with only a couple remaining open any more. A lot of this has happened in the west: the gold fevers of Alaska and California; the 1920's stock market boom; the downfall of the whole economy starting in 1929 and years after that. I guess not everything should be built on one thing like uranium was, but that's the style of the west, Kaarina. Take all you can from the discovery and go forward again. No one could have predicted this, any more than they could have predicted the accident. Now people there are closing up their houses and boarding up their windows so that they wouldn't be broken. I wonder if Elliot Lake will be the first ghost town of the uranium age? Listen, there are a lot of them, these ghost towns here in the west. I wonder if anyone even knows where they all are, these ghost towns? They were so busy in the beginning and people populated them so readily; and then when the work ended, the people had to leave everything. That's the history of the west. The riches are taken and the people go somewhere else to look for the next discovery. It's the eternal thought of the new west. Yes, that's what it is. There is always a new west somewhere, and you have to go there, use it and benefit from it, and go forward again."

"I guess, it is so," Kaarina agreed. "But it's hard. People in these places live their ordinary lives and suddenly it ends. What happens to them and where do they go? It all seems so cruel. Think about Margaret and Pekka and how they had to leave their new home there!"

"I guess it's some kind of a law of the west; this continuous going and moving and clearing and settling of new places. People just have to get used to it."

"It's hard for me to accept it. I mean at home in Finland, everything was more orderly and people stayed more in their places, and perhaps felt more secure than they do here."

"I guess that's how it is. Europe is more orderly. Perhaps things will become more orderly and secure here once enough time has passed, but if you think of the time of the First and Second World Wars, then it seemed more safe and secure here." Albert argued.

Kaarina agreed: "I guess it is so. I didn't think about that. You know more about these matters than what I do."

"Well, I better go. I'll come and get you on Saturday." Albert went home.

The Saturday evening movie was called *Anatomy of a Murder.* The picture started with black body parts being displayed on the large white movie screen, accompanied by shrill jazz music which told about an underworld story, like a drinking bar and a young wife who had made a habit of visiting the bar on evenings, when her husband slept; and about a murder the husband was being accused of now. The husband had apparently shot the bar owner, who had been accused of raping her, in her words, after she had received a ride home from him that night. The further the movie plot developed on the movie screen, the harder it was for the jury and the movie audience in the theatre, to guess what the verdict would be; so cleverly was the defending lawyer able to present his case. When the final verdict was heard: apparently the husband had momentarily lost his mind, he had short term insanity, when he had heard about his wife's rape.

Was it possible to become momentarily insane? Who was right, and who was wrong? And no one knew the final right answer.

"You can't even tell if this was right," Kaarina said to Albert on the way home.

"I can't. The case was so difficult and the lawyers so clever in presenting their cases. So, it was Kaarina. The husband was made to look like a Korean war hero and the husband of this beautiful wife, and the wife was presented as a very clean and good wife. But we were not able to hear how she behaved in the bar or in the car that evening."

"And the couple had left the trailer park where they had lived and I guess no one will find them again." Kaarina thought aloud.

"I guess not. You're right about that," Albert agreed, "and did you notice how at first the movie was so distinctly black and white, and as it progressed, it became more and more gray?" Albert noted.

"I guess that's how real life is too, more gray than starkly black and white." Kaarina determined.

When Albert kissed and hugged her at the gate, Kaarina was surprised, but kissed him gently in return.

- - - - - - - - - -

Like Margaret and Pekka in the winter, Albert returned home in the spring, after the school where he had taught, closed. He was hired at the Golden Avenue Public School and moved back in with his parents.

That same spring Sylvi again received a letter from Lempi: "Father is not well any more. The doctor says that he may have had a small stroke because he can't remember much and just sits by the window and talks to himself, that he should go and do something; put potatoes in the ground or chop some wood, but he can't remember where the potatoes or the wood are, and his walking has slowed down. Come at least to visit soon if you possibly can. He misses you so."

Aarne and Sylvi counted all their money at home and in the bank that evening, and Sylvi had to write to Lempi that they didn't have enough money for Sylvi to travel to Finland. Marja's school fees and board and room had to be paid and she had to go to school in order to get a good job. Sylvi wrote in the letter that she understood that the original two years that they had intended to stay, had now stretched to seven years, but there just wasn't enough money. They just couldn't save enough money in the New Country any more than they had been able to save in the Old Country, and it would still be some time before they could return home. Sylvi didn't know what she could say about the fact that pappa would now be left for Lempi to care for, perhaps for the rest of his life, and that she would send parcels whenever she could, but she couldn't do anything more just now.

"This is a cold fact about the west, I would say!" Aarne emphasized: "You're not going to leave here any time you want!"

"And who wanted to come here in the first place? I didn't for sure," Sylvi replied angrily.

But when Aarne thought later that evening about the letter Sylvi had written, all the Finland memories flooded into his mind: the time of leaving, the letters his brother Matti had written and all the changes that had taken place in Finland after their leaving. Urho Kekkonen had become president in 1956 and the Finns seemed to like him for the foreseeable future. President Kekkonen's open, somewhat square, friendly face seemed to look trustingly into Finland's good future. Just as his predecessor, Juho Paasikivi, Kekkonen seemed to be continuing a peaceful path. The Soviet Union had declared Finland's neutrality in 1956 and Finland had trading partners in the east and the west. People had work. New houses and apartments were being built in all areas of Finland. Aarne's brother Matti had been able to move into a new condominium with the help of an Arava loan. Aarne wiped his moist eyes and stared into the darkening evening and asked himself quietly: "Why did I really leave to come here, and will we ever all get back there again?"

Otherwise spring and summer arrived at the Golden City as always and Albert came to get Kaarina to go to movies, and for drives, and gave rides to Aarne and Sylvi to stores, to the church, or just for Sunday drives; and if before the radio, and then the television, had changed the Kalliokoskis lives in wonderous ways, now the car started to change their lives outside the home.

Aarne himself could not think about getting a driver's license. How could he possibly learn all the rules of the road in a strange language and with what money would he be able to buy a car? Jussi didn't have a car but his son Martin gave them rides wherever they needed to go. And then the fact that a car demanded money; they needed it for repairs and up-keep and for gas. Then all his money would go into a car. Aarne thought to himself.

One evening in the middle of July Aarne was watching television with great interest. He had been following the American politics for some time now and knew that Richard Nixon, an experienced politician, was the republican candidate and that this particular evening, the democratic candidate's name would be declared. When the news were read, and the name of John Kennedy was announced as the democratic candidate and the camera focused on his face, Aarne thought that he was youthful looking, with a round face and an open smile. Kaarina came to the living room to translate the man's age and other particulars that were given on the television.

"Well, he is close to my age," Aarne laughed and felt himself to be younger and stronger than what he had felt for a long time and added: "If he is planning to go to the White House, then I guess I can build that one house here in the Gold Camp. That's what I'm telling you!" Aarne declared to Sylvi who smiled when she saw and heard his excitement.

The next day Pekka dropped in at Kaarina's work to tell her that Margaret had given birth to a girl that morning at one o'clock: "Eight pounds and a big healthy girl. Now I'm going to tell mother at the boarding house and then I'm going home to sleep."

That Saturday Kaarina and Sylvi bought a soft blanket and a summer dress to give as gifts to the new arrival as soon as the mother and baby arrived home.

The more Albert visited Kaarina, the more Aarne and Sylvi liked him. The young man took the steps upstairs lightly, knocked on the door and greeted Aarne and Sylvi in the living room. He asked them how they were doing and talked about the weather and news before he spoke to Kaarina. Marja liked Albert too. But Aarne still thought that a Finnish man might be more interested in going back to Finland, when that time came, and he determined to talk to Kaarina about this issue before things developed any further.

"Can you not find a Finnish man?" Aarne asked the following evening.

"I guess I can find one at the hall but then they are older, or they're from a place in Finland where they speak with a different dialect."

"I don't mean that you have to get married now. I only meant that if we return to Finland, a Finnish man might be more interested in returning there, whereas a Canadian would be interested in staying here. Albert is a nice man but it would be easier to speak to a Finnish man. Our English is still not good."

"I'm not getting married now. You speak well enough," Kaarina replied and the matter was left there.

Kaarina and Albert attended church often. Kaarina prayed for Billy's soul and Albert tried to support her in her still changing feelings about everything. Other times they also visited Albert's family's church.

The whole family was satisfied that Kaarina had someone with whom she could speak about everything: the uncertainty of life, the history of the west, the local issues. None of them really knew anything more about the New Country than what the issues were around school, work and everyday life. Now that Kaarina was able to go further with Albert and his car, she became more familiar with the roads, the beaches, the landscapes and the people of the area, and she could speak with more certainty about its history and people.

Once Albert asked: "What is the history of the Finns here in Canada? Do you know anything about that Kaarina? I know a lot of Finns and you more closely but I really don't know much about your history."

"I don't know either. Does anyone know that? Has it even been written? I don't know if there was much more than rumours and gossip about immigration in Finland even; and then people like my father came here to carve gold. The streets here were supposedly made out of gold. Perhaps it's been the same for all immigrants."

"It's really tragic but probably true for all immigrants. They come with huge hopes and the hardships here are great, at least at the beginning. The world changes and goes forward all the time. Think about it all Kaarina! How long do you think that the Golden City has been here? And one day it's going to be gone: when the gold runs out, or when a rich owner decides to leave the rest of the gold in the ground, and to continue later when the price of gold is really high. We are only going to have this one life Kaarina. That's what I think. Billy has died and you have to start living your own life."

Kaarina was surprised about Albert's words and she turned away but Albert took her shoulders and turned her towards himself: "May I think that our future would perhaps be together? Tell me that Kaarina!"

"I don't know Albert; I don't know anything about the future yet," Kaarina felt herself to be at a crossroads.

"I'll leave it there now but please think about it. I have liked you for a long time Kaarina, already when we were going to school but you were always so crazy about Billy."

Albert kissed her tenderly and Kaarina kissed him back thoughtfully.

But from that time on Kaarina thought about Albert and the future often. Perhaps Albert would be her best future and perhaps with him she would have a home and children and a secure life. She liked Albert a lot but would their good friendship change into love; she couldn't tell yet.

"Think about October and Thanksgiving Kaarina. We could get engaged then and have a wedding at Christmas. I'm already 23 and you're 21 years old," Albert suggested one lovely Sunday.

"Hey, we are not in any rush. We're not over the hill yet," Kaarina laughed with surprise, but then became serious when she thought about her relationship with Billy and determined to tell about that to Albert right away: "Albert, listen! You had better know that my relationship with Billy went pretty far."

Albert looked at her seriously and said: "I thought that. I also had a close relationship at Elliot Lake but she chose another person. They were childhood friends. Kaarina, we also have a good friendship. Perhaps I can't present my case so well but I do love you and I would try hard to make you happy."

"Well, I'll think about October and you should think if you want to be with us Finns for the rest of your life. We should be going to the church picnic next Sunday. It's on Labour Day. Do you want to go? We haven't had a chance to go before because we don't have a car but now if you gave us a ride, we could go together with my parents. And I should tell you that usually the older people at these events only speak Finnish to each other."

"I have noticed that. It doesn't bother me. Let's just go with your parents and shall we tell them about our engagement plan?" Albert put his arm around Kaarina's waist.

"Are we in a rush? Will you then love me forever and forever?" Kaarina teased him, laughing at the same time.

"Yes, yes, always and forever," Albert replied

also laughing.

Everyone was welcome to the late summer picnic at the Niemi's cottage. The only request was a contribution to the food being served at the event.

"What can we bring there?" Sylvi asked Kaarina.

"They said at the church that you could bring a cake or some sandwiches. I'll make sandwiches and you make a cake," Kaarina suggested.

At the picnic when Kaarina introduced Albert to their Finnish family friends, she noticed that people knew who Albert was and seemed to like him. She also remembered that Billy hadn't often wanted to attend the Finnish events, or if he had gone, he hadn't enjoyed being there. Perhaps he had just been that *Dream Lover* in the song and their relationship would not have lasted if they had lived an ordinary life.

When they were driving home, Kaarina and Albert told Aarne and Sylvi about their plans to get engaged.

Both parents were surprised about the news, but at home Aarne searched for his long-ago bought red wine bottle, opened it, and they all took a small glass of wine to celebrate. Sylvi touched her wine with the tip of her tongue and gave it back to Aarne.

"We are getting engaged in October, at Thanksgiving time," Kaarina told and Albert smiled beside her.

"Are you thinking of getting married soon?" Aarne asked and sat down on the kitchen chair. He was so surprised about the whole issue.

"Albert would like to get married at Christmas-time," Kaarina felt herself becoming sure about their plans as she spoke about them to her parents.

"We'll get engaged at Thanksgiving and married at Christmas," Albert announced in English.

"Well, why not. Did he say that you wanted to get married at Christmas?" Aarne asked.

"Yes, he did say Christmas," Kaarina laughed: "That's what we have planned."

"Well, hopefully you'll stay here in the Golden City?" Sylvi asked. "Marja is leaving at the beginning of September to go to teachers' college. I hope you're not planning to go away from here?"

"We'll stay here because we both have our jobs here," Kaarina replied.

"Well, congratulations then," Sylvi hugged Kaarina and touched Albert's shoulder.

"Yes. Congratulations then. Congratulations!" Aarne repeated still somewhat surprised when he shook Kaarina's and Albert's hands.

That evening Kaarina asked Marja to be her maid of honour and they started to plan their dresses. They had seen short and long wedding dresses in magazines, but Kaarina thought that an ordinary short, white dress and a short veil, would be appropriate for her and Marja suggested a light blue colour for her simple dress. The next week they chose Sylvi's best dress from her closet, and a light beige felt hat to complete her outfit. Aarne would be dressed in his best dark gray suit. Albert also had a dark blue suit to wear. His best teacher friend, Walter, had agreed to be his best man.

Marja was packing her suit cases. She would be leaving for teachers' college at the beginning of September. She organised her clothes in the large suitcase and her books in the small one. Aarne and Marja together had visited the bank together to certify a cheque for paying the school fees and her room and board. They had also already purchased her ticket for the train travel. Marja, along with her four good friends who were also going to attend teachers' college, would travel together. Marja felt herself to be very excited when she thought about her future life without the everyday support of her parents and the togetherness of their family. She also felt unsure about the fact that she would now be leaving and Kaarina would leave at Christmas and then their parents would be left to live on their own.

While she was watching Marja's face as she packed, Kaarina asked: "You look excited. Are you excited?"

"Yes, I'm tense and excited. Everything is changing now. Well, are you not afraid about getting married?"

"Somewhat! It's a big commitment. You can't just leave it like that. Albert wants to get married and I want to get married too but he wants it more."

The whole family together were driven to the station in a taxi and Aarne carried the big suitcase into the train as Marja carried the small one. Marja's school friends also arrived there with their families and suitcases. Soon the train was filled with youngsters who were all leaving for their schooling far away from the Golden City.

The following Saturday Kaarina and Albert were buying their engagement and wedding rings.

In the New Country it was the style to buy a diamond ring for the engagement ring but Kaarina and Albert made up their minds to buy simple gold bands instead.

"Like my mother has," Kaarina whispered into Albert's ear.

"Yes, they are a fine memory of the Golden City for us both, if we ever leave here," Albert commented. They smiled at each other. On Sunday they spoke to the Finnish pastor after the service and he told them that the Saturday before Christmas would also be suitable for him to marry them. All the details at the

church were finalised and the pastor promised to an-
nounce the upcoming marriage three times at the
church before the actual ceremony.

Kaarina felt that time was once again spinning
away from her hands: there was so much to do before
the wedding. When she visited Margaret, they together
admired Kaarina's ring and talked about the wedding.
Baby Elizabeth was a good baby, Margaret declared,
even though she was still waking up at night. Otherwise Margaret was satisfied with her life in that they
had a roof over their heads and that they were able to
live cheaply in Pekka's former room.

When Pekka returned home he explained to
Kaarina that he had been able to negotiate an agreement with the bank, that the bank had taken the
house back and that they would lose all their invested
money in it, but would no longer have to make payments on the house.

Margaret added: "Sometime later we can buy a
small house here. I can't think about this matter any
more. I have cried my eyes dry over losing it and
Pekka is angry over losing our down payment and
monthly payments. The car we were able to keep, because it had already been paid, and the furniture.
Pekka has already picked them up in a trailer," Margaret wiped her eyes.

Kaarina nodded her head in reply and thought

momentarily about adult responsibilities she would also be facing soon.

"Do you love Albert, Kaarina?" Margaret asked when they were left alone.

"I do love him in a different way than I loved Billy. With Billy everything was always exciting but unsure at the same time, and only now I can understand that you can't build your life on that."

"Albert is a good and trustworthy man, what I know about him from our school years, and teachers are usually able to find a job even though the pay may not be all that high."

"I understand more fully now that an ordinary secure life, is the best life."

"Only after you have children, will you understand it finally," Margaret replied seriously.

In the evening Aarne showed his diminishing bank account balance to Sylvi.

"So that's all we have left!" Sylvi looked at Aarne with round eyes.

"And we still have to give some money to Kaarina for a wedding gift," Aarne shook his head.

"Oh my God!" Sylvi said quietly.

Thinking by himself, Aarne thought that it would be Kaarina and Marja that would truly be able to live the awaited New Country's future, and that he himself would not be able to buy any lot or build any house for a long time to come.

"Let's just be quiet until this wedding is over and then save whatever we can," Aarne told Sylvi before they went to sleep that night.

The next time Aarne and Sylvi looked at the television, the newscaster was talking about the promises of both presidential candidates: It was hoped that the country's economy would grow to double what it had grown in the past seven years. Bank interest rates would be kept in check. The country's defence would be strengthened. The blacks would be given more civil rights. Aarne tried to keep up with all the promises that were given but finally he had to tell Sylvi that he really wasn't sure about any of it.

A few times John Kannedy's beautiful, young wife was also shown on television.

Aarne laughed at Sylvi: "This man who is the same age as me, has a young wife, only thirty-one; Kaarina told me."

"But she is beautiful, this Jackie Kennedy. Kaarina also said that the brother of John Kennedy, Robert Kennedy, is the head of this election campaign," Sylvi added importantly.

"Well, let him just be that, as long as I don't have to do it," Aarne joked.

"And, Kaarina also said that it's not so easy because this John Kennedy is a catholic, and they haven't had a catholic president before in America."

"Well, I really don't know much about any of this, except that this man is young and healthy looking."

"And I hear that they are also rich people, these Kennedy's. That's what Kaarina told that had been written somewhere," Sylvi added.

"Well, these kind of election campaigns demand money," Aarne mentioned on his own behalf.

At the end of September Aarne and Sylvi settled to watch a debate on television between the two main presidential candidates. Neither one of them understood enough about American politics so that they would have known what they were talking about, but John Kennedy looked official and important in his dark suit, whereas Richard Nixon looked nervous and sweaty. It seemed that television itself had given a boost to John Kennedy, even though everyone understood that the road to the White House, was only just beginning.

Sylvi and Aarne were invited to Albert's home for a dinner on a fall Sunday. Conversation was difficult because of their poor English, but approving smiles on all faces on both sides, and good will, allowed everyone to feel that the coming union would be welcome on both sides.

In November Albert suggested to Kaarina that

it would be a good time to look for a small place to rent. He had seen one ad in the newspaper and had heard about another place from a teacher friend. Now they went to see both. The first place took up the whole first floor of a large house, and was too expensive for them; but the second place was suitable, an upstairs living room and kitchen with a small bedroom and a bathroom; and since the rent was reasonable, they decided to take it. Albert's parents promised them a couch for the living room and a table with two chairs for the kitchen. Aarne and Sylvi announced that they would be giving bedsheets and woollen blankets and pillows for the bed.

America's most important news in November told the world that the democratic presidential candidate, John Kennedy, had won the presidential election. Aarne told this to Sylvi and Kaarina, but at the same time he noticed, that their full attention was taken up by the wedding preparations.

One November weekend Albert and Kaarina cleaned their rented apartment and organised all the gifts and furniture that they had received from their parents. After this initial work they made plans to purchase a bed in the middle of December.

"Of course, we have to buy a bed. Where would we sleep and what about all that loving we are planning to do every night?" Albert laughed and grabbed

Kaarina into an embrace, and they kissed and continued embracing until they were both laying beside one another on the floor. "We better stop before we go too far. Let's get up Kaarina. Only a few weeks any more."

"You're right," Kaarina knew that she loved Albert more and more.

"I love you; I love you" Albert repeated several times.

Kaarina replied again: "I love you too. Soon we are married."

A couple of days before the wedding Marja travelled home on the train, and the next day they planned all the final details of the wedding with Kaarina. The ceremony would take place at the Finnish Church and the wedding party would be held at a hotel as requested by Albert's parents. Forty guests had been invited there. Margaret and Vieno had held a shower and Albert's mother and aunt had been there. Kaarina had received many towels, several table cloths and small kitchen appliances as gifts.

Everything was ready for the wedding day. Kaarina carried a bouquet of red roses and Marja a smaller bouquet of pink roses; pink flowers decorated Sylvi's dress, and red roses the men's suit lapels. They all arrived at the church. Margaret, Pekka, Elizabeth, and Eikka, Vieno and Mikko Kuronen all arrived in their best finery as the last guests before the ceremony started. Both Kaarina and Albert sighed a sigh of relief once it was over. Everything had gone well. Margaret stood by Kaarina's side as the guests congratulated her. Many of the guests patted baby-Elizabeth's head in passing.

A wedding dinner was served at the hotel and Albert led Kaarina to the first dance. People behaved quietly and danced slow waltzes and tangos while a small band played music. At twelve Albert pulled Kaarina towards him and together they thanked everyone for their gifts and well wishes, and invited the guests to visit their home during the coming winter.

In the car Albert kissed Kaarina deeply and they drove home. He grabbed Kaarina and carried her over the threshold to the bedroom, turned her gently and unzipped her dress which fell on the floor. "Lay on the bed, on the bed," he repeated and pushed himself fully into her and they quickly made love. After a little while they embraced and made love again. "This was everything and more," Albert said and gently caressed Kaarina's head.

They slept the first night in their new home.

"Should we be using something Albert?" Kaarina asked the next week.

"Don't say anything. I don't want to use anything," Albert didn't want to hear Kaarina's warnings and they continued making love almost every night through January.

Every now and then Kaarina asked: "Could we use something so I wouldn't get pregnant right away, Albert?"

But Albert didn't listen. "If you get pregnant, then you get pregnant; we're married and of course we are going to have children. It's normal. We have everything: a small apartment and we are young and healthy. We have food and I'm working, and if you get pregnant then you'll be staying home. My mother didn't work. She got married right from school and father went to work and mother stayed at home. Let's save what we can, and in about three years we'll have enough to put a down payment on a small house. We have everything we want. We need a television but we'll buy it right in the spring when the weather warms up; when it's not wet any more and the men can carry it upstairs without getting everything wet on the stairs and the entryway downstairs."

"It would be good to have a television but I guess it costs a lot of money. Well, we have a radio. Turn it on louder, Albert! They are playing Elvis' last year's record: *Are You Lonesome Tonight*? It's such a lovely ballad."

"I'm going to make sure that you're not lonely any night. Come and sit beside me on the couch."

At the Kalliokoski's home, both Aarne and Sylvi

together thought about how quickly everything had changed. In the spring their family had still been together and now in January both of the girls had moved away from home.

Chapter Seventeen

The new president's inauguration day was an ordinary very cold winter day in the Golden City, but in Washington it was an unusually cold and snowy day. The main streets were cleared through the night into the morning hours from the fallen snow, so that everyone could attend the ceremony, but the majority of people were sitting in front of the television sets in their living rooms. In spite of the cold the youthful-looking president-elect seemed to be dressed lightly in a dark dress-coat and carried a black silk hat in his hands. But he appeared the whole time with no hat on his head, the same as the vice-presidential candidate.

"Oh, they're a beautiful family," Sylvi said to Aarne when they were together watching the ceremony.

"Do they paint these people?" Aarne thought aloud.

"Oh, yes they paint or make them up and fix their hair so that they look really good," Sylvi said. "That's what I think. Even though on television you can only see black and white but if you're there in person, then you can see all the colours too."

"Well, it's kind of like a play or a movie that we are watching," Aarne determined.

"It's kind of like a film or a play; on television they can make people look lovely like you can make them in movies too."

"It's odd when you think about it. This is what we watch every evening but we don't see everything. We only see what they want us to see."

"Yes," Sylvi hesitated and wasn't really sure any more if she understood it correctly.

"I guess you don't understand?"

"I don't know what you mean, but I think it almost has to be true, what they show."

"That's what I'm thinking aloud that this is only a part of what's happening; the same way that newspapers write according to how they think."

"Well, I understand now what you mean but I don't think so much about these issues. I've always got something else to do."

When Kaarina and Albert visited later, Kaarina explained to Aarne and Sylvi that the new president had talked about a New Frontier, and had asked that the citizens would not ask about what the country can do for them, but instead should ask about what they can do for their country.

Already the next week he held a news conference which was televised and to which all the important news reporters had been invited. He appeared friendly and replied affirmatively to questions that the reporters asked him.

"Oh, he knows everything so well," Sylvi declared.

"Well, yes," Aarne allowed.

"As long as it stays peaceful, so that there would be no other war than the Vietnam War," Sylvi replied.

"Well, that's true. These places used to seem to be far away but today we get news from there almost every day."

Of course, Aarne had read about the Vietnam War. He remembered that in the Geneva peace treaty of 1954 Vietnam had been temporarily divided into two along the 17th latitude and a communist government was established in North Vietnam; whereas South-Vietnam had a democratic government supported by France. The country's natural mining resources and the main factories were all situated in North Vietnam, and it had been rebuilt with the help of China and the Soviet Union. Farming and small factories were located in South Vietnam, and America and the western countries had accepted its independence. In December 1960 the South Vietnamese guerilla forces had organized into a freedom army so that a united government could be established in Saigon.

The Soviet Union let it be known that they would give assistance to countries that wanted to fight to establish their independence; whereas the American president declared that America would help those countries that wanted peace and freedom.

"Well, let's hope that they don't find a place where they start fighting again," Aarne commented.

"Don't say anything more. I guess not when they are so far away from each other," Sylvi said uncertainly.

"Well, America and the Soviet Union are far away from each other but Cuba is just a little bit south of America, and now they are saying that they want that Castro out of there," Aarne added.

"I can't understand any of that. I want peace," Sylvi declared on her own behalf.

"Well, time will tell what's going to happen there," Aarne determined.

The regular love-making in Kaarina's and Albert's home continued and at the end of February Kaarina was sure that she was pregnant when a nauseous feeling repeated for three mornings.

"I think I'm pregnant Albert," she said to Albert.

"I hope we have a boy first," Albert replied and smiled.

Kaarina laughed: "A boy or a girl, as long as it's healthy! Do we have enough money for a child? Do you never think that we are poor?"

"We are not poor Kaarina. We have everything we want. I have you and you have me and we'll have more happiness when we have a child."

"Yes, I only thought about the fact that my father is always talking about being poor." Kaarina replied.

"He is not poor either. He only thinks that he is poor. There is a difference," Albert said.

"He wants to build a house and sell it and go back to Finland with his money. I have a feeling that he is never going to have enough money," Kaarina continued.

"I wonder if he's going to be able to do that because you girls are not returning there. You are not going. We are married and you are going to stay here. Soon you'll be looking after a citizen of this country. Yes, have you even applied to become a Canadian citizen Kaarina?"

"No, I haven't Albert. We never seemed to have a need for that. I guess I should do that sometime. We have been on our way back, the whole family I mean, but I guess Marja can't go back either. She's been educated here and she'll be starting to work here. We have always tried to live by the wishes of our parents and haven't really thought independently."

"I don't think that it's really going to work in your family's case any more, I mean the going back. Think now! How could your parents go back when the most important people in their lives would stay here? Your father just doesn't want to accept that, but I don't think that they can go back either. I'll ask about those papers next week and you can apply to become a citizen before the baby is born. Isn't that so Kaarina?"

"Yes, we'll do that," Kaarina agreed.

That winter and spring the newspapers wrote a lot about the new president and his wife and about their three-year old daughter and the son born in November.

The couple was interviewed on television but mostly the president was seen alone. If his wife was seen somewhere, she was stylishly dressed and the simple styles preferred by her, were becoming popular all over the world. It was also heard that the president's wife had taken on the historical restoration of the White House as her special project.

Canada's economy had slowed down and the newspapers wrote that unemployment had again risen to the same 7% during 1960 as what it had been in

1958 and 1959 and the beginning of 1961 did not look any better.

During the winter Sylvi cleaned the whole apartment but left the girls' room as it had always been. She hoped that Marja would come back in the spring and would look for her first job in the Golden City. Then she could live at home and the whole family could once again be near to each other. It just seemed so quiet when she and Aarne settled down to watch television in the evenings. There was no one to read history, no one to interpret anything; the radio was no longer playing music all the time, like it had when the girls had danced wildly in their teenage years. Kaarina dropped in once a week on her way home from work, and they visited each other on the weekends. Marja wrote once a week, but over all their life was quieter than it had been before.

At the beginning of April Kaarina and Albert told Aarne and Sylvi about the baby coming in November, and the following week Kaarina told Margaret.

"That's wonderful Kaarina. The first child is usually wanted but I really don't want another just right now; I want to be in our own house before we have any more children. It's all so uncertain," Margaret said to Kaarina.

"So it is," Kaarina agreed.

After Sylvi had cleaned the flat she decided that

she would try once again to talk to Aarne about a phone. "Let's get that phone now because I feel that we need to talk to Marja, just to hear her voice, and Kaarina and Albert are going to have a child and then we would need a phone, in case she needs some help fast."

"Well, how expensive is that going to be if you're going to call Marja every day? You have to have some kind of a limit to all this," Aarne started to tell Sylvi.

"I'm not phoning every day, only once a week or once every second week, and Kaarina's phone calls here are not going to cost anything," Sylvi defended herself.

"Well, I was really thinking of it for the house," Aarne tried again. "We could save that money now that every penny is really needed."

"It's not going to be that expensive. You brought me here and I haven't got any other family left except the girls and you. I don't know if I'll ever see pappa and Lempi again," Sylvi demanded, starting to cry at the same time. "You always talk about when we get the house, and when we get that and something else, only three more are then needed to make five. I haven't got any other life except this one and I want a phone and I want it now!" Sylvi blew her nose loudly, and noted from the corner of her eye that Aarne was ready to get the phone.

And it was almost like when they got the television, they needed to look for a suitable place for the phone, so that it would be easy to reach but wouldn't wake them up in the middle of the night. Finally, they decided to put it in the girls' old room, and Aarne went to order the phone with Kaarina. As soon it was put in its place, Sylvi took the receiver in her hand and pressed it against her ear while listening.

"Well, does it work?" Aarne demanded.

"I guess it works because there is a noise there that says, hmmm. We might try to phone Kaarina!" Sylvi was unsure.

"Well, give me that thing and I'll call!" Aarne ordered.

After a couple of tries, and after Sylvi had read the number and Aarne had twirled the number with his finger, all of a sudden Aarne yelled: "Kaarina is that you? Well, it's me!"

"Let me talk too," Sylvi wanted.

"Your mother is going to talk. Well, there is nothing else except that we have this phone now," Aarne sighed with relief and gave the receiver to Sylvi.

"Can you hear me when I'm talking?" Sylvi started and from that began Sylvi's and the girls, and also Aarne's phone calls to each other; and soon they all felt that the distances between them had shortened to almost nothing.

Sometimes Aarne thought about rumours and promises and how they both were matters you couldn't trust. Some rumour could start from nothing and spread like a wildfire through the small city, and perhaps the same was true with bigger issues, when they started to spread in the bigger world. Promises again came back to the person who had promised something, especially if that promise couldn't be kept; like Aarne's own promises to Sylvi and the girls came back to his mind, about a better life and riches which they all could enjoy in the New Country.

Cuba had signed an agreement to buy oil from the Soviet Union at the beginning of 1960 but when the American-owned refineries in Cuba, refused to clean that oil; then Cuba had declared that they owned the refineries and all the banks, sugar and oil refineries, factories and privately-owned properties in Cuba. America had then stopped all diplomatic relations with Cuba. By the time the new president took on his responsibilities at the beginning of 1961, it was felt that the Cuban government might be supporting revolutionary activities in other Southern American countries and now everyone lived with the fear that the other Southern American countries might follow Cuba's sample.

In April 1961 the president announced that America would be against all spreading of communism and it would help other countries in stopping the spreading of communism. Firstly, this support was promised to Cuba, who apparently wanted to take power away from Castro. In high circles people were sure about the rumours that the ordinary Cubans were waiting for America's help and would join a coup to take power, if given the opportunity, but when a group of about 1,400 men who had originally escaped from Cuba and supported America, landed at the Bay of Pigs shore, twenty thousand Cuban soldiers confronted them and the whole fiasco ended there. This was counted as a failure against the American president, even though he had inherited its beginning from the previous government.

Fidel Castro advised that Cuba would make positive purchase agreements with the Soviet Union, China and North-Korea, and that Cuba was now a socialist country and they would no longer hold elections there.

The president announced at the same time that the American government was ready to attack the Cuban government, if it was necessary, and the ordinary Americans sighed a sigh of relief when they heard this.

At this same time that all this was happening in the world, the demands of blacks continued in the American South. Brave black students had ordered a meal at a local lunch counter but they had been refused service.

"It has never been done here in the South." Both the lunch counter owner and the waitress had said: "Go and eat somewhere where they are serving blacks!"

"We were able to buy items in your store on the other side and they took our money there." The young blacks had proposed and stayed to wait for their lunch. They had listened to their new leader Martin Lutcher King Junior's message, when he had requested for them to ask for their rights in a calm manner. He had asked for them not to organize riots, and instead to follow the sample of Gandhi in India, and demand for their rights without violence.

When days and weeks went by while they were waiting for service at the lunch counter, people started to collect around them and the news writers took pictures which were published in newspapers, and the matter was discussed on television, and the sit-ins spread across America's South: to stores, to restaurants and to many public places. Finally, after six months of waiting, the four students were served a meal at the lunch counter and they were able to eat together with the whites.

Early in 1961 the highest court in Virginia continued to uphold the 1946 statute stating that everyone had the right to travel on the Southern buses, and use the restaurants and washrooms at the bus terminals. Now the black leaders felt that it was the right time to free the bus service from all segregation and in April 1961 they announced their intentions publicly. Shortly after that, two small groups of people, blacks and whites, stepped into public buses in Washington. The issue had sounded easy when they had discussed it but the reality turned out to be different. All buses followed a predetermined route, and now arrived at places where they were met with agitators, who had been coerced or paid to beat and thrash the travellers. Many felt that these freedom rides should be stopped because they brought with them riots; but the trips continued and several travellers who stayed on the buses all the way to Mississippi, were taken to prisons in the Southern heat. On the news it was felt that the government did not want to take sides on this issue, perhaps hoping that patience would be the best strategy.

In April the president with his wife visited Ottawa in Canada and it was shown on the news that the public there received them with open arms. At the beginning of July, they travelled to visit with the president of France, and from there they would continue to Vienna where the president would be talking to the Soviet Union's leader.

Aarne followed the news on television, and talked to Sylvi about his own feelings about these issues: "And who knows yet what trouble there might be waiting for him in the world and in these talks, but the world will educate him too."

Aarne's thoughts and predictions hit a sore spot when the president's serious face was shown on the television screen in the following days, and the news revealed that there had been many difficult issues to discuss: like Cuba, Vietnam and space. On top of all these, the escapees from east to west in Berlin, was now becoming an issue of dispute between the two sides. For sometime now it had been noted, that almost every day, close to a thousand East-Berliners escaped over the border to the western side in hopes of finding a better future, and the escapees were well-educated and skilled workers who could not easily be replaced. So far, no easy solution had been found for this problem.

When the president arrived back in America, he often spoke of the Cold War and atomic weapons, and that every American citizen needed to build a bomb shelter into their own home. Large bomb shelters were already being planned into many important places and one of these shelters would soon be built in Canada's capital in Ottawa.

Aarne declared: "It's the Cold War. They are

switching from one idea to another, threatening with this and that, but let's just hope that the real war doesn't come. I know for sure that I'm going to build a bomb shelter into that house that we are planning, and I'm telling you that now."

When Aarne said this, Sylvi looked at him and nodded her head in agreement but couldn't find anything else to say. That much she knew within herself that it was hard to think about the future in the atomic age.

In the spring Marja graduated from school and she was hired as a teacher in the mining city of Sudbury. Once she arrived home, she announced to Kaarina: "I'm so happy I was able to get a teaching position in Sudbury. It's close, but far enough that I don't have to live at home."

During the summer Albert painted their whole apartment.

In August Aarne, Sylvi and Marja together travelled with a bus to Sudbury to look for a place for Marja to live. They had a weekend to do that, and there was not much money to stay in a cheap hotel, and riffle through an unfamiliar newspaper, and try to think of where the rooms and apartments listed might be located in a strange city. Marja found two possibilities, phoned both of them and they went to see them. The first was a damp basement room with a bathroom, and after thanking the owner for showing them, they left to see the next place. There a middle-aged lady waited for them at the door, telling them she was going to work, and she showed them upstairs. A small bed-room, living room and a kitchen with a bathroom, seemed right from the start. The rent was reasonable and when the lady explained that she had lived in the house almost all her life, and alone after her hus-band's passing, that also seemed right. The furniture came with the apartment. Marja rented the place.

In August the world learned that a high barb-wire fence had been erected between east and west Berlin, which divided the city in two, and cut the east Berliners road to the western side.

Kaarina and Albert estimated that Kaarina would be able to work until the end of September. Each payday Kaarina purchased one or two baby clothes and stored them in the bottom dresser drawer; and when Albert noticed the growing collection of baby clothes, he looked at Kaarina and asked: "I guess we'll soon be needing a dresser and a bed for the baby. Should we buy them now?"

"A little bit later," Kaarina wanted to leave the purchase of a crib closer to the baby's birth.

"Let's do that," Albert agreed.

When Kaarina thought about the past year, she felt that her world had changed almost too much, and not only her own but also the Kalliokoski family's. Aarne and Sylvi now lived on their own, and were planning the purchase of a lot and the building of a house. Aarne grew their bank balance like a pig before Christmas, and with time, Sylvi also started to firmly believe in building the house. Nowadays her homesickness only came into her mind when she received a letter from Lempi. Lempi's letters were now more and more full of their life, and their girls' achievements, and pappa's losses; but still when Sylvi replied, a homesickness invaded her mind, but she had got used to that.

Kaarina felt more and more tired when fall came, and was satisfied when she was able to stay at home, after Albert returned to school to teach in September. It was easier to wait for the child's birth in peace. Almost every Saturday they visited Aarne and Sylvi and on Sundays Albert's parents. Almost every time the main topic of conversation now was the child's name. It was a Canadian custom to name the first boy after the father, and almost every family had a John and John Junior, and this was hard for the Kalliokoskis to understand.

"Now, why must everyone have the same name? What sense is there in that, and what kind of name is this Junior exactly?" Aarne queried.

"I don't know. They have a custom like that,"

Kaarina felt that she had been left between her parents and Albert's parents. "Albert Junior is like Albert, the younger."

"What were your parents asking about?" Albert asked when they got in the car.

"They were just hoping that if the child is a boy, that he wouldn't be called, Albert, because then there would be the three of you with the same name, your father, you and the boy," Kaarina said.

"Yes, but the boy needs our name. He can be Junior," Albert stated looking surprised.

"I don't like Junior at all, Albert," Kaarina said stubbornly.

"Well, but it is so, that if the child is a boy, then he is going to be Albert Junior." Albert repeated.

From that ensued an argument between them.

"You are already Albert Junior; so how many of them must there be?" Kaarina felt herself becoming angry, but also tired at the same time, and she went to bed instead.

In the morning Albert tried to smooth things over with words: "Why don't you think about giving the child a second name, or even two, but let me keep Albert Junior."

Kaarina laughed and replied: "I'll think about that. And that second name is going to be Aarne, so that I also have a reason to call the child Junior, because he is also named after my father."

"Yes, why don't we do that," Albert seemed to become happy when he felt that the argument was settled, until Kaarina announced: "If the child is a girl, I'm going to call her Annabel."

"In God's name Kaarina, where are you finding these names? From old romance books, for sure."

Kaarina started to cry and went back to bed.

Albert came after her: "I never meant anything. Just name the girl Annabel and let's give her an easier second name. Then she can use that for every day, and use Annabel here at home. I think you are tired. I can see it in everything and it's best if you rest now."

Later Kaarina laughed at the argument, but also felt that there were many things to think about in the future. Would Albert allow her to teach the child Finnish, and what language would Sylvi and Aarne speak to the child, if not Finnish? When she thought about the issue further, she felt that the whole Kalliokoski family like many first-generation immigrants, still lived according to their old customs and culture. Name-days were celebrated but they were not a part of the Canadian or the American customs, any more than Finnish celebration days were, along with other customs that were different, without even mentioning the language. All these issues turned in Kaarina's head during that fall as she was starting to accept the fact that the child would grow up to be a Canadian.

Kaarina and Marja wrote to one another and Kaarina learned that there were many new things in Marja's life: she lived in her new apartment, she bought new outfits regularly so that she would soon have a reasonably professional wardrobe, she had new friends and she had a new boyfriend with whom she went on walks. Her teenage years which she had lived in the Golden City, were left behind and, her childhood memories from Finland, were now a part of long-gone history. Her first boyfriend Fred had joined the navy after he had left school and had travelled to the east coast to work. He had sent a couple of cards from there, but then she had not heard from him again.

Kaarina's birthing pains started at nine o'clock on the evening of the last day in November. Albert held her hand as they rushed down the stairs and into the car, but already at the hospital door, he was turned away, and Kaarina was put into a hospital bed. The pains came closer and closer, and by the time it was midnight, Kaarina felt herself to be holding the young nurse's hands tighter and tighter as she tried to help with her breathing process. She felt that she was trying her hardest but soon begged for help: "Please give me something for the pain. I didn't know it would be so hard. Please give me something now!"

In the delivery room she was told: "Push, push, push," until someone slapped a mask over her face and she lost consciousness.

"It's a boy, it's a boy. Can you hear Kaarina, wake up now!" She heard the doctor say in a loud voice. And Kaarina replied: "It's Albert Aarne Junior," and laughed happily to everyone.

Chapter Eighteen

Kaarina's and Albert's son was baptized at the Finnish Church during the church service at the end of January. In this way the whole congregation was able to see the child and congratulate the parents and grandparents after the service.

Albert Aarne Junior stared at his Godparents with his big blue eyes until the minister wiped his head with water; after that he closed them and started to scream loudly. The Godparents, Marja and Albert's best friend Walter, were relieved when the parents started to try to calm him, but they were not successful either. Finally, Sylvi and Albert's mother took the boy into their hands, dressed him warmly against the cold, and carried him into Albert's father's car and the little boy calmed down and fell asleep in Sylvi's arms. Most of the people left for home but the invited guests went to Albert's parent's home.

The people relaxed and started to smile to each

other over their coffee or teacups and talked about how much the boy resembled his father and both of his grandfathers and that he seemed good-natured. The immediate families were sure about the fact that he seemed to have his own mind and a loud voice. Sylvi and Kaarina had agreed from the beginning that he might look like his father and his grandfathers, but he was very much like Aarne in his determination and stubbornness. However, they were all very satisfied with him; after all he was the first grandchild into both families.

Margaret and Vieno had held the usual baby shower at the end of October and Kaarina had received a collection of baby clothes, blankets and diapers. Now at the christening, the Godparents and invited guests gave silver dollars, silver spoons and a special child's plate and cup.

February 1962 millions of people sat down in front of their televisions to watch and hear the president's wife's presentation of the White House. Walking from room to room and followed by television cameras, she introduced the historically renewed White House, and thanked everyone who had contributed original furniture and paintings so that a historically correct final achievement had been possible. The president joined his wife at the end, and said a few grateful words in thanks for the work she had done.

"And how beautiful it is there. So that's what the White House looks like!" Sylvi praised as she poured coffee into her cup.

"Well, there it is. Of course, it's finer when you see all the colours there as well, but this is good enough." Aarne said.

"Well, she has spent a lot of time and effort working on it all," Sylvi added.

"People like this. It seems that these people come closer to everyone when you see them on television. Ordinary people like this president, but it's hard for him to get anything important passed, because there is a republican majority in the congress there."

"Oh, I don't understand anything about that," Sylvi declared on her own behalf.

"It might be that you don't understand but that's what it is," Aarne defended himself and the matter was left there.

The president's speeches about the great new society, and the news from Vietnam, were everyday contradictions in the lives of ordinary Americans. The older people remembered the Second World War shortages, which were not far behind, but the young people wanted to live their own lives with no restrictions. They wanted everything that belonged in the good new life: a new place to live, and good pay, and more time for themselves; and they didn't want to hear about the older people's warnings about problems that might be waiting for them behind the next corner.

And even though the time didn't seem right, once he had seen his grandson, Aarne had determined that he would buy the building lot now; he felt firmly that this early spring would be the right time because the money was saved in the bank now. There was a little bit of snow on the ground and it was slippery on the streets; and the temperature still fell below zero at nights; but Aarne walked the streets once again in search of a suitable lot.

"Well, buy it right away if you find the right one," Sylvi supported him,"and if we have enough money."

"Well, there'll never be enough of that, but now I'm buying it!" Aarne inspired himself and Sylvi, although he was afraid of the whole building idea, when he thought about his own and Sylvi's ages, forty-five, and their small wages. When he thought further back and all that they had done, it had been different; like leaving Finland, even though he had had to take a loan, they had been able to pay it back within two years; and the girls' educations which had seemed to be behind a solid rock, they had been able to do that. But now they would have to risk everything: all the saved money and take a loan on top of that, if he was going to build anything while he was still healthy. He also felt that the dream of being able to rest and relax might not ever come for him; and he didn't really even know if he could build the house, but he would have to try.

That important day when he found the lot in May, and took Sylvi to see it, and they together determined that the lot was the exact right one in every way; that was scary too; but now it was behind them and they owned the lot. He had visited a lawyer with Kaarina and Albert to sign the purchase paper, and had given a certified cheque, and later he had picked up the papers. Now Sylvi and he together visited the lot every Sunday. All their money had been spent to purchase it.

Where would he get the money to build the house? That was still a guess. That's what he thought about every waking moment now. If he saved for two years, he might be able to save two thousand dollars in the bank. But then he would be that much older, almost fifty. Then again, if he saved just one year and took a loan, he would have a house and a loan which he could pay off over a few years.

"And that might be the best," Sylvi guessed, but Aarne was not yet ready to say yes or no.

Sylvi was now sure that she wanted her own house. The more she thought about it, the more she felt that a house would be a payment for all her losses.

Moving to Canada, all the hardships of the first years and the knowledge that the girls would not be returning were all losses in her life. Their lives had changed greatly in the past few years when the girls had finished their schooling; Kaarina had married and become a mother; and Marja had become a teacher and moved away. Inside herself Sylvi knew that the girls would not be returning to Finland any more and if the girls would not be returning how could the two of them return then.

When she thought about it all further, little Albert was the main reason for her new way of thinking. When would they see little Albert and all the important firsts in his life if they moved away? And if they lived in Finland, how could they find enough money to travel back and forth to visit the girls and their children? Now she had to accept this new way of looking at everything and the thought seemed enormous to accept.

Sylvi cried almost every time she thought about her father and Lempi, and still missed them, and if she thought about all the familiar places she had travelled daily: the market square at Turku, the streetcar which rolled past the Turku Cathedral, all the familiar stores, weekly visits to Lempi; then she became angry at Aarne because she felt that he was the cause of their leaving; but at the same time she knew that there was no point in talking about it any more.

Aarne defended the leaving by stating that the girls had perhaps gained a better future in the New Country; but they both also knew that this was an accepted lie in both their minds, because Aarne had not really thought about the girls at that time; he had thought about himself or perhaps the whole family. Now that was all behind too.

"Now we have to think about the future," Aarne declared each time, if Sylvi started to talk about the past or he stated: "Stay with the ideas of today and don't always think about the past."

In early June when the frost was gone and the ground dry, they raked the lot and started to plan the house more closely. They had decided together that the house would be situated in the middle of the lot, and the main entrance would be in the middle of the house. Now they decided that the living room, dining room and the master bedroom windows would look on the street, and the kitchen, washroom and the two smaller bedrooms' windows would look on the back. There would be room on the side for parking a car, if it was needed later, and enough room in the back for a vegetable garden and a clothes-line.

Aarne put these plans on paper and showed them to Jussi and Vilho, both of whom encouraged him to build right now when he had the lot; but no one seemed to be sure about where he would get the money.

"Build it but I haven't got money to loan you. Where did you get that idea?" Jussi lifted his eyes and glanced at Aarne from under his eyebrows, "it's good if I can get enough together so I don't have to work for the rest of my life. I haven't got any other hope left. I've got this cough all the time now."

"Well, I didn't think that," Aarne replied, "I was just talking."

"You know that all my money went on the fixing of this house. Good thing I didn't have to take a loan myself. And I should save even now," Vilho explained as he stretched his arms, and Aarne nodded his head because he knew it as well as Vilho.

"But tell me then where I'm going to get the money from?"

"Come on in and let's think about this. Does Eikka have money?"

"Eikka doesn't have any money. His son, Pekka, came back from Elliot Lake and they lost their house there, so Eikka's money will go to helping them," Aarne stated.

"I guess that's true but what about Korpis Niilo? He's got his own house and a rental house and he gets a nice amount of money from rent every month. Ask him," Vilho became enthusiastic.

"I wonder if he would give a loan and what percentage of interest would he ask?" Aarne started to guess.

"Let's go ask him. I'll come with you. Maybe he would give a couple of thousand or three against your lot. He's given loans to others. Somebody said that he is giving them at six or six and half percent now, and that's the same as what the banks are charging," Vilho told Aarne.

"I think that I'll leave it till next spring," Aarne retreated when he started to think about the size of the loan and the fact that he would have to give his lot for collateral. "What if I save for another year yet and ask then, I could build the house ready outside and move in and finish it off when I had more money."

"So it is. I'll ask Niilo now so he can keep some money ready for you."

"Let's do that," Aarne agreed. He walked back towards home and thought about the size of the loan he needed and asked himself: "Do I really need such a large loan? And how is Sylvi going to pay it off if I'm not able to finish the house? Behind every corner there is always another problem!"

But when he spoke to Sylvi about the loan, Sylvi seemed unusually calm: "I think we have to do it. Otherwise we won't get the house."

And then Aarne spoke to Kaarina and Albert,

and Albert encouraged him on: "I will back you if you can't get it otherwise. I will back you at the bank or with an individual. I have a permanent job and they will accept me because I'm a teacher."

Kaarina smiled as a sign of her support.

"You are rich!" Aarne joked in English to Albert. "You rich!"

"I'm not rich but if something happens to you, then we can live together in the house until it's paid for, and pay for it that way."

"Yes, he is right," Sylvi said and they all looked at Albert with new respect.

"Get the loan that you need and then I will come and look over the papers and back you up," Albert patted Aarne on his shoulder.

"I'm saving more through the winter and then we'll get the loan in the spring," Aarne explained the issue to Kaarina so that she would explain it to Albert.

He had not expected that Albert would back him. When Kaarina visited later Aarne asked her directly about it: "Will Albert back me up if I can get the loan at the bank?"

"Yes, he will. We discussed it at home," Kaarina ascertained.

"Well, we can see about it in the early spring," Aarne said with relief and it was left there. He ordered the plans for the house with the help of Kaarina and

Albert so that they would all be able to study them in peace.

With Sylvi he familiarised himself with the plans and they started to each put forth their own ideas about the house.

"And in the basement I'm going to build that bomb shelter," Aarne planned: "They're talking about them all the time in the newspapers and on television. Then we can think about shelves and beds and storing of food and water, of course."

"Well, we have to put a toilet in there too?" Sylvi thought.

"It's going to have everything: a chemical toilet and a primus-cooker, like we had in Finland," Aarne added further: "We can't tell yet what's going to happen. They talk about these shelters on television and in newspapers all the time. And there is always somewhere in the world a lit piece of coal, that's just waiting for someone to blow it to a full fire!"

Sylvi shook her head and left the table. She didn't really want to hear about the bad news of the world.

Little Albert moved around on his blanket on the floor, and laughed at his parents who smiled back at him, and thought that he was the world's most wonderful baby.

"He follows the clouds and the large branches

and leaves on the tree which he can see through the window. He is doing something new almost every day," Kaarina explained happily to Albert.

"So it is. We have to buy him a stroller so that you can bring him outside to see everything now that it's getting warmer," Albert planned.

"Let's do that. We can go to the store on Saturday, when you're home. Then we can carry him in turns. I can't carry him for very long any more," Kaarina said and continued: "Now Margaret pushes Elizabeth in the stroller that they have, but she can't loan it to us because they're already expecting a new baby. Margaret told me. They really didn't want one yet but I guess their birth control methods didn't work that well."

"I guess not if they're already expecting another one. It would be easier for us if we didn't have another one in the upstairs rooms. How would you cope with carrying two up and down? It wouldn't work out."

"I guess not. Let's hope we don't have another one yet. Right?"

"Let's hope for that," Albert agreed.

Kaarina noted that Albert was no longer the young man who had wanted to make love without thinking of the consequences; now he seemed to know full well the responsibility he carried for his family.

But in the case of Margaret and Pekka, a second child was now expected and they had already for some time looked for a small house that they could settle in. They found it in June, and now they were fixing it up so they could move in during the summer.

"The house has to be fixed but we didn't have enough money for a better or a bigger one. The house is good from the outside and the roof is good, but we have to paint it inside," Margaret explained to Kaarina.

"Ask us to come and help paint. You can look after the children and make something to eat and I will paint with Pekka and Albert," Kaarina suggested. "You can't paint any more in your condition."

"That would be wonderful," Margaret was enthusiastic. "I'm just tired and I have gained too much weight. Pekka has to already help my shoes on."

After Pekka and Margaret had the house in their names, Kaarina and Albert went to help them. Walking there was easy now because of the stroller they had bought for little Albert.

Pekka had already painted the ceilings and fixed the walls inside earlier in the week and now he started to paint the lower walls, while Albert painted the higher parts of the walls, and Kaarina kneeled and painted the walls close to the floors. Elizabeth played on the kitchen floor while little Albert slept, and Margaret started to make the dinner.

The painting turned out well and made the

whole house inside look brighter. Pekka said that he would be painting the two bedrooms' walls during the week and after that he would clean the floors, and then they could move in.

"Wonderful! We can hardly fit into the upstairs bedroom at Pekka's old home, and the baby won't fit in there at all." Margaret said.

Later in the evening Albert, Kaarina and little Albert were returning home tired. After little Albert was put to bed, Kaarina laid down beside Albert on the living room floor and they stayed there to listen to the music coming from radio, and to talk about everything that had happened during the day.

"Margaret told me that Pekka would like her to teach Elizabeth some Finnish," Kaarina started.

"How can she do that when she can only speak a few words of Finnish? You told me that she only speaks a few words. How can she teach it to others?" Albert asked.

"Pekka doesn't understand that. I guess he thinks that Margaret has learned more Finnish be-cause all the Kuronens speak Finnish. I was going to start teaching little Albert Finnish," Kaarina turned to Albert.

"But will he benefit from that very much?" Now Albert turned to look more carefully at Kaarina.

"He is half-Finn. I have to teach him Finnish

so that he can speak to mom and dad."

"I didn't think about that so much. I guess I must have thought that you parents would learn more English as little Albert started to learn it."

"I really don't believe it. It's been very slow, their learning of English."

At the same time as they spoke Kaarina listened to the ballad coming from the radio and started to think about the words: "You give your hand to me and then you say Hello, , , and those that see us think that we know each other, but you don't know me, , ,"2 Kaarina lay back to think about the message in the song and said to Albert: "Perhaps we should have spoken about many more things earlier, when we were going together?" Only now in the marriage she felt that she had learned to know Albert more closely and found in him many more good points which made her respect and love him more than before.

Albert squeezed her hand: "Only in marriage does everyone learn more about the other person and ordinary life. Perhaps marriage is the boat into which we both step and float on the sea of life, and we don't know beforehand about the winds and storms, that the churning of the sea is going to throw in our way. Go ahead and teach him Finnish. He will learn English when he goes to school. That's what all kids do. I've noticed that."

They both listened quietly to the song.

In the late fifties and early sixties Aarne noted that the Canadian government and the provinces, were more and more in agreement about needing more social services for the population. The old-age pension had been raised and the age limit for receiving it had been lowered. This summer in Saskatchewan, a suitable hospital insurance idea had been introduced, and even though doctors there had gone on a three-week strike, after that the hospital insurance had been accepted. When Aarne thought about his brother Jussi, the reasonable hospital insurance would not be coming any time too soon. Jussi was now having to stay home from work, sometimes even two days a week. If Aarne dropped in to visit him on those days, he often found Jussi sitting on his garden bench, just trying to breath deeply.

"Martin is goinna take me for an Xray. It's not goinna get better just by me sitting here. I guess it's that silicosis. I guess it's that. I wonder if there is a medicine for it?" Jussi kept glancing at Aarne while he was talking.

"I really don't know. It's best if you ask a doctor. Maybe they have some medicine for it or they'll put you in the hospital."

"Well, let them put me in the hospital! But who is going to support Aune if I have to go to the hospital?"

"I guess she might be getting some help money and if Martin and his wife could help. I really don't' know. I guess they must have some money if you can't work? Don't you know anything about that?"

"I don't know about it because I didn't think I was goinna get sick," Jussi left the topic there.

When Aune visited Aarne and Sylvi after three weeks, she told Aarne that Jussi would be going to the tuberculosis hospital in the next week; and Aarne was not surprised, but asked instead if Aune would be needing help.

"Well, time will tell. Come and visit before he leaves," Aune asked.

"Well, yes. We'll come tomorrow evening," Aarne replied.

When they visited the following evening, Aarne thought that Jussi looked relieved now that he knew that he would going to the hospital.

"Martin and Nancy are going to move in here to help us out. We can't manage otherwise for very long," Aune explained, "they'll give me a little income."

"I guess that would be best," Aarne agreed. "I can't really do much when all my money is tied up in building the house but I'll come and help Jussi when he gets home."

"That sounds good," Aune also seemed to be more peaceful now that it sounded like there would be help on the way.

"I wonder how it's all going to turn out?" Aarne asked Sylvi when they were alone.

"Well, you really don't know about it until you see it," Sylvi was equally puzzled. "What money is a person going to get if they can't work? I just don't know. But I guess they would get something. I think so."

"No one else seems to know much about it either," Aarne continued more uncertain, "today's life is such that you start to go crazy. Who controls what they put on that television? You can't tell what is a lie, and what is the truth?" Aarne announced to Sylvi.

"I can't tell what they're talking about. You have to know a lot more English than what I have. I look at those musical programs and fun movies," Sylvi explained.

"And I look at the news. Read from this paper if you're not planning to watch the news," Aarne encouraged.

"Well, I'm going to read after I have my coffee. I come home so late and I should really be starting to knit a sweater and a hat for little Albert and I haven't got time for all the news. It's going to be winter soon and he needs a sweater and a hat. And all these kinds of news come like a surprise from the clear sky. You can't expect them at all!"

But in the middle of October Sylvi sat beside Aarne with her knitting in her hands and stared at the television screen when they together listened to the American president's serious talk.

"Will you call Kaarina now so that she could ask Albert what that president is talking about, and why he is looking like that?" Sylvi asked.

Aarne rushed to the phone and soon came back to tell Sylvi that Albert had explained, that the president had announced that American airplanes had taken photographs of the Soviet Union building bomb and atomic missile basis in Cuba. Albert had said that this was starting to sound threatening because the island of Cuba was only a short distance from Florida.

"It's so close!" Sylvi was alarmed.

"That's what I told you, that there is always somewhere a smouldering piece of coal, that's waiting for someone to blow on it to start a really big fire. Let's see what they say tomorrow."

Very soon the president announced that he had given the order to surround the island of Cuba, so that no more missile basis could be built there. The American ambassador was taking the photographs, taken from the air, to the United Nations' meeting, and it was starting to feel that the news were pushing the world closer and closer to war. American students were already being taught how to protect themselves. Finally, at the end of October, the Soviet Union promised to remove the missiles from Cuba, if America promised to remove its missiles stationed in Turkey. The United Nations representatives would be able to come and check that the removal was taking place, and America had promised not to attack Cuba at this time. The whole world seemed to sigh a huge sigh of relief.

"And who knew that the Americans had installed their own missiles in Turkey already earlier? No one has said anything about that until now?" Aarne asked the television.

"Well, is it all over now?" Sylvi asked Aarne when the news seemed to be calming down and now explained more about the concessions each side was willing to make.

"It's over for now but I can't say anything about the future. It just seems that each country wants to be ready if some differences of opinion should develop."

"Sometimes I think about Marja being out there in the world and if she would be able to find a bomb shelter if something happens."

"I don't know if there is any really safe place left in this world. You might be in that decrepit boarding house, and I would already be underground in the mine, if an atom bomb drops. That much I heard from Vilho, that these big bosses are planning some kind of a hot-wire phone on which they could phone one another if something happens again, so that no one else can interfere with their talking."

Like always Christmas came everywhere in the world and Marja drove to the Golden City in her new car. They had promised more snow for the evening, and for that reason Aarne and Sylvi rushed right out to look at her car. They admired its beautiful colour and checked everything inside closely. Later in the evening they asked Marja more about her new life, and work, and pay; and then both Aarne and Sylvi stopped for a moment to think about the fact that Marja's pay was already now more than Aarne's, without even thinking about Sylvi's low pay. Kaarina had often told them that Albert's pay was enough for them to live on, but only now, after having heard about Marja's pay; did they truly understand what a difference it made for a person to be able to understand and speak the language, and to have an education.

The next day they all drove to visit Albert and Kaarina, to show the car and to see little Albert. Little Albert struggled to stand up beside the sofa, and then walked a few steps from one adult to another, and according to Kaarina, had already taken a few steps on his own.

The grandparents stayed to look after little Albert and Marja took Kaarina for a drive. They drove directly to Smithy's restaurant like in the old days. The parking lot was full of cars, and the restaurant was full of young people, who had all come from different places in Canada to celebrate Christmas with their parents.

In the middle of it all former friends called out to one another: "Hi! How are you?" Was heard everywhere, and after that there were questions: "Where do you live now? What are you doing? Did you get a good job?"

Marja spoke to her friends and told them about her new life. Kaarina greeted her friends and replied to their questions. At the same time, she looked for Anita and Warren, who also came to the restaurant.

"Great to see each other again! It's wonderful that you have time to write me. I'll reply as soon as I get time. Last year it was so busy because I attended teachers' college and, I already told you, that I got a job. I'll stay home when we have children. We really love Toronto. It's a big city. The expenses are more there and the distances are long, but there is just not enough work here for everyone. Albert had good luck when he was able to get a job here when Elliot Lake ended. Mother and father said that little Albert is starting to walk," Anita started to talk to Kaarina.

Kaarina admired Anita's new coat and exquisite boots, and asked them to visit if they would have time.

"Let's see now," Warren replied on behalf of Anita. "I don't really know. Our parents are hanging hard onto to us. We only see them so rarely any more because the distances are so long."

"So it is," Kaarina replied.

"I'll write and send pictures of our home as soon as we return to Toronto. Make sure you reply as soon as you can and send pictures of little Albert," Anita urged.

"I will write and I'll send photos too."

Marja was ecstatic when she saw her childhood friend Donna after a long while. Their paths had parted when Donna had gone to Montreal to become a registered nurse, and had got her first job there. Donna said that she was very happy to be in her new home city, and in her new job, and was now learning the French language because there were a lot of French-speaking people living there.

"Come and visit me as soon as you can. It would be nice to see you in the coming summer. Montreal is a big and beautiful city, and there is a lot to see and do there," Donna invited and Marja replied that she would think about it, and come as soon as she could get the time.

By the time it was five o'clock, people started to leave, waving their hands once more, promising to write to one another; they hurried back to their childhood homes. It was almost dark already. Marja and Kaarina left with the others.

"Almost everyone has moved away. Are there any of yours or Albert's former friends still living here?" Marja asked Kaarina.

"Not very many. Some stayed here and some came back. Mostly everyone has moved away, and each Christmas when we meet at Smithy's to see our old friends, there'll be fewer of them returning. You don't see people over forty any more. They don't come any more. This is just a phase we are living through. After their parents have died, they don't return here. Their lives are elsewhere. It's a long way to come here. After people move away from here, they always complain about the long trip. Hey, let's not think about such dark things; that our parents have gone; that friends wouldn't be coming back here any more. It's Christmas now! Let's go home! Tomorrow we can celebrate Christmas with father and mother and Albert, and little Albert." Kaarina replied.

"Let's go. You're right. Tomorrow is Christmas," Marja agreed.

Chapter Nineteen

Winter came north as fierce and angry as always. It had already started at the end of October, and had thrown snow into the forests and on the fields, and had locked the northern lakes under a thick cover of ice and the people inside. During Christmas and January, the snow started to collect on the streets and yards of the small city. The city ploughs cleared them and the citizens shoveled clean their own paths; everyone had to carry the wood and the coal into their homes every day.

That winter almost every time that Aarne carried another pile of wood or a pail of coal to the upstairs landing, he said to Sylvi: "Is this the last winter that I'm carrying these woods and coal to this God-damned upstairs?"

"Well, I'll carry more tomorrow before I go to work," Sylvi tried to calm him.

"Well, that's good to hear."

"Well, you're getting nervous about it."

"Well, I've carried these already, pretty soon for ten years. Are these not enough?"

"They're enough. Don't swear any more. It's Sunday now."

Margaret gave birth to a boy at the beginning of January and Pekka gave cigars to his friends as was the custom when a boy was born.

"Does the boy have a name yet?" Kaarina and Albert questioned when they visited to see them.

"Pekka wants to call him Erik which is a little bit like his father Eikka's name," Margaret replied. "Then they would be Elizabeth and Erik. I like the name Erik."

"I think Erik is a good name," Pekka said to Albert.

"Erik is a good name; a Scandinavian name and it's easy to say," Albert continued.

Margaret made coffee and they spent a few moments together. She was overwhelmingly happy in her new home.

"I'm so happy. Now we have our own home. Let's look at every room," she showed the visitors around. "I'm not moving from here any more."

Pekka smiled: "I won't be moving either. This is a good place for us."

It also seemed that the president was looking

forward with hope to the year 1963. When he spoke to the nation at the beginning of January, he proposed a $13.5 billion tax cut so that the economic outlook would improve, and the unemployment, which had already gone down, would go down further.

But everyone was not satisfied with his aims or accomplishments; the blacks especially were disappointed as they had wanted to hear something truly promising. They were disappointed with the president's promise that the vote would be given to all. They felt that this promise did not go far enough; and it did not give the blacks the same rights that the whites had in schools and at work.

Their leader Martin Luther King Jr had not himself experienced racial injustices because his parents had shielded him from them. He had been educated as a minister. In 1953 he had married Coretta Scott and together they had dedicated their lives to bettering the lives of the blacks in the American South. He had been chosen as the leader of the Southern Christian Association, and with his encouragement, the Southern black churches and their leaders had started a campaign to stop all injustices.

They had made up their minds to bring their campaign to a conclusion without violence. They appealed to their religion and to the fact that the original immigrants had travelled to America in the hopes that they would be able to practise their religion in peace. From the time that the famous Mayflower ship had brought the first immigrants from Plymouth in England, to the New World, religion and politics had gone forth hand in hand. King always pointed out to the fact that both the blacks and whites would benefit if racial segregation was ended.

Almost every week Aarne and Sylvi studied the house plans and Aarne started to add the upcoming expenses. At the end of March, he received the good news that he would be given a mortgage. He visited the bank with Kaarina and Albert, and they together signed the necessary papers for a mortgage of three thousand dollars with six percent interest. Now all the monies were waiting at the bank. With Vilho he visited the man who would dig the hole for the house, and he promised to come as soon as the frost was gone at the beginning of June.

Now in April of 1963 the black leaders made up their minds to start a campaign against all segregation in the city of Birmingham, and in addition to that they demanded that blacks be given jobs in the city's stores and factories. With the encouragement of their leaders, young blacks there were soon marching with placards in their hands in front of department stores, to let everyone know about their campaign.

The Birmingham city leaders prohibited all

campaigning, but the black protestors did not listen to
them any more. Soon they were taken to the city jail.
This was Martin Luther King Jr's thirteenth arrest,
and he was thrown alone into a small jail cell, but after
a few days, a black lawyer visited him to tell him that
a famous black singer, Harry Belafonte, had collected
thousands of dollars to have him freed. After this visit,
the conditions in the jail cells were improved and Dr.
King was able to phone his wife. But when he saw the
newspapers, where the white religious leaders were
critical of their campaign, King started to write an ex-
planatory letter about all the aims of the blacks. He
wrote on the sides of newspapers and on pieces of
paper, and his visitors secretly brought the letter outside, and it was all published in newspapers. In his
letter King appealed that the American constitution
had promised all immigrants civil rights, and that the
blacks had already waited three hundred years in
order to receive the same rights as the whites. He repeated Thomas Aquino's words when he wrote that all
laws that approved and uplifted civil rights, were good
laws.

By the time it was the middle of May the general
feeling in the city of Birmingham demanded that the
black protestors be freed from jail. In June the president spoke on television and promised to bring to the
congress, a bill demanding that all segregation be

ended in public places, in travel, in education and in employment.

The best news that Aarne and Sylvi heard that spring were the news that Lester Pearson was chosen as Canada's prime minister.

"That's the same man that received the Nobel peace prize," Aarne remembered.

"Well, he is already famous then. I remember that," Sylvi added.

In the same month of June Aarne and Sylvi stood beside their lot, looking on, as a small digging machine started to dig the hole for their house. Every now and then as he turned, the man on the machine waved his hand to them, to let them know that the work was proceeding well. Aarne thought that the hole would be dug by the time it was evening and he would then only have to pay for the one day's work. At four o'clock the man drove his machine back on the flatbed, and Aarne paid him off. On Sunday Vilho would be coming to measure everything with him, and the following weekend they would pour the cement footing for the house.

"There is the hole now," Aarne commented to Sylvi.

"Well, there it is. How long is it going to take to build the house?" Sylvi asked.

"Don't start rushing! It's going to take the

whole summer. It's a good thing if we can get inside in the late fall. Or it would be best, so that we wouldn't have to pay rent through the winter any more, because there are going to be the taxes and all kinds of other expenses to pay on this house by that time." Aarne replied.

"Do you mean October or November?" Sylvi still asked.

"Well, I can't put it on the exact day but late in the fall."

The large basement blocks were delivered to the lot the next week, and Aarne and Vilho organised them into rows on the sides of the lot.

"And this is where it starts," Vilho spoke with enthusiasm the following Saturday, when they were finishing nailing together the wooden trough, in which to mix the cement.

"This is where it starts," Aarne agreed as they started to mix the cement. "Is this right?" Aarne asked many times, "you have to know because I'm not a cement professor."

"I'm not either but we made this according to the instructions on the bag and I've done this before. This is good," Vilho replied.

Aarne laughed with relief.

The day was spent in mixing the cement and pouring it into the form for the footing of the basement.

By the time it was evening, the footing was poured and they both went home.

"I am so tired; first working all day and now all weekend on this house," Aarne said as he fell on the bed.

"And this building has only just begun," Sylvi agreed.

"You better come and start carrying those big basement blocks when we start the basement. Vilho can't help the whole time and I'll have to pay him too if he has to come every evening after work."

"Well, I'll come but I'm wondering how many of those big blocks I'll be able to carry? What if we asked Albert to come?" Sylvi suggested.

"Well, we'll ask Kaarina first, so that they both know about it. If we could get this basement done; then the worst would be over. This is the heaviest part," Aarne said, "or when we get the roof on top of the whole thing, then the worst will really be over. Good if we can get it ready by the time it's late fall. You have to help the whole time. It's not going to get ready without everyone's help. Do what you can, and you'll lose some weight at the same time."

"And I thought that I would make food for you while you're building the house," Sylvi started to con-tradict Aarne.

"This is the kind of work that both men and

women can do," Aarne replied stubbornly.

At the end of June, the American president travelled with his entourage to Europe, and everyone watched on television how excited the people there were, when they welcomed him and threw flowers onto the streets of West-Berlin. That evening Aarne and Sylvi sat down to watch as the president spoke to the masses of people who had collected around the Berlin Wall; the wall had been erected in 1962 in the hopes that it would finally end the escape of the people to the west. He spoke about freedom and the right of all people to think freely, and his hope that in the future the whole of humankind would be able to live in peace.

"It's such a fine speech; what I can understand about it. Look how everyone is yelling hurrah, hurrah," Sylvi was excited as she spoke to Aarne.

"It's probably a good speech but it just doesn't happen like that. It takes time for all people to think alike, like in the American South."

"Well, I can understand that. But at least he has taken that proposal to the congress so that everyone could get the same rights. That's what you told me," Sylvi added still.

"That's what they said on television," Aarne agreed.

"Everyone seems to like him even though he can't really change everyone's life all that much," Sylvi thought aloud.

"So it is. Well, if nothing else, this president gives hope for freedom and a better life that we all want, whether they are living east of west. And, of course, that all people would be equal."

At the end of the television program, it was announced that the president's trip would continue to Ireland, from where his family had immigrated to America.

"It's so in this world, that people who take on these important positions, don't really have much time to live their own lives because they have to always be going or settling some big issues somewhere." Aarne concluded that evening when they were going to sleep. "There are these riots in the American South and the Vietnam War on top of all his problems; and everything else is underneath these."

The Vietnam War continued. At first there had been hope that the war would be short and America and South-Vietnam would win, but now it seemed that the fighting had become caught in the difficult terrain of Vietnam, and the guerilla warfare. The issues came to a head in the spring of 1963 when Diem's older brother Ngo Dinh Thuc was given permission to celebrate with public display of flags, his own rise to an archbishop 25 years previously; but when the Buddha-believers asked permission to celebrate their leader's 2,527 anniversary date, that was forbidden. At the same time Diem's younger brother Ngo Din Nhu and his wife, robbed more and more power for themselves and the secret police under their direction, controlled the life of everyone soon. America informed Diem that he needed to free himself from Nhu, and gain the support of the best politicians in South-Vietnam and the support of the people, and he needed to free the jailed Buddha monks, but Diem didn't listen to these warnings. In the summer of 1963, the leaders of South Vietnam's army started to plan an attack against the Diem and Nhu government.

Aarne took a three-week holiday in July and he was able, with the help of Albert, to bring all the walls up and, by the end of the month Aarne, Vilho and Albert together raised the roof and nailed the roof-tiles on. That afternoon Aarne rushed to buy a bottle of liquor to offer a small drink to everyone who came to help. The rest of the day he walked around the house repeating in Finnish and English: "Nyt meillä on katto päällä, Albert! Now we have a roof on top, Albert!" And Albert smiled at him with satisfaction.

Many of Aarne's friends visited the building site, and a few of them came with their tools, and helped Aarne with whatever part of the house he was working on at that time. Everyone knew that the summer in the north ended in September and after a short fall, winter might begin around the middle of October.

Aarne started to work on the window frames; the windows were already waiting inside.

In the middle of all his work Aarne visited Aune to ask her how Jussi was doing, and Aune told him that Martin had been told that Jussi was doing fairly well and would likely be able to come home sometime in the fall. One thing was sure that Jussi's silicosis was a permanent illness; now the doctors were only trying to find the right drugs to enable him to live at home; he would never be able to return to work.

"So, that's what happened," Aarne said sadly to Aune.

"That's what happened. He is never going to recover from that silicosis but at least if he could come home. I knew when he went there that he would never be able to return to work," Aune lamented.

And Aarne didn't say anything about Jussi's future either. Whether he would be able to live long with the help of medicines, was also an unknown. All the men they knew who had become ill with silicosis, had lived a year or two after their hospitalisation, and then died with pneumonia or from not being able to breathe.

Aarne walked home deep in his own thoughts; he thought about his own busy life with the building of the house, and how little time he had for anything else; but he made up his mind that he would try to help Aune and Jussi after his brother returned home.

Marja came home on a holiday at the beginning of August, and like everyone else in the family, she started to help with the house. Together with Sylvi they carried building materials: flooring, nails or screws; all that Aarne and Albert asked for; and after Sylvi went to work, Marja continued the work on her own, and swept floors as they needed it. While doing this she thought about her own future. Perhaps already in two years she would be going to university to get her bachelor's degree, and then her master's degree, and after that hopefully she would be able to get a job teaching in high school. She had new friends; many of whom were going to universities to get more education, and then some other friends who travelled the world. The world that so many people had seen in the movies and on television, now beckoned many to travel and to meet people in other parts of the world.

Kaarina spoke and taught little Albert Finnish, the same as Aarne and Sylvi did. Albert and his parents spoke English to him. Often Kaarina thought how it would be wonderful for little Albert to have a playmate. He walked around the building site like some kind of a prince, and carried left-over little pieces of wood into his own play, and messed up everything as he wanted, and never listened to any orders no matter who gave them. Kaarina and Albert were planning the purchase of a house the next spring, and hoped to have another child after that. Kaarina and Leena still wrote to one another, and she sent birthday and Christmas cards to her grandfather and aunts and cousins; but her previous life was left more and more behind. Even so she was still hoping to visit Finland and Albert also seemed interested in going there.

Sylvi was still sometimes homesick for her old life, but her thoughts were more and more connected to their new house now, and how she would place the furniture in it. She planned to buy new curtains and perhaps a new kitchen table and chairs after the house was finished. Like before, she wrote to Lempi and told her about everything that they were doing. And neither of them ever mentioned anything about travelling across the ocean any more. Lempi was just too timid for such a long trip and Sylvi didn't have enough money yet. They might travel there in five years or so, Aarne had promised.

Nowadays when Aarne thought about his brother Matti, he seemed far away. Matti had stayed in the Old Country and Aarne's return there had changed into building a house. He still wrote to Matti and sometimes sent pictures but now he understood that they would not be moving back there. He was tied to the life in the New Country more and more; through

Kaarina and Marja and especially through little Albert.

Jussi was now an ill man, and might not even live long any more; that much Aarne felt he knew about the men who had become ill with silicosis. And he had never really got to know Jussi well, that's how different their personalities and outlook on life were. Jussi had tried to give him directions and helpful ideas about life, but they had all been too old-fashioned for today's life that had a much faster tempo. You couldn't think long about anything, or you lost your only chance. You had to take chances with new ideas and take risks. Aarne felt that the New Country and its difficulties had honed him into steel that endured more effectively in today's fast-paced life.

Aarne was sure that he knew a lot about all that was happening around him, even though he really didn't know that much English, but he had read newspapers, had listened to the radio and had watched television. That was the good thing about these means of communication that he was able to stay on top of things. It was a person's own duty to find his own way. Through the building of his house he had achieved a part of what he had come to get from the New World. He also knew that many people had helped him in this endeavour. Now he had the house which he could change into money and go forward again. He might even be able to leave the mining work.

When his supervisor had visited the house, he had told Aarne that he could organise work on the surface of the mine for him, and this would be work in a healthier environment.

In the larger world England had let it be known that the most important issue for both England and America would be to find a way to stop experimenting with atom bombs.

The presidential couple was now expecting their third child and the president's wife had already left all her official duties.

Philip Randolph and Bayard Rustin together were planning a march to Washington. They were hoping to achieve new laws that would finally ensure equal civil rights to all the citizens. The date of the march was organized for the end of August and anyone that wanted could take part in the march.

News reporters travelled to Washington for the day of the march, and later it was reported that there were hundreds of reporters taking photos, writing and interviewing those who took part in the march. Close to 300,000 marchers had arrived at Abraham Lincoln's statue when Martin Luther King Jr started to speak: "I have a dream that the American blacks would be able to get the same rights as the whites and that they could all together sing the old song of the blacks: 'Free at last! Free at last! Thank God almighty, we are free at last'"3 and 4

The news from Vietnam informed the world that Diem and Nhu had both been shot in the battle that had begun at the beginning of November. After that it was announced that America would try to help the South-Vietnam government to gain a better support from its citizens, and it was hoped that the new leaders in South Vietnam would be able to end the war soon.

It seemed that life was increasingly busy and there seemed to be more knowledge about everything, Aarne thought. There was always something happening somewhere and the news that followed pulled all the people in the world into thinking about the news. When he thought back, he realised that he had lived through a wonderful ten-year period in the world's history. When did all the busyness and the spreading of news start? Did it start with the airplanes that had begun to travel all over the world in the 1920's and 1930's; or did it start with the phones that allowed peoples' voices to travel in a matter of moments from one place to another? Or was it the radio that had started to tell everyone about all the news, or in all finality, the television which now sent communications and pictures all over the world? When he thought about the millions of people that collected to see the televisions around the world, he started to understand that they all had the same opportunity to think and take part in the same issues and knowledge, and how wonderful it was that even all ordinary people could take part in this.

On top of this he thought about how hard his own life sometimes was, but was not even close to the difficult life that the president had, and the pressures and responsibilities that he had. The president's hoped-for third child had been born but had only lived for one day. Every day news told more about Vietnam, the Cold War, the blacks Civil Rights campaign, Berlin, and now also about the president's plans to start a new campaign so that he could again become the president in the 1964 elections.

At the end of September Aarne noted that summer was turning to fall and he felt good that all his plans had worked out. When he looked out from the flat's upstairs window, he could see that the last leaves of the trees were flying in the wind, some still green but most were yellow and red leaves that had completed their work and they soon covered the ground in bright colours.

In October Aarne and Sylvi completed the walls and the floors. One Saturday they went to order a new electric stove. They often looked at the house from across the street and sometimes Aarne grabbed Sylvi's arm like he had when they were young; and Sylvi might lean on his shoulder for a moment and say: "It turned out to be a fine house!"

And Aarne felt that his life was very good.

In the news they were talking more and more about the fact that the president would travel to the American Southern cities to lay a foundation for his 1964 presidential campaign. Why he would want to continue, was a puzzle to Aarne, because it seemed to him that the lives of these important people were more and more full of problems. Was there much family-life when the job of being a president would already take all of his time and energy?

In November they painted the closets and varnished the kitchen cabinets' doors. Winter was coming again and there was already a cover of snow on the ground. The next week they would be moving all the furniture into the new house. Aarne had already informed the landlord that they would be moving at the end of the month.

Eikka, Toni and John came to help with the move. Thursday evening after work they carried the furniture down the steps into a small truck that John had been able to loan from a friend. At the house they carried in and organised the furniture in the way that Aarne asked. Aarne offered beer and Sylvi made coffee and sandwiches and coffee bread for the men.

On Friday Sylvi and Aarne started to put all the small things into their places in the house. The sofa, a chair and a small table had already been put in the living room and the television had been placed across from the sofa. Now they would take the girls steel beds for their own use, and sometime when they had collected money again, they would buy a dresser to go there too. The new electric stove had been carried into the kitchen and the old fridge and a table and chairs were placed there too.

It was snowing outside. After lunch Aarne and Sylvi sat down together in front of the television. Nowadays the programs started at noon.

"Well, here we are now," Sylvi said.

"Well, here we are inside our own house. Now the winter and snow can come and I don't need to carry the wood and the coal up those stairs any more," Aarne commented.

"Don't' say anything more. It's warm and wonderful here," Sylvi continued.

Aarne got up and turned the television on. They would watch the daily news.

The familiar news anchor already sat on the television screen looking very serious. He took off his glasses, wiped his eyes, and put his glasses back on and then told the world that on that day the American president had been shot in the city of Dallas in the American South, and he had died without regaining consciousness.

It was an unusual day in the history of the world at the end of November 1963; but the world turned forward as always; measuring time and history from now to eternity.

About the Author

Sirpa T. Kaukinen was born in Finland and was educated both in Finland and Canada. Her writings have been published in Finnish and English. She lives in Canada.

The First Winter, written in Finnish, 2nd prize winner in a book, Lännen Kultaan Kurkottamassa – Reaching for the Western Gold, Werner Söderström Oy. 1979, Finland.

Muuttolinnut ja Kukkopillit – Migratory Birds and Clay Whistles, written in Finnish and English, 3rd place winner, was published in the Canadan Sanomat, 2007.

No Place for a Woman, written in English, 1st place winner, was published in the Kippis Internet Journal, 2009, in USA.

Greetings from Canada – Terveisiä Kanadasta, was published 2012 – UPS Printing.

Finnish Canadian Heritage Recipes 2004 and **The Finnish Canadian Cookbook 2017** were written in English and published by Gateway Rasmussen in Manitoba, Canada.

Kultakaupunki, a novel, written in Finnish, was published on Amazon.com 2019.

Golden City, a novel, written in English, was published on Amazon.com 2020.

A List of Sources Consulted

Books:

Gioia,Ted. Jazz – The History of Jazz, Oxford University Press Inc., New York, 1997.

Granatstein, J. L., Irving M. Abella, David J. Bercuson, R. Craig Brown, and H. Blair Neatly. Twentieth Century Canada, McGraw – Hill Ryerson Limited, 1983.

Hearden, Patrick J. The Tragedy of Vietnam, Causes and Consequences, Pearson Longman, New York, U S, 2006.

Jenkins, Philip. A History of The United States, St. Martin's Press, New York, 1997.

Lonn, George. The Mine Finders, Pitt Publishing Company Limited, Toronto, 1966.

Miller, John and Aaron Kenedi, Ed. Inside Cuba, The History, Culture, and Politics of an Outlaw Nation, Marlowe & Company, An Inprint of Avalon Publishing Group Inc., 2003.

Raivio, Yrjö. Kanadan Suomalaisten Historia, - The Canadian Finnish History, New West Press Co. Ltd., Vancouver, B.C. 1975.

Simpson, Paul. The Rough Guide to Elvis, Published by Rough Guides Ltd., 2004.

Sitkoff, Harvard. The Struggle for Black Equality 1954 – 1980, McGraw – Hill Ryerson Ltd. 1981.

Archives: Barrie Public Library:

Toronto Daily Star – newspaper articles 1953 – 1963

The Globe and Mail Weekly – newspaper articles 1953 – 1963

Vapaa Sana Press – newspaper articles - 1953 – 1963

Articles:

Jalava, Mauri A. Lempi Johnson, 54th Finnish Canadian Grand Festival Program, Town Press, Toronto, 1993

Saarinen, Oiva W. Ph.D: Book Review: Varpu Lindstrom: From Heroes to Enemies: Finns in Canada, 1937-1947, Journal of Finnish Studies, Aspasia Books, Beaverton, 2000.

Quotations:

1 - Chapter 11, page 244 – Toronto Daily Star - October 24, 1956 newspaper.

2 – Chapter 18, page 416 - Charles, Ray, You Give Your Hand to me, copyright 1962 by Sony/ATV Music Publishing, LLC. Writer/s: Cindy Walker Eddy Arnold.

3 – Chapter 19, page 441 and 442 - Stephen B. Oates: Let the Trumpet Sound – A Life of Martin Luther King, Jr. Harper Perennial – A Division of Harper Collins Publishers, 1994.
and
4 – Chapter 19, page 441 and 442 – John Wesley Work, Jr., African American collector of folk songs and spirituals and included in his book New Jubilee Songs and Folk Songs of the American Negro, 1907

Music

Anka, Paul, "Diana", Lyrics by Joe Sherman and Paul Anka, copyright 1957 by Sony/ATV Music Publishing LLC, Universal Music Publishing Group.

Charles, Ray, "You Give Your Hand to me", copyright 1962 by Sony/ATV Music Publishing, LLC. Writer/s: Cindy Walker, Eddy Arnold.

Crosby, Bing, "I'm Dreaming of a White Christmas", "Christmas Carols", copyright 1942 – Kim Darby Singers and the John Scott Trotter Orchestra.

Darin, Bobby, "Dream Lover", "Darin at the Copa", copyright 1959 by Atlantic Records.

Ford, Tennessee Ernie, "You Load Sixteen Tons", copyright 1955 by Capitol – songwriter Merle Travis 1946.

Gershwin, George, "'S Wonderful, 'S Marvellous", copyright 1927, Lyrics by Ira Gershwin.

Haley, Bill and His Comets, "One, Two, Three O'clock, Four O'clock, Rock" copyright 1954, lyrics by Max C. Freedman and James E. Myers 1952.

Jurva, Matti, music, Tatu Pekkarinen, words, "Tää On Vain Maailmaa"- "This is only the World"

"Herra Johtajan Harha-Askel"-"Mr. Boss' Sidestep"-(1940) – copyright Filmistudio Oy, Finland.

King, Pee Wee, "Tennessee Waltz", copyright 1949 – lyrics by Redd Stewart, 1949.

Linna, Kaarlo Kullervo, "Kultainen Nuoruus" – "Golden Youth", copyright 1949 – Finland.

Malmsten, Eugen, "Vanha Merimies Muistelee" – "An Old Sailor Remembers" - copyright 1938 by Columbia Tanssiorkesteri- Finland.

Page, Patti, "Mockingbird Hill"copyright 1951, composer Vaughan Horton 1960.

Presley, Elvis, "That's All Right Mama", copyright 1954 – originally written and performed in 1946 by Arthur Crudup.

Presley, Elvis, "Blue Moon of Kentucky", copyright 1954 – originally written and performed in 1946 by Bill Monroe.

Presley, Elvis, "Don't Be Cruel", copyright by RCA Victor 1956 – lyrics by Otis Blackwell.

Presley, Elvis, "Are You Lonesome Tonight", copyright 1960 by RCA Victor. Originally recorded in 1926 - music by Lou Handman and lyrics by Roy Turk, Harmony Records.

Rautavaara, Tapio, "Kulkurin Valssi" – "Vagabond Waltz", recorded and lyrics copyright 1957 – Originally Pentti Lääveri, trad.arr. Kansansävelmä, and J. Alfred Tanner, words, copyright 1926.

Rautavaara, Tapio, words "Jos Sais Kerran Reissullansa"- "If I Could Just Once on My Travels",copyright 1970 – Kansansävelmä - Finland.

Rautavaara, Tapio, "Isontalon Antti ja Rannanjärvi" – "Big-house Antti and Rannanjärvi", words, Lääveri, Pentti, trad.,arr. Kansansävelmä, copyright 1967 – Finland.

Sibelius, Jean, "Finlandia" copyright 1899 revised 1900, Lyrics by V. A. Koskenniemi, – Finland.

Valens, Ritchie, "Donna"and"La Bamba"– copyright 1958 by Del-Fi Records 4110.

Vesterinen, Vili, "Säkkijärven Polkka", "Säkkijärvi Polka", recording and lyrics – copyright 1939 - Finland.

Virta, Olavi, "Metsäkukkia" - "Forest Flowers", recording and lyrics – copyright 1952 – Finland.